THE SEVEN DAY SWITCH

MEG CHRONIS

MC

ISBN (paperback): *978-0-6397-5799-5*

ISBN (ebook): *978-0-6397-5800-8*

To contact the author, visit www.megchronis.com

Cover designed by Tallulah Lucy (www.tallulahlucy.com).

Additional illustrations by Nada Qamber (www.qamberdesigns.com) and Gregg Davies (www.greggdavies.com).

To the keepers of my heart, Theo and Ash and Anna.

And to my mom Chanel, for everything you've done, and everything you continue to do for me...every single day.

1

#RescueMission

"We need two pairs of tiger-print panties."

"Knickers, Dot. Knickers." Standing on the other side of The Rickford London's gleaming marble concierge desk, the shorter of the two American guests swatted her friend on the arm. "Speak British! No wonder they don't know what you're blathering on about."

Becca Stratton smiled at the flustered trainee beside her. "I'll take it from here, Amy." She slid her notepad towards her as the trainee scurried off. Not even the smallest muscle twitched in her face. And why would it? Before she hit thirty next year, she planned on being inducted into the ranks of the Society of the Golden Keys, the most prestigious and exclusive concierge association in the world. Her application was already in. Soon, her lapels would bear the distinctive badge of two crossed golden keys that would single her out as an elite concierge. It would take a great deal more than sparkly underwear to fluster Becca.

"Course she understands 'panties'," said the taller of the two. "She's not British. I can tell these things. She's a New Zealander."

Becca smiled. Right hemisphere, wrong country, but then she was used to people being confused by her South African accent, softened somewhat but still as robust as ever, even after almost seven years in London.

She asked for the women's room number, then wrote in neat script under The Rickford London's embossed emblem: *Rm 1136, 2 x tiger-print panties*. She'd put in a call to Jess at Harrods. "I'll have a range of sizes sent over by this afternoon and brought to your room."

The taller guest nudged her friend. "I wish we got service like this back home."

Back home. Becca's gut clenched with anxiety and she swallowed hard against the pin-dotted silk scarf knotted at her throat. By this time tomorrow, she'd be back in Johannesburg, on a rescue mission for her identical twin sister.

Usually such a pro when it came to saying the right thing, her celebrity twin had landed herself in a social media disaster, complete with enraged animal rights activists calling for her job...and her head. And while Gem was no stranger to the vitriol that flowed when people had a computer screen to hide behind, this time, it had knocked her sister's feet out from under her.

Becca shoved aside the gnawing worry and smiled across the counter. "Is there anything else I can do for you?" Please say no. She had to wrap things up here if she was going to get to Heathrow in the next hour. She shouldn't even be at work this morning. She knew the team would manage without her—she'd trained them well—but it didn't stop her feeling guilty about her unplanned time off.

One of the guests leaned an elbow on the counter. "Aren't you curious though?"

Becca squashed an urge to sigh and inclined her head. "Curious, ma'am?" She'd learned long ago not to be curious about guests' peculiar requests.

"About the panties! The *knickers*!" The two women tittered.

Becca suppressed a smile, her gaze taking in the women's white T-shirts with the words "You're the most beautiful woman in the WORLD" printed on the front. Copies of the tee worn by Spike in the movie *Notting Hill*, though most likely without the "FANCY A FUCK?" punchline on the back. She inclined her head and tapped her lips with one finger as if deep in thought. She hadn't worked this long behind the concierge desk at an Earl's Court hotel without picking up on all the trivia for *Notting Hill* and every other British romcom besides.

The woman waggled her eyebrows. "You give up?"

"Let me guess. Today you visited the film locations for *Notting Hill*. And tomorrow, it's Bridget Jones's turn. You're off to the Montblanc Boutique at the Royal Exchange where Mark Darcy kissed Bridget in her tiger-print panties."

Both women sucked in their breath and their eyes grew wide, as if she'd levitated in front of them. "They do train them well, don't they, Vera?"

Her companion nodded earnestly, and Becca felt the usual glow that seeped under her skin whenever she impressed a guest.

"We like to get into the spirit of it, don't we, Vera?" the woman jabbered on, to more earnest nodding. "We did *Pride & Prejudice* too. We found Victorian bonnets on eBay for when we visited Pemberley yesterday. So quaint. We felt positively British, didn't we, Vera?"

"Oh for God's sake!" a voice bellowed behind the pair, and a woman shoved her way to the counter, barging aside the two Americans. She held a bichon frisé captive in the crook of one arm, the little dog so perfectly groomed it appeared to be constructed from white wool pom-poms. "Some of us have actual problems we need attended to," she said, and thrust out her mobile phone at Becca. "You're sorry, but you couldn't get me a table?"

She spoke as if she were trying to make sense of a particularly difficult theorem in a quantum mechanics textbook.

Becca upped the wattage of her smile. "Ma'am, I'd be happy to assist you once I've finished with—"

A hand heavy with ostentatious rings thrust the phone over the counter into Becca's hands. "What do you say to this?"

Becca scanned the email that was open on the screen. So this was the guest from Room 67. The email had come through to the concierge inbox less than an hour ago, written in much the same tone as God had likely used when he'd commanded, 'Let there be light'. *Book me a table for six at Le Gavroche for lunch today. 12:30 p.m. And a dog sitter for Lady Anastasia.*

The disgruntled American guests were gathering their shopping, their angry gazes hurling more daggers than a knife-thrower in a Vegas stage show. "Have a wonderful day tomorrow, ladies," Becca said, flashing her most conciliatory smile. They stalked away with much aggrieved muttering, and Becca returned her attention to the seething woman across the counter.

She arranged her face into a mask of calm civility, glad for the scarf at her throat that hid the fast tick of her pulse. "Regretfully, ma'am, I wasn't able to book your first choice." Even her remarkable people-pleasing powers hadn't extended to securing an eleventh-hour booking at one of London's top French restaurants. "As I mentioned in my reply email however, I've made provisional bookings at a number of excellent alternatives, assuming it's specifically French cuisine you want."

"What I want, *specifically,*" the woman said, throwing Becca's own word back at her with a sneer, "is Le. Gav. Roche." She mouthed the syllables like a singer warming up her lips before a performance. Then she extended her thumb and pinkie finger beside her ear as if making an imaginary phone call. "Call them. Now."

Becca felt her smile slip and she hiked it up, using the trick Mom had always reminded her and Gem of before they stepped out onto a pageant stage: *press your tongues behind your teeth, girls!* Becca twiddled the mouse on the desk under the counter and her computer blinked awake. She tapped the restaurant's name into Google and clicked to open Le Gavroche's online booking page. "I see there's still a slot open at four thirty."

The woman bunched her eyebrows. "I don't know how you people in New Zealand or wherever the hell you're from do it, but where I'm from, civilized people do not eat lunch at four thirty. Did you ask the maitre d'? They always make plans for you people."

Becca smiled back impassively. She might have to take guests' rudeness, but nowhere in the concierge code did it say she had to do it lying down. "I generally find London maitre d's are only willing to make plans where famous people are involved, ma'am."

The woman looked affronted. "How do you know I'm not famous? I could be married to a movie star."

"*Are* you married to a movie star, ma'am?" Becca said. "Because that would certainly give me something to work with."

The woman gave Becca such a heated stare it was a wonder the bichon frisé's dandelion head didn't burst into flames. A be-ringed hand smacked the counter. "I want to speak to the head concierge."

"I am the head concierge, ma'am." Another reason why she'd come in this morning, despite her fast-approaching flight.

"You? Are you even qualified?"

"I have a post-graduate degree in Hotel Management, ma'am."

The woman scoffed. "From some trashy little college, no doubt."

Best hospitality school in the world. "And yet I'm no less in charge, ma'am," Becca said, pointing to her name badge with her title displayed prominently beneath it.

The woman peered at the badge. "Becca Stratton," she read. She exchanged a look with her dog. "Remember that name, dumpling, because Mommy's going to need it for her review on Tripadvisor."

Becca's pulse accelerated. No bad review was going to get in the way of her becoming a Golden Keys concierge. There was always a way to please any guest, even this one. She just had to think.

Two pairs of eyes stared at her. Becca chose the least hostile of the two and fixed her gaze on the bichon frisé's polished black marbles. *A table at Le Gavroche and a dog sitter for the dumpling.* She needed to get creative.

Becca grinned. Good old superpower. "Délicieux isn't as popular with tourists, but it's the place any real Londoner wants to go." She tapped the side of her nose and winked. "But best of all? It's dog-friendly."

Five minutes later, she'd booked a table for six—plus one dog—at Délicieux. As another satisfied guest left the counter, Becca loosened the knot of her scarf with a finger and inhaled slowly. There was no need to have misgivings about the coming week; if she could handle rabid guests like that one, she could handle a few wild animals.

Across the lobby, one of the sets of lift doors opened and Shahid Hussain, the hotel's general manager, stepped out. Impeccable in a double-breasted charcoal suit and silk tie, his bald head gleaming as bright as the gold fixtures in the lobby, he hurried towards the concierge desk, a branded carrier bag from the hotel's gift shop in one hand. "I was worried you'd have left already," he said when he drew up.

Becca's answering smile was warm and genuine, not the polite one she reserved for guests. She'd known Shahid almost as long as she'd been in London, meeting him back in the days when she'd been in Housekeeping. As she'd rocketed through the hotel ranks, her sights set on management until she'd discovered her true calling behind the concierge desk, Shahid had become more mentor and friend than boss. "I'm heading out as soon as I finish the revised duty roster."

Shahid nodded. "Ever the professional." He reached into the carrier bag and produced a glossy black box secured with a shiny silver ribbon: The Rickford London's decadent chocolates. "For Gem." He laid the box on the counter. "I know she's going through a tough time right now."

She curled her fingers over the box, touched by Shahid's gesture. "She's really got herself in deep this time."

Shahid patted her hand affectionately. "Some sisterly support and good quality chocolate should do her the world of good."

Prickles of heat darted over Becca's skin and she averted her gaze. She hadn't told Shahid exactly what form her support was going to take. Something told her identity theft had most definitely not crossed his mind.

NEWS 24/7

First to break the news.

Embattled *Luxe Life* presenter given final chance

Wednesday, 3 August

After throwing in the towel two days into her community service sentence, TV presenter Gem Stratton has been granted one last extension before her contract is terminated.

Katleho Productions, production company of popular TV magazine show *Luxe Life* and much-anticipated renovation reality show *From Hell to Hotel*, released a statement today following appeals received from Ms Stratton's agent and family. In the spirit of restorative justice, the company's board has agreed to allow the TV presenter one more week to complete her community service at Winterberg Wildlife Rescue and Sanctuary.

The suspended *Luxe Life* TV host, former Miss South Africa, and girlfriend of Springbok rugby captain, Mandla Ndungane, walked out yesterday on the wildlife sanctuary where she was doing community service to make amends for an Instagram post that had the South African public up in arms.

Ms Stratton sparked outrage on social media platforms last week when she posted a photo on Instagram of her cuddling a leopard cub at the Ingwe Sanctuary in Cape Town, with the caption: "Isn't this baby leopard too gorgeous!! Love love love its coat!! Do you think my Jimmy Choo pumps would match?"

When animal rights activists took to social media to condemn what they called Ms Stratton's endorsement of fur wearing, the celebrity fired back with another photo of herself and the leopard cub, captioned: "I have never worn fur!! It's so cruel! Imagine anyone wanting to skin this sweet baby! And what would be the point...its pelt isn't even big enough for a handbag!! Just joking!"

Following public outcry, Katleho Productions suspended Ms Stratton and gave the presenter fourteen days to complete 50 hours of animal-related community service, or face dismissal. At the time of her walkout yesterday, Ms Stratton had completed only nine hours of her sentence.

Dr Sullivan Scott, chief veterinarian at Winterberg Wildlife Rescue and Sanctuary, declined to comment, but other sanctuary workers told News24/7 that no one was surprised by Ms Stratton's flight. A source who preferred to remain anonymous said, "Anyone who wears stilettos to do manual labour can't have been serious to begin with".

The celebrity's agent, Mr Alek de Abreu, told a press conference held this morning that Ms Stratton is "suffering from extreme stress", but that her family is rallying around her to ensure she returns to the sanctuary to "prove her commitment to animal welfare and show her deep remorse for her recent social media posts".

News24/7 was unable to reach Ms Stratton for comment.

ALSO READ: Tearful Gem insists her Insta post was "taken the wrong way", and Public labels Gem's apology as "insincere and unacceptable"

Sign in to join the conversation
Showing Comments (74)

Warrior64
No!! Don't give her another chance! Defenseless animals in the fur trade don't get another chance. #furiscruel #gemmustfall
Like Reply Report

JontyM
I'm glad Mandla Ndungane is off playing in Australia with the Springboks. Last thing we need is the captain's girlfriend taking his focus off the game with all this drama.
Like Reply Report

SirJohn75
No more chances! Fire the bitch now!! #luxelife #furkiller #gemmustfall
Like Reply Report

2

#SisterSwitch

This must be what it felt like to be hit by a bus. Slumped on her haunches against the wall of the toilet stall beside her weekender bag, Becca dropped her chin to her chest and let her eyes drift shut. Flying via Addis Ababa might have been the cheapest way to get from London to Johannesburg, but it certainly hadn't been the quickest. The layover had wiped her out, and she could quite happily have gone to sleep right here and now on the floor, if the floor didn't happen to be in the Arrivals Hall restrooms of Johannesburg's OR Tambo International Airport.

She jerked at a knock on the stall door, almost overbalancing onto her butt.

"Becca? It's us."

Mom. Becca scrambled to her feet, her exhaustion momentarily forgotten as she unlocked the stall door and flung it open.

Her smile fell away. Standing behind their mother was her sister, looking even worse than she had a few days ago on their last video call. Skin scrubbed free of makeup, shapeless grey sweats swallowing her curves and a baseball cap pulled low over her eyes, Gem was barely recognisable.

"Sis." Becca's voice broke in anguish and she opened her arms.

Gem stumbled past Mom and into Becca's embrace in the doorway of the stall. "You have no idea how happy I am to see you." Gem's voice was a muffled croak in Becca's neck.

Arms wrapped tight around her sister, Becca caught their mother's eye.

Mom dipped her chin and raised her eyebrows: *Told you it was an emergency.* Immaculately dressed in taupe tailored trousers, a black blouse and stylish black parka, Cecelia Stratton looked every bit the mother of a beauty queen. It was a role she still loved to play, even years after Gem had handed over her crown to the next Miss South Africa. "In we go, girls." Mom herded them, still entwined, into the family-sized stall. She locked the door, hung a black leather duffel bag on a hook behind the door, and turned. Reaching out, Mom drew them into a group hug. "It's been too long since I've had you two together."

Becca leaned her head against Mom's encircling arm. "Missed you too, Mom."

"I just wish it was under better circumstances," Mom said.

Gem gulped back a sob.

"Hey!" Becca pulled back from the hug enough that she could look into Gem's drawn face. "I'm here now. I'll sort everything out."

Gem's lips compressed as if she were biting back tears. "I feel so bad we've made you do this."

"You're not making me do anything. I offered."

"And we're so grateful," Mom said. "But now, lovely as this reunion is, we have work to do." Mom broke up their bonding session and stepped as far back as she could in the confines of the stall, training an assessing eye over the length of Becca's body. "You can start by taking that hideous thing off your head."

Becca patted the curly blond wig she'd worn ever since she'd climbed onto the plane at Heathrow. "You don't think this look is quite me?"

Gem aimed a scowl at Becca's head. "Where'd you get that repulsive thing anyway?"

"Costume shop near work." Becca unpinned the blond wig and shook out her shoulder-length brown hair. She dumped the wig on top of her weekender bag. "Considering what we're about to do, I didn't want anyone spotting your clone arriving in the country and plastering the evidence all over social media."

Gem gave a weak grimace. "Especially not when you look like that. You know you can be arrested for appearing in public in Crocs?"

Becca patted her sweatpants, glad to see a spark of Gem's usual feistiness. "Haven't you heard? Sweatpants and Crocs are de rigueur in Economy Class these days."

"Precisely why we prefer Business Class," Mom added in an undertone. She waggled a hand at Becca's sunny yellow Crocs. "Take those off. Right now. We have an image to maintain."

Mom always used the plural when talking about Gem's career, as if it were hers too. In a way it was, considering all the time she'd sunk into getting Gem all those auditions, callbacks and modelling shoots over the years.

Becca stuck out one foot as if she were posing at the end of a fashion show runway. "Zooey Deschanel rocked Crocs."

"When you're being paid millions to be their brand ambassador, you can wear them too. Now get changed." Mom turned to get the duffel bag.

"Wait." Gem's face was tense with worry. "I'm still not convinced about this plan. Maybe I should go back and try again. I should pull myself together—"

"We've discussed this, darling," Mom said, all confident assurance. "You barely lasted two days at that sanctuary. You're hardly likely to handle another seven. Frankly, you're in no state to return. You're back on Xanax, and if it weren't for the sleeping tablets, you wouldn't be getting a wink of sleep." Mom clutched the duffel bag to her chest. "Personally, I blame Alek. As your agent, he should've known his sister's setup in the middle of nowhere would be a terrible fit for you."

"It's not his fault none of the Joburg animal shelters wanted to risk the negative press of having me there."

"Still. He could've insisted they go easy on you. Especially that awful vet." Mom shook her head in disgust.

Gem fiddled with the neck of her sweatshirt, clutching the fabric into her fist and tugging at it like it was a noose. "But what if someone works out that Bex isn't me?"

"They won't, darling. Even your father and I get confused by the two of you at times."

Gem tugged a pale lip between her teeth and chewed it for a moment. "But what if they do? If something goes wrong, I'll be even worse off than I am now. The public would crucify me for a deception like this." Gem's eyes met Becca's. "A whole week, Bex? It was tricky enough when we'd switch places for a few lessons at school. Now you're going to be me for a whole week?"

Mom gave a long-suffering sigh as if she'd been over this ground before with Gem. "Even if Becca doesn't act precisely like you, nobody will suspect a twin switch. This isn't the movies, darling. They'll assume it's stress. Hardly anyone even remembers you're a twin."

"She has a point, Gem," Becca said. Gem's social media feeds were carefully planned, curated and photographed to best portray her personal brand. Family photos seldom made the cut. She put a reassuring hand on Gem's shoulder. "It'll be fine. You were there for such a short time that no one at the sanctuary really knows how the real Gem is supposed to act. It's not like someone working there is one of our old school friends who knows about our childhood switches."

Gem held Becca's gaze, anxiety crimping the skin around her pale blue eyes. "Have you even thought about yourself though? If this whole mad scheme goes south, imagine the fallout for your work."

Exactly what Becca had said when Mom had first pitched the plan two nights ago, after Gem had fled the sanctuary, putting her job in jeopardy.

Mom snorted a laugh. "No one in the UK is interested in what happens at an obscure wildlife sanctuary in rural South Africa."

Becca jostled Gem encouragingly by the shoulder. "Mom's got a point." At least she hoped Mom did. "Don't worry about me. It's worth the risk to ensure you get your job back so Dad can have his operation. Besides"—she grinned—"what are twin sisters for if not to get each other out of trouble?"

Gem's eyes welled and she smiled a smile as pale and thin as weak tea. "Okay." Gem rubbed at her eyes with the cuff of a sleeve. "Thanks, Bex. You've always had my back."

They hugged again until Mom pried them apart. "Now that's all settled, can we please get a move on, girls?" She thrust the duffel bag into Gem's arms. "Alek's deal with the production company was that you'd be back in Winterberg by five today."

Gem went on her haunches, unzipped the duffel and pulled clothing into her lap. A pair of spray-on-tight faux leather leggings appeared, followed by a luxurious cashmere top in a soft camel shade. Towering high heels appeared next. Gem looked at Mom. "Tell me you packed more sensible outfits than this."

Mom's mouth tensed. "That's one of your classic looks."

Gem sighed in exasperation. "For Fashion Week, yes. But we both know what's waiting for her there."

Becca remembered Gem's video call on her first day at the Winterberg sanctuary. Gem had been expecting cutesy bottle-feeding sessions with mewling lion cubs and orphaned baby rhinos. Instead Gem and her Instagram-worthy outfit had found themselves tackling a clean-up job in a hyena enclosure that would've been better suited to full Hazmat gear.

Mom shrugged, unapologetic. "I thought it might force that awful vet to give her less strenuous jobs."

"No, it'll force her to muck out animal enclosures in her bare feet." Gem shot Becca an apologetic look. "I'm sorry, Bex. I should've packed for you myself, but I was so..." She huffed an exhausted sigh and dangled a shoe by its precipitous heel. "You'll just have to wear your own shoes."

"I didn't bring any. I knew I'd be wearing your clothes, so I chucked in undies, warm PJs and a few toiletries and..." Becca looked at her Crocs lying higgledy-piggledy on the stall floor.

"Don't even think about it," warned Mom. "The last thing we need is a repeat of *People Magazine*."

That had been Gem's first taste of the ugly side of fame. Someone had sneaked photos of Becca at the mall in ragged jeans and an outsized character tee, thinking she was her famous sister. The subsequent magazine cover had screamed in huge-lettered glee: *Miss South Africa...from FAB to DRAB.*

Becca pulled her gaze from her own shoes and poked the high heel on Gem's finger, making it see-saw. "I'll buy something more suitable once I'm in Winterberg. But for now, I'd better get changed." She pulled her T-shirt over her head.

Eventually, after much wiggling and shimmying to insert herself into the circulation-restricting leggings, and a hasty session of hair, makeup and nails—she'd forgotten how much effort went into being glamorous—Becca stood transformed before her sister and mother.

Mom stepped closer and examined her face. "Beautiful job covering those dark circles, Gem." Mom fussed with Becca's hair, settling the dark waves just so around her shoulders. It took Becca right back to the days when she and Gem had stood side by side in front of illuminated backstage mirrors doing last-minute touch-ups, exchanging exasperated looks as Mom fluffed out their frilly skirts and pinched colour into their cheeks before they went out on stage for Little Miss Wherever.

Mom pulled the cashmere knit down to reveal one of Becca's shoulders, her head tipping to the side, shaped brows bunching. "Are you always so pasty white?"

Becca covered her exposed shoulder with a hand. "I spend twelve hours a day behind a concierge desk in a hotel lobby."

"They don't do spray tans in London?"

"Leave her, Mom," Gem batted away Mom's primping hands and pulled the cashmere top back onto Becca's shoulder. "She can't wear it like that anyway, or have you forgotten my tattoo?"

Becca inhaled. The black floral wreath tattoo, a little smaller than the size of a palm, positioned on the cap of Gem's shoulder. "I can't believe we never thought of that."

"You can't see it unless I wear something off-the-shoulder, so unless you're planning on getting your sexy on when you're cleaning out animal pens, you should be fine."

Becca relaxed. "I wasn't planning on it. Unless sexy is all you packed for me, Mom." She gave Mom a dark look as she worked a finger under the band of the leggings where it cut into her waist. Probably shouldn't have done all that comfort eating after she'd tossed that bastard Kevin out on his lying, cheating arse.

Mom looked down her nose at Becca. "Sexy never hurts, darling. I packed your sister's signature polish. Be sure to touch up any chips."

"No problem." Becca splayed her freshly manicured fingers. "I'm sure that moody vet you keep telling me about won't mind one bit if I stop in between shovelling poo and spraying down animal runs to touch up my nails."

Gem grimaced. "Yeah, he'll love that. I've never met a man more determined to be a dickhead than Sullivan Scott. He forced me to do such gross work and then had zero sympathy for what I was going through."

"Dreadful man." Mom scooped up Becca's discarded T-shirt and sweats and dumped them unceremoniously into the duffel bag. "Strutting about like he owns the place."

"But he does," Becca said. "Didn't you tell me he and Alek's sister are co-owners?"

Mom was unimpressed. "Did I tell you how he made Gem clean out a pigsty?"

Becca chuckled. "Numerous times."

Mom shut the duffel bag with a force that threatened to tear off the zipper. "The man is a disagreeable arse."

"Can we please stop talking about him?" Gem slumped back against the stall wall. "He's vile. Trust me, you'll never please Sully."

"Sounds like a challenge," Becca said.

"I'm serious, Bex. Don't waste your people-pleasing powers on him. Rather direct all your people-pleasing skills at Clare, the other vet I told you about. She seems nice enough, even though I'm pretty sure she has a thing for the dickhead. No accounting for people's taste. Ask Jo if you can report to Clare instead, then you won't have to have him glowering over you all week. Oh, and a little trick...there are a bunch of foreign volunteers there who pay for the chance to work with wild African animals. If you ask the guys nicely, they'll help you with your chores, and believe me, you'll be glad for some male biceps after a few hours of wielding a manure fork." Gem toed Becca on the shin with her trainer. "Plus some of them are pretty hot. There's this one German—"

"I'm not here to find a man, sis."

"No, right. Sorry. Still too soon after Kevin." Gem's expression darkened. "Seems we both have a knack for finding douchebags. Well, good luck to Mandla, finding someone better than me." Her face turned hard at her mention of her famous rugby-captain boyfriend.

Becca stiffened. This was news. She knew Mandla hadn't been impressed with Gem's publicity *faux pas*, worried it would tarnish his reputation as the golden boy of South African rugby, but a breakup? "You've ended it? What if he spills about the switch to get back at you?"

Mom clicked her tongue. "We didn't tell him. The fewer people who know, the better. And it's not a breakup. Just another one of their fights."

Anxiety was sharp in Becca's gut. "But a fight's even worse! What am I meant to do if Mandla comes to the sanctuary wanting to put things right? I draw the line at having make-up sex with your boyfriend!"

Gem's eyes shimmered. "He's in Australia with the Springboks. They've got match fixtures all week. They're only due home the week after you fly back. And then he's got so much grovelling to do..." Gem hugged herself and seemed to shrink into her sweatshirt. "Are we done yet?"

Mom consulted the elegant gold watch on her wrist. "We'd better be, or we're going to be late for our flight."

Unease crowded into Becca's chest. "I still think you should lie low at home."

Mom shivered. "If I have to read one more death threat from another internet troll..." She shook her head. "You've been insulated from it all in London, but for your sister and I, it's been a terrible few weeks. We need to get away from it all. Recharge."

"Can't you recharge at home?" Instead of on an all-expenses-paid trip to a yoga retreat in Thailand, a sweetener from one of Gem's sponsors that her sister had never got around to using. "What if something happens and I need you?"

Mom smiled and stroked a hand down Becca's cashmere-clad arm. "Nothing will happen, not now you're handling things." Mom pointed at Becca's weekender bag. "Is your passport in there?"

"Why?" Becca asked. "Are you worried they'll work me so hard I'll be tempted to go AWOL too?"

Mom bent to pick up the bag. "You're not the only one who thought about a disguise."

"What have you done, Mother?" Gem asked.

"I booked everything in Becca's name." Bag squashed against her chest, Mom unzipped an outside pocket.

Gem's mouth fell open. "I can't fly on her passport! It's illegal."

"I couldn't very well have you flying off to Thailand when you're meant to be in Winterberg," Mom said, inspecting the pocket's contents. "I told your sponsor you'd donated the trip to your sister and me."

"Tell me you've heard of biometrics?" Becca said. "Fingerprint scanning?"

Mom tut-tutted and zipped shut the pocket. "It's Thailand, not England. It'll be fine."

Becca exchanged a look with Gem that said there was no use arguing. Their mother hadn't gained her reputation as a pageant mom by not knowing how to stand her ground. "Inside compartment, beneath my underwear," Becca said.

Mom located the green South African passport. "Thank you." She handed over the weekender bag. "And don't scowl, darling. You'll get premature wrinkles."

Becca swung the bag onto a shoulder. "If Gem lands in a Thai jail, you'd better pray there's a real-life Mark Darcy out there who can bail her out, because I'm not coming to the rescue."

Mom laughed and waggled the passport. "Not without this, you won't be. And now we really must go." Mom handed over the keys to Gem's car. "I wrote the bay number on the parking ticket. The rest of the things you'll need are in the car. And here's some money." She handed Becca a fistful of South African rand. "Gem, give Becca your phone."

"Why would I want her mobile?" Becca said. "What if I need to contact you?"

Mom tsk-ed. "It's not called a 'mobile' here. Pay attention, darling. And the retreat doesn't allow cellphones. We're going to completely disconnect from this ugly world for a whole week."

Gem handed over her phone. "Don't post anything, okay? I've scheduled content to post while I'm away."

"Keys. Cash." Mom was patting her pockets. "Oh, and we decided not to tell Alek about the switch. Don't gape at me, Becca Stratton. His sister owns the sanctuary, how's he going to keep it from her if he knew? The fewer people who know about this, the better."

"And he'd only have a fit if he knew," Gem said.

As if this coming week wasn't going to be hard enough, now she had to lie to Gem's agent too. "He's going to call me, you know? To find out how things are going. Then what?"

Mom shoved the duffel into Becca's arms. "If I confuse you two on the phone, so will Alek." Mom stooped to collect the blond wig and Crocs. "I'll keep these. Best not to tempt you," she said with a wink. Then she pulled Becca into a hug. "Thank you for doing this, darling." Mom pulled back and cupped Becca's face with a hand. "We've always been able to count on you."

"Which isn't always a good thing," Gem said. She touched Becca's arm. "Are you sure about this? *Luxe Life* isn't the only job in the world."

"Of course she's sure," Mom answered. "Because it's not just *Luxe Life* we're talking about here. It's future work too. If you lose *Luxe Life*, they're not going to want you presenting *From Hell to Hotel* next year. And there are your sponsors to consider too."

Becca caught Gem's eye and a subtle mutual eye-roll passed between them.

"You can say no," Gem mouthed.

But she wouldn't. Everyone in this toilet stall knew that. Gem didn't need any more things to worry about. It was time to dig out the proverbial big-girl panties. Becca reached for the lock on the stall door and turned it. "Would you stop worrying? Nothing will go wrong." She stepped back to swing open the door. "Compared to the crap I have to deal with at work, a week handling actual crap will be a total breeze."

3

#Busted

The silver Audi hit the gravel shoulder along the country road and crunched to a skidding halt. There it was. Winterberg.

Becca gripped the steering wheel and stared through the bug-spattered windscreen at a picturesque diorama of country life: the little town nestled partly obscured by trees in the valley ahead, the mountains of the Drakensberg range a protective wall in the near distance. Her chest constricted and nerves exploded in her stomach. In a few short minutes, she was going to drive into that town and have to act like someone else for a week. Be the famous, sparkling Gem Stratton for seven...whole...days.

Becca flung open the car door and stumbled out. Bracing her hands on her knees, she gulped down lungfuls of warm air sweetened with the scent of wild grass from the field beside the road. She must have been nuts to go along with this plan. This wasn't a switch. This was *The Parent Trap* meets *The Perfect Storm*. If she messed up and the truth got out, the hate Gem was already dealing with online would feel like a welcome-home ticker tape parade.

A pickup truck roared past, so close the hot wind off its metallic body lifted her hair and filled her nose with exhaust fumes. She straightened and picked her way over the loose stones to the bonnet where she'd be less likely to become road kill. That pickup had been going way too fast. No, that *bakkie* had been going way too fast! She couldn't even get the local lingo right.

She sat on the edge of the bonnet. How would it look if 'Gem Stratton' marched into town speaking like a Brit? Gem, a former Miss South Africa, as South African as rusks and redbush tea—Becca exhaled on a moan and slumped, hanging her head off tense shoulders. It was *rooibos* tea. Nobody here said 'redbush'. It was always the little things that gave away a switch. She was going to get busted, for sure.

This was how it had felt when Mom had urged her out onto pageant stages with Gem, her small clammy hand clutched in her sister's, her whole body shaking, as they trotted (Gem) and shuffled (her) down the little ramps set up in the centre courts of shopping malls and in school and community halls. Then the heart-pounding pose at the end. Her, standing there quaking, hand clawed around whatever prop Mom had teamed with their outfits—a stuffed toy giraffe for the safari kit...a glittery wand for the fairy ensemble—and Gem letting go of her hand to sashay closer and beam at the smiling, clapping audience.

Becca flattened her palms against the hot metal and splayed her fingers. Her fingertips bumped over hard raised patches on the metalwork. She looked down at the splashes of red enamel paint baked onto Gem's bonnet, the handiwork of animal rights protesters who'd broken into her sister's complex the week before and done an impersonation of PETA at a fur convention. It was incomprehensible what complete strangers felt justified in doing to Gem over two misconstrued social media posts.

A jolt of anger reminded Becca why she was here. Gem needed her. Desperately. And Dad too. He'd been unemployed for almost two years now, living off a retrenchment package that hadn't been as generous as he'd led them all to believe. By the time she and

Gem had found out how tight things were, Dad had already cashed out his pension and liquidated most of his stocks to keep afloat. The book-keeping Mom had done over the years in between sewing pageant costumes and carting Gem around to auditions and catalogue photo shoots helped, but it wasn't nearly enough.

And then when Dad's hip had given out after years of niggling pain, and he'd admitted that maybe, just maybe, he might need a hip replacement, she and Gem had discovered he'd stopped his medical cover too.

They'd chipped in—Gem more than her—to help their parents keep the lights on and pick up Dad's medical cover again. Gem wasn't living large like her overseas celeb counterparts, but her TV presenter's salary and brand endorsement deals easily eclipsed Becca's take-home after rent and living expenses and student loan repayments.

But those months of missed premiums meant Dad now had to wait a year before the medical insurance would even consider covering the operation. Which meant pay for it themselves, or have Dad continue to live in pain.

That was why this community service couldn't be put off until Gem was feeling strong enough to do it herself. There was no going back now without losing Gem her job and likely her endorsement deals, and then Becca would have to go on seeing the barely concealed pain in Dad's eyes at every video call. Someone had to do the community service, and if it couldn't be Gem, it would have to be her.

She took a measured breath and held it until her head pounded and her lungs burned. She exhaled in a rush. She could do this. It wasn't as if she was trying to impersonate Gem in her usual environment, in front of audiences and cameras. Nobody really knew how Gem Stratton should act when it came to doing manual labour at a wildlife sanctuary. She just needed to calm down.

She concentrated on the chattering of unseen birds in the surrounding fields. On the wind in the new spring grass. On the cattle calling to each other, hazy black and white blobs in a far-off field.

Squinting against the sinking afternoon sun, Becca followed the road that spooled out ahead of her past fields and pastures before it dipped into the town. Behind the tall spire of a church peeking above the trees, the Drakensberg Mountains rose from soft green foothills into a muted purple and grey vista of sheer cliffs, rugged peaks and table-top plateaus that formed the imposing wall of the vast escarpment that ran like a great, jagged scar through the country.

It was beautiful here.

Peaceful.

Nothing like the frenetic, never-sleep pace of London. Despite the circumstances, it was good to be home. She straightened her back and rolled her shoulders before pushing to her feet and returning to the driver's door. As she climbed in, a white van with the yellow and blue stripes of the South African Police Services crested the low rise ahead of her, coming from town. The two occupants, heads panning, stared at her as they cruised past.

She shut the door and reached for the seat belt. Gem's phone was propped against the dashboard, the navigation app waiting patiently to guide her the last few kilometres to her fate. She went to start the car, but the bark of a siren behind her made her heart kick and she looked up.

The police van filled her rearview mirror. It must have stopped and turned in the road behind her. Though she knew she'd done nothing wrong, her pulse shot up.

The police van's doors creaked open and the two men climbed out. One was large and bald, a tank of a man in his mid-forties. The second didn't look old enough to have grown the ginger moustache that quivered above his lip. Both wore navy SAPS uniforms, guns holstered at their hips.

Becca twisted in her seat to follow Ginger Moustache as he swaggered up the passenger side of Gem's car to crouch at the front bumper. There was a loud rapping on her window. She whipped her head around to find a heavyset torso clad in regulation blue. The torso bent at the waist and Officer Tank's head ducked into view, the thick folds in his neck like those of the enormous bulls they bred out in this part of the country.

Becca's heart knocked against her ribs. "Is there a problem, officer?"

Officer Tank motioned with a stubby finger for her to roll down her window.

She pressed the window button. Nothing happened. The car was off. She clicked her tongue in annoyance and turned the ignition key. The car jerked forward as if it had a learner driver at the wheel.

A yelp erupted from the front of the car.

Oh God, she'd run over a cop. The clutch! It had been so long since she'd driven a car.

Officer Tank thundered to the front of the Audi, one thick hand clamped to the top of his bald head.

Hands clawed on the steering wheel, her heart thrashing about like a fish in a net, Becca held her breath. *Please don't let him be dead.*

Two hands appeared on the bonnet and Ginger Moustache pulled himself upright, his eyes screwed into outraged slits.

Her relief at seeing him alive was so strong it brought tears to her eyes. She sagged forward until her forehead touched the steering wheel.

Officer Tank was beside her again. “Out!”

She hadn’t even reached the town, let alone the sanctuary, and already things were going wrong. With fumbling fingers she undid the seatbelt and opened the door. She climbed out on wobbling legs and pressed herself against the car’s back door. “I’m so sorry! I left it in gear, and then I forgot about the clutch.”

A meaty finger thrust into the air and she shut her mouth so fast her teeth clicked.

Officer Tank leaned in. “That’s assault of a police officer.”

She stared at him in horror.

“Constable!” he bellowed, and Ginger Moustache bounced to attention.

“Yes, Captain Mabuza?”

Captain? Oh shit.

“Have you examined the bumper of this car?”

“I have, sir.”

The captain side-eyed her as he spoke. “And what did you find?”

“There’s a large dent and paint marks that match the paint scraped off our police van, sir.”

Captain Mabuza whistled through his teeth. “Do you know what the penalty is for a hit-and-run?”

Becca swallowed hard and shook her head. Gem hadn’t said anything about an accident.

“We have a witness that saw your vehicle parked behind our van outside the Brewhouse on Tuesday evening.”

Ginger Moustache shivered in apparent anticipation, his moustache bristling over his scrawny lip. “Come we arrest her, sir!” he said, mangling word order in his excitement, translating his native Afrikaans into direct English.

Becca's heart bucked. Now they were just trying to scare her. She lifted her chin. "You can't arrest me for bumping your van."

Captain Mabuza pounced. "So you admit to hitting the police van. Constable, are you making a note of this confession?"

"That's not what I said," Becca squeaked. "I meant you can't arrest someone for scraping a bumper. It's a misdemeanour, at best."

The captain sing-song-whistled through his teeth again. "A misdemeanour. Someone has been watching too much American TV, don't you think, Constable?"

Ginger Moustache snickered at his superior officer.

The captain propped an enormous hand above the gun holstered at his hip. "I don't know what the law says in America, but here in South Africa, if you drive into another vehicle and don't stop, it's a hit-and-run. And it's even more serious if that hit-and-run involves a state vehicle." He thrust out his hand. "Driver's licence."

How her knees remained locked beneath her, Becca didn't know. She pressed clammy palms against the car door at her back. Her South African driver's licence card was back in her flat in Aylesbury. Hold on though. She wasn't Becca now. She was Gem. And Gem kept her driver's licence..."On my keys!"

Captain Mabuza gestured for her to get them.

She ducked in at the Audi's door and removed Gem's key from the ignition. A black leather zip pouch was attached to the key ring. She unzipped it to find it packed tight with plastic store cards. She wiggled one free, then another. The stares of the two men were a physical weight. "I'm sure it's in here." Her fingers trembled, making it even harder to sort through the stack.

Ginger Moustache jangled a set of handcuffs hooked at his waist. "Looks like stalling tactics to me, Captain."

She pulled the last few cards from the purse and thrust them all into Captain Mabuza's hands. "There. It's one of those. Have a look."

The big man fanned through them with stocky digits. Then his fingers stilled. He clicked his tongue and held up a folded orange banknote. "Two hundred rand." He unfolded the banknote as if he'd stumbled upon a map to the fabled missing Kruger millions. "So, we can add bribing a police officer to the charge sheet."

Becca's breath seized in her chest. She reached out to him, but stopped abruptly when both men closed their hands on their guns. She lifted her hands, palms up, into the air. "It's not a bribe, I swear."

"Bribing a police officer is a serious offence," intoned the captain.

"Why would I need to bribe you?" One eye on the holstered gun, she pointed at the cards on his palm, the edge of Gem's laminated driver's licence clearly visible. "My licence is right there. Look."

He made a low whistling sound out the side of his mouth. "I can't see anything past this." He wafted the banknote in her face.

"That's money she keeps—I keep!—in case."

"In case you need to bribe a police officer?"

"In case I need to buy bread or milk." Her voice was shrill, slicing across the hushed fields.

The captain swung his bald head. "Constable, I think we are going to need those handcuffs."

4

#JailhouseJock

Becca stopped pacing and wrapped her fingers around the icy bars of the prison cell's battered door. The blood-tang of metal assaulted her nostrils as she pushed her face between the bars and angled her head in a vain attempt to peer up the fluorescent-bright corridor beyond.

"Hey! I'm still waiting for my phone call. And my jacket." She listened. Nothing. "This is a clear abuse of police power!" No response. "I know people at *Carte Blanche*! You don't want to end up on TV in one of their exposés!" The empty corridor remained empty. "You could at least bring me something to eat." A chocolate cake with a file in it would be great. Becca gave a frustrated cry and tugged hard on the bars. The locked gate clanked and her aching brain rattled in her skull. "And two Aspirins." That niggle she'd had when they'd first turned the key on her was developing into a full-blown tension headache.

She released the bars and crossed to the slatted metal bench at the back of the cell. She sat, wincing as the cold metal bit through the faux-leather leggings. Any longer in here and her extremities were going to turn black and fall off. It might technically be almost spring in South Africa, but in early August, the nights here in the shadow of the mountains were still icy.

With one hand, she kneaded her tight neck muscles while rubbing warmth into her freezing legs with the other. For the umpteenth time that night, she eyed the rough blanket folded at the end of the bench. She bet it would glow in the dark if exposed to one of those blue lights they used to find bodily fluids in TV show crime-scenes.

A bone-deep shiver passed up her spine, tensing her tired muscles and sending a spasm through her aching head. Hypothermia was worse than whatever she might catch from that blanket. Her huff of resignation was white in the frigid air. She leaned over and snagged the blanket between thumb and forefinger. It unfolded stiffly as if it had been starched. With a shudder, she pulled the grime-stiff fabric about her shoulders. It was impossible not to notice the smell: pee with base notes of stale beer. Those months on rotation in Housekeeping, back in the early days when she'd been cycling through various hotel departments before she'd found her perfect fit behind the concierge desk, had trained her nose too well.

She leaned back against the whitewashed wall, her shoulders tensing at the first kiss of the cold bricks, even through the blanket. Her fingers tingled from the cold. She pulled her hands into the long sleeves of the cashmere top. At least she could no longer feel her bum, although on second thoughts, that might be a bad sign...frost-bite might already have set in.

Ironic, really, how only this morning she'd told Mom they'd better pray there was a real-life Mark Darcy waiting in the wings if they got nabbed by the Thai police, and now here she sat, in need of some heroic assistance herself. Not that she wanted to be indebted to some heroic Mark-Darcy type. Though to be honest, if the universe did see fit to send some gorgeous hero to rescue her from this barred meat locker, she'd be prepared to shelve her dignity if it meant preventing her nose from turning black and falling off like some frostbitten Everest adventurer's.

As Mom kept telling her this morning though, this wasn't the movies. No one was coming to her rescue. She'd just have to wait. Eventually someone would have to come down that corridor, and then she'd bombard them with uncomfortable questions about how keen they were to have charges of unlawful detention on their service records.

A soft clicking, like fingernails on a chalkboard, sounded from the end of the corridor. At last! Becca pushed to her feet and crossed to the cell door, clutching the blanket at her throat.

The noise grew louder, an ambling clickety-click, coming steadily closer.

"Hello?"

A large chocolate Labrador trotted into view, its tail swishing rhythmically. The dog saw her and stopped.

Not quite the rescuer she'd had in mind. The universe could at least have sent a St Bernard with one of those little barrels of warming brandy hanging from its collar. "Have you come to bail me out?"

The Labrador wagged its tail harder and worked something to the front of its jaw before letting it drop to the ground with a wet thwock: a raw potato, covered in tooth marks and bubbles of spit.

Becca screwed up her nose and took a step back.

The dog beamed at her wide-mouthed and sat with a satisfied harrumph, one back leg sliding sideways into an easy slouch.

If she had a pen and a scrap of paper, she could write a message and slip it under the dog's collar. *Help. Wrongfully incarcerated. Send lawyer.*

The deep vibrations of a male voice sounded in the corridor. The dog's ears perked up. Heavy footsteps echoed and the Lab scrambled to its feet and snatched the potato from the floor.

A human. Hopefully one with a key for this— Damn! If she'd known the universe had been listening when she said she'd be up for being rescued by a gorgeous hero, she'd have asked for the winning lottery numbers too.

The dog gave a happy whine around its potato and looked up adoringly at a man in his early thirties. He was taller than her, even in Gem's Eiffel-esque heels. A bulky navy jacket was zipped over a broad chest. Big arms filled the jacket's sleeves, the kind of arms that suggested he'd be able to pick up that dog as if it were no more than a puppy. Faded jeans covered long, muscled legs, and scuffed work boots gave the man a rugged, outdoorsy look.

The Labbie beamed at him around the potato and wiggled its rump excitedly. Becca felt a similar urge herself to break into excited wiggles. It was all that thick dark hair. His. Not the Labrador's. And those deep brown eyes that hinted at warmth despite the frowning set of his eyebrows.

The man leaned down to pat the dog's plush head before straightening to face her. He folded his arms. "Gem Stratton."

Another cop sent to hassle her? No uniform, but he could be off duty. She arranged her face into a neutral expression while she awaited more clues.

"Back in town in the nick of time." He had the kind of voice best eaten with a spoon. "And with a police escort, no less."

Or licked off skin like body chocolate.

An involuntary shot of lust zinged up from parts neglected since Kevin's unceremonious expulsion from her flat. She mirrored the man's arrogant stance, folding her arms as best she could without dropping the blanket. "You sound surprised."

"I am." The man's scowl deepened and he made a tsk-ing noise. "And even more surprising"—his voice lifted, as if he were announcing an extra discount on an already too-good-to-be-true offer—"she's not throwing a fit." He looked down at the dog, who looked up at him with eyebrows bobbing. "Can you believe it, girl? No tragic lip trembling and not a single tear."

Becca stiffened and lifted her chin. This guy had definitely crossed paths with Gem. Pity the sanctuary's website had nothing but photos of animals on it, then she might recognise this charmer. One of the foreign volunteers? Gem had said some of them were hot. But Mr Snide here had a South African accent.

Whoever he was though, he had a point: she wasn't acting like Gem. Her sister would not have tolerated this jail cell quietly. She'd have been indignant. Aggrieved. 'Extra', as only Gem could be. "Would you prefer it if I were ranting and raving? How about if I dragged a tin cup across the bars?"

A hint of a smile played across the man's lips and he folded his arms across his broad chest. "It would certainly be more entertaining."

She glared at him. If he thought he could cow her, he could think again. She'd dealt with way worse at The Rickford, though it wasn't easy having a stare-off with someone whose dark eyes were doing odd things to her stomach. Something banged against the bars and she looked down.

The dog had dropped her potato against the barred door. With a jerk of her muzzle, the dog nudged the potato against the bottom rung and looked up with a floppy-tongued grin as if she'd just nosed the key under the cell door. Becca dropped a cautious hand between the bars and the Labrador extended her snout and sniffed.

"Look at that, Ella," he said, looking aghast at the dog. "Her Royal Highness has at last deigned to acknowledge your presence. Seems all your efforts to win her over this week have paid off."

So he *was* from the sanctuary. The disagreeable vet? But Gem had said Sullivan Scott was vile, and while this guy was many things, vile was not one of them.

The dog gave her a lick with a slobbery tongue and Becca whipped her hand away.

"Careful, you might catch something," the mystery man said.

Becca wiped the back of her hand on the cell blanket. "Thanks for the concern, but I've had all my vaccinations."

"I was talking to Ella."

Becca upped her glare to a full glower.

He grinned back, unperturbed. Enjoying it even. "I reckon you've got an excellent chance of catching something from that though." He indicated the blanket with a jerk of his stubbled chin.

She shifted her shoulders beneath the blanket as if she were posing in a Chanel silk wrap. "Better than freezing to death."

His mouth twitched. "More surprises. Imagine, Gem Stratton, choosing to commit a fashion atrocity over suffering a hypothermic death."

"Haven't you heard?" She cocked her head. "Grunge is making a huge comeback."

He laughed. "As is scabies." The dog returned to lean into his thigh, gazing up at him, tail wagging, as if sharing in her master's unexpected enjoyment.

Becca clenched the blanket. "Is there a reason you're here trying to get a rise out of me? Boring Friday night at home alone, watching the parliamentary channel?"

His eyebrows arched. "Home shopping channel actually. I was about to phone in for one of those incredible Floor Whizz thingies when Jo called me. Alek raised the alarm when he phoned to check you'd arrived and a cop answered your cellphone." He held his arms out wide. “So here I am. The cavalry, at Your Majesty’s service.”

Thank God for agents. Although... “Alek only called now to check on me?”

The man shook his head. “He called a few hours ago. But I was busy.”

Bastard. “I haven’t done anything wrong, you know.”

“Of course you haven’t. You’re a good girl.” He drew out the syllables of the last words so that Ella thumped her tail on the floor. He smiled at the dog and brushed the tips of his fingers over her ears. “And you’re a good girl too, but then that’s never been in question.”

For an arse, he was rather sweet with the dog. “That bribery thing was a total misunderstanding. And if it was my car that dinged their police van, then that’s news to me.”

His laugh was disdainful. “Considering the state you were in the last night you were here, I wouldn’t expect you to remember a thing.”

She was too cold and tired to try and work out what that meant. “Look, the sooner you bail me out, the quicker you can get your hands on that super-duper Floor Whizz you’ve had your eye on for so long.”

There was that lip quirk again. “First, answer one question for me. If I get you out, am I going to have to put up with you bitching and moaning all week, prancing about like an aggrieved princess?”

Becca hardened her gaze and wrapped a hand around a bar. “I’m no princess. And I never prance.”

He closed the space between them and clamped his hand above hers. “You would put a bloody Lippizaner to shame.” His low voice sent tingles across her skin. He leaned in, so close she could feel his heat radiating off him and smell hints of his deodorant. “Now answer the question, princess. Because I'm quite happy to leave you here."

She set her jaw and gave him another glare for good measure. "No."

"No what?" Another smirk.

Remind her to give this guy a wide berth when she got to the sanctuary. She released the bar and gave him a mock salute with her free hand. "No, sir!"

His grin intensified. "I meant, 'no, I won't prance about like an aggrieved princess', but 'no, sir' will do." He clicked his fingers for the dog. "I'll go and sort out getting you released."

She gave him another salute. "Yes, sir, thank you, sir!"

He let go of the bar and tipped his head in contemplation. "Sir. I rather like that." He smirked at her. "From now on, be sure you call me 'Dr Scott, sir'."

5

#DazedAndConfused

It was hard to keep up with Dr Smugness in Gem's heels. His more practical boots devoured the gravel in the car park outside the police station, outpacing her mincing jog as he headed for a large white Ford Ranger.

"Dr Smu— Dr Scott!" God, she still couldn't believe this was Sullivan Scott, the dickhead incarnate. Gem must have really loathed him to not once have mentioned the word 'hot' in connection to him. "How much was the bail?"

He didn't break stride. "I thought we agreed you'd call me 'Dr Scott, sir'."

Bite me. "I need to repay you." Not a chance was she going to be in his debt.

"Only courts grant bail."

Her feet halted abruptly. "I have to appear in court?" Not only was that going to play havoc with her schedule for raking in Gem's hours, but the press would have a field day.

"Relax." He aimed his key fob at the Ranger and the pickup's orange lights flashed. "They aren't going to charge you."

"They're not?"

"They were messing with the big-city celeb. It's too hard to make the bribery charge stick, and it's hardly worth the paperwork to go after you for that little scrape." He threw open the driver's door and stood aside so Ella could leap up into the cab. "But next time you go on a tequila bender, you shouldn't drive the next morning, even if you're fleeing town. Drinking and driving's a harder charge to talk your way out of."

That didn't sound like her sister. Gem seldom drank alcohol. Aside from being fattening, it took the glow out of her complexion and led to undesirable exposure on social media.

Dr Smugness stepped onto the runner board. "Now stop glaring at me and get your car. I'm tired and we've got an early start tomorrow."

She straightened her shoulders. "I can find my own way back, thank you very much."

"I'm sure you can. But Alek said to make sure your little spell in jail didn't prompt you to do another runner. Though if you really want to"—his voice dropped into a conspiratorial whisper—"it would make my life a hell of a lot easier." He pointed into the darkness. "Freeway's that way."

She lifted her chin and stared him down. "Sorry to disappoint, but I'm not going anywhere."

"Until I make you get your hands dirty again," he said, and swung into the cab.

Her mouth fell open, but he thunked the door shut before her incensed mind could come up with an appropriate comeback. Mom had been right about his being a disagreeable arse. This was going to be a long and trying seven days.

She stalked to Gem's car as best she could without twisting an ankle and giving him the satisfaction of watching her face-plant in the gravel.

He revved the Ranger, impatient.

Just a quick stop to open the boot to get out a nice warm jumper—oops, jersey...better get her South African vocab right. She rummaged about in the duffel bag. No jerseys, only a soft thin cardie, but there was a black blazer folded neatly at the bottom. She pulled it on, slowing her movements when he revved the engine again. Then she shut the boot, climbed into the car and took her sweet time putting on the seat belt and preening her hair in the rearview mirror in the light cast by his waiting headlights.

The Ranger growled again and she smiled at herself in the mirror and gave her dark hair a final flick. Her head responded with a burst of pain. She pressed her fingertips into throbbing temples. Forget tension headache, this was heading into migraine territory.

There was a generic pill bottle in the compartment beside the handbrake, the label worn and illegible. She flipped the cap to see familiar white tablets: paracetamol. Hallelujah. She tipped out two and threw them into the back of her mouth, dry-swallowing and grimacing at the taste on her tongue. Then she started the Audi.

The big pickup spat gravel as Dr Smugness accelerated out of the car park and onto the road. Industrial buildings gave way after a minute or so to tree-lined residential streets. Another turn put them onto a road lined with dark shops that curved around a large central grassed oval. The village pub was still open, people smoking outside on the pavement.

Her stomach growled, reminding her she hadn't eaten since that chicken pie she'd bought at the One Stop on the drive from Joburg. Probably why she was beginning to feel so groggy; her blood sugar must be tanking.

The Ranger's left indicator came on. She followed the pickup onto a road that seemed to be heading out of town and into the dark countryside beyond. The taillights were smudged red, bleeding like streamers into the black night. They drove, curving this way and that into the foothills.

Her head nodded and she jerked it up with a sharp intake of breath. The journey from England was starting to catch up with her. What she needed was a blast of cold mountain air. She buzzed down the window and trained her gaze on the hypnotic weaving trail of the Ranger's lights. Her eyelids drooped and she blinked them open in time to see the blaze of brake lights.

She stomped on a pedal, heart drumming. That was close. Imagine the flack if she'd driven into his pickup. A large signboard stood on the side of the road. *Winterberg Wildlife Rescue and Sanctuary.* The black letters seemed to jostle about like popcorn kernels in a hot pan. She gave herself a shake.

The Ranger turned at the sign onto a deserted dirt road. She followed, engulfed by the cloud of dust that spewed from his wheels and poured like abrasive smoke into her car. Coughing and squinting through the airborne grit, she fumbled for the window button. The car veered and she pulled it back with a jerk of the steering wheel, making the world outside blur and sway even after the car straightened out.

She had to pull over right now, before she drove off the road. But the dirt road was bordered by a barbed-wire fence. There was nowhere to pull off. A flare of orange signalled another turn, this time onto a driveway of sorts, just two tracks worn into the earth.

They must be almost there. She forced her eyes open and gritted her teeth as tight as her grip on the steering wheel. It couldn't be much longer now.

She jolted up the track behind the pickup, bouncing in the seat to keep herself awake until the brakes ahead flared and the Ranger swung onto a stretch of lawn and parked in front of a wooden fence.

Thank God. Becca yanked on the steering wheel to follow, throwing the car into a turn worthy of a stunt driver and bumping up onto the grass. In a rapidly darkening section of her mind came the suggestion that braking might be a good idea. Her foot kicked at the brake.

The fence leaped at her.

Crunch.

She pitched forward and the seat belt locked, jarring air out of her lungs. Her feet lost their grip on the pedals and the car stalled with a lurch. Befuddled, Becca stared out the windscreen, waiting for her mind to catch up. She turned her head at movement beside her.

Dr Smugness looked in at her window, his eyes wide in what-the-hell-just-happened astonishment.

She would have laughed at his expression if she hadn't been so focused on diverting all her energy to keeping her head upright. "My brakes failed."

"More like your coordination failed." He wrenched open her door. "You hit the accelerator instead of the brakes."

"Only because your pickup turned off so quickly. You startled me."

He reached in, turned the ignition key and the headlights cut off.

Blissful darkness. How nice would it be to shut her eyes—

"Are you drunk?"

She jerked her head and looked up at him, standing in the car's doorway, all glowering, looming, bristling male. "Course not." She lifted her right hand and poked the tip of her nose with her index finger. "Perfec—" For a moment she couldn't quite get her tongue to navigate the word. "Perfectly." Better. "Sober."

"Say that without slurring and I might believe you."

"That without slurring," she said, staring him down in challenge until an immense yawn ruined her bravado. Flattening her hand against her mouth, she looked away out the windscreen. That was odd. "Why is there a fence on my car?"

"Because you drove into it. Come on. Out!"

Second time today some macho male had ordered her out of her car. She leaned towards the open door and poked out a leg. Something held her back. Her brow furrowed. "I'm stuck."

"Undo your seat belt."

She inspected the belt across her chest. Right. Twisting her shoulders, she squinted at the seat belt clip. Tipped her head for a better view. What was she— Oh right, getting out the car. The seat belt. Undo it. One hand smothering another tonsil-exposing yawn, she jabbed the red release button with the other. Why wouldn't it release? She tried again. Still stuck. Applying both hands to the task, she gave the buckle a sharp tug. "I can't undo it."

"It's fine, boys, thanks."

Abandoning the seat belt, she looked up. Still standing in the open door of her car, Dr Smugness had his forearms resting on the roof now, his big torso filling the space. A boy's voice drifted from somewhere behind her.

"Minor accident, but I've got it under control." Dr Smugness had a nice voice when he wasn't smirking. Commanding. In control.

A bright light flashed. A teenage boy wearing a baseball cap the wrong way round looked at her through the windscreen. He was holding up a cellphone. Another flash blinded her and she covered her face.

"Enough, Gabe. Go on now."

Dr Smugness and his deep, hypnotic voice. Becca sighed, leaned her forehead on the steering wheel, and shut her eyes.

"Sit back."

She jolted awake as a hand nudged her against the seat. Dr Smugness leaned in over her, his shoulder skimming past her face.

She inhaled deeply and slowly, drawing in faded notes of deodorant, another scent that was slightly stingy and astringent, and fabric heated on warm skin. The smell loosed something twitchy and giddy inside her. There was a soft snick and the belt released.

He straightened out of her car and looked down at her with undisguised irritation. “Anytime today, princess.”

If her eyes hadn’t been so sleepy she’d have rolled them. She forced herself to stagger from the car, holding onto the door to steady herself. “Are you mad at me?”

“Nothing like Jo’s going to be when she sees her fence tomorrow.”

Something brown and panting appeared around the car door. His dog. Emma. No, Ella. She gave herself a mental high five, as if remembering a simple name was somehow remarkable, though the way her head was feeling right now, it was a feat worthy of instant MENSA membership. Ella thumped her tail. “At least somebody around here likes me.”

“Ella would wag her tail for a guy in a balaclava holding a shotgun.”

She was too tired to dredge up the energy needed for the filthy look that comment deserved. “You have a thing for princesses. Me.” She hooked her chin at the Lab. “Cinderella over there.”

“It’s short for Nutella. And I most definitely don’t have a thing for you.”

Mmm. Hazelnut chocolate spread. On toast. No, on him. *Down, girl.* “You ever had the Nutella cupcakes at the Hummingbird Bakery? Tiny place on Portobello Road?”

He looked at her as if she were speaking Martian.

“In Notting Hill?” she prompted.

“The movie?”

Clueless. "The district." Still no sign he knew what she was talking about. "Of West London?"

"Ah." He nodded sagely. "I often shoot through to London in my Learjet when I'm feeling peckish."

Fortunately exhaustion stopped her from physically face-palming herself. "I mean I read about them. Online. The cupcakes." She was rambling—she knew she was—but couldn't seem to stop the words from spilling out. "I didn't actually go there myself." Stop. "Why would I?" Stop! "It's in London and I live here!"

He boxed her in then between car and door, bringing his face close to hers, which mercifully shut off her switch-wrecking monologue mid-spew. He leaned in and her pulse took flight. Was he trying to...to kiss her? The twitchy, giddy thing took off again. But he couldn't kiss her. He didn't like her. And she didn't like him. No, no, no, she did not. Although she couldn't quite remember why. Her brain felt like it was running on a backup generator.

His fingers closed on her jaw then and she jumped. He was so close. She put a hand on his chest to push him back, but electricity fizzed through her and she forgot why she'd lifted her hand in the first place. He was so solid. *Dr Sturdy.* Dr Sexy too. So, so sexy. Suddenly she was up on her toes, her mouth pressed to his.

For the space of a heartbeat, he tensed, then he released her jaw as if a live current had passed through it. He fell backwards, almost toppling over Ella. "What the hell are you doing?" His hand went up to his mouth as if he were assessing the damage from a well-placed right hook.

"I..." What the hell *was* she doing? "I'm sorry. I lost my"—*mind*—"my balance." Sure. Losing her balance had caused her to fall upwards into his lips. "Don't glare at me like that. You wanted it first!"

"Wanted what?"

"To kiss me."

His eyes pulled wide with indignation. "I was smelling your breath for alcohol."

She felt for the side of the car and concentrated all her energy on assembling her thoughts into a vaguely straight line. "Look, I'm knackered. I want to go to bed." *With you.* "By myself!"

"I wasn't offering."

Of course he wasn't. "Good night."

"Can I carry anything for you?"

You can carry me. "Nope! You just run along to your pickup now."

His eyes narrowed. "That's the second time you've called my bakkie a pickup. And why does your accent go all BBC every now and then?"

Adrenalin shot a dose of focus into her brain like an espresso in the morning. "I'm—" Calm down. Speaking with the odd British inflection didn't mean she wasn't Gem. "I'm auditioning for a small part in an English movie. Crikey, guv'ner. Fancy a spo' o' char?" Gawd, now she was Dick van Dyke in the original *Mary Poppins*. She clapped her hands like she meant business. "Right then, I'm off to Bedfordshire." *Doing it again.* Her lips rolled off her teeth into a frozen grin and she gave him a little wave.

He threw her one last inscrutable look, shook his head in confusion, and headed for his pickup. His bakkie! Bakkie! How hard was it? Gosh, but she was too tired for all this linguistic gymnastics. In a final Herculean feat of mind over bone-crushing exhaustion, Becca kept her head erect and watched him drive off.

When she could no longer see his taillights, she let her knees unlock and slumped onto the edge of the driver's seat. She dropped her head into her hands, the motion making her brain slosh about like a paper boat on an incoming tide.

She dragged her legs back into the car and felt on the passenger seat for the room key Gem had omitted to return when she'd high-tailed it from town. She picked it up and squinted until the letters engraved on the metal tag came into focus. *Volunteer Block, Room 3*. She looked through the slats in the fence at the lights winking across the dark lawn from buildings dotted about in the blackness. She clutched the key in her fist. Shouldn't be too hard to find Gem's room.

A yawn attempted to dislocate her jaw. She shut her eyes.

Just for five minutes.

Twitter

Sexy.AF.Gabe
@gabe.deabreu

Check out this photo! I caught #GemStratton pulling! Wish I was sucking face with a HOT AF chick like Gem. Respect, Doc! But if #MandlaNdungane plays like kak tomorrow, you know why! #cheatingbae #2timing #cheaters

10:03 PM **1567** Retweets 468 Likes

Jo_Girl@jobarker 1h
Replying to @gabe.deabreu

Wait whoa what?!?! That's not Mandla Ndungane!!! Who's the guy she's kissing? And does Mandla know?!? OMG!!

MapuleB@mapulebabes 1h
Replying to @gabe.deabreu

This girl!! Mandla isn't enough for her?!? She must mess with other men as soon as Mandla is away? Slut.

6

#SearchAndRescue

A rough snort snatched at the back of Becca's throat as she jerked awake. She grimaced and rubbed the knee she'd whacked on the steering wheel.

The rapping sound came again.

It felt like sections of her aching brain had yet to come online. She turned a stiff neck to look out the drizzle-spattered driver's window and groaned at the face on the other side. Dr Flipping Smugness, one arm braced on the car's roof, looking in at her with an expression as leaden as the sky beyond.

Becca pressed her fingers into her eye sockets and tipped back her head against the headrest. Details of the previous night jostled into her groggy mind. Jail. Attractive yet infuriating vets on white horses. Or white Rangers. Potato-carrying dogs. A white-knuckle drive. The rest was nothing but torn fragments of memory. Her brakes had failed. Or her foot had failed. Something like that. And there was a vague recollection of mashing her face into a certain someone's stubble. Please let that last bit be a fatigue-induced hallucination.

Rap rap rap. "Fifteen minutes, princess!" Dr Smugness's voice was muffled through the glass.

Becca opened one eye and turned her head. The stubble was gone, but the mouth was awfully familiar. Her stomach tipped. Not a hallucination then. She felt for the key in the ignition and turned it one click so she could buzz down the window. "Fifteen minutes until?" Her voice was thick with sleep.

"Until seven o'clock, when I leave here without you and you don't get to complete any hours today."

She scrunched up her face. "So early? But it's Saturday."

Dr Smugness's eyes hardened. "Animals don't care about days of the week."

Forget Dr Smugness. Today he was Dr Surly. And Mom hadn't been exaggerating that he was a taskmaster. "Go without me. I don't want to hold you up. I'll find someone else to help today." *Anyone but you.*

He straightened and took a step back from her window. Drizzle misted the shoulders of his navy fleece and collected into bright drops in his dark hair. "Believe me, after this last week, I'm as keen as you are for us not to work together. But Clare's in Howick this morning, so it's work with me or sit in your room and paint your nails." The lift of his eyebrows said he was hoping she'd choose the manicure.

Fat chance he was getting rid of her that easily. "Guess it's you and me then."

His eyebrows hooded and he glanced at a heavy metal watch on his wrist. "Fourteen minutes."

Her concierge training kept her eyeballs from rolling back into her head. Instead she graced him with a smile that hinted he was her favourite person on the planet. "I'll be ready in ten, Dr Scott, sir."

Irritation sharpened his gaze and without another word, he turned and stomped off towards the buildings beyond the parking area, gravel grinding under his boots.

Becca pressed the heels of her hands into her eyes and groaned. Her head was stuffed full of cotton wool and when she opened her eyes, the world outside the car seemed to be tipping ever so slightly. On a hunch, she found the bottle of medicine she'd tossed on the passenger seat and shook one onto her palm. She flipped it over to read the letters stamped into one side. *AMB.* Whatever it was, it wasn't paracetamol. What was the bet these were Gem's sleeping pills? And she'd taken not one, but two.

She stacked her arms on the steering wheel and rested her head on her forearms. No wonder she felt so groggy; she had a medically induced sleep hangover.

With the sort of effort it took to drag herself to the gym on a winter's morning, Becca collected Gem's room key and phone and heaved herself from the car. It took some juggling to get Gem's suitcase, the duffel bag and her weekender bag marshalled, but eventually she was staggering towards the sanctuary's buildings, slowing only to take a guilty look at the toppled section of fence in front of the car.

The wheeled case juddered as it hit the concrete path. A fork to the left led to an expansive single-storey brick building with a gabled roof entrance over double glass doors. *Rehabilitation Centre*, said lettering on the gable. Becca scanned a directional sign at the split and kept straight for the volunteer block.

Past the rehab centre, more buildings were dotted across a wide lawn that was greening in patches as the grass came back to life after winter. Signs over cottage-pane doors marked out the main office, a communal dining room, a laundry. What was presumably staff housing, some single units and others semi-detached, stretched away up the slope behind the admin buildings. Over the tiled roofs, decades-tall trees stretched winter-bare branches not yet revived from hibernation. And rising up behind it all was the flank of the mountain.

The suitcase bumped into Becca's calves as she stopped and gazed up at the mountain, its foothills folded into bands of rock that rose into a steel sky. A blanket of descending cloud obscured the topmost peaks, spooling over the cliffs to drain into steep-sided ravines made dark and mysterious with wet vegetation.

She stood like that for a moment, ignoring the soft drizzle, letting the stillness of the place steal across her jangled nerves like a deep breath. Then she tightened her grip on the suitcase's handle and broke into a shuffling jog.

The volunteer block was a wide two-storey block at the end of the path, one side sheltered by a massive oak. Two women in jeans and bulky jackets exited the stairwell on the far end, turning their faces towards her without breaking off their conversation. A door opened on the ground floor and a man hurried out, waving at the women before shoving his hands deep into his jacket pockets and dashing off the way Becca had come.

Finding Gem's room on the ground floor, Becca parked the suitcase beside the door and took the room key from a pocket. The door swung open onto a room that, but for its lack of cleaning equipment, could well have been a broom closet in a past life. Against one wall stood a single bed draped in a white duvet tinged yellow by chlorine bleaching, with a thick navy blanket folded across the foot. Beside the bed was a small blocky bedside table. A portable heater stood on the carpet before a double-doored wooden wardrobe. And through an open arch was a cramped bathroom with a loo, basin and shower. Not the sort of digs Gem was used to.

As Becca parked the suitcase beside the narrow bed and dumped the rest of her bags on the duvet, she leaned to look out the postage-stamp window, finding a view onto neat lush gardens of rain-glistened hydrangeas and agapanthus. While the boss here might leave much to be desired, the scenery couldn't be faulted.

She lifted Gem's phone to fire off a text before she remembered that her mother and sister were incommunicado. It was a strange feeling, to not have Gem just a video call away. She set the phone on the bedside table and heaved the suitcase onto the bed. No time for a shower. She'd have to make do with fresh deodorant and clean clothes.

A rummage through the suitcase unearthed spaghetti-strap tops. Off-the-shoulder dresses. Silky blouses. Two T-shirts, but both white. Their mother was too much. She wriggled into skinny jeans, threw on a silky black blouse that would hide her glaring lack of a shoulder tattoo, and shrugged into one of her sister's blazers. Then she brushed her dishevelled hair into a ponytail and reached for Gem's makeup bag.

Minutes later, she pocketed Gem's phone, snatched up an ungainly pair of death heels from the suitcase, locked the room door behind her, and set off at a run, bare feet slapping on the wet concrete.

The Ranger was already idling when she huffed into the parking lot, a stitch stabbing her between the ribs. She hauled open the passenger door and tossed Gem's heels onto the cabin floor.

Dr Surly's eyes darted to the shoes and his mouth gave a contemptuous twist. "You don't own a pair of *takkies*?"

Sneakers...if only. "My wardrobe consultant did all the packing," she said, hopping up into the cab.

Dr Surly put the big vehicle into reverse. "More fashion sense than common sense. And you're late."

"By a minute." She banged shut the passenger door with more force than was necessary.

"More like ten. I'll dock it from your hours."

She gave his snide comment the same reaction she would've given had she been standing behind the concierge desk: she was Switzerland, majestic in her neutrality, as she fastened the seat belt.

The Ranger surged backwards, Dr Surly's gaze focused on his mirrors. "Need any help with that?"

"With the seat belt?"

"That most mystifying of all safety devices," he said, his big hands flexing and crossing on the steering wheel as he backed into the dirt road.

Why would she need help fastening a seat belt? He jabbed the Ranger into first with the heel of his hand and the scent of him stole into her nose, unlocking a drug-dimmed memory. Dr Surly leaning over her when she'd been too woozy to figure out the seat belt.

Her cheeks heated in embarrassment. She'd *sniffed* him. Inhaled his warm male scent with a great sigh. Well, that ended now. Yes, he was attractive, but he was equally disagreeable. And she had one goal this week, a goal that had nothing to do with thirsting over men, good-looking as they may be. She turned in her seat to look at him. "I'm sorry about last night. About everything."

Silence. Nothing but the bump and clatter of the bakkie on the dirt road.

"I wasn't in my right mind. I found some pills in my car that I thought were painkillers, but they were sleeping pills."

"Uh huh." Dr Surly stared straight ahead.

She gave up and instead reached down for Gem's heels, peering out the side window at the wire-fenced enclosures that lined the road as she slid each shoe on. "What's that buck called?" she said, tipping her head in the direction of a large antelope with a jet-black coat and two pointed horns scooping dramatically backwards over its head.

"Sable." The Ranger powered through a puddle, spraying water past her window.

"Why's it here?"

"Road accident."

First job of the morning: pulling conversational teeth. She hugged her arms around her body and returned to looking out the side window. In the next camp, two zebras and a donkey watched them drive past. "Is it true zebras have the strongest kick on Earth?" An Australian guest had told her that once, while she was booking him tickets for a kickboxing championship. She turned her head to look at Dr Surly, but she might as well not have been buckled into the passenger seat for all the attention he gave her. The swish-swish of the wipers chopped the icy silence into blocks of vibrating tension. It was a wonder her breath wasn't coming out all white and frosty. "Where are we off to?" she said.

Dr Surly turned onto the main dirt road outside the sanctuary. "I don't remember you being so chatty the last time you were here."

A complete sentence this time, with a verb and everything. "Look, I tried to apologise. I didn't mean to kiss you."

His hand fisted on the gear lever as he up-shifted.

"It was the sleeping pills I took," she said. "Temporary insanity."

"If you say so." He slowed and checked for traffic before he joined the municipal road. "Though I doubt that excuse will make your boyfriend feel less cheated on."

She stiffened. Kevin was the cheat, not her. "Not that it's any of your business, but I don't have a boyfriend—" She pressed her lips together and clenched one hand into a fist in her lap. She didn't have a boyfriend. But Gem did. First rule of a twin switch: remember which damned twin you were meant to be.

Becca uncurled her fingers and smoothed both palms on her jeans. "Mandla and I...we're not together."

Dr Surly scrutinised her face.

"What, you don't believe me?"

His eyes hooded. "Can you ever really believe a cheat?"

Something in his eyes made her think he was speaking from experience. "I'm not a cheat. And I'm also not Mandla's girlfriend." She signed a cross over her heart with her index finger. It was the God's-honest truth. Just not Gem's truth.

He turned his attention back to the road and they drove in silence for several more minutes, the road winding through uninterrupted expanses of natural grassland until the GPS on his phone announced they'd reached their destination. Dr Surly pulled the Ranger onto the hard shoulder and killed the engine. He retrieved his phone before climbing out and going round to the back of the bakkie. The tailgate dropped with a thunk, and Becca heard him scrabbling about in the back. She craned around in her seat and saw him lift out a large black plastic toolbox before he banged the tailgate shut.

She hopped down and joined him as he strode past her, toolbox in one hand and a thin metal pole in the other, towards the rusted barbed wire fence that separated the hard shoulder from the veld. "What are we doing here?"

"You? Getting in my way. Me? My job."

And there he went again, earning himself another nickname. Dr Sarcastic dumped the holdall and pole at his feet, then he stamped one heavy leather boot on the bottom strand of spiked wire, stomping it into the muddy ground. He positioned both hands between the spikes on the next strand up and lifted, looking at her expectantly.

Becca directed a pointed look at the wet stone-strewn ground, then at the gap in the sharp wire. "I'll climb over."

"In those heels?" he said, without breaking eye contact to look at the footwear in question.

Becca blinked away the drizzled mist of rain gathering in her eyes. "So you want me to crawl through there instead?"

"No. I thought I might stand like this all morning for my own entertainment."

Maintaining her placid expression with difficulty, she smiled benignly at him and dropped into a squat on the wet ground. Hands in the mud, she clambered through the gap he'd made in the fence with about as much grace as a newborn foal on ice, careful not to skewer herself on a rusty barb.

He passed the pole and plastic toolbox through the fence, seemingly unconcerned about getting jabbed by wire himself through his thick fleece. Then he held down the topmost piece of wire and swung one long leg over, then the other. The fence vibrated along its length as he released the top strand. Then he stooped to retrieve his things and walked off into the open veld without a backward glance.

Becca fell in behind him, but it wasn't easy keeping up. Even if she hadn't been wearing shoes less wholly unsuited to the terrain than Gem's heels were, Dr Surly made no effort to shorten his stride for her. "If you don't slow down, you're going to be carrying me out of here with a twisted ankle." What an unappealing thought, being pressed up against that unforgiving chest.

He stopped; not for her sake it would seem, but to check the GPS on his phone. He scanned the veld, then set off again at the same break-neck speed, altering his course towards a thicket of brush and small trees.

Becca scowled at his back before returning her concentration to picking her way through the clumps of winter-yellowed wild grass, so heavy with rain they soaked the bottom of her jeans and filled her shoes with water, making her squelch as she walked. A few minutes later, she almost bumped into Dr Surly and had to throw out her arms when she looked up to find him halted right in front of her.

"Could you please not make threatening movements like that?" he said in an annoyed whisper.

She pulled a rude face at his back before she stepped around him to see why he'd stopped. A few metres away, huddled low under the cover of a rangy bush, was a large wild cat with short reddish fur made slick by the rain. "Is that a lynx?" she whispered, taking in the black smudges above the big cat's oval eyes, and its long pointed ears rimmed with black and tipped with flamboyant black tufts.

"Similar. It's a caracal."

The animal bared its teeth at them in silent warning, but didn't attempt to flee. "It's beautiful," she said.

"It'd be more beautiful without the snare."

Becca saw it then: the noose of thick wire around the caracal's neck, the fur bloodied beneath it. "Poor thing." Her voice caught, and her stomach lurched at the sight of its torn flesh, but she didn't look away. If she could survive the annual ZombieCon held at The Rickford, with the inevitable requests from delegates to source them an extra lifelike severed hand or reposition a fake bloodied axe in a head, she could cope with the real thing now. She steadied herself with arms wrapped tight about her. "It must be in such pain."

"It is." He was on his haunches before the open toolbox of vet equipment, drawing liquid into a syringe from a glass vial. "But that's why I'm here." He secured the syringe to the front of the pole he'd been carrying, then he lengthened the pole and tightened it in place with a sharp twist of his hand that made the muscles flex beneath the leather and metal bracelets cuffed at one wrist.

Staying low on his haunches, he approached the cat. It hissed at him, eyes straining in its head as it tried to keep him in sight without pulling on the wire. Dr Surly held out the pole, inching the syringe towards the wild cat's flank. He made a stabbing motion and the cat fought against the wire noose for a moment before sinking back into the grass, eyes wide and frightened. He capped the syringe and disposed of it in his holdall. "Give it a minute," he said, settling onto his haunches, his eyes trained on the caracal.

As he waited, he fiddled with the bracelets on one wrist, his fingers playing over the woven black leather and silver. Becca snapped her gaze away and looked instead at the cat, feeling the soft drizzle curling strands of her ponytail around her neck as the tension slowly drained from the animal's muscular body and it eventually slumped into the thick grass.

"Right." Dr Surly stood and shoved a hand up to push the dark wet hair off his forehead. "Time to work." He caught up his holdall and strode off ahead of her to where the prone animal lay. On his haunches again, he snapped on surgical gloves before easing the cat's tongue out the side of its jaw. With quick movements, he clipped a wire lead to the lolling tongue and a portable monitor he'd produced beeped into life.

Becca came closer and squatted beside him, balancing on the balls of her feet so her heels wouldn't sink into the soaked ground. She side-eyed the caracal's neck. The wire had cut cruelly into the animal's flesh, so deep she suspected it was bone she could make out from the corner of her eye. She swallowed an uprising of nausea. “That wound looks terrible. Will you have to put it out of its misery?”

He stopped fiddling with the monitor and looked at her. “I never give up without a fight. Everything deserves a second chance. And everyone.” His eyebrows lifted in a clear double meaning. “Or don’t you agree?”

“No, I do.”

“Then pass me the wire cutters.”

Becca swivelled on the balls of her feet to the holdall behind them and lifted out a pair of battered wire cutters that were lying on top. She held them out to him. “Let’s save it.”

His eyes played over her face for a moment, then he hefted the cutters, inserted one pointed tip under the wire snare and clenched his large hand. The wire parted with a snap.

Something in Becca’s chest released with it and she sighed.

“Don’t worry.” He handed her the cutters. “We’ve got this.”

Their eyes met again and she shifted, uneasy under his gaze. She twisted away to return the cutters to the holdall, and when she turned back, she was relieved to find his attention focused once more on the injured caracal.

With efficient yet gentle movements, he examined the wound, turning the animal’s heavy head to better see. His brow creased. “The wire’s cut really deep here.”

Becca put a hand on his leg to balance herself on Gem’s heels as she leaned in to take a closer look. She winced and looked up into his face. “Will you be able to fix it?”

He didn’t answer immediately, his gaze focused on where she was touching his leg.

Heat flared up her neck and she snatched away her hand as if his jeans were on fire. She’d been so absorbed she hadn’t even noticed the unconscious gesture. She steeled herself for the inevitable snide comments, but he spared her further embarrassment by swivelling abruptly on his toes to his holdall.

Smoothing her hot damp neck with her palm, Becca kept her eyes on the far-off mountains as he dug around in his holdall like someone inspecting the top kitchen drawer for a missing potato peeler.

When he turned back, he was holding a faded, much-washed green towel. Without another glance at Becca, he rolled the bedraggled unconscious feline into the towel and tucked the still-beeping monitor into a fold. He crouched and slid his arms beneath the caracal. "Can you carry that?" he said, standing, and nodded at his vet's things with the caracel swaddled in his arms.

Becca snapped shut the holdall, grabbed the pole and hurried after his fast-retreating form.

An hour later, engulfed in borrowed scrubs large enough to fit Gem's rugby-playing boyfriend, surgical mask around her neck, and wearing a disposable hair net that would have made her sister weep, she stood beside a stainless steel surgical table in one of the rehab centre's brightly lit operating theatres, with the injured caracal stretched out motionless before her.

"Suits you," Dr Surly said from across the table, his surgical mask hiding the smirk that the glee in his eyes gave away. The assistant busy setting up a tray of sterile instruments turned her head away too late to disguise a snort of mirth.

"Thanks," Becca said, patting the blue gauze puffed around her head. "The colour really brings out my eyes." She pulled the surgical mask over her mouth and nose and met his taunting gaze with a pointed look of her own to his uncovered head that told him she knew precisely what he was up to, and that it wasn't going to work. Gem Stratton was going nowhere.

"Couldn't expect the princess to wear an uncoordinated outfit." His gaze was hard over the top of his mask, but Becca faced him down like any other difficult guest she'd dealt with at The Rickford. After a few seconds, he broke eye contact, picked up a scalpel from the tray on the table, and set to work.

The irritation that had Becca grinding down on her teeth made way for prickles of anxiety. ZombieCon was all well and good, but the red liquid welling up beneath Dr Surly's scalpel wasn't cornstarch and food colouring. She dipped her head and fastened her gaze on the caracal's rump that was sticking out from the sterile draping around its neck. A slow measured breath through clamped teeth sucked the bite of disinfectant into her mouth, and she swayed back almost imperceptibly before she stiffened her back. The last thing she wanted to do was faint around him and give him more proof that Gem couldn't cut it.

"You don't have to watch."

Now he was Dr Perceptive. She shoved her hands—triple gloved for everyone in the operating theatre's amusement—deep into the pockets of the scrub pants. "I'm perfectly fine, thanks."

"Sure?" His eyes had narrowed over his surgical mask. "Because I don't want to have to stitch your head when you faint and crack it open."

She'd rather bleed out. "All good. Cut away." She just wouldn't look at the caracal. Or at Dr Surly's scalpel-wielding hands. Instead she'd look a little higher. Somewhere where she could avoid the gore without giving him the satisfaction of thinking she couldn't bear to watch. His bracelets. Copper and steel and leather banded around one thick, sinewed wrist. Muscles flexing beneath tanned skin as he twisted his forearm to change the blade's angle.

Becca sighed inwardly and looked away from the hypnotic practiced motion of his hands. Gem's cellphone rang then, and she smothered a relieved exhalation and fished the phone out of a pocket. The name on the lock screen put an instant damper on her relief. "Can I...?" She hovered a finger over the answer button and looked across the operating table at him.

"Wouldn't want to keep you from your adoring public," he said, without looking up.

"It's my agent. Alek."

"I know who your agent is."

Of course he did. "I'll just..." The screen didn't register her touch through the layers of latex, so she hooked a finger in at her right palm and stripped off the gloves. "Hey, Alek," she said, lifting the phone to her ear.

"Don't 'Hey, Alek' me, Gem."

Apprehension tightened her fingers around the phone and she glanced across the table at Dr Surly's dark head, bent over his work.

"What the hell are you doing?" Alek's voice grated.

"Trying to perform surgery," Dr Surly muttered to himself.

"Hang on, Alek," Becca said, and pressed the phone to her chest as she stepped away from the table. She marched off—admittedly more shuffle than march, thanks to the surgical shoe covers she wore over Gem's heels—into the scrub room at the end of the operating theatre and nudged the door shut with her hip. "Sorry, Alek," she said, lifting the phone to her ear again. "We rescued a caracal in the veld and—"

"Have you completely lost it?" Alek cut in. "Jesus, Gem! You can't cheat on the Springbok rugby captain and expect the public to forgive you."

Becca's mouth went instantly dry. She dragged the surgical mask off her face and croaked out a strangled "What?"

"Don't you check Twitter anymore? My idiot nephew Gabe took a photo of you last night kissing fucking Sullivan."

She had a patchy memory of Dr Surly talking to a bunch of teens, and of a camera flash making her cover her face. "Your nephew?"

"Jo's kid. My sister. Who runs the sanctuary with the man you decided to throw yourself at last night."

Becca blinked. "I was not throwing myself at him," she said, mortification making her cheeks heat. "I tripped."

"Into his face?"

It could happen. "I'm not cheating on Mandla. We had a fight and now we're taking a break."

"And you never thought to tell me this? Even if you and Mandla are through, could you not make your rebound quite so public?"

"I'm not on the rebound. That wasn't even a real kiss."

"What was the point then? If you're going to get mauled by the public for cheating on their rugby hero, you should at least get some real action for your trouble." Alek sighed heavily. "Look, I'll deal with the press. You do your hours and no more hot and heavy, okay? And no repeats of Tuesday night either, you hear me? My sister was less than amused." And he hung up without saying goodbye.

Becca found Twitter on Gem's home screen and typed in her sister's name as a hashtag.

Oh God. There it was.

She tapped to enlarge the grainy photo and grimaced. She was plastered to Dr Surly's face like one of those sucker fish on an aquarium wall. Her head felt hot, as if she'd been sitting under Mom's portable hooded hairdryer before a beauty pageant.

The operating room door opened and the vet assistant stuck her head out. "Sully wants to know if you plan to earn hours today or stand around playing Candy Crush."

"I'm not—"

The woman's head retracted.

"—playing Candy Crush." Shoving Gem's phone into a pocket, she returned to the operating theatre and slipped back into position beside the table.

"Discussing the sob story Alek is going to use when you make your next escape?" he said, his gaze catching hers over his mask.

Discussing her alibi when she stuck him with that scalpel. "Have you seen Twitter today?"

He returned his attention to the anaesthetised animal. "I don't do social media."

Odd, but thank God. At least he hadn't seen the photo. Probably the only South African who hadn't by now. What would Mandla do when he saw that tweet? Her stomach rolled and a weird prickling heat spread up her arms and into her chest. She felt suddenly ill, and the blood and that scalpel of his, glinting as he cut away damaged tissue, were not helping. She gripped the edge of the table.

"Gem!"

She looked up to find serious eyes regarding her.

"I said, are you okay?" he said slowly, like he was repeating himself. "You don't look good."

She hadn't looked good in that photo either. Gem was not going to be pleased. "I'm fine." Her free hand tugged her mask back up over her chin before joining the other in a death-grip on the edge of the surgical table, ungloved fingertips blanching white from the pressure. Everything would be fine. Alek would handle the press. She'd handle Mandla if needs be. Everything would work out. She should stop worrying and make herself useful, like the nurses did on TV. "You need any of these?" Still holding the table for support with her gloved hand, she snatched for the instrument tray beside him.

His hand shot out. "No!"

Becca pulled away in surprise and caught the edge of the tray with a flailing hand, knocking it off the table. Surgical instruments clattered to the floor.

She covered her mouth with her hands and he sighed in exasperation. "You can't touch sterile instruments without gloves," he said.

She knew that. Everyone knew that. She balled her ungloved hand into a fist and pressed it against her stomach as she backed away from the table. "Maybe you should put me to work somewhere less clean."

He accepted a new sterile tray from his assistant. "Somewhere less clean..." He reached for some sort of clampy thing and bowed his head over the prone animal. "I'm sure that could be arranged."

7

#WontQuit4Shit

A juvenile vervet monkey scolded Becca from a high leafy branch that jutted across the large cage. From inside the double-gated entryway of the cage, Becca stuck out her tongue at it, but the gesture was lost behind the two surgical masks she wore. It was an old trick she'd learned, handy to cut the smell wafting from her metal clean-up bucket.

"Thought you'd break me, huh?" So did Dr Surly, but she had news for him. He could assign her every filthy job there was and she still wouldn't quit.

More of the sleek-furred poo machines dashed into the foliage as they piled out of the sleeping area at the back where they'd been holed up while she cleaned. They looked like they were wearing fitted grey onesies with hoods edged in white fur, so that just their charcoal grey faces peeped out. The branches shivered as the lithe bodies sped along them, long tails bobbing like dexterous question marks.

From the safety of the gated entryway, Becca watched the energetic little creatures pursuing each other through their freshly cleaned cage. Another up-close encounter with the sanctuary's wild animals, and she'd aced it. She picked up the spade and the poo-filled bucket at her feet. "I'm going now. Try not to trash the place before I come back tomorrow. Otherwise I might be forced to feed you to..." What ate long-tailed poo factories?

"Leopards."

Becca almost dropped the bucket, she spun so violently. For a big man, Dr Surly could move silently when he wanted to.

He lounged outside the cage, one shoulder propped against an upright metal post as he looked through the steel mesh. "Though humans with pellet guns are a bigger threat to vervets than leopards are. And then there are also cars and dogs." His own dog sniffed the ground behind him, following a scent near his boots.

The drizzle had cleared an hour ago and the sun was now attempting to nose its way from behind the clouds. The fleece he'd worn that morning was gone, revealing a black T-shirt that hugged his chest. The fingers of one hand were hooked loosely through the mesh, his collection of leather and metal bracelets low on his wrist.

The bucket's wire handle slipped in Becca's damp palm and the bucket clanked and rocked. It was so irritating how her body kept responding to him. Annoyed with herself, she banged open the external gate and clumped from the cage, letting the spring-fitted gate bang shut behind her. The oversized wellies lent to her by a vet tech flapped about on her feet. She'd get blisters at this rate, but they were better than high heels.

Dr Surly's head dipped as he directed his gaze to her feet. "You're going to trip and break your neck in those."

She clanked the bucket onto the ground and leaned the spade against an upright cage pole. "If the shops are still open in town when I'm done, I'll go and buy something more suitable. Until then though"—she waggled a foot at him—"these wellingtons will have to do."

"Wellingtons, huh?" His gaze was sharp with scrutiny.

It took her a few moments to catch his drift. "Gumboots! You know what I mean. That's what comes from bingewatching *Bridgerton.*"

"All those lords and ladies have a lot of conversations involving rubber footwear, do they?"

Dr Smart-Arse. She eyed him, trying to work out if he was teasing her or if that was real suspicion in his eyes. "Of course. It rains a lot in England."

He held her gaze a moment longer, then swivelled away to rest his back against the mesh. "You scared you'll catch something from the monkeys?" He gestured to her face with a tip of his head.

"Nope." She slid the masks off her face so they hung from their ties around her neck. "Maybe you haven't noticed, but monkey poo smells gross."

The weight of his shoulders made the mesh flex. "A surgical mask is useless for cutting smells."

"Not if you use two and squeeze toothpaste between the layers. Or Vicks Vaporub. Your receptionist had some in her drawer. Works brilliantly." She snapped the thin ties, balled up the masks and shoved them into a baggy pocket. She'd learned that nostril-saving life hack years ago from The Rickford's housekeeping manager. The filthy things guests could do to their rooms... To this day, she couldn't look at a toilet brush without an involuntary shiver.

"They do teach you odd things at beauty-queen school, princess."

The amused way he was looking at her was having a strange effect on her ability to breathe. She broke eye contact and looked away into the cage. "What happened to that one?" She indicated a one-eyed, one-eared monkey sitting inside a bucket swing.

He shifted to look over his shoulder at the monkey she'd pointed out. "Jeremy." His expression softened and he turned back to face the cage. "Dog attack. Took almost two hours to sew him back together." Ella sidled up to him and he leaned sideways to drag his fingertips through her dense fur. "I thought we'd lose him." The Labbie pressed her snout to the mesh, potato wedged in one floppy cheek, her eyebrows dancing as she watched the monkey leap from the clanking hanging bucket and shimmy up the rope tied to the handle. "Lucky for him he had a fighting spirit."

"And a determined vet." Becca felt his gaze on her, but she kept her eyes trained on the monkey that was now hanging from the suspended bucket on one sinuous arm.

A gate banged further up the row of cages and she followed the sound. A man in a Dallas Cowboys T-shirt tossed a spade into a wheelbarrow full of dirty straw and grasped the handles. As he passed, he greeted them both with a jaunty "Hiya!" in a broad American accent, but he reserved the long slow sweep of his gaze for Becca. Must be one of the foreign volunteers Gem had told her about.

Dr Scott's gaze moved from the departing man to the Lab, who was investigating the bushes beside the road that ran behind the cages, her potato discarded on the ground near his feet. "I'm surprised you didn't twist Cooper's arm to help you with the monkeys."

As Gem had suggested she do. "This is the all-new Gem Stratton."

His gaze found hers again. "So you keep telling me. It's just odd, this amazing new work ethic of yours." He inclined his head to look at the bucket of monkey poo. "First the caracal and all that gore. Now monkey crap. Yet the last time you were here, you couldn't get muddy without having a meltdown."

Becca's heart bucked.

He folded his arms and scrutinised her face. "I'm surprised you haven't yet demanded I hit you up with a horse tranquilliser."

She closed a hand around her throat to hide the racing pulse that ticked just beneath the skin. "I'm holding out for the elephant tranqs," she said, with what she hoped was a disarming smile.

It didn't work. He was still looking at her the way people did when they ran into an old friend who'd shaved off their beard and they were trying to put their finger on what had changed about them.

Becca brushed away a strand of hair that had escaped her ponytail. She had to end this. Stop him questioning her every move. "I wasn't myself the first time I was here. Did you see all the stuff people were posting online about the villainous Gem Stratton?"

He shook his head. "I told you, I don't do social media. Jo's always on at me to post stuff to promote the sanctuary. Photos of our cases, that sort of thing. But when I'm trying to save an animal, taking photos for social media is the last thing on my mind."

She hooked a finger through the mesh like he had done. "You're not missing out, believe me. It isn't all pretty photos with filters and funny cat videos. People say the most vicious things online, as if their screens grant them some sort of exemption from following the basic rules of society. And they seem to enjoy it more if it's a successful woman they're trashing." She glanced at him, leaning once more with his back against the mesh and watching her with a surprising softness in his eyes that soothed some of the bitterness from her words. "I know that post was stupid, but it was never meant the way everyone took it. It certainly didn't deserve the brutal backlash it got."

She broke eye contact and trained her gaze instead on the swoop and dash of energetic monkeys. She swallowed against a lump in her throat. Putting herself in Gem's position was eviscerating. "After that shit storm, you can't really blame a girl for being a hot mess. But that was then. Now, I'm committed to getting those hours, no matter what you throw at me."

"You love your job that much?"

"It's more than that. My dad got retrenched and let his medical aid lapse. Now he needs a hip replacement, which isn't cheap, but I'm going to make sure he gets it. Which is why losing *Luxe Life* isn't an option." She straightened under his contemplative gaze. "I'm not going anywhere until those hours are done. Just point me in the direction of the next filthy thing you want cleaned."

His eyebrows arched. "Fighting talk."

"I mean it, Dr Scott. Nothing you do is going to make me quit again."

"I believe you." He unfolded his arms. "And it's just 'Sully'. That's what everyone here calls me."

Her stomach flipped.

Sully.

She held his gaze a second longer before looking away, her eyes skimming the ground until she noticed the clean-up bucket. "I'd better empty that." She hurried from him and grabbed the bucket. A wave of nauseating stink hit her full in her unmasked face. Her stomach did a disgusted somersault and she scrunched her nose and clamped her lips tight.

Sully appeared at her elbow. "Give me that." He removed the bucket from her hand. "I have no desire to get vomit all over my clothing again." He tramped off with the bucket down the line of cages.

She peered after him, stumped by his veiled comment. Something had gone on when Gem was last here. Something to do with tequila benders.

Before she could think more about it, three dogs on leads came straining down the dirt road that ran past the cages, towing a pair of teenage boys engrossed in their cellphones.

When a delighted Ella emerged from the shrubs to greet them, the canine procession paused, bodies stiff and tails wagging. The boy with the backward-facing baseball cap looked up as Sully, minus the clean-up bucket, rejoined Becca.

The boy scowled. He said something to the other boy and they yanked on the leads in their hands, breaking up the canine meet-n-greet as they hurried away.

"What was that about?" Becca said.

Sully chuckled, his eyes fixed on the departing boys. "Gabe's got a bug up his nose. His mother's given him extra chores for tweeting that photo."

So that was the kid who'd snapped that photo of her drug-induced kissing spree. "You've seen it now?"

"He didn't get my good side," he said, his mouth curving up on one side.

As if he had only one. "So now they're dog walking," Becca said, to head off her own thoughts.

"Grooming. Jo runs a grooming parlour on the side to bring in extra income for the sanctuary. They'll be taking those three back to their owners in town." He watched the boys for a moment longer, then he brought his gaze back to her. "Let's pick this up again tomorrow." He patted his thigh. "El! Let's go, girl. Kick-off's at two and I want to get a good seat at the Brewhouse." Ella bounded over to him, scooping up her potato en route.

Becca checked Gem's phone. Almost one. She did some sums in her head. "Thirty-five hours left, and six more days to do them in. I reckon I can afford to take the afternoon off."

"Mental arithmetic not your thing?" Sully asked.

She eyed him. "Six hours today, plus the nine I worked earlier this week—"

"I thought you knew. Jo found out you'd got her boys and a bunch of the foreign volunteers to do most of your work. She docked all those hours you worked."

Becca frowned. "You mean I'm starting again from zero?"

He nodded.

Now that was an unexpected spanner in the works. But she routinely pulled sixty-hour weeks, and that didn't even include weekends. Fifty hours would be a cinch. Still, she didn't want to leave things to chance, not with a deadline that couldn't be extended and her family's welfare on the line. "Can't you assign me something else before you go then? There must be more cages I can clean."

"It's Saturday," he said, walking backwards as he spoke.

She followed him, falling in beside Ella. "I thought animals didn't care about the days of the week."

He grinned at her repetition of his words. "They also don't care about rugby, but I do. South Africa's playing Australia. You're not going to watch your ex play?"

"I only need a few more hours."

He stopped, took a step towards her and sniffed. "What you need is a shower." His gaze flicked to her shirt. "That mark? It's not mud." He snapped his fingers for Ella. "Tomorrow, princess. Bright and early." He strode off with a backward wave.

Becca peered down her front, wrinkling her nose at the brown smear on the top's hem. Gross. A shower sounded like heaven. But falling behind on her daily quota of hours on the very first day wasn't a great start.

She glanced back at the row of cages, then away up the slope towards the large animal enclosures. This was a big sanctuary. Surely Sully wasn't the only one here who could do with her help?

8

#SinkOrSwim

Convincing the two teenagers to let her help with their chores and hand over their canine charges had been the easy part. It was controlling her freshly groomed charges that was proving to be somewhat more difficult. At this rate, with all the detours the dogs insisted on taking and all the surfaces they seemed determined to pee on, returning them to their owners in town could easily take her a couple of hours. Which was precisely the idea.

"Would you lot slow down?" Arm stretched out in front of her at a shoulder-dislocating angle, she gave the golden retriever's lead a tug. Behind her, the spaniel jerked away in the direction they'd come, half choking itself as it strained against its collar. "No, not that way!" The spaniel changed course. "Now you've got yourself all tangled." Becca bent to extricate the dog's leg from the lead.

Perhaps if she'd walked that bulldog herself for those Swedish guests last month, she'd have been better equipped to handle these energetic dogs now. She could've at least practised a few dog-walking commands. Instead she'd charmed one of the porters to take the huffing, chuffing beast into the streets of Earl's Court for her.

The Scottie peered up at her as if it could see into her soul. "Fine, so I'm as bad as my sister. It's just that bulldog slobber's not a good look on a concierge's uniform." The Scottie barked at her as if to say it agreed with her. "Thank you. Now let's go before it starts raining again. I'm sure your owners don't want you back all wet."

She pulled on the leads. "My car's this way." The spaniel and Scottie ignored her and added their weight to the straining retriever's. She dug in her heels, but the combined muscle power of three dogs towed her off the path.

She stumbled and tripped across the spongy lawn in the oversized gumboots behind the determined hounds who were heading towards a large dam at the bottom of the slope. A pair of Egyptian geese paddled about and dunked their heads beneath the surface. The golden retriever whined, its feathery tail waving like a frayed silk scarf.

One of the paddling geese steered itself to the water's edge and flapped up onto the raised bank. The retriever barked and bore down on the lead, hacking against its collar. Then the spaniel joined in, which set off the Scottie. "Stop pulling, all of you. No!" Becca fumbled with the leads in her hand. "Heel!"

As if she'd brandished a sword in the air and roared "Charge!", the retriever yanked its lead from her hand and careened off towards the dam. Becca gaped after it in horror for a second before her head mobilised her to give chase. The world tilted and she toppled onto the grass, the spaniel's lead wrapped like ivy around her calves. She clawed at the woven strap that had felled her. "Hold still!" The spaniel rabbitted about on the lead. "No! Sit! You're only making it tighter."

She struggled free as the retriever flung itself into the dark water, sending the goose scrabbling into the air, honking in noisy protest. The spaniel whined in frustration and with a backward jerk, pulled itself free of its collar. Becca made a grab for the dog, succeeding only in somehow letting go of the straining Scottie too. Both dogs tore off across the grass to join their escaped friend.

The spaniel splashed into the dam, sending the second goose into the air with a clatter of wings. And there went the Scottie.

Fantastic. Three previously clean dogs swimming about in a dam full of pond weed and fish poo, getting all sopping wet and smelly. Becca put her hand to her forehead in exasperation. She could see an afternoon of re-washing and blow-drying three dogs in her future. Hopefully Jo would let her count that towards her hours.

She squinted out at the dam. The retriever and spaniel were paddling about in lazy circles. But there was no Scottie. She scanned the banks. Out in the middle of the dam, a black head broke the surface. Frantic paws churned the dark water and then the Scottie was swallowed up again.

Adrenalin roared through her. She kicked off the gumboots and ran. She hit the bank at full pelt and skidded onto her bum to negotiate the drop into the shallows, only dimly registering the bite of the frigid water. The muddy bottom sloped away until several metres in she found she could kick off the silty bottom and swim.

The Scottie broke the surface a few metres from her. Its eyes bugged like a panicked cow's, then down it went again.

Becca thrashed out to where she'd seen it go under, her legs fighting against the pull of her clothes. She sucked a frantic breath into burning lungs and submerged. The water was so murky she couldn't see a thing. A strap brushed her arm. The lead! She thrust out her arms and felt fur. A solid body.

They broke the surface together. The Scottie gasped for air, its short legs beating at the water, even though she was doing all the real work of keeping them afloat. "I've got you." Her words stuttered on a ragged breath. "You're safe." Relief coursed through her, so strong her whole body trembled. Although that could also be from the cold, working its way into her bones. Second time since she'd got here that she was courting hypothermia.

Scissoring her legs, she rotated in the water to see to her dismay that she had attracted an audience. A small crowd stood clustered on the bank. There was the guy in the Dallas Cowboys shirt. A handful of people in blue overalls. The vet assistant who'd helped Sully with the caracal surgery this morning. And far too many upraised hands holding camera phones.

Great. More grist for the social media mill. "*Gem Stratton rehearses a canine adaptation of* Baywatch." Becca felt sorely tempted to stop kicking and let the water close over her head, but the Scottie had done nothing to deserve a watery grave.

Gabe rammed his way to the water's edge and spiked his fingers into his hair, knocking his rear-facing baseball cap to the ground. He swore loudly. "We spent all morning grooming those dogs!"

She didn't reply. Couldn't. A stitch in her side was making breathing difficult, and Gem's jeans seemed to have grown even tighter in the water, making it hard to stay afloat. The bank seemed suddenly much too far away, and a surge of panic sent new energy to her limbs.

Something moved at the edge of her vision. A brown head glistening with water powered towards her. Ella, swimming in a tight curve, her thick tail flexing like a rudder.

Becca cast her gaze back to the bank and groaned softly. There was Sully, legs braced wide, hands on his hips, the very picture of angry maleness. As if the universe simply had to have him witness her humiliation.

Beside him, a woman a few years younger than Becca in a pink puffer jacket and jeans, shook her head in disbelief at the scene playing out in the dam, a high blonde ponytail swinging about her ears.

Sully stepped to the edge of the water. "What the bloody hell are you doing?"

Cancelling out any Brownie points she'd earned with him earlier today, that's what. "Helping." Becca spat out the word, along with a mouthful of water.

"I told you to go and shower, not take a flippen swim."

"Needed"—her chin dipped under the surface and she kicked hard—"hours."

"Drowning Jo's customers doesn't count as community service," he shouted back.

The Scottie struggled in her arms, its back claws gouging into her stomach. "Not drowning." Her chin skimmed the water again. "Saving it!"

"Is that what you're calling it? Now I'm going to miss the ruddy kick-off." Sully shrugged off his fleece and dumped it on the grass. Then he bent to untie one of his boots.

Oh hell no. She did not need a hero. She was perfectly capable of looking after herself, despite how it may look.

The first boot hit the grass, followed by a black sock, and then Sully turned his attention to the next boot.

Becca tucked the Scottie under her left arm and began to swim in earnest, doing a lopsided breaststroke with her free arm, legs churning up the water.

Sully reached over his head and pulled off his black T-shirt.

Becca's legs slowed. That tight-fitting tee had not been overselling what was underneath it. Water lapped at her chin and the Scottie delivered a panicked kick to her gut. Her legs jerked back into motion.

Clad now only in his jeans, Sully strode to the edge of the raised bank. He placed one hand on the ground and hopped off the bank into the calf-deep water. His hips and his muscled arms worked as he forged his way through the deepening water.

Becca swallowed hard. Not a chance was she being rescued by *that*. Dragged to the bank in the arms of a man who looked like he could be on the cover of an erotic romance novel? Imagine the comments if that got online. Mandla would be on the next plane home. She had to reach the shallows before he could get to her, but he was already up to his waist now. "Don't bother." She glugged another mouthful of water. "Almost there."

"Stay afloat for another minute." Sully threw himself forward and struck out into the deep water. It took him less than that to reach her and the dog. Wet hair clung to his forehead. Treading water, he pushed it aside. "You need a bloody babysitter, princess." Ella swam past them, her paws paddling in an easy rhythm.

"I would've...made it...back."

"Of course you would've. Dead bodies always wash up eventually." He brushed water from his eyes with an angry swipe. "You keep hold of MacTavish and I'll tow you both."

She scissored her legs to move away from him. After last night's Twitter debacle, Alek would kill her if another photo of her and anyone who wasn't Mandla found its way onto the internet. Especially when that someone looked like Sully. "I'm fine."

"No you're not." Sully took her by the shoulder and pulled her towards him, ripples of water breaking against his bare chest. "Don't be so stubborn. You're freezing."

How was his hand so warm? She imagined him hooking that strong arm around her shoulders, pulling her tight against his chest, his powerful legs kicking beneath her, then dragging her up onto the bank. #GemStratton, trending again. She thrust the struggling Scottie into Sully's arms. "Take him." It was like shrugging off a backpack filled with dumbbells. "I'll swim back myself."

She winced as a gasped breath stabbed a needle of pain between her ribs.

Sully scowled at her over the Scottie's head. "If you drown, you should know I'm not legally allowed to resuscitate humans."

Kneeling over her. His mouth covering hers. His warm breath filling her lungs. She splashed at him with paddling hands. "Just go. Please."

He hooked the Scottie's front paws over one muscular shoulder, then whistled for the rest of the canine swim team. "Ella! Jasmine! Jasper! Come!" He kicked away, swimming backwards towards the bank with his gaze fixed firmly on Becca.

Her cramping legs berated her for passing on his help, but it was better this way. No need to stoke the rumour mills after what had happened last night. And the bank wasn't far off. She could make it, now she wasn't clutching an hysterical Scottie that had the buoyancy properties of a brick.

On the bank, the woman in the pink puffer jacket rushed up as Sully waded towards her though the shallows. She had the kind of stand-back-I'm-a-doctor vibe of someone who knew what she was doing in a crisis. Most likely Clare, the other vet.

Sully handed up the Scottie to her, before helping the rest of the dogs scramble out of the water. They stood on the edge, shaking their coats in his face as he planted one hand on the grass and boosted himself out, water sluicing off his contoured back.

Becca looked for the Scottie, but the onlookers had pressed in tight, obscuring her view of whatever the woman she suspected was Clare was doing with the rescued dog.

Sully stood on the bank watching her, wet jeans clinging to his thighs, his expression thunderous.

Dr Scowling.

He should put on his shirt; all that exposed skin wasn't helping her breathing. A few more exhausted strokes and she was at last able to touch the bottom. Each step felt like she was dragging herself through syrup.

She stopped at the raised bank and pushed a sodden clump of hair from her cheek. Her breathing was a staccato of shallow gasps between thumping heartbeats. She looked up at Sully. "How's...the Scottie?"

"He'll live." He turned still-damp shoulders to look back for a moment at the knot of onlookers gathered around the dog. "Clare's checking him over now. He'll need observation, but he should be fine."

Relief made her legs wobble like cooked noodles. "I'm so sorry." Her teeth chattered. "I never knew he"—a wracking shiver—"couldn't swim."

"Most Scotties are bad swimmers. It's the short legs and dense coat." Sully bent and held out his hand.

She looked from his hand to the bank. She could probably drag herself out without his help. Beneath her, her legs quivered with exhaustion. His fingers twitched, beckoning to her. Perhaps now was the time to accept a little help. She put her hand in his.

"On three, jump," he instructed. "One. Two. Three." His fingers flexed and his arm powered upwards, yanking her from the water and onto the bank. She collided with his bare chest, her breath expelling in a whoosh and her fingers splaying out to brake her against hard, chilled muscle.

He circled her with his free arm, pinning her to him. "I've got you."

Breathing hard, she looked up into his face. His damp hair tipped over his forehead as he angled his head. His gaze locked with hers and his arm around her back drew her closer to him. Her heart smacked against her ribs, so hard he must have been able to feel it.

"Sully."

At the sound of his name, he jerked his head around, breaking eye contact. "Jo." He sounded bewildered, as if his head was playing catch-up. He looked back at Becca and released her so unexpectedly her legs only just caught her.

Becca turned her head to see a woman with short black hair standing a few paces away, hands on her hips, radiating anger. Becca had seen Gem's agent in photos, and this woman was a female version of Alek, and from the looks of it, as formidable as her brother.

"We need to talk," Jo said, her voice taut.

That sounded ominous. Game-over ominous.

"Sure," he said. "Let me grab my shirt." Sully scooped up his T-shirt from the ground. He dragged it on, only to yank it off again and turn it around before slipping it once more over his head.

Ignoring the body shakes that rattled her down to her frozen bones, Becca staggered over to Jo. "I'm really sorry about the Scottie." Her voice wobbled with cold.

Jo looked at her with contempt. "I agreed to let you do your hours here last week as a favour to my little brother. But after this? MacTavish could've drowned."

Becca's hands were clenched in front of her in shivering supplication. "What can I do to make this right?"

"If it were up to me, you'd be packing your bags. But fortunately for you, Alek is not above bribery." Jo looked up at Sully as he joined them, his fleece and boots in hand. She waved her phone at him. "That was Alek. I told him I've had enough of the celebrity chaos." Jo's gaze scorched over Becca. "But he says if we let Gem stay and make sure she finishes her hours, he'll give us the shortfall for the long-term housing for the small predators."

Sully's eyebrows lifted. "He must really want her to finish her community service."

"If she doesn't, he loses one of his biggest earners." Jo turned to Becca. "Looks like my little brother bought you a stay of execution."

Becca was effusive in her thanks, though worry seeped into her mind. From Sully's reaction, Alek's bribe was a sizable amount, one he would likely expect Gem to repay. A shiver jolted up her back and set her teeth clacking. What a mess she'd made. The whole point of the switch was to save Gem's income, not tie it up in bribe money.

Warmth settled around her and she looked to see Sully's fleece draped about her shoulders. "I'll get it wet," she said to him, and made to pull it off, but stopped when his brows pinched. All this sudden concern. He probably didn't want her getting sick and jeopardising his payout from Alek. She slid damp arms into the too-long sleeves.

Jo speared her with a critical eye before facing Sully. "She needs to be under constant supervision if she's going to stay."

Sully frowned and looked up from knotting a boot lace. "We're a sanctuary, Jo, not a babysitting service."

"What if she does something that costs us our permit? When this gets out, I guarantee you we're going to have an SPCA inspector on the phone asking questions."

Both Jo and Sully looked at her then, and she dropped her gaze to her chilled feet. *Just heap on the humiliation.*

Jo threw out suggestions. "She could shadow Lerato. Or what about Andile?"

Sully thought for a moment, his brow furrowing. "From a liability point of view, it's better if I do it."

Becca's head jerked up. What a positively crap idea!

"No, let me." Her pink puffer jacket rustling, Clare bobbed up to Sully's elbow with the Scottie dog wrapped in a blanket in her arms. Her eyes darted to the fleece engulfing Becca and her smile seemed to stutter for a second or two. "The last thing you need is a TV celeb getting under your feet all day."

Despite the offhand insult, Becca smiled at Clare, relieved to be saved from a week of hell with Dr Surly.

"And it'll be fun." Clare shifted the Scottie so she had a hand free to place on Sully's forearm. "She can be in my vlog. It would be awesome for my YouTube views."

Sully slid his hand into the back pocket of his wet jeans, dislodging Clare's grip. "I'm the head vet, Clare. She'll work with me."

Clare stiffened almost imperceptibly. "But your time's too valuable. You have so much to do."

"It's only until Friday. I'll manage. And since the small predator housing is my project, it seems only fair I should be the one to suffer for it."

That made Clare's smile a little less brittle.

Jo tapped on her cellphone. "I'd better phone our broker to check the insurance covers us against celebrities."

9

#TheBoyIsMine

"He's going to be okay, isn't he?" Becca looked over her shoulder to where the Scottie lay in a dog crate on the back seat of Clare's car.

"He should be." Clare stopped at the end of the dirt road. "But he needs to be monitored by a vet for any complications arising from water inhalation. We don't have facilities to over-night domestic animals, so I'm taking him to his vet in town." She checked for traffic with a side-to-side flick of her high ponytail that wafted shampoo-freshness around the car, then she pulled onto the road leading to town.

Becca gave the woebegone dog a last apologetic look before swivelling in her seat. "I'll pick up the bill, of course." Yet more expense. "And I'll explain to his owners." Sully had sent her off to her room to get out of her wet clothes before she caught her death, but instead she had run after Clare and tagged along. No reason why Clare should be expected to deal with the Scottie's owners, when it wasn't her mess to clean up.

She squirmed on the towel protecting Clare's upholstery from her uncomfortable damp clothes. Making her more uncomfortable though was Sully's fleece. It had that earthy, I-just-roped-a-steer, rumpled bed-sheet-y smell only men could brew up, and perversely, a part of her wanted to gather the material to her face and inhale. If she wasn't so cold, she'd take it off.

"It's a pity he won't let us work together," Clare said. "It would've been fun."

Becca smiled at the young vet. "Certainly more fun than I'll be having with him." There'd been a bit of a thaw between them outside the monkey cage, but forcing him to play life-saver in an icy dam had frozen things right back up again. "Just think, a whole week chained to Dr Surly." Becca flinched and glanced at Clare. "Sorry, I shouldn't have called him that out loud."

Clare snorted a laugh. "That's exactly how he is with you. You've really got his hackles up. Not surprising, considering you threw up on him."

Becca jerked her shoulders to face Clare dead-on. "I what?"

Clare dipped her chin and looked at her. "You don't remember?" A shrug. "Also not surprising, considering how wrecked you were. We found you passed out in your room.

"Alone?"

"Uh huh. Just you and the tequila bottle." Clare side-eyed her. "Not a great look."

Becca was mortified on Gem's behalf. "I'm not usually like that."

Clare laughed. "I should hope not. You'd have cirrhosis." Clare's laugh tapered into a snicker and she shook her head in remembered disbelief. "That night was chaotic. The volunteer from Norway was freaking out about the cops coming to arrest him because he'd bashed a cop van going on your little booze run. Jo was swearing and yelling into her brother's voicemail. Sully was calling an ambulance to take you to get your stomach pumped. And then you hurled all over him." Clare feigned vomiting over her steering wheel, her gaze locked on Becca's in obvious mirth. "If they ever do a remake of *The Exorcist*, you should audition."

Becca cringed back against the passenger door, the arm-rest jamming into her arm. She'd known the social media fiasco had hit Gem hard, but she hadn't realised Gem was hurting so badly she'd let her usual iron control slip like that. She'd been right to come back home to fix this mess for her sister.

Clare took her eyes off the road to look at Becca. "If you hadn't run away the next morning, I swear Sully would've packed your bags for you and thrown you out. I'd have thought you'd be more used to booze, what with all the partying you celebs must do."

They'd reached the outskirts of town and Becca looked out the window at the houses spooling past. "I'm a TV presenter, not a member of Metallica. I hardly ever drink."

Clare's answering snicker lifted the hairs on Becca's neck. "Could've fooled us. Does Mandla approve of you drinking like that?"

"Mandla and I aren't together." The words slipped out. She looked away from the window to see the teasing smile playing across Clare's face falter.

"You've broken up? I didn't see anything about that online."

Becca dug her fingernails into her palm, annoyed with herself for blabbing the lie she'd meant only for Sully. "We haven't made it public." And now she'd given Clare a juicy bit of gossip for her YouTube vlog. "We'd prefer to keep it that way, if you don't mind."

Clare ran her finger along the seam of her lips and mimed locking a key at the corner.

"What's your vlog about?" Becca said.

Clare pulled up at the stop sign at the intersection with the high street that circled the town oval. "Vet things. A day in the life. It's called *The Blonde Vet*."

Becca allowed herself to breathe again. A vet vlog wasn't the place to drop celeb gossip. "You have a lot of subscribers?"

"Almost five thousand." Clare turned onto the ring road lined with shops and small businesses on one side. A coffee shop. A hole-in-the-wall boutique. A hardware store. "Why did you and Mandla split?"

Dog with a bone, this one. "The usual couple problems," Becca said to the window. "Five thousand subscribers isn't bad."

Clare made a dismissive sound. "It's nothing compared to what you've got. That's why I wanted to work with you this week. The others say having a celeb guest appearance is great for the numbers."

Becca looked over her shoulder at Clare. "Others?"

"I'm in a group for local YouTubers. We get together to discuss trends, marketing, that sort of thing."

Now here was a topic that could likely get them all the way to the town vet without circling back to Gem. "What channels do the others have?"

"A few gamers. Makeup tutorials. Gardening. Dave does fitness videos, weight training programmes—you should see the abs on him. And there's Devon. He's a male stripper."

Becca grinned. "Now *that* I'd like to see."

"He does dance routines to horny songs, but he keeps it PG, obviously. Do you think you and Mandla will get back together?"

What was Clare's obsession with the state of Gem's love life? Unless she was trying to suss out whether or not Gem was a threat. That possessive hand on Sully's arm back at the dam... Were they an item? "What about you? Are you seeing anyone?"

Clare flicked on her indicator and turned into a road that ran down the side of an imposing brick church with a spire with aspirations of reaching clean into heaven. Just when Becca thought she wasn't going to answer, Clare took her eye off the road and said, "Nobody else knows, so you can't say anything to anyone."

"Who would I even tell?"

"You can't let on you know, not even to him."

"Him being...Sully?"

Clare turned down a side road, catching Becca's eye. "We're keeping it quiet for now, because of the whole workplace thing, and him being my boss. He'll be annoyed if he finds out I told you, so not a word. Okay?"

Becca mimicked the lip-zipping gesture Clare had made earlier. "Sure." Discussing Sully's love life with him sounded about as appealing as getting back into the dam for a couple of leisurely laps. "Did you meet at the sanctuary?"

"Uh huh. I was on my first vet practical, when I was still a student. I took one look at him and I knew." Clare slowed outside a converted house with a large signboard outside saying *Winterberg Veterinary Clinic*.

Consulting hours listed below showed the afternoon consult only began at five, which was still a few hours off.

"You didn't answer me about Mandla," Clare said, persistent. "You think you two will get back together?"

Becca gave the answer she suspected Clare was desperate to hear. "We usually do."

Some of the tension left Clare's face. She pulled into a parking bay outside the practice and twisted her shoulders to look at the dog on her back seat. "We're here, boy."

They climbed from the car and Clare opened the back door to retrieve the Scottie. Despite the weight of the dog and crate, she still managed to bounce as she crossed the paving and negotiated the stairs up to reception.

A young woman stood in the open doorway. Clare greeted her and turned to make introductions. "Gem, this is Steph-Marie. She's the practice manager here."

Becca took the woman's outstretched hand. "Sorry you had to open up especially for us."

Steph-Marie gave a quick lift of her shoulder. "It can't be helped with an emergency. Dr Nomsa's on her way." She stepped back to let them through into the reception area. "And anyway, I was around the corner at the church." She spoke with an Afrikaans accent, rolling her r's and flattening her vowels. "We have a ribbon-cutting ceremony tomorrow for the new Sunday School classrooms. I was setting up tables with the catering committee."

Clare set the dog crate on the floor. "Her dad's the *dominee.*"

Steph-Marie stifled a laugh. "Lucky for you he is, because you're going to need someone to preach at your funeral once the Van Ecks get here." She went on her haunches to look in at the Scottie. "Your *ma*'s very protective of her baby, isn't she, *liefie*?" Her expression grew pained. "And once I tell her Kurt van Jaarsveld's cancelled for the ribbon-cutting tomorrow, she's going to be even more upset."

Clare frowned. "At such short notice?"

Steph-Marie rose from the floor. "I suppose that's how it is with famous people. Even ones who you'd think would remember they got their start in singing in our church choir." Steph-Marie looked almost accusingly at Becca, as if she somehow had a hand in the sins of her kind. "Mrs Van Eck runs our Sunday School, and she sent out invitations promising Kurt was going to be doing the honours. Now we're going to have all these guests expecting a celebrity and getting my dad instead."

Clare extended a finger and twiddled it in Becca's direction. "You could do it."

Sure she could, if she wanted to blow the switch sky-high. "No, that would be a bad idea," Becca said.

Steph-Marie's face was suffused with relief. "No, it's a great idea! You're not a singer or anything, but at least you're a celebrity."

"Not South Africa's favourite celebrity these days."

"We don't mind," Steph-Marie said.

But Becca did. Very much. "I can't."

"Why not?" Clare said.

An excellent question. One that required an iron-clad answer. Becca shuffled her feet and jammed her hands into the pockets of Sully's fleece. That was it. "Sully's not going to be happy with me if I run off during my community service."

Clare's eyes darted sideways before she returned her gaze to Becca. "Why would he even have to know? He'll be at his own church tomorrow morning."

Excitement bloomed on Steph-Marie's face. "Our ribbon cutting's at nine."

Clare cocked her head and grinned. "Right in the middle of St Matthew's service. And he always stays for tea afterwards."

Both hands held up, Becca retreated a step. "Ordinarily, I'd be more than happy to help you, but—"

"It's not like you can do any hours when Sully's away," Clare said. "You'll be sitting around doing nothing anyway until he gets back."

Head shaking emphatically, Becca said, "I still have to say no." Even if Sully wouldn't be put out, Alek was sure to be.

Clare leaned an elbow on the reception counter and eyed Steph-Marie. "Don't MacTavish's owners go to your church?"

The two women exchanged a meaningful glance, and Steph-Marie's eyes took on a calculating glitter. "They do. Mr Van Eck is an elder. And Mrs Van Eck is the chairlady for the ribbon-cutting ceremony."

Back in the depths of Sully's fleece pockets, Becca's hands fisted at her sides. She chewed on the inside of her cheek. How could she say no? But imitating Gem in a public role? It was crazy to even contemplate pulling that off. Although it was just a little ribbon-cutting ceremony at a church in an under-the-radar small town. She smothered her misgivings and looked at Steph-Marie. "Will I have to make a speech?"

From the crate on the floor, the Scottie whined.

Facebook

Elzette van Eck added 3 new photos.
Yesterday at 5:16 pm

Our dear little Scottie almost drowned today, after Gem Stratton let him loose in a dam! Thank you, Dr Scott, for swimming out to rescue our poor baby. Also a big thank you to Dr Nomsa Gumede, who's caring for our baby now. Please people, Scotties aren't good swimmers! They should never be left near water!
79 comments

Jonathan James
She wasn't happy talking about killing animals, now she's actually doing it. Can't believe she let this dog drown! Time to report this bitch to the SPCA.
15 h Like Reply

Marty Clifford Nel Can't you understand English? She said "almost drowned". The vet saved it. It's fine!
15 h Like Reply

Dev Randall
How could she have let it drown? She's a terrible human being. I'm shocked. I wish people like her would die, instead of the innocent animals.
15 h Like Reply

10

#SundayScandals

A sliver of morning sun striped the end of Becca's bed. Propped against the wall that served as the headboard, she read through the speech she'd prepared the night before on Gem's phone. Her twin would have winged it, charming the ribbon-cutting crowd completely off the cuff, but then Gem had always been the one who was good behind a microphone.

A few words, Steph-Marie had said. A bit of a euphemism that. It had taken a good number of sentences to get from the opening greetings to declaring the Sunday School classrooms officially open. But the final speech was still short enough that Becca could get in and out as fast as possible before anyone had a chance to suspect something was amiss with this version of the Gem they all knew and (usually) loved.

She settled against the pillow folded double behind her back and pulled the duvet up around her chest against the morning chill. If only she could send the speech to Gem. Check it was suitable for the intended audience.

An incoming call notification obscured the screen.

Alek.

Becca's fingers clenched around the phone and her stomach yanked into a knot.

The green answer button pulsed.

She flipped the phone, screen down, onto the duvet. There was no need to answer to know why he was calling, and she didn't have the energy to face him this early on a Sunday morning. Not with a certain video clip doing the rounds faster than a veld fire in winter, of her thrashing about in the dam to Britney Spears's "Oops!...I Did It Again". Thank the stars Mom and Gem were on a media blackout.

The ringing stopped. She eyed the phone nervously. When the ringing started again, she swore she saw the phone jump on the covers, but that could've just been her. She waited it out. One minute and several missed calls later, the phone dinged. She picked it up.

A message notification filled the screen. *"Are you trying to ruin us both! I've had the press calling me all morning. Call me back! NOW!"*

That was the problem with show business: a person's life could be ruined by something as simple as a stumble on stage. An outfit with the wrong shoes was a disaster warranting pages of editorial comment. And there was Gem, day in and day out, trying to stay on the right side of a fickle public.

Guilt flooded Becca's chest. She was meant to be fixing things for Gem, but instead, all she'd done was make things worse. This wasn't how she rolled. Becca Stratton put things right. She made plans. She pulled strings. She made people happy. And Gem would be far from happy if she found out what was going on at the sanctuary.

Becca blew out a breath, then focused again on the speech on Gem's phone. She couldn't let anything else go wrong on her watch, and that meant she'd better be able to trot out this speech as casually as Gem would've done. She'd already made her twin look bad enough.

There was a curt rap on her room door. She straightened against the pillow. "Hello?"

"Room service," said an unfamiliar voice in a thready falsetto.

Mercenary as it was, her stomach threw off its nervous tangle and growled hopefully. Breakfast in bed was an unexpected treat. She hopped up and crossed the room in a few short steps to open the door. "That's so kind of—"

Sully stood outside on the concrete walkway in his work boots and faded jeans, a grey fleece zipped against the morning cold. Beside him, his Labrador vibrated with canine enthusiasm, mouth wide around a fresh potato in a beaming 'good morning'.

Sully's expression was less welcoming. He ran a critical eye over her long-sleeve pyjama top, and she folded her arms, aware that she wasn't wearing a bra.

His gaze didn't linger though. It thundered down the length of her, before shifting to Ella. "Oh no, girl." The dog swung her head to look at him. "It seems we've disturbed Her Majesty on her morning off." Ella spat out her potato as if in mutual shock and horror.

Becca bridled at the condescension in his voice. "But you're supposed to be going to church. Clare said you go every Sunday."

"I do." He folded his arms, mirroring her own defensive stance. "When I'm not on shift, which I am today."

Of all the weekends for Clare to get her boyfriend's schedule mixed up. Becca hugged herself tighter. "Any chance I could start a bit later today? It is Sunday, after all."

Sully thrust out a leg, spiking the heel into the concrete floor, and bowed low over it. "Oh, but of course, Highness," he said, with an elaborate flourish of his hand. He straightened. "What was I thinking, El?" The dog waved her tail. "We'd better go home and wait like obedient serfs to be summoned when Her Majesty is ready to get started." He levelled a sardonic glance at Becca.

"A simple 'no' would've sufficed."

"But would it have been as satisfying?" Sully tipped his head at her, and Becca thought she caught a hint of amusement muting the irritation in his eyes.

She hoped so, considering what she was about to ask him. If only she wasn't having to do this in her baggy jammies with her bare boobs squashed beneath her arms. She squared her shoulders. "I have something I need to do this morning, before I can get started on my hours."

The glower was back. "Spit it out, princess."

"The singer who was meant to open the new Sunday School buildings at Steph-Marie's church cancelled at the last minute, and seeing as the Scottie's owner is an elder there, I thought the least I could do was fill in."

Sully gave a slow head shake, like she really was too much. He cocked an eyebrow. "I am seriously questioning your commitment to your community service."

"I won't be long. Call it an early tea break. I'll say my little speech and head straight back to the sanctuary."

"What time's it at?"

"Nine. But I want to leave half an hour before."

He flipped over his wrist to consult his watch. "Then you can put in half an hour of work before you go."

"But I'm not even dressed!"

He took in her pyjamas with another flick of his eyes. "Best you get moving then." He patted his thigh for Ella and strode down the path without another word.

Becca had to restrain herself from banging the door shut. In a replay of her first morning at the sanctuary, she tore through the suitcase of clothing she'd been too exhausted last night to unpack. She flung aside the more unsuitable items—honestly Mom, a faux fur jacket? And Gem's leopard-print pumps, after the post that had caused all this trouble? A halter top. A cold-shoulder shirt. Was there anything in this suitcase that wouldn't show off her tattoo-less shoulders? She settled on skinny jeans, a long-sleeved black bodysuit, camel blazer and Gem's nude heels. Mascara and lipstick would have to do. It was a church function after all. No need to turn on the glam. She brushed out her hair and slid Gem's phone into a back pocket. A last look in the mirror to check she was on spec (albeit roughly) for Gem and she was done. She left her room at a run. Well, more of a scamper in Gem's heels.

By the time she burst through the front door of the rehab centre, her heart was pounding against her ribs. At this rate, she was going to be ready for the London Marathon when she got back. Despite being a Sunday, the reception was busy. A woman seated in one of the plastic chairs placed along the walls held something small and quivering wrapped up in a towel. A few seats away, a little boy pressed an eye to an air hole poked into a cardboard box on his father's lap and asked him if the birdie inside was sleeping. At the reception desk, a man stopped filling out a form to explain to someone in a sanctuary uniform where he'd found the squirrel secured in the shoebox at his elbow.

Becca stepped in beside the man and smiled at the receptionist in her hunter-green sanctuary tunic. "Excuse me."

The woman looked up from her computer only long enough to see who was interrupting her. "He's in his consult room."

Not one of the rooms she'd discovered yesterday, but she'd find him. She hurried across reception and shoved through the pair of internal swinging doors marked 'Staff Only', almost colliding with Clare who was coming the other way.

"Gem!" Clare stepped back as if surprised to see her.

"Finally!" came Sully's voice from higher up the corridor. "The princess graces us with her presence."

Clare grimaced. "I'm so sorry. I got all confused about the shifts. And now I've got you into trouble." She glanced back in the direction where Sully's voice had come. "He doesn't sound very impressed with you."

"Is he ever?" Becca said, looking over Clare's shoulder up the corridor.

"At least you only have to endure him for a few more days," Clare said. "I've got to run. Good luck." A quick consoling pat on the shoulder and Clare was through the doors into reception.

Becca didn't need luck. She needed to get her act together and start acting like the professional, problem-solving concierge that she was. Yes, her first day at the sanctuary had been less than stellar, but today, things would be different.

She clicked up the corridor, checking each room she passed until she found Sully in one at the end. A high steel table stood in the centre of the room. A counter ran the length of a wall, a laptop open on one end, shelves above packed with veterinary books.

Sully stood with his back to her, arms braced on the counter, head bowed over something he was reading. Ella was no longer with him. Probably in the storeroom at the back of the clinic, sleeping in the wicker basket Becca had seen yesterday.

She stepped into the room. "Reporting for duty, boss," she said, speaking to his back. In her pocket, Gem's phone rang, but she ignored it.

When the ringing stopped, Sully straightened and dumped the page he'd been reading into an overflowing in-tray. "Got an injured hyena I need to put back together. You can come and help us prep."

Her pocket rang again.

Sully's eyebrows lifted.

She ignored the call. "It can go to voicemail."

"Answer it. It's distracting."

She took out Gem's phone. Just as she'd thought. Alek. She couldn't ignore him forever. She answered and he cut her off mid-greeting.

"Why didn't you call me back?" he snapped.

"I've been working."

"Is that what they're calling it these days?"

"Excuse me?"

"You've been doing a shitload more than working, Gem, if *The Sunday Star* is anything to go by. Did you not hear a thing I said yesterday?"

Foreboding snaked into her gut. "*The Sunday Star*?" That was national. "What did they print?"

A sound came over the phone like Alek was being garrotted by a trained assassin with a length of piano wire. "You don't know? Your career is going down the toilet and you don't know?"

Her mouth went dry, as if she'd been chewing on the little packets of silica gel that came in medicine bottles. She glanced up to find Sully watching her, his brows drawn slightly together. "It was only a silly video of me swimming in a dam. How can it be that bad?"

Now Alek was making the sort of gargled laughter better suited to a villain in a Batman movie. "Look online," he brayed. "Do it now. I'll hold."

Doors clattered open down the corridor and before Becca could get Gem's browser open, a breathless Clare barrelled into the consult room. An iPad was clutched to her chest. Clare fired off a look at Becca, then turned her attention to Sully. "You're not going to like this." She passed the iPad to him, and Becca caught a glimpse of *The Sunday Star*'s prominent masthead.

Sully's eyes scanned the screen. He frowned. "You seen this?" He thrust the iPad at Becca.

Oh God. Heat exploded over her skin and her heart went into a free-fall. No wonder Alek had sounded like he was about to give birth to his own spleen. The headline was in attention-seeking red. *Pariah celeb caught 'wet-handed'.* Beneath it was a large photo of her, wet and bedraggled, pressed against Sully's bare chest, her palms flat on his defined pecs, looking up into his face like a swooning damsel. All the photo needed was a title in a flouncy font—*His Brazen Hussey*— and it could be the sultry cover of an eighties bodice ripper.

The caption below the photo swam, then came into focus as Becca forced herself to read the bold text.

"WHILE THE CAT'S AWAY? With boyfriend and Springbok rugby captain Mandla Ndungane off battling the Wallabies this week, TV presenter Gem Stratton cosies up to Winterberg vet, Dr Sullivan Scott, after almost drowning a local's dog in the dam yesterday at Winterberg Wildlife Rescue and Sanctuary. The pair was also the subject of a tweet that has been lighting up social media, showing them locked in an illicit kiss earlier this week. Read more..."

Becca's cheeks were on fire. Her lungs were a furnace. Every breath felt like she was inhaling lit paraffin.

Someone was calling Gem's name from far away.

"Your phone." Sully indicated the device in her hand.

She'd forgotten all about Alek. And about Clare, standing there lapping up her humiliation with one hip leaned against the consult table, looking like she wished she had a bowl of popcorn in her gleeful little hands.

Becca's gaze caught Sully's, and for a second, she thought she glimpsed sympathy in his eyes. Then he took the iPad from her grip and with a jerk of his head towards the door, he motioned for Clare to follow him out.

Alek's incensed voice sounded again in the now-empty room. Becca sagged against the consult table and pressed the phone to her ear. "Alek?" Her voice trembled. "It's not what it looks like. They've taken it completely out of context."

"Nobody cares about context, Gem," Alek snapped. "You know this game is all about looks. And what it looks like to the South African public is that instead of being suitably punished for wanting to make accessories out of leopard cub pelt, you're off having a good time cheating on the captain of the Springboks." Alek's voice was sandpaper.

"I'm not cheating on Mandla! Can't you call the paper and tell them what really happened? We should demand a retraction."

Alek snorted in derision. "Are you shitting me? Their editor's a card-carrying member of the World Wildlife Fund. You think she gives a rat's arse about your side of the story? All she's thinking is here's the perfect photo to sell her front page while at the same time shaming the woman who thought a joke about skinning a leopard cub would go down well."

Her head drooped. "I'm sorry, Alek."

"Tell that to the people who pay your salary. *Luxe Life* won't put up with more drama. And if you lose that gig, you can kiss *From Hell to Hotel* goodbye too. As for your sponsors, I've already had Clearly Beautiful on the phone. Nobody likes a cheat, Gem."

"I'm not, I promise."

"You might not be cheating, but something sure as shit is going on with you. I know all this has been hard on you, but if you don't get back in form fast, not even the best PR spin in the world is going to help you."

"Don't worry, Alek, I'll make it right," she said, stung by his words.

"No, you'll leave it to the publicist. Your job is not to sort things out. Your job is to look hot and finish your hours without getting yourself dragged by the media. You think you can do that?"

Becca nodded and forced an affirmative from her aching throat. Probably not a good time to tell him about her impending celebrity appearance, and backing out at the eleventh hour would tarnish Gem's image even more. A ribbon-cutting ceremony at an out-of-the-way church wasn't the sort of event that would ever make the news. And what Alek didn't know wouldn't hurt him.

11

#LostInTranslation

Becca gave Gem's car a last wistful glance in the passenger wing mirror of Sully's Ranger. "I could've driven myself to the church." Embarrassment was still warm on her cheeks.

"And deny Ella a trip in the bakkie?" Sully's hand tensed on the steering wheel as a deep rut in the dirt road threw the Ranger to one side. Behind him, Ella's heavy bulk slid across the back seat and a thunk on the floor suggested the dog had lost her grip on her beloved root vegetable. "Sorry, girl." Sully snaked one arm backwards to check on his pet.

Becca smiled at the affectionate gesture. "You should stay and help that hyena. Let me go by myself to the ceremony." One less witness.

"Clare will sort out the hyena. Right now, I don't trust you to get to the church in one piece." He accelerated onto the municipal road and Ella shoved her head through the gap between the front seats, staring delightedly through the windscreen. He gave the dog a rough stroke on the head, then glanced over at Becca and cast a clinical eye over her. "You feeling better?"

Becca lifted a hand off her thigh and extended her fingers. Only the faintest tremor remained. "That was quite the ambush this morning. Whoever sent that photo to the press outdid themselves. I really am sorry. You didn't sign up to be paraded half-dressed around the country."

He shrugged and turned on the car radio. "One of my secret dreams is to be a newspaper pin-up." He draped an affectionate arm over Ella's thick neck and burrowed his fingers into her heavy ruff. "Is it always like that? With the media?"

She caught his eye over Ella's head. "Yep. Not always this gleefully vicious, but yeah, there's always something. And it doesn't even need to be as scintillating as you and me in a misconstrued embrace. Going out in public without a full face of makeup is usually enough to awaken the tabloid beast."

"Aren't they supposed to get the whole story?"

Becca laughed. "The public doesn't want the whole story. They want to be entertained."

"Even at your expense?"

"There's nothing more fun than dragging a celebrity off her pedestal." She imagined she saw a flash of sympathy in his dark eyes, but just as quickly he lifted his arm off Ella's neck and returned his attention to the road.

She looked away too, staring through the window at the dew-wet foothills that darkened into mountains hunched under banks of white cloud. Surly, she could handle. Smug too. But the way he'd looked at her then, as if he were genuinely concerned for her, and not because she was his ticket to getting Alek's money...that had knocked her off balance. And she couldn't afford to lose her balance, especially not over a man who was involved with someone else. Like Alek had said, nobody liked a cheat.

In the distance, a church spire was visible above the trees. A tremor of anxiety simmered through her veins. "I'd better go over my speech. You want to hear it?"

"Not particularly," Sully said, but he lowered the volume on the car radio.

"Ladies and gentlemen..." She ran through the speech, doing her best to mimic Gem's measured, easy cadence and confident, assured tone, and the way Gem always spoke with a smile in her voice. "And now, ladies and gentlemen, it gives me great pleasure to declare your new Sunday School classrooms"—*pause, two, three*—"open!" With a flourish worthy of her sister, she lifted a pair of imaginary scissors and made a snipping gesture with her fingers.

Sully remained silent for a moment, as if digesting her words. "You know Steph-Marie goes to a Dutch Reformed Church?"

"Oh. So?"

"So they speak Afrikaans in the Dutch Reformed Churches, not English."

Becca's heart sank. It hadn't even crossed her mind, but now it was so obvious. Steph-Marie's slight accent. Her father, the *dominee*, not the minister. Which meant she should be doing the speech in Afrikaans. *Crap!* "Course I know," she said breezily, and opened the speech on Gem's phone. "I was saying it in English for your benefit."

He upped the radio's volume. "I speak fluent Afrikaans."

As did so many South Africans. She, however, did not. She hadn't spoken Afrikaans in years, not since high school, and even then, she'd never been very good at it. And since moving to the UK, the most she said these days were a few Afrikaans phrases here and there when a South African guest recognised her accent, and then it was only silly things like telling them to enjoy their holiday. *Geniet jou vakansie* was of zero use to her today.

She turned to the window and stared in desperation at her reflection. There was no way that Gem, who'd been in an Afrikaans soapie before her *Luxe Life* days and who'd done countless bilingual appearances at events, would make an announcement to an Afrikaans congregation in English.

She'd just have to try. She thought for a moment, the scenery outside blurring. The online translator! The one she used at the hotel when dealing with guests with shaky English. She swiped the phone awake, found the translator online, and copied and pasted her speech into it. She selected Afrikaans as the result language and scanned through the translation.

A pro like Gem would never read a speech, but there was no way she could commit all this to memory, not with the outlying houses of the town already whipping past her window. Reading it would have to do, and she wasn't even sure she'd be able to do *that* properly.

She spent the rest of the drive reminding her brain how Afrikaans worked, sounding out the rusty words in her head, until the imposing brick facade of Winterberg's Dutch Reformed Church loomed in the Ranger's windscreen.

Sully parked on a side road in the only open space left. "Show time, princess."

Becca feared her answering smile had a tinge of terror to it. She unfastened her seat belt and pocketed Gem's phone.

Sully was waiting for her on the pavement, Ella sniffing the concrete beside him. He gestured to Becca to precede him and she stepped onto a neat-clipped lawn that fronted the spired church. She sent up a silent prayer that despite Mrs van Eck's invitations, new Sunday School buildings wouldn't be the highlight of the Winterberg social calendar and that she'd only have a small audience to contend with.

But apparently the Almighty wasn't on her side today. Outside a sparkling new brick building stood what might well have been the town's entire population. And front and centre was the glinting all-seeing lens of a press photographer.

Becca's anxiety exploded into full-blown dread. It hadn't even crossed her mind that if Steph-Marie had organised a well-known singer to open their Sunday School, she might also have organised a photographer or two.

Becca masked her dismay with a bright smile that had her cheeks aching by the time Steph-Marie had finished with all the introductions. And then the *dominee* called everyone to silence. While he droned away in Afrikaans to the crowd, Becca focused on slowing her breathing. Adjusted her stance. Stomach in. Shoulders back and loose. Chin parallel to the ground. And smile. The crowd laughed and she startled back to attention. The *dominee* had stopped speaking and was looking at her expectantly.

Her turn.

Her heart was beating so hard she could feel her pulse in her neck. She could do this. She had to. She'd sat in on enough of Gem's public-speaking classes, sitting cross-legged on the floor doing both their homework while Gem learned the tricks of wowing pageant judges in the Q&A sections. It was all about poise. Confidence. And hiding the fact that her stomach was so full of butterflies she was about to float right out of Gem's heels. "*Dames en here...*" She sneaked a look at the next sentence on Gem's phone. Her tongue, out of practice with the language, stumbled over the guttural syllables.

The photographer fired off a shot.

She stood a little straighter. Smiled her confident, capable concierge smile, and launched into the translation of her speech. A minute or two later, she checked the phone for the last line, then lifted the scissors. "*Ek verklaar hierdie gebou oop!*" She snicked the blades shut with the kind of flourish that promised that somewhere close by, a clutch of rabbits had just appeared in a hat.

As the ends of the purple ribbon fluttered to the ground, the onlookers broke into polite applause. Lucky for her this was a church-going crowd; forgiveness of her dodgy pronunciation was likely mandatory. Throwing out a Gem-bright smile, Becca clapped her hands together like her sister would've done and dispensed with the Afrikaans. "Please join us for tea in the hall."

And for those requiring something stronger, we'll be raiding the altar wine.

Inside the church hall, Becca made a beeline for Sully, who was standing at a central row of tables laden with platters of eats. "I'm ready to get back to work." She scanned the hall for the photographer.

Sully picked up a plate. "I haven't had breakfast."

She eyed the cake forks on the table and imagined jabbing him with one. "Let's take something to go." She picked up a paper serviette and took a homemade muffin from the platter he'd been eying. She popped the muffin onto the serviette. "You want anything else?"

He moved the muffin from her hand to his plate. "You were good out there. Wasn't sure what language you were speaking at times, but you made up for it with sparkle." He bit into the muffin and chewed, his gaze contemplative. He swallowed. "I don't know how you do it. Stand in front of people like that. I would freeze up."

She'd always hated it too, being on stage, with all those eyes trained on her. "Good thing you work with animals then." She picked up a scone, snagged the muffin off his plate, and wrapped both in the serviette. She waved his breakfast to-go at him. "You should go and check on that hyena."

Empty plate in hand, Sully ignored her and instead cruised the table, inspecting the treats on offer. "The only thing I should do is get myself some of this." He gestured with his empty plate at some sort of upside-down tart decorated with slices of orange beneath a sticky glaze. "It's the dominee's grandmother's specialty." He lifted a generous slice onto his plate.

"I'm serious, Sully."

He stabbed a cake fork into the tart and shovelled a large bite into his mouth. "So am I," he said, with his mouth full. "You should try some. It's her marmalade tart. It's won first place in annual fete's baking competition for the last three years."

"No thanks."

"You don't eat baked goods unless they come from some fancy Joburg bakery?"

"I don't eat baked goods slathered in marmalade."

"Too much sugar?" he said, forking another huge bite into his mouth.

"Too much orange rind. I can't stand the stuff. Look, shouldn't we be more concerned about this hyena?"

A soft thumping rose from the floor by his side. Sully sliced a bit off the remaining tart with the edge of his fork and prodded it off his plate onto the floor. Ella dropped her potato and set about hoovering noisily around his boots. "The hyena's in good hands, and even if you aren't hungry, Ella and I are. Aren't we, girl?" He consulted Ella and she panted up at him in adoring assent.

"Please, Sully." Becca laid a hand on his forearm. "There's a press photographer here." Sully's gaze flicked to her hand and she removed her fingers smartly before she found herself the subject of another out-of-context photo. She made an anxious scan of the hall, searching for a camera.

Sully seemed to be weighing his options, cake fork poised over his plate. "Fine," he grumbled. He took a forkful of tart and jammed it in his mouth, then he dumped his plate on the table.

The knot in her stomach loosened a little, but she wasn't in the clear yet. She resisted the urge to grab Sully by the hand and drag him behind her to the door.

"Gem! Gem!" A woman was elbowing her way through the milling crowd, with the photographer Becca had been trying to avoid in her wake.

Becca glanced at a set of double doors that lead out of the hall. Too far to make a break for it. She pinned a smile on her face and turned to the woman. Calm and professional. Just another day behind the concierge desk. *How may I help you, ma'am?*

"Gem! Cassie Govender from *Hot*," the woman said.

Just as she'd feared...the local celebrity magazine.

The woman thrust out a petite hand, her wrist jingling with gold bracelets. "We met at that launch party for the new Lamborghini."

Becca clasped the woman's hand in hers as the photographer raised his camera. "Of course! Cassie!" she gushed. "Fabulous launch, wasn't it?"

Cassie's rapacious grin faltered. "The car caught fire."

And this was why switches were like carrying around a hand grenade with the pin pulled out. "Sarcasm, Cassie."

Ka-shik, ka-shik, went the camera.

"Oh. Funny!" Dark, assessing eyes regarded Becca from behind a pair of trendy red-framed glasses, then Cassie Govender turned her focus to Sully. Her red-glossed mouth pulled into a beguiling smile as she gave him a slow and thorough inspection. She flipped a sheet of shining black hair over her shoulder. "I recognise you." Beguiling smile became appreciative smirk. "You're the hottie from the paper this morning. Dr Sullivan Scott. Even sexier in person." Cassie's voice was a sultry purr. The gossip columnist snapped her attention back to Becca and gave her a sly look. "Our readers are dying for all the juicy deets."

Becca kept her expression neutral. "Then you've wasted a trip, I hate to tell you. Unless you think shovelling manure is the sort of juiciness your readers enjoy."

Sully's hand closed on her shoulder and he leaned in. "We need to go. You've got work to do."

The camera whirred before Becca even thought to shrug away from his touch.

"So was it love at first sight?" Cassie fired off. "Or lust?" She waggled her eyebrows. "And who could blame you? Two gorgeous people, thrown together by circumstance..." Cassie tapped an icon on her phone. "You don't mind if I record this, do you?"

Sully's hand on Becca's shoulder tightened. "There's nothing going on between Gem and me."

Cassie gave him a conspiratorial wink, her gaze darting to his hand, and tapped the side of her nose.

Becca lowered her shoulder until Sully's hand slipped off.

Cassie grinned. "So is this a one-night stand? A fling?" She held out her phone towards them. "What have you told Mandla Ndungane?" She eyed Sully. "You're a brave man having an affair with the Springbok rugby captain's girlfriend."

Sully tipped his head in annoyance. "I'm not having an affair with anyone. And I don't get what the scandal is about. She's not even *with* Mandla anymore."

Shoot me now. The knot in Becca's stomach jerked tight.

Cassie couldn't have looked more stoked if Sully'd announced that Chris Hemsworth had arrived and was setting up a kissing booth in the foyer. "When did you break up? Was it amicable or ugly? Did he catch you cheating? Or was it because *he* was cheating...we hear you had a fight before he left for Australia on tour. Is this payback?"

Becca did a shaky imitation of Gem's tinkling laugh. "You gossip columnists..." She shook her head in feigned indulgent amusement. "Always jumping to conclusions. I'd love to chat more, but I have community service hours I need to get back to." She spun away from the press duo.

"But Gem!"

She felt Cassie's long fingernails graze her arm, but she lengthened her stride and shook her off. She angled this way and that to avoid the chattering, tea-drinking congregants. Sully had better be bringing up the rear, because if he wasn't, she'd chuck a brick through the Ranger's window and hot-wire the damn thing.

The *dominee* stood near the doors that led out of the hall, talking to a stern-faced woman on the stage who held a small child hostage by the hand. Becca grimaced. Mrs van Eck. The Scottie's owner who'd torn a strip off her yesterday at the town vet's.

Becca eyed the *dominee*, then the doorway. If she went wide, she could circle around him and sneak away, but Mrs van Eck glowered down at her from the stage and the *dominee* turned to see who was getting the full force of her death stare.

"You're not leaving us already, Miss Stratton?" he said.

Becca put on a look of abject disappointment. "I'm so sorry, but I must."

Sully appeared at her side. "Emergency at the sanctuary."

The *dominee* looked crestfallen. "But the Sunday School children want to sing for us."

Becca cast a look at the captive child. More had filed onto the stage, and were standing in neat rows in height order, the tallest at the back. "How lovely, but I really do have to go."

"They've practised very hard. One song?" The *dominee* waved a hand at the assembly on the stage, and Mrs van Eck clapped her hands to bring the children to attention.

Becca caught Sully's eye and he shrugged in defeat. "One song," he said.

The *dominee* pressed Becca into a chair at one of the round tables set up at the foot of the stage. "This is my wife, Hermien," he said, introducing Becca to a willowy woman in a demure floral dress, "and this is my grandmother, *Ouma* Irmi. She's ninety-four and doesn't hear so well."

"But she still bakes the best tart in Winterberg," Sully said, leaning around Becca and raising his voice a little. When the old woman blinked at him, he repeated what he'd said in Afrikaans and a smile creased her lined face.

Cups of tea had appeared in front of them, and Sully set about heaping sugar into his. And then the dominee's grandmother reached a bird-thin arm to a platter of scones topped with lashings of chunky, glistening—what else, but marmalade—and offered it to them.

Sully took two, but Becca smiled and shook her head. "No thank you."

Not to be put off, the dominee's grandmother selected the biggest scone and placed it on the plate in front of Becca. "*Proe,*" she said. "*Dis heerlik.*"

Delicious as it may well be, Becca did not want to taste it. "Thanks," she said, trying to return the scone to the platter, which the old woman was deftly keeping out of her reach," but I'm not a big fan of marmalade."

"*Proe.*"

Tasting wouldn't make any difference, but Becca picked up the scone anyway and nibbled on an edge devoid of preserves.

The old lady wasn't fooled. She jutted out her chin in silent command. Apparently rejection of said preserves was not an option.

Maybe if she said in the woman's home tongue, like Sully had done. Going the extra mile was something Becca did, and she had, after all, aced the speech, hadn't she? Telling the scone pusher that she didn't like marmalade wouldn't be that hard to say. *I don't like marmalade.* Easy. "*Ek hou nie van...*" She didn't know what 'marmalade' was in Afrikaans, so she just said it in English.

The preacher's granny just stared at her. Then at the scone. Then back at her.

Becca huffed softly. "It's the peel, you see. It's so bitter. *Ek hou nie van...*" It seemed her rusty vocabulary was going to let her down when it came to *peel* too. For the life of her, she couldn't think what the Afrikaans word for *peel* was.

Steph-Marie popped up then at Becca's side and jammed a microphone into her hands. "The Sunday School kids are ready. We want you to announce them."

Great! More microphone work. "Sure, er..." Becca stood, mic in her hand. She patted the old woman on the shoulder. "Sorry, but *ek hou nie van* peel *nie*." The mic was on. Her voice bounced around the hall, booming out of the stage speakers.

Sully sprayed a mouthful of tea over the arrangement of daisies in the centre of the table. The chatter in the hall shut off as if someone somewhere had hit a mute button. On the stage, Mrs van Eck put her hands over the ears of the child closest to her, and the *dominee*'s gran's eyes boggled so she looked like a Pug in a floral dress.

Becca's blood chilled. She looked at Sully, who was bashing the flat of his hand against his chest as he spluttered and choked on laughter and inhaled tea. "Did I say something wrong?"

All he could do was nod, his eyes watering.

Sound crashed back into the hall like gravity being restored on a spaceship. A hand closed on Becca's arm and she jumped and looked down, almost dropping the mic. Cassie's fingers were wrapped around her forearm. "Is that it, Gem?" Cassie gasped, and the photographer fired off a few shots in Becca's startled face. "Is that why you and Mandla broke up? Are you coming out officially?" She leaned in closer. "Are you a lesbian?" she said, the mic bouncing her words around the hall.

Becca's mouth fell open. "No!" She switched off the mic. "Why would you—"

"You look horrified at the thought, Gem," Cassie said. "Is there something wrong with being gay? Do you not support the LGBTQIA+ community?"

Shit! What? "No! That's not at all what I was saying!"

Firm hands closed on her upper arms. "The door's this way." Sully's voice in her ear was the only calm thing in the agitated hall.

"We've got to get back to work," he said to whoever was close enough to hear, then he turned her by the shoulders and steered her ahead of him.

Stumbling along before him in Gem's rickety high heels, Becca glanced over her shoulder. "What exactly did I say?"

He leaned close to her ear. "You said you don't like dick."

12

#WrongPlaceWrongTime

"Hurry, or they'll catch up with us." Sully stopped on the pavement behind the church and looked back at Becca.

She clenched her toes to keep Gem's shoes on her feet. "I don't see you wearing heels."

"Want me to chuck you over my shoulder?"

She turned a harried expression on him. "Ooh, yes please. I'm dying to crack the front page again."

The grin he'd had on his face ever since they'd escaped through the back door of the hall intensified. "We'll have to wait until the coast is clear and we can get back to the bakkie." He whistled for Ella, who'd barrelled off along the pavement as if they were playing a rousing game of catchers. The dog turned and lollopped back, huffing in excitement around her potato.

"In here." Sully unlatched a wire gate set into a brick wall and ushered Becca through into a small garden, shutting the gate once Ella had lumbered in.

A pretty stone building with a grey zinc-plate roof and arched stained-glass windows was set against a backdrop of flower beds and trees just beginning to flaunt their spring foliage. From inside came the sound of a piano thumping out an opening refrain, then voices joined in to sing a hymn Becca remembered from school assemblies. "Is this your church?"

He nodded. "St Matthew's. Come on, off the path, or they'll spot you through the gate."

She followed him across a patch of thick grass, heels sinking into the lawn so she had to hobble after him on the balls of her feet.

He stopped out of view of the gate beside a dense swath of shrubbery and Becca paused beside him. Without the sound of their hurried footsteps to cover it, Becca could hear her own heart now, smacking against her breastbone. She glanced behind her in the direction of the gate. "*Hot* is going to make such a meal of this." Her legs were trembling as much as her voice and she wobbled on her toes. "It was an innocent mistake."

Sully took her arm to steady her, his long fingers cupping her elbow. "There's nothing innocent about announcing to an entire congregation of conservative Afrikaners that you don't like dick."

She tipped her head back and groaned. "How was I supposed to know that 'peel' in English sounds exactly like the Afrikaans word for 'dick'?"

He gave her a look of amused disbelief. "Come on. You seriously want me to believe you didn't know that *piel* meant 'dick'? Weren't you in an Afrikaans soapie once?"

She twitched against his supporting hand. "That was a long time ago, and it was a PG show."

Footsteps pounded beyond the walled garden and Cassie's voice echoed in the street. "Hurry up! This way!"

Becca caught her breath on a gasp and her gaze whipped to meet Sully's. Without letting go of her arm, he raised a silent finger to his lips.

"They can't have gotten far." Cassie's voice was shrill. Excited. A hound locked onto a scent. "You take that road. I'll check this one."

There were more footsteps, then silence.

Sully's breath eased from his chest.

A second scraped by.

Then another.

The wire gate rattled.

Becca's gaze met Sully's in an expression of horror. He glanced in the direction of the gate, caught her gaze again, and then the hand on her elbow shot out to hook around her back and with apparently no effort, he lifted her off her feet and against his chest.

She squeaked in surprise, but he shook his head, signalling for her to be silent. He stepped backwards off the lawn into the flower bed, shoving aside branches with his free arm as he reversed with her through the foliage until he pulled her in behind an azalea bush, its branches heavy with showy white blooms.

"Down," he whispered to Ella, and the Lab sank immediately into the fragrant blanket of wet leaves at their feet.

A second passed.

And another.

The gate banged with a rattle against its post.

Becca tensed, and so did Sully's arm that held her tight against him. She couldn't tell if it was her heart or his, jack-hammering against her ribs like that.

Footsteps tapped on the path, and Sully snaked another arm around Becca's waist as he stepped back deeper into the foliage.

Something plopped into the leaves at their feet and the footsteps stopped. Sully shook his head at Ella. "Bloody potato," he breathed into Becca's ear, his warm breath lifting the hair at her temple.

A snatch of pop music blared mere metres away and Becca jerked against him.

The music cut off. A ringtone. "Hello?" Cassie's voice.

Becca turned her forehead into Sully's chest and bit her lip.

"Where? Okay, I'll go look." Footsteps. The click of a latch. The protesting squeak of the gate swinging open. Then a hollow clash of metal on metal and Cassie's footsteps broke into a run on the pavement outside.

Becca lifted her head and listened. Nothing, except the drone of the priest inside the church. She sagged against Sully's chest, expelling the breath she'd been holding for an eternity. "God, that was close." She inhaled, filling her head with the scent of crushed wet greenery and surgical disinfectant and...warm male. Awareness surged through her. She was flattened against him, her breasts squashed against his chest, his strong arms locked around her body, the hard lines of his thighs pressed against hers. Electricity sparked low in her stomach and her pulse, already racing, accelerated.

She felt with her foot to step away but found her feet weren't on the ground. She squirmed and pushed against Sully's chest. He loosened the band of muscle around her, and she inched down his body until her feet met spongy leaf litter.

Their eyes made contact and Becca stumbled back from him, almost tripping over a reclining Labrador.

A song swelled in the church behind them. *God bless Africa. Godddd blesssss Aaaafffrica.*

Sully cleared his throat and checked his watch. "The service will be coming out soon. Best not to get caught in the bushes with me." His eyes found hers again before he shifted his feet and looked away to the church building. "I could do with a cup of tea I won't have to snort through my nose. Or do you think you might feel compelled to also announce to this congregation that you're not big on dick?" The amused smirk was back.

She gave him a frosty look. "You're never going to let me forget that, are you?"

"Nope."

Unlikely that anyone else would either, not once *Hot* splashed it across the gossip pages. Her stomach clenched as if it were being crushed by a giant fist. Alek was going to lose his head over this. And she couldn't bear to think what Gem was going to say about all this once she got back. Or Mom. She pressed a tight fist to her mouth and breathed in slowly through her nose.

"Princess."

Sully's voice from the other side of the bushes shook her from her rising panic. She blew out a quick breath and made her way out of the shrubbery.

They crossed the lawn and ducked in through a side door of the church, where they joined the tail end of the column of parishioners filing out into a foyer. People stooped to pat Ella's broad back, and Sully greeted them with a laid-back tone she hadn't heard him use before, certainly not where she was concerned.

In the small foyer, congregants gathered around a hatch where tea and coffee had been laid out.

Sully touched her arm. "You want?"

She shook her head, not convinced her churning stomach could keep anything down.

Sully picked up a mug and sloshed milk into it. "I'm so parched from all that hide-and-seek I could just *peel* my tongue off my palate."

"You really are the most smug man alive."

He chuckled and amusement lit his eyes. "You bring out the worst in me, princess." He greeted a woman wielding a large metal teapot and held out his mug. As he stepped away from the hatch, steering Becca with his fingertips in the small of her back towards an open section of floor, he leaned in close to her shoulder. "Who knew that royal life was this exciting?"

She twisted to scowl up at him and earned herself a delighted chuckle. "I'm glad my imminent repeat humiliation in the press is so amusing to you."

Sully stopped and removed his hand from her back. Ella sat at his feet and plonked her bottom squarely on one of his boots, contorting her neck so she could stare up at him. Amber eyes met brown, and he smiled at the dog. "Fine, I'll stop teasing her." He lifted his head and took a noisy swig of tea, holding Becca's gaze over the rim of his mug. "Even though it's such fun." He took another sip.

"Yoo hoo! Dr Scott!"

Sully spat tea into his mug and his gaze shot away over Becca's shoulder.

Becca spun, her heart in her mouth, expecting to see someone with a camera bearing down on them. Instead it was a woman in her seventies hurrying towards them, a clipboard clamped under one arm.

He swore softly, and Ella's tail thumped energetically on the grey vinyl floor. He wiped his mouth on the back of his hand. "Now I remember why I wasn't coming to church today."

The woman bustled up and pressed a hand to her chest in an overblown show of relief. "Sullivan!"

Sully curved his lips into a smile so tight it seemed in danger of twanging right off his face and knocking the woman's black-framed reading glasses from their perch on the end of her nose. "Mrs Abrams."

"Do you know what you are, young man?"

Sully flinched under the woman's zealous gaze. "A sacrificial lamb?"

The woman tittered and patted his arm, making his back stiffen. "You're the answer to my prayers. When I didn't see you in church this morning, I said to the man upstairs that if it was his will, he should make it happen. And here you are. With a celebrity in tow." The woman angled sharply to face Becca. "Edwina Abrams. Head of the charity committee."

Out thrust a hand and Becca shook it. "Nice to meet you."

"I saw you in the newspaper this morning." One eye narrowed slyly. "Very cosy. If you want him though, you're going to have to pay for him. Isn't that right, Sullivan?"

Sully's gaze skittered to the door behind Mrs Abrams and his throat flexed on a hard swallow. "I can't do it again, not after last year."

Mrs Abrams tsk-ed. "It wasn't so bad."

"I almost had a heart attack with everyone ogling me like that." Tea slopped on the floor and Sully righted his tipping mug. He glanced at Ella, who was crawling forward on her belly to clean the floor with her pink tongue. The colour had drained from his face as if a memory playing behind his eyes was making him light-headed. "And then Reverend Adele made me take off my shirt." He shuddered.

A flush crept up Mrs Abrams's pleated neck and she squeezed Sully's arm. "It was all for a good cause. And we made an absolute killing off you."

"And almost offed me in the process. I hate being the centre of attention. There's a reason I work with animals and not people." He shook his head vehemently. "You'll have to count me out this year."

Mrs Abrams tipped her chin and eyed him from beneath raised eyebrows. "I don't see what the fuss is about, not now the entire country's seen your bare chest." She did a slow, appreciative survey of Sully's fleece-wrapped torso, freeing her clipboard and fanning herself with it while her gaze roved. "After that photo in *The Sunday Star*, we're going to have our best turnout ever."

Becca peered at the flapping clipboard. Between flaps, she made out *St Matthew's Anglican Women's Association* on the page clamped to the top. And—she moved her head with the motion of the clipboard—*Annual Bachelor Auction.* So the women of Winterberg were hot for Dr Smug 'n Sexy, were they? Becca smirked and looked at Sully with undisguised enjoyment. Not that he looked all that smug right now.

He caught her gaze, and the pure desperation that flashed through his eyes caused a swell of sympathy to wipe the grin off her face. Fun as it was to see him in hot water, she'd been in a similar tight spot not too long ago herself, and he'd stepped in to help her. The least she could do was not gloat. Better yet, she could rescue him and even the score. "Shouldn't we get back and check on that hyena?"

Sully's eye lit. "Yes." He threw the last of his tea—likely ice-cold by now—down his throat. "Sorry, Mrs Abrams. Medical emergency." He took a determined step sideways, but Mrs Abrams leaped forward to grasp his wrist, dislodging her reading glasses so they swung from their beaded spectacle cord onto her chest.

"You do know we're raising funds for the underprivileged kiddies in the Thandanani informal settlement? For the informal school there? And if we don't make our target"—Mrs Abrams gazed up into Sully's eyes and sighed as if the task of achieving world peace had been laid at her door—"we won't have enough to buy the new playground equipment we promised them. You wouldn't want to let down the children. Or your church. The church that welcomed you into its midst when you moved here. That supported you when your fiancée left you at the altar for that farmer."

Becca stiffened in surprise and looked at Sully. Well that might just explain where all that surly energy came from.

"Thanks," he said, irritation twining through his voice, "I needed to be reminded of that." His gaze found Becca and held for the briefest of moments before he snapped it away.

Mrs Abrams hoisted up her reading glasses on their cord, jammed them on her face and unclipped a pen from the clipboard. "That's settled then." She chiselled Sully's name in block letters onto a list of what were presumably the other hapless bachelors. "I'll see you at the church on Tuesday. We start promptly at noon."

Becca glanced at Sully. His stricken expression knifed her between the ribs. He should tell this pushy woman that he had a girlfriend, but in a small town like this and with someone like Mrs Abrams, his secret would likely make its way back to the sanctuary before the tea in the parishioners' mugs grew cold. She returned her gaze to Mrs Abrams and adjusted her posture to concierge-erect. "You said Tuesday? He can't make it. We'll be at work."

Sully drew himself up like a horse in a desert that had smelled water. "Right. I have to supervise Gem's community service."

Mrs Abrams pursed her lips. "Tuesday is a public holiday, so you'll have the day off."

"Animals don't take holidays," Becca said solemnly, earning a thankful glance from Sully. "And nor can I. I'm on a tight schedule, and I can't do my community service without him."

Mrs Abrams eyed Becca, one eye screwing shut. "Then I'll put you down as the MC and you can work your community service hours at our charity auction."

Becca took an involuntary step back. That hadn't gone as she'd planned. Not a chance was she getting behind a microphone again.

She adopted her best guest-wrangling tone. "I'd love to, but my agent said not to set foot from the sanctuary."

Mrs Abrams looked down her nose at Becca. "And yet here you are. I'm sure Sullivan will count MC-ing a charity event towards your hours."

Becca turned to Sully, mouth open to toss out her next objection, when he blurted out, "I'll make it double hours if she promises she won't let anyone pressure me into taking off my shirt."

"I— No!" Becca gaped at him. "I'm not hosting a bachelor auction."

"I've rescued you twice, princess. Time to return the favour. Triple hours, and I don't have to take anything off or answer any embarrassing questions on stage."

"Deal," Mrs Abrams said.

Becca bridled in protest. "No deal."

Mrs Abrams shoved her clipboard under her arm. "There will be no removal of clothing, no uncomfortable questions, and I will see you both on Tuesday." Her head whipped towards the tea hatch. "Oh! Yoo hoo! Patrick!" Mrs Abrams set off across the room, wafting her clipboard at a young man who looked as if he'd just noticed the red dot of a sniper's laser sight on his chest.

Becca thrust out a hand to try and stay the departing woman. "But my agent..."

"Save your breath." Sully blew out a sigh.

Becca turned on him. "You rolled over like a good little dog."

"Not a chance was she ever going to let me off the hook. At least this way, I get to walk off the stage with all of my clothing and some of my dignity intact."

"But I can't do it." Becca's head was shaking in time to the *Nonononononono* soundtrack playing on an endless loop in her head. "That ribbon ceremony was bad enough. I can't be MC."

Sully tipped his head, curiosity suffusing his gaze. "Why not? It's what you do."

She stiffened and sent her gaze skipping away. "Yeah, I know. But after what happened this morning..."

Sully placed a hand on her shoulder. "You'll be fine. So long as nobody offers you anything with marmalade on it."

13

#Heart2Heart

"You missed a spot." Arms folded atop the chest-high stone wall overlooking a section of the pig enclosure, Sully pointed at the concrete floor.

Becca dutifully aimed the hosepipe where he'd indicated and scrubbed the toe of her borrowed gumboot on a muddy smear. Since they'd returned from the church, she'd been working flat-out to catch up on her hours. She'd emptied and scrubbed out a concrete pond for a pelican with a broken wing. She'd disinfected food and water bowls—enough to provision an ark. And now, with the afternoon sun throwing long shadows, she was on clean-up patrol in the pigs' night shelter.

Her body ached, her hands were red and chapped, and her nails were so battered and filthy it looked like the name of Gem's signature polish might very well be *Sewer Rat.*

She gazed enviously at two enormous potbellied pigs lying stretched out on their sides at the far end of the spacious pasture, a shrinking patch of sunlight toasting their broad black paunches. "Why do you even have pigs at a wildlife sanctuary?"

"Is there some rule against it?"

She looked back at him. "I could understand if they were warthogs or wild bush pigs. But those are domestic pigs. Hardly endangered wildlife."

His head inclined. "Not wild, but still endangered. I went to pick up an injured bat from the vet in town, and found those two about to be put down because they'd grown too big and their owner didn't want them."

Becca frowned. "That's gross. Just kill your pets when you're tired of them?"

He tipped his chin. "There are times when I'm ashamed to be a human."

"But you're one of the good ones." She caught his eye and gulped. Where had that come from? She whipped her gaze away to the pigs and laughed. "Dr Scott, saving the world one pig at a time."

He gave a dismissive shrug. "It's what I do. Helping animals has always been my thing."

"In that case, why don't you help this animal with her chores?" She poked herself in the chest.

His face grew incredulous. "And risk breaking a nail?"

"And you call me the princess." She eyed him lounging against the wall. Looked at the hose in her hand. If she flicked her wrist—

"Don't even think about it, princess. Not unless you want to try scrubbing out the shelter with a toothbrush."

His voice was a low burr that sent goosebumps prickling along her thighs. "A toothbrush is a great idea." She did a neat pirouette away and redirected the water to the opposite end of the shelter. "So much easier to get into all those hard-to-reach places."

Sully angled his head at the dirt road that ran past the pigs' enclosure. "My house is around that bend, if you want me to fetch you one."

The boyish mischief in his eyes made her stomach quiver. She turned away sharply and aimed her hosepipe at a section of concrete she'd already cleaned. "My sister and I once dressed as tooth fairies for a pageant." She blanched inwardly at the nervous tumble of words and glanced at him over her shoulder, hoping he hadn't heard her over the splash of water.

But he was watching her expectantly. "Go on."

She could've kicked herself. "That's it. That's the story. There's nothing to tell." She shut the hose nozzle with a purposeful twist and let the hosepipe fall. "I'd better fetch the clean straw."

"No, you'd better spill. You can't blurt out something like that and then leave me hanging."

The amusement in his voice was doing strange things to her ability to breathe. She scrubbed damp palms on Gem's filthy jeans. "You don't really want to know about kids' beauty pageants."

"I don't?" Stubble-darkened jaw propped in his hand, Sully tapped a finger on his bottom lip, as if pondering a great mystery. "The princess, dressed as a tooth fairy?" He grinned. "Oh, I very much want to know about that."

"I'm here to work, not chat." The fresh hay bales to replace the pigs' used straw were stacked beneath a green tarpaulin along the outside wall of the shelter. She eyed them pointedly before looking back at him. Brows raised, he had the look of a man prepared to wait a very long time to get what he wanted. "Fine." She aimed a finger at him. "But if you mock me about it, remember who's in charge of the microphone at your bachelor auction."

His head gave the smallest nod. "Fair enough. Now tell me about tooth fairies."

She flopped her arms at her sides, in case he wasn't crystal clear how reluctant she was to tell this story. He waved an imperious hand for her to continue. "It was for a pageant sponsored by a toothpaste brand. Mom thought it would improve our chances of placing if we dressed appropriately, so she made us sparkly tutus and got those dress-up fairy wings. You know the gauzy, sparkly ones that hook over your shoulders with elastic?"

Sully's mouth quirked with undisguised mirth. "Can't say I've ever worn any myself."

The image of him, bare-chested like he'd been at the dam, with a set of fairy wings secured over those broad shoulders, made a chuckle rise in her throat.

And a slow heat spread through her chest.

She dropped her gaze to her feet and wet her lips. Her foot prodded the hosepipe nozzle as she tried to remember what she'd been saying. *Fairy wings.* "Mom rounded off our outfits with tiaras that she'd hot-glued toothbrushes to, and then she made giant toothbrushes out of pool noodles with dustpan brushes shoved in at the end."

Sully laughed. Not the snide, taunting laugh she'd have expected from him yesterday, but a genuine laugh that made her stomach roll over like a dopey puppy. She caught his gaze and the humour in his eyes only added to the heat now creeping into her neck. "You promised you wouldn't laugh," she said, hoping he'd read the flush on her skin as embarrassment.

"I promised I wouldn't mock you." His smile was disarming. "And I'm not."

She wished he was, then she could feel annoyed, rather than this slipping, sliding, off-kilter attraction. She crossed to the hay and tugged off the tarp, dropping it on the ground beside her.

"How old were you?"

"Five."

"And your sister?"

Becca hesitated, her chest growing instantly tight. She skimmed one hand down the rough face of the bales stacked as high as her chin. She should lie. Tell him that she was younger, which technically wasn't a lie: Gem had been born eight minutes before her. But the more lies she told, the more complicated the switch became. Even if he knew she had a twin, it didn't mean he'd make the fanciful leap that they'd switched places.

"It's not a trick question, princess."

That's what you think. She fingered the white plastic strapping that bound the top bale, her pulse picking up speed. She faced him. "I—Becca is younger." Her mouth grew sticky as she lined up the next words. "If you count eight minutes as being younger."

Sully didn't reply immediately, but from the twitch of his eyebrows and the movement of his eyes, she could almost see the gears turning in his head. His hand fell away from his chin and he straightened against the wall. "You're twins?"

And there it was. "Yep."

Eyes narrowed, he surveyed her face. "Fraternal or identical?"

She turned away and took hold of the top bale. "Identical." She gave a sharp tug, jolting the heavy bale towards her. "Go on, ask me."

"Ask you what?"

She hopped backwards as the bale crashed to the ground at her feet. Her breath was hard and quick, and not just from the exertion. "If we feel each other's pain. Or if we can read each other's minds."

Sully angled his head as if what she said might make more sense that way. "Why would I ask you that?"

The strapping had bitten into her fingers and she rubbed them absently on her thighs. "People always ask things like that when they find out I have an identical twin. Like do we have a secret language? Do we share boyfriends?" She hesitated, considering the question that was poised on the tip of her tongue. *Just say it.* "Of course my favourite question is whether we're always switching places and getting up to all kinds of hysterical shenanigans." She rolled her eyes, as if this was the most ludicrous question of them all.

"And do you? Switch?"

It was hard to maintain eye contact. "No!" She looked off over Sully's shoulder. *Not 'always', anyway.*

"Do you have a photo of her?"

She should've anticipated that. People always wanted to see for themselves whether she and Gem were as indistinguishable as the label 'twin' implied. She chewed the inside of her lip. This was a good thing though. If she showed him a photo of herself looking nothing like the Gem he knew, it could only help reinforce that she was 'Gem'. That photo of her on The Rickford's website, with her grey uniform, modest makeup and efficient chignon, the concierge team ranged behind her.

She called up the hotel's website on Gem's phone and scrolled down. Her team smiled out from the screen, and she felt a pang again at abandoning them like she had. "Here." She crossed to the stone wall and handed him the phone. "That's m—" She gave herself a mental slap; she'd almost said 'me'. "That's my sister. The Rickford London's head concierge."

His eyebrows lifted and he scrolled the screen a little before returning to the photo. "How does someone become a concierge?"

"By chance, in Becca's case," Becca said. "She has a degree in hotel management, and worked across all sorts of hotel divisions in the beginning. Originally she had dreams of ending up running a hotel, working her way up to general manager, but she landed a guest relations job at the Rickford and found herself behind the concierge desk, and she never left." Gosh, it was weird talking about herself in the third person. "She'd have signed up for the junior management programme, but she was so good with guests, nobody high up at the Rickford wanted her to leave. So she stayed and now she's the head concierge."

"Isn't she rather young to be a head concierge? What are you? Thirty-five? Thirty-six?"

"Twenty-nine," Becca spluttered.

He smiled as if he'd known that and had just wanted to poke fun at her. "Even more impressive then. You're quite the talented double act."

A cord tightened low inside her and she broke eye contact as the unexpected praise caused a strange, charged tension to span through her chest and down through her body.

Sully looked between her and the photo, as if he were doing a Spot the Difference puzzle. He handed back the phone. "If you told me it was you in this photo, I'd believe you."

Her fingers clawed around the phone and she gulped. "Even our parents get us mixed up at times."

He smiled. "The hazards of being identical."

"You have no idea," she said, relief making her voice all gushy. She returned his smile and pocketed the phone. "One of Mom's cousins still calls both Gem and I 'Bemma' because he can never tell who's who."

Sully's head inclined. "Gem and I?"

It took her a moment, but when understanding came, it came like a full-speed collision into a nose-shatteringly clean glass sliding door. Her stomach plummeted, but years of training kept her smile from taking a similarly precipitous nose-dive off her face. She gave an exasperated snort and smacked a damp palm to her forehead, shaking loose a manic titter. "You see? Even I get confused!"

She spun on one booted foot and forced nonchalance into her stride as she walked to the stacked bales. *Even I get confused?* She was such. An. Idiot. "Do your pigs have names?" Her hands shook as she snatched at the strapping on the topmost bale, her breath trapped in her chest, waiting for his response.

A beat. "Harry and Beatrix." He paused. "Trotter."

A knee-melting relief sluiced through her and she almost slumped against the hay bales, clutching at her racing heart. He was letting her glitch slide. She gathered herself and looked over her shoulder at him. "You're kidding."

"What? It's genius." His smile sparked humour into his eyes.

"That is the worst pun I ever heard."

His smile deepened. "It was better than 'Pork' and 'Sausage', which was Jo's contribution."

She laughed. "Yeah, that's worse." She gave the plastic strapping a great heave and dislodged the second heavy bale. It bounced off the first and landed a little way away.

"Did you both win?" Sully asked. "At the tooth fairy pageant."

Becca hesitated. "Twins don't compete as a team. I took first princess." Might as well stick with the truth.

There was the amused smirk again. "How appropriate."

She tossed her head and gave an affronted snort, which made him chuckle.

"And your sister? Where'd she come?"

While they might have looked identical in their matching outfits, Gem's brimming confidence, even at five, and her too-cute wiggle had been irresistible. "She took home the crown that time."

"The tooth fairy pageant wasn't a one-off?"

Becca scoffed. "At five we were already seasoned pageant pros." She brought another bale crashing to the floor. "We won our first competition for cutest newborn, for some or other baby formula brand. Mom was on the front page of the local community paper with us. After that, she was hooked, and us along with her. Mom entered us into every competition she could find."

Sully shifted on the wall, taking his weight on both elbows and letting his hands dangle off the edge. "So you were one of those kids you see on *Toddlers and Tiaras.*"

"Mom would've loved that, but Dad didn't like seeing us glammed up, so she stuck to the less over-the-top competitions." Becca's gaze drifted from his attentive eyes. He'd taken off his fleece hours ago, revealing a khaki T-shirt that fitted snugly across his chest. Her eyes played over the outlines of muscle until the wall interrupted the view and sent her gaze veering off along a tanned forearm. Over the bracelets at his wrist. Down the lazy, dangled hand.

A tingling sensation prickled up the back of her neck. She bent sharply and latched onto one of the fallen bales. Using her knees as leverage, she hauled it up, expelling a lungful of air with a ragged grunt. Bugger, the bale had to weigh a good twenty kilos. And she had four of them to move. She was going to need a back massage after this.

Her eyes found Sully's dangling hand again. Even relaxed, she could see the thick muscles at the base of his thumb. The tendons spanning from wrist to knuckle. His strong fingers that would work out the knots in her shoulders with smooth, firm strokes.

Her breath skipped and her own fingers forgot how to stay flexed. The bale landed with a rustling thud on her feet. "Gosh, that's heavy." She hoped flustered breathing looked much the same as exhausted breathing. "Phew!" She fanned her face. "I need to catch my breath."

Sully straightened and braced his hand on the wall as if he intended to vault over. "Let me do it."

"No!" She flapped a frantic hand at him. "I'll do it." *You stay there while I beat my ovaries back into submission.*

"Are you always this stubborn?" Before she could answer, he leaped the wall in one fluid, powerful movement that made her pulse skip, landing with a heavy thump of boots on concrete.

"Step aside, princess." His arm brushed hers as he stepped around her to get to the bale.

"Really, I can do it myself."

His reply was to close his hands on her waist and lift her off her feet, swinging her through the air and up onto the wall as if she were lighter than a bag of dog food. "I'm sure you can, princess. But do me a favour and let me help you."

He shoved his fingers under the strapping and lifted the bale, his biceps bunching as he threw the bale effortlessly across the shelter into the corner where the pigs slept.

Becca's hands fisted on the wall's edge. Not even a Tazer and enough teargas to equip a SWAT team could've subdued her ovaries now. Thank goodness she was leaving on Friday.

WhatsApp

Mandla
Sunday 10:37 p.m.

What's going on, baby?!?!? We have a fight and now you're with some other guy?

Babe?

Hello? Gem? Baby?

Are you cheating on me?

I know you're reading my texts, girl. I can see you're online.

Ghosting me won't make this go away.

Fine, you want to ignore me? We'll talk when I get back.

And I'm gonna assume that photo in *The Sunday Star* is fake news because we both know the press.

Please don't let me find out it's not, baby.

Coz I know you say I'm your teddy bear, but swear to God, I will kick. His. Arse!

14

#MondayBlues

Becca tested the glass door of the rehab centre and found it unlocked. She leaned on the door and stepped into an empty reception. Quarter to seven on a chilly Monday morning, and 'Gem' was reporting for duty seemingly even before the paid employees. After yesterday's public-relations disaster at the church, the least Becca could do was demonstrate just how hard-working and committed her twin could be.

Time to put the weekend's calamities behind her and sort this community service like she did everything else.

She pushed through the internal swinging doors. Before she could get a few metres down the corridor, Sully called Gem's name from one of the side rooms. Impossible to be a stealth ninja in Gem's heels. "Be there in a second," she called back, and turned off into the store room where yesterday she'd stowed the borrowed wellies— Gumboots! No more slips of the tongue today.

"Oh, hey, Ella." The Labbie's tail thumped on the overstuffed cushion in her wicker basket, and she scrambled to her feet, ducking her head to snatch up a chewed, saliva-slick potato.

Becca crossed to the dog and patted the velvet head, eliciting a happy chuffing that made her smile. "You're a sweetie, aren't you?" Much like the dog's owner, once you got past all the gruffness. She switched Gem's stilettos for the outsized gumboots, blew a kiss to Ella and hurried out into the corridor.

She found Sully in a room full of cages built into one wall. He stood in front of a cage, a faded green towel draped over the bars to shield the occupant. When he didn't turn immediately, she took the opportunity to give his shoulders an appreciative look. Bidding was going to be fierce at tomorrow's auction.

She stole closer, curious to see what animal or bird was inside the cage, but he turned then and she stumbled back in the too-large boots. He caught her arm and she looked into his face, feeling a flutter in her chest.

He frowned at her feet. "You really need more suitable footwear."

"Sully?" Clare stopped in the doorway and placed a casual hand on the door jamb. "You're in early." Her gaze zeroed in on Sully's hand, still closed around Becca's arm.

"Still way too many hours until I get my hands on that money," he said.

Becca extricated herself and shoved her hands into her jeans pockets, smoothing her face into a mask of innocence. Not that she'd done anything that crossed a line, but she hadn't come to Winterberg to break up relationships.

Clare slid her phone from the pocket of her vet's tunic top and tapped at the screen. "You might need to rethink how badly you want that cash once you've seen this." As she handed him her phone, she caught Becca's gaze, her eyes cold as a shark's.

Sully signed in exasperation. "Now what?"

Becca didn't need to see the screen to guess what he was reading. Embarrassment chased through her. It had been a vain hope that Sully wouldn't see *Hot*'s report on yesterday's lost-in-translation slip.

Sully's finger scrolled up the screen, exasperation turning to a frown that deepened with each flick of his finger. Which mortifying photo was he on now? The one where the dominee was fanning his shocked mother slumped in a chair, parishioners gathered round, all shooting each other scandalised looks? Or was it the photo where Sully had his hand on her shoulder, another moment caught out of context so it looked like he had been moving in to kiss her neck. His head slightly tilted. Eyes closed on a blink. Lips parted. And the caption: some salacious crap about how Gem had been seen getting up close and personal with "her rebound man" moments before announcing an apparent change of sexuality to a room full of conservative church people.

Becca cringed, hollowing into herself at the memory of last night's infuriated phone call from Alek.

Clare had tucked herself into Sully's side, perusing the screen around his arm. Sully made an annoyed sound at something he saw and Clare stroked a soothing hand down his arm. He seemed not to notice, too distracted by the dirt on *Hot*'s website.

He handed Clare her phone and widened the gap between them with a side step. "They must have a pretty large legal budget, if they make a habit of publishing *kak* like that."

Becca looked up at him, her face contorted with shame. "I'm used to this kind of thing, but you never signed up for this. I'm really sorry you got dragged into the media all over again."

"I'd be furious if it were me." Clare kept her gaze locked on Sully's. "I hope the sanctuary won't get negative press from this. Maybe you should call off this arrangement with Jo's brother."

"Eye on the prize, Clare." His gaze flicked to Becca. "And it's not her fault the press is unscrupulous."

Clare's eyebrows climbed and she opened her mouth to speak, but someone shouting Sully's name up the corridor cut her off.

"Sully. Officer Khalil to see you," called the voice.

His expression grew instantly serious and he and Clare looked at each other.

Becca's pulse accelerated. "If I'm going back to jail, promise me you'll bail me out."

"Relax," Sully said. "Imraan is with the Endangered Species Unit. He works animal poaching and trafficking." He gestured to Becca to follow him and Clare. "Let's go see what he's brought us this time."

Outside the rehab centre, a skinny, middle-aged man in police blues stood at the open back of a parked police van. Another officer sat behind the wheel, one elbow on the open window sill.

The officer behind the van stepped forward. His surname was printed in capitals above the SAPS crest on his left breast. Officer Khalil nodded at Becca, greeted Clare, and then clapped Sully's hand in his as if they were old friends. "We've got work for you today, doc." He tipped his head at a large box in the back. "We confiscated them at the Ultra City on the freeway. The guy was showing them off to the petrol attendants. We got three this time."

Sully approached the box, Clare hovering at his elbow. "How long did he have them?"

"He said a week, maybe two." Officer Khalil moved to make room inside the open van doors. "He got them from a poacher up in Mpumalanga."

The box was a beat-up packing box. Sully lifted one flap and looked in, and Becca stretched in a vain attempt to see over his shoulder.

He shifted something inside, his eyes sharp and assessing. "You get the buyer?" He looked at the cop.

Officer Khalil shook his head, regret lining his forehead. "We have an address in Durban. The team's been watching this guy for a while. We'll go to the drop-off point and see if we can arrest him before he gets wind that we've seized his cargo."

Clare tucked herself in next to Sully so she could look into the box. "I want to cry when I see things like this," she murmured, turning her face up to his and giving him a sad little pout.

Sully hesitated, then gave her a quick side-on hug with one arm slung around her shoulders. "Good thing they've got us then." He removed his arm swiftly. "Will you get the team together?"

Clare sniffed. "I'll set up exam room two."

He nodded and turned to Becca. "You ever seen a pangolin?"

"A pango-what?"

He crooked a finger at her.

Becca threw a quick glance at Clare, not wanting to tread on any toes, but Clare was already jogging back to the rehab centre. Sully angled his body to give her room in front of the box. She peeked under the flap that he held up for her.

On a grubby towel lay three basketball-sized creatures with hard overlapping scales like a stegosaurus's armoured plates. "Those are animals?"

"Pangolins," said Officer Khalil, hand holding the top of the van door. "They're sort of like armoured ant eaters."

One of the little balls shuddered and the heavy scales shifted as the animal underneath curled up tighter.

Sully closed the flap. "They roll up like that to defend themselves, but that only works against lions and leopards. Against humans, it makes them sitting ducks. Poachers simply scoop them up." Sully crouched to encircle the box with his arms and lift it out of the van. He turned. "Thanks, Imraan." He shifted the box slightly so he could free one hand which he held out to the cop.

The doors of the police van clattered shut behind them as they walked back to the rehab centre.

"What's wrong with the pangolins?" Becca said, skip-stepping at his side to keep up. "Have the traffickers hurt them?"

Sully's eyes hardened. "Usually by the time we get to a poached pangolin, it's almost dead from starvation and dehydration. Pangolins eat ants and termites exclusively, and poachers aren't about to collect ants for them to eat, not when they're going to kill them anyway."

Becca pushed open the reception door and held it for him. "They're not being sold as exotic pets?"

"Nope. Pangolin's a luxury meat in Asia, and their scales are used for traditional medicine, both here and in Asia."

He stepped past her, skirting round a woman standing at the reception desk with a covered bird cage at her feet.

But Becca stalled in her tracks. The hydraulic door closer shut the door against her back so she had to take a little step forward to keep her balance. "You mean they kill them just to grind up their scales?" She swallowed against a lump in her throat. "Like rhino horns?"

Sully stopped before the internal doors and turned back to look at her. "Only worse. Pangolins are the most trafficked animal in the world. The Asian sub-species are almost entirely extinct, so now traffickers are coming for our indigenous ones. We estimate we're losing almost three million African pangolins a year to the black market trade."

Becca gaped at him. "Then you have to save these ones!"

He smiled and reversed into the internal swing doors, parting them behind him. "That's the plan."

For the rest of the morning, the sanctuary team worked on the stricken pangolins, running through a well-rehearsed rescue protocol. Everyone knew exactly what to do. Where to insert the drip. What vitals to check for. What drugs to administer.

Now, the last of the curled pangolins slowly unfurled under Sully's insistent but gentle touch, its flat prehistoric-looking tail unfolding onto the padding of towels that lay on the steel examining table. A small black eye slid open and a pointed nose tested the air.

Becca felt a silly smile creep over her face. A few hours ago, she didn't even know what a pangolin was, and now she was rooting for each little animal like a Super Bowl cheerleader.

"More alert than the last two," Sully said, in the low voice he'd adopted since they'd all piled into the examining room. He tilted the conical snout, scrutinising the confused face. "Okay, Gem," he said, without looking up from the pangolin.

Positioned at the head of the table, Becca had been tasked with controlling the rubber mask that delivered a constant hiss of sedating gas. Now she took careful hold of the pangolin's thick neck and fitted the mask over its snout. She shifted her grip to keep the mask in place as the gas took effect and the pangolin's short limbs turned to rubber.

Sully moved aside a scaled front leg with its three long digging claws like ossified fingers. He sifted through the soft belly fur. "Snare injury." With quick, sure fingers he examined a wound.

Clare leaned in from the other side of the table, her head almost touching his. "Bad?"

"No. We'll disinfect it to be certain. Gem, can you hold this leg out the way for me? Ya, like that." His hand closed on Becca's as he adjusted the leg's position in her grip. "Keep it there for me."

Clare caught Becca's eye and raised her eyebrows.

Becca averted her gaze, fixing it on the gas mask she held with one hand, and carefully avoiding looking at Sully as he swabbed the injury.

Or trying to. She kept noticing him out the corner of her eye. The efficient yet gentle way he tended to the little animal's wound. The slight frown on his brow, as if he somehow felt the pain of the prone creature before him. It made her chest feel strangely light, as if she were breathing in some of the gas hissing around the pangolin's snout.

Sully made one more pass with the swab over the wound before dropping it into a kidney bowl on the table. "You can remove the mask now, Gem."

Becca placed the mask into a vet tech's gloved hand and stepped back from the table, as much to give herself space from Sully as to give a tech room to lift the pangolin and curl it into a wooden box with air holes on two sides. "What happens to them now?"

Sully checked the drip line. "Once I'm sure they're stable, they'll go to a rehab centre in Mpumalanga that specialises in releasing rescued pangolins."

"You can't release them here?"

"They're not endemic to this part of KwaZulu-Natal."

"Which means they're not from here," Clare chipped in. Her gaze clashed with Becca's, a hard, unyielding knife blade of barely concealed meaning. "They don't belong."

Time to put some space between her and Sully before Clare shanked her with a scalpel. Becca headed for the door. "I need some air after all that excitement."

Down the corridor, she stepped aside for one of the vet nurses coming out of the intensive care room.

"They finished?" he asked, glancing in the direction she'd come.

"Yep." As the nurse hurried away, Becca looked in at the door. The wooden crates of the first two pangolins stood on a counter opposite a bank of wall cages. She stepped inside and put an eye to one of the air holes, but it was too dark inside to see the pangolin.

She cracked the lid of the crate and peeped in at the animal, curled tight in a nest of clean towels as if trying to lock out the terrifying world it found itself in. The thought of what would've happened to the little animals if the police hadn't found them made her skin crawl. To think she hadn't even known they existed, let alone were facing extinction. Perhaps she could do something about that. Posting a photo of the pangolin on Gem's massive social media platforms would be great for awareness. And it might even drum up some donations for pangolin conservation and the sanctuary.

She wasn't meant to post anything though. But this was a chance to do some real good. She rolled her bottom lip between her teeth. One photo. How could that hurt Gem's carefully curated image? And it could make such a difference to these persecuted creatures. Might even rub off some goodwill onto Gem. Win-win, really.

She lifted the lid of the box and set it aside on the counter top. "Hello," she whispered into the crate. The pangolin was carved stone, hard scales interleaved in a defensive ball. "Do you mind if I take a photo?" A few minutes later, with every pangolin hashtag she could come up with and a plea to Gem's fans to dig deep for animal conservation, Becca shared the post.

15

#PerfectFit

The rehab centre's bat room was warm and cosy, and after the frantic pace of the morning's work, Becca was relieved to be able to sit for a while. Nestled in her lap, wrapped up like a furry burrito, was a velvety black bat. It squeaked at her in its high-pitched, rapid-fire bat language, and she popped a nugget of soft fruit into its chattering mouth.

All around her, volunteers sat in chairs feeding morsels of fruit or mealworms to injured and orphaned bats that were hooked onto the knitted gloves they each wore on one hand. There was even one tiny bat pup lapping milk off a sponge.

Sully stood at a counter beside a volunteer in a *Walking Dead* T-shirt, his head bent over a brown bat that lay on a folded towel before him. He inserted a fine needle under the skin on the bat's back and injected something he'd called 'Ringers' to the observing volunteer. "Once they're dehydrated like this, it's the only way to get fluids into them," he said. "Twenty-five gauge needle, and always subcutaneous." The volunteer looked on intently.

Further along the counter, a young woman in a lilac fleece looked up from the digital scale where she'd been weighing a bat wrapped in a soft cloth. "He's a gram off fifty now," she said, beaming up at Sully.

He smiled back. "Almost big enough to release."

The volunteer grinned at the bat and touched her little finger to a teeny head. "My little star," she crooned, before returning the bat to its temporary home, a sturdy fabric pet carrier with sides of see-through black mesh that the bat hooked itself upside down to.

Sully set aside the syringe and was passing the bat on its towel to Mr *Walking Dead* when the door opened and a uniformed vet tech darted in. "Bat Squad call-out, guys. Colony of long-tails, by the sound of it. The homeowner says if they're not gone in an hour, he's sealing them in."

The room erupted into disgusted groaning peppered with multilingual swearing. The woman who'd been funneling mealworms into a large bat that clung to her polka-dotted glove stood in a rush and banged the bowl of live mealworms she'd had in her lap onto the counter. "The more I do this job, the more I hate people," she said, nabbing a mealworm that had been bounced out of the bowl and dumping it back with the others.

Sully motioned with one hand for her to give him the bat, while he felt about in his pockets with the other. "Lerato's off in the sanctuary bakkie," he said to the woman, producing his keys. "Take mine."

"You're not coming?" the volunteer said, passing him a knitted glove from a box on the counter.

He pulled the glove onto his left hand. "I need to stay with the pangolins."

The woman nodded and addressed the room while unhooking her bat's minute claws from her glove and transferring the little creature to Sully's large hand. "Let's move, everyone. We've got crates to load."

A few seconds of frantic activity later, and the door shut on the departing team.

Quiet descended on the room, broken only by the soft squeaks and rustles of the bats. "What did she mean they'd get sealed in?" Becca said.

Leaning against the counter, Sully ran his little finger along the downy back of the bat on his hand and selected a mealworm from a bowl. "Long-tail bats roost in roofs and people don't like that." He offered the worm to the bat.

"I think it must be rather cool to have bats," Becca said. "They'd eat all the mosquitoes."

"People don't like the droppings," Sully said. "And some of them think they'll get rabies from bats, but our local bats seldom transmit it." He stroked the downy head before fishing out another mealworm. "Whatever the reason, they want them out." In went the mealworm. "If they can't chase them out, they just seal in all the gaps in the roof. And since humans work during the day when bats are all asleep in their roosts, the whole colony gets sealed in."

Becca turned appalled eyes on him. "But that's inhumane!"

He dipped his chin in agreement. "That's why the Bat Squad exists." He held out another mealworm and the bat chomped it up greedily. "We'll remove the bats, bring them back here for a once-over, and then relocate the whole colony somewhere safe."

Becca's bat demanded more fruit with a sharp chirrup. "How many bats have you got here now?"

"Thirty-two at the moment. We'll have even more soon, once baby season gets properly underway."

"And that one?" The bat on Sully's hand had one wing folded and strapped. "What happened to it?"

"Someone brought her in with a broken radius." He tapped the thumb-side of his forearm in explanation. "I had to use a suture needle to make a pin fixator to hold her all together." He turned his gloved hand so he could look into the tiny bat's face. "And now you're almost all better, aren't you? Won't be able to go through metal detectors again, but that's a small price to pay."

Becca's bat chirruped again, and she felt absentmindedly in the bowl in her lap, unable to take her attention off this big man crooning to a scrap of fur and bone he could so easily crush in his fist.

"Your bat's getting antsy," Sully said. He looked up and caught her watching him.

Becca looked away sharply and fumbled for a piece of fruit, inserting it into her impatient customer's mouth. She angled in her chair so she could see less of Sully in her peripheral vision. Seeing that tiny bat in those big hands was doing something odd to her insides. "You ready for the auction tomorrow?"

He growled—literally—and she laughed.

"Mrs Abrams emailed me questions, but I'm not answering them," he said.

"You'd better. Everyone else has." Last night, Gem's inbox had been swamped with forwarded emails from bachelors, and she'd spent the evening planning her intros.

Sully sent another mealworm to its doom. "The deal was I didn't have to answer any embarrassing questions."

"How am I meant to introduce you to all those eager bidders tomorrow if I don't know at least some juicy details?" Becca snagged more fruit from the bowl for her bat and swivelled back in her chair to face him. She almost laughed again, this time at the sulky look on his face.

"I really don't see why the audience needs to know things about me."

"Do you want to be the only bachelor with the old clichéd age-height-occupation intro?" Chomp, chomp, went her bat.

"Ya, I'm cool with that. Thirty-three, six two, vet. Enough said."

Mmmm, enough said indeed. Her gaze swept the length of him before she roped it back in and focused on the bat. "You'll never be able to strut your stuff after an introduction that boring."

"I promise you, princess, I will not be strutting."

No, he'd be glowering, which would only make him all the more appealing. "You prefer prancing, pony-like?" She levelled a smirk at him and was rewarded with a glare that sent a delicious shiver over her skin.

He fed the bat another mealworm, then transferred it, still chewing, to a bat carrier. "Say I love sunsets, long walks on the beach, and listening to Barry White ballads."

She pulled a face.

"What?" he said, in mock offense. "Not strong, silent and troubled enough for you?" He leaned against the counter, arms folded, eyes thoughtful. "Say I love French noir films and in my spare time, I ride out on my motorbike on lonely mountain roads in a bid to escape my own tortured soul."

She scoffed and rolled her eyes. "Now you sound like someone from a telenovela. Why don't you ask Clare to help you with your intro?"

"Why would I do that?" His question was full of guileless curiosity.

She back-pedalled. She'd forgotten that his relationship wasn't common knowledge yet. "I only meant because she works with you, that she might know some redeeming qualities we could highlight."

"I'd rather keep my colleagues out of this. It's embarrassing enough that half the town will be there, without bringing the sanctuary into it too."

Becca felt in the fruit bowl. Empty. "This bat's full." She slid her hand from the glove and passed it, bat and all, to Sully. "Let's do it now."

He took a carrier from a shelf and flipped it open. "Do what?"

"Mrs Abrams's questionnaire."

"I don't remember the questions," he said with his back to her as he settled the bat in its carrier.

"I bet you've got her email on your phone," Becca said.

One hand dropped protectively to the pocket of his jeans.

She smiled knowingly and clicked her fingers. "Hand it over."

He ignored her.

The sound of a zipper being dragged closed tooth by tooth made her chuckle in amusement. "I'll still be sitting here when you eventually turn around, you know."

He lifted the closed carrier onto the shelf, then grumbling, reached for his phone. He turned, settling back against the edge of the counter, his index finger swiping and tapping on the screen. "Why are you so persistent?" He grudgingly relinquished his phone to her.

"It's for your own good." He narrowed his eyes which only made her giggle. "Okay, let's see." She kicked off her gumboots and folded one leg under her in the chair as she scanned the list of questions. "Age. Height. We've covered that. Pets: a Labrador called Ella."

"I have six dogs."

Becca shot him a surprised look. "Six?" Lucky his girlfriend was a vet.

He shrugged and settled against the counter again, hands clamped on the edge on either side of him. "They wash up on my shore and I take them in."

"Wash up from where?"

"Rescued from puppy mills, like Ella. Emigrating owners. Strays."

"You never say no?"

He gave a non-committal grunt. "I've got a big garden."

And a big heart. She shoved the thought aside. "What's next...gosh, but some of these questions take me right back to my pageant days." She did a little shimmy in the chair. "Ooh, here's an interesting one. What's the most embarrassing thing you've ever done?"

She laughed at his answering frown. If he knew how sexy he looked when he pulled his brows tight like that, he'd stop doing it.

He pushed off the edge of the counter and took a bat carrier from one of the shelves lining a wall. "According to the terms of our agreement, I get to skip that one."

She grinned. "Chicken."

"I happen to like chickens." He lifted a tiny black bat from the carrier. He peered into the animal's puckered face. "And bats."

And I like you. She blinked, several quick flutters as if to sweep the thought clean from her head. "If you were a superhero, what power would you want?"

His phone rang in her hands and a single word flashed on the screen. *Mom.* "Saved by your mom." Bat in one hand, Sully extended the other to Becca, but she held the phone away from him and waggled a finger. "Keep it short, Dr Scott. I'm trying to run an interrogation here." His brows lifted and she smirked, but returned his phone.

"To answer your question, invisibility." He lifted his phone to his ear. "Hey, Mom." He held her gaze as he talked. "No, I'm not busy. In fact, we haven't spoken in a few days, so you'd better tell me all your news, and don't leave out a single detail." He answered Becca's scolding look with a self-satisfied smile. "Ya, I booked last night. I emailed you the flight details. No, arriving Thursday. The flights are cheaper then, and I thought we could all spend some time together before the party."

He positioned the phone between shoulder and ear and moved the bat in his hand onto the digital scale. A smile crept over his face and he gave a long-suffering sigh. "It's Roh's birthday, Mom, not his wedding. I'm sure a plus-one isn't a prerequisite." He checked the scale's display and entered the results onto a clipboard on the counter. "Do you give him this much grief about grandchildren?" Whatever his mother said next made him laugh. He picked up the bat and returned it to its carrier. As he drew the zipper closed, he gave a good-natured groan. "I'm going to hang up now, Mom, because believe it or not, I'd rather answer bachelor auction questions. No, don't even ask. Ya, like last year, for the church auction." He laughed again. "You wish! I love you too."

He ended the call and returned his phone to his pocket.

"Hey," Becca protested, holding out her hand to demand the return of his phone. "We're not finished."

"Oh yes we are, princess. Here, make yourself useful." He checked a whiteboard on the wall and selected a carrier from the shelf. "This guy needs topping up." He handed her a glove, waited for her to pull it on, and then hooked a palm-sized bat onto her palm. "Bat." He handed her a prepared bowl of food from the small fridge under the counter. "Banana."

She smiled as the little animal's mouth flipped open eagerly for the fruit. "Who's Roh?"

"My younger brother. Rohan." Sully's eyes lifted to her face from where he'd been watching her hands. "He's flying in from Austria after the grand prix next week to celebrate his birthday."

She made an impressed face at her bat. "Formula One?"

Sully shook his head, and lounged back against the counter, his hands loosely clasped on the edge. "He races motorbikes in MotoGP. The premier class. They've got a two-week gap before the next grand prix so he's flying home for the weekend."

"Are you close?"

"As close as we can be when he spends most of his time in Europe. At least there are video calls."

Becca selected a chunk of banana and popped it into her bat. Its cheeks filled up like a hamster's and she chuckled. Funny little thing. "Yeah, but it's not the same seeing them online. I talk to my sister almost every day, but sometimes, like with all this drama over those Instagram posts, I wish I could reach through the screen and hug her."

He hummed in understanding. "It's easier for me because I'm always so busy here. But I know Mom really misses us. She could come and live here at the sanctuary if she wanted, but she's happy in Cape Town. All her friends are there. She still gets lonely though."

A bit of banana had escaped the bat's mouth and clung to the fur of its jaw. Becca eased it into its mouth with her baby finger. "Where's your dad?"

Sully shifted his weight, straightening a little to shove his hands into his jeans pockets. "He passed away."

She stiffened and unfolded her bent leg in a rush, making the little bat squeak at the sudden movement. "I'm so sorry."

"It's fine, princess." His head dropped and he stared at his boots for a moment before lifting his gaze back to hers. "It was a while ago. I still miss him, but I don't collapse in a heap anymore when I talk about him."

"How did it happen?"

A big exhale said it was still painful for him to talk about. "Car accident. He was in a head-on collision on Sir Lowry's Pass one night. He died at the scene."

Becca pressed her free hand to her chest, squashing a bit of banana onto her shirt. "That's awful." Her throat felt impossibly thick. "I can't imagine being without my dad."

Sully's mouth pressed into a hard line, his eyes on the floor. "It's tough. It's been years now, but I still forget he's gone." He looked up and his gaze found hers. "I'll want to tell him something and pick up my phone and then I'll remember."

Becca felt an overwhelming urge to stand up and hug him. Instead she stretched out her leg and slid her bare foot forward until her toes bumped against the toe of his boot. Their eyes met and he smiled at her, just the corners of his mouth tipping up in a way that made her chest ache.

"Feed your bat," he said.

She slid her foot back and tucked it under her leg again. "Were they very close, your parents?" Her bat stretched out a delicate wing and began clawing its way up her glove.

"She'd been with my dad since high school. He was her world."

"That's so sad." She tried to head off the escaping animal with another piece of banana, but it kept climbing up her fingers.

Sully pushed off the counter and crossed to her, holding out his hand for the bat. "Those were very dark, very rough months. Mom went to pieces." He scanned the room with its chittering bats in their temporary roosts as she carefully slipped the glove from her hand and held it out to him with its winged passenger. "That's actually how I came to be here. I resigned from private practice and moved to Cape Town to be with her."

Becca looked at him in surprise. "You gave up your job?"

His back was to her now, as he set about transferring the bat to a carrier. “It wasn’t as heroic as it sounds. Private practice wasn’t a good fit for me. Pet owners can be...” He paused, lifting his head as if he were searching for the right words in the air. “Let’s just say they can be hard on the soul.” He closed the carrier and stowed it before turning around again. “Mom needed someone, and I needed time to figure out my life, so it made sense. Rohan came out for the funeral, but he couldn’t stay long. He’d recently been signed to a MotoGP team. It had taken years of racing to get to that point, and Dad wouldn’t have wanted him to risk losing his seat. At least Dad got to watch him race in the big leagues before he died.”

Now she needed a hug too. Becca swiped at her welling eyes. “It must be really hard on your mom, having a son who does something so dangerous after what happened to your dad.”

“She has her moments. Still does, I’m sure. But racing is Roh’s life, like being a vet is mine. He could no less give up the track than I could give up the sanctuary.”

“How did you get from Cape Town to here?”

“After a few weeks at my parents’, a tanker wrecked off Robben Island. Hundreds of African penguins got covered in oil, so I went to help, along with other volunteers. Jo was one of them. We were put together on a cleaning team and spent weeks together rehabbing the penguins, getting them strong enough to go back into the sea. She told me about the place she’d inherited where she wanted to start up a rehab clinic. When she found out I had no plans of my own, she asked me to join her. And here I am.”

Becca looked out the window at the massive bird aviary visible through the trees, where rehabbed birds went to grow strong before release. She brought her gaze back to his. “You’ve done an amazing job putting this place together. You must really love it here."

A shrug. "Sometimes I question whether I have it in me to keep doing it." He turned his head to look at the rows of carriers, lifting a hand to touch a fingertip to a bat hanging against one black-meshed side. "It can be hard on the soul, especially when it's human-induced suffering, which it so often is." He looked back at her. "But it's what I'm meant to do. And where I'm meant to be."

The door of the bat room opened then, and Becca looked to see Clare bounce into the room.

"Oh, there you are," Clare said, shutting the door behind her. "Bat Squad's off again, I see." She held a plastic shopping bag in one hand.

"Long-tails in a roof." He slid his hand from the glove and transferred the bat to its carrier.

Clare came up behind him. "The Farm City delivery came."

"Good." He zipped shut the carrier and turned. He seemed surprised to find Clare so close behind him that he had to crowd back against the counter not to knock her over.

"Thanks for remembering that hoof-rot spray I needed." Clare tilted her head and peered up into his hair. "There's something in your..." Her arm shot up and she flicked her fingers through the hair flopped over Sully's forehead. "There. All gone. Milk formula or something."

He aimed a guarded look at her, then glanced over at Becca, but she looked away, not wanting him to think she'd seen Clare's subtle gesture of possession.

Clare stepped back, swinging the shopping bag in her hand. "They made a mistake on the order though. I tried to get them to take it back, but they insisted you'd asked for this." She dumped the plastic packet on the counter.

It made a heavy thunk.

"Those are for Gem," Sully said.

Clare hesitated for a split second before her mouth curved into a flirty smile. "Did you bring me a gift too?"

His eyebrows lifted. "Hoof-rot spray not enough?"

Clare brayed a laugh in answer and handed over the plastic bag to Becca like she'd been forced to relinquish a kidney.

Becca set the bag on the floor and with her bat-free hand, removed a black trainer. "Shoes?" She looked at Sully in surprise.

"Don't get all sentimental about it. It's for purely selfish reasons." He toed one of the gumboots lying discarded on the floor by her chair. "I don't want to waste a morning having to drive you to hospital when you break your neck in those gumboots."

Becca hefted the trainer in her hand. "It's heavy."

"They're safety shoes. Boots like mine would feel too heavy for you. These are lighter, but they've also got steel toe caps in case something large steps on you."

Becca gave Clare a nervous side-eye. Bad enough that he was buying her things, but he was putting some thought into it too. "They're even the right size," she added under her breath.

"You leave your heels lying all over the storeroom. It's a bit hard not to notice."

"Aren't you a lucky girl?" The friendly note in Clare's voice wobbled, as if she had to work to keep it there.

Becca gave her an apologetic look and dropped the shoe into the bag. Men could be such idiots. Could he not have saved his gift, unsentimental as it may be in his eyes, for when his girlfriend wasn't around?

"There should be socks in there too," he said, his back to them both as he gave his rapt attention to the figures on the clipboard.

Clare plucked the plastic packet from the floor and rooted around in it. She drew out a bulk pack of black socks, scowled at them, then thwacked Becca on the arm with them in a seemingly playful gesture that nonetheless made Becca glad it was only socks in Clare's hand and not a steel pipe. "Good thinking, actually," Clare said. "If she injures herself in those gumboots, we won't get the cash, and then having her here would've been a total waste of time."

Ouch.

"Exactly." Sully set aside the clipboard and turned. "Come on," he said, suddenly brusque and impatient. "We've got work to do, and sitting around talking doesn't count as community service."

16

#LevellingUp

The shower Becca had taken after dinner had been heavenly, the hot water pounding away the aches and pains of an exhausting day. Now, sitting cross-legged on the narrow bed in her pyjamas, she scrolled through some of the responses from Gem's fan base to her pangolin post. *Always knew you were an animal lover, Gem. Sent a donation.* And another: *I donated to that pangolin charity like you asked*. Result!

A knock at the door made her look up. "Hello?"

"It's Sully."

A spark of electricity zipped through her. "One sec." She slipped off the bed to open the door.

Sully's gaze took in her pyjamas and his expression turned apologetic. "Did I wake you?"

She hooked a chunk of hair behind an ear. "I was checking my social media feeds."

He looked past her, his gaze distracted as he scanned her room. "A kudu's caught in the fence in one of the back enclosures." He returned his eyes to hers. "I thought you might like to come help.

"Sure. I'm always game for more hours. At this rate, I'll be out of your hair long before Friday."

There was a moment's hesitation before his mouth pulled into a grin that didn't quite reach his eyes. "What are we waiting for then?"

"Let me put on my shoes." She picked up one of her new safety shoes from the floor and plonked onto the edge of the bed, working at the laces. Sully watched her from the door as she manoeuvred her foot into a shoe. The amused tilt to his mouth made him look even more attractive than usual. She bent her head to her task.

Once her shoes were on, she hopped up from the bed and plucked Gem's bomber jacket off the wardrobe door-knob. "Right, let's go," she said.

But Sully remained planted in the doorway.

She made a little hurry-up gesture with a hand. "Don't we have a kudu to rescue?"

He inspected her. "You don't think slippers might match your outfit better?"

It took her a second to realise what he meant. She was still in her pyjamas. She squeaked in embarrassment and swung the door shut on his laughter.

Several minutes later, Becca was seated in the passenger seat, clad in more suitable jeans and a warm top. She put on her seat belt and checked Gem's fluffy bomber jacket was zipped all the way up. "Is the enclosure far?"

Sully reversed the Ranger from the visitors parking onto the internal dirt road. "Couple minutes' drive." He jabbed at the dash and the cabin's heater kicked in. "The big antelope camps form the back boundary of our property."

She rubbed her hands together in the jet of warm air. "I forgot how cold it can get out here." Evidently, despite its fluffiness, Gem's bomber jacket was meant more for fashion than function. "Do you often get called out at night?"

"Quite often." Sully directed a vent to blow towards her. "Collisions mainly. Animals that have been blinded by headlights and then flee across the road."

His hand dropped between them to change gears, then stayed on the gear lever.

Her gaze strayed over his hand and down to his fingers, hanging loose and relaxed over the gear shift. "Didn't Clare want to come with you instead tonight?"

"Why would she?"

She didn't know why she'd said anything. Her filter never seemed to work when he was around. "No reason."

He side-eyed her. "Spit it out, princess."

She hesitated and fiddled unnecessarily with the heating vent. "I know you guys are dating."

He pulled his attention off the road to look at her, eyebrows drawn together in confusion. "Where'd you hear that?"

"Just...around. I shouldn't have said anything. I'm sorry."

He shook his head and focused once more on driving. "You of all people should know not to believe every bit of gossip you hear."

She looked at him in surprise. "You mean you're not?"

"Nope. Never have. Never will."

Clare had lied. And then backed it up with the sneaky arm strokes. The leaning in close. The hair touching. All those subtle little gestures to warn Becca off.

Sully was looking at her again. "But seriously? Me and Clare? If that's how I act around a partner, you must think I'm an emotionally stunted arsehole."

"Or just keeping an office romance quiet." Becca lifted a shoulder in an offhand gesture and huffed a small laugh. It seemed deceit was going around. "You don't seem like the demonstrative type anyway."

"Oh, I can be demonstrative. Just not with Clare." The look he gave her made her want to unclip her seat belt and climb into his lap.

Unnerved as much by her own reaction as by what she saw in his eyes, Becca shifted in her seat and stared out her side window. If she could've done so without getting a bruise from the jolting ride, she would've pressed her hot forehead against the cold glass. Instead she focused on the dark shapes appearing and disappearing in the sweep of the headlights. Perhaps she'd swallowed everything Clare had fed her because she'd wanted Sully to be off limits. It had been better that way, with a line drawn sharply between them to keep her growing admiration from tipping over into something more. Something that could only end in tears.

A building loomed in the moonlight, vast and sprawling, like the manor houses on the wine estates in the Cape. A distinctive Cape-Dutch gabled entrance stood front and centre, flanked by two wings punctuated by dark shuttered windows.

"That's the old manor house," Sully said. "It's derelict."

"It must have been beautiful once."

"It was. Jo has old photos from when her grandparents were here. It was a dairy farm back then."

She turned in her seat to look at him. "You've never considered restoring it?"

"All our funding goes to the animals. It's hard enough paying the bills with what we make from the foreign volunteer programme and the donations Jo drums up, without adding building restoration to the budget." He negotiated a tight corner and down-shifted as the road began to climb. "We did initially consider turning it into the rehab centre, but the layout was all wrong. And it was too big for Jo and her family to live in, so we left it. Plus there's a colony of bats living in the chimney of one of the lounges, and they've got full squatters' rights."

"Jo lives here at the sanctuary?"

"In the gatehouse. A lot of our staff lives here. There are cottages and houses out near the dam and behind admin."

He slowed and turned the bakkie through a stone gateway, the low wrought-iron gates standing open. "This is me. Used to be the farm manager's place." The headlights lit the front of a single-storey house in the same style as the manor house, but with twin gables separated by a softly lit verandah. Light poured from the large bay window in one of the gabled ends, revealing a pack of dogs crowding to look out of the cottage panes.

"Your dogs stay inside?"

"When I'm not home at night. I lost a dog once to a leopard." He parked in front of a detached garage. "Won't be long." He hopped from the bakkie.

He crossed the wide lawn at a run and took the stone steps to the verandah two at a time. He disappeared into the house, only to emerge several seconds later with something bulky under one arm. He nudged a Jack Russell back through the door with his foot before locking the door and running back to the bakkie. He climbed in and dumped a khaki hooded parka into her lap. "For you. It'll be too big, but it's better than that." He gestured with a jerk of his chin at Gem's bomber jacket.

She looked from the parka to him and smiled, touched by his unexpected concern for her.

He buckled up and started the bakkie. His gaze met hers en route to his rearview mirror. "Can't have you freezing to death."

She smoothed her fingers over the padded fabric. "Wouldn't want that. Not when there's Alek's bribe money on the line."

He gave her a quick, enigmatic look, then he thunked the bakkie into reverse. "There's that too."

She shucked off the bomber jacket and rammed her arm into a too-long sleeve. She twisted in her seat to tug the parka around her, releasing the scent of wood smoke and disinfectant.

And him.

A spark ignited deep in her belly. *Don't go there.* Even with Clare out of the equation, giving rein to this attraction she felt for him was sheer futility. Come the end of a week of deception, she would transform back into Becca and the Gem he thought he knew would cease to exist. She busied herself with rolling the parka's too-long sleeves, trying not to focus on the smell of him that each movement released. She had one job. Finish the hours. There was no room for distractions. Not even delicious-smelling ones.

The road straightened out to run along a towering fence. "We're here." Sully killed the headlights and drove the last few metres by moonlight. "I don't want to spook him," he said, in reply to her questioning look.

She leaned forward to peer through the windscreen at the high fence. "You keeping a T-Rex in there?"

He chuckled. "It takes a high fence to keep a kudu in. They can clear two metres in a standing jump without even breaking a sweat." Sully pulled the Ranger to a halt beside two other vehicles. "Zip up that parka."

Becca followed him out of the bakkie into a cold wind that had her wishing she was back in bed. She pulled up the parka's hood. It cut the wind immediately but also enveloped her head in Sully's scent. She shoved it off. After years in London, she could handle a little cold. There wasn't even snow to contend with.

Ignoring the bite of the wind, she took in the silver-washed thickets of dense bush and swathes of wild grass inside the enclosure, with the deep shadows of the mountain looming behind.

Outside the camp, three men leaned against the front of a bakkie with the sanctuary's logo on the door. She smiled and nodded at them. Two more men stood with Sully at the back of the Ranger, stamping their feet to keep warm. They spoke in low voices and one pointed off into the enclosure. A lot of nodding ensued, and then one man set off through the enclosure's gate with a roll of fence wire and heavy-duty pliers.

Sully looked up as she joined them. "Someone's cut the fence and come in through this camp. That's probably what spooked the bull."

She eyed the dark enclosure and a nip of fear bit at her spine. "Poachers?"

"Could be. Or rustlers." Sully leaned over the open tailgate and dragged a flat case towards him. He flipped the catches on the case. Inside was a rifle.

Becca's heart kicked. "Is that for whoever broke in?"

He set the rifle on the tailgate and pulled his black plastic holdall closer. "For the kudu."

She swallowed noisily. It must be too badly hurt. "I'd better stay here then. I don't want to watch you euthenase it."

He glanced at her, brief bemusement giving way to a chuckle. He held up a dart with a fluffy neon pink end. "I'm going to sedate him."

She noticed the silver gas canister then, screwed into the rifle in front of the trigger, and relaxed.

He loaded the dart gun and handed her a heavy metal torch. "Let's do this."

Inside the enclosure, they waded through the grass for several metres before Sully held out an arm to stop her. "This is close enough." His voice was a whisper. "Kudus are really skittish. If he panics and breaks a leg, I might really have to euthenase him." He nodded to the torch in her hand. "I need you to shine the light so I can place the dart properly."

She lifted the torch. A beam of strong light sliced through the dark enclosure to reveal a kudu bull hanging partially suspended in the high fence by its back legs. Big as a stag, the huge antelope's back hooves were snarled in the fence wire, its elegant front legs lying akimbo in the dirt.

Sully tipped his head this way, then that. "How the hell did he get himself caught like that?"

The only sign the antelope was alive was the frantic rise and fall of the white vertical stripes that looked like paint had dribbled down its blue-grey sides from its spine. Suddenly it jerked and thrashed its head. Its magnificent horns, easily a metre long with their distinctive corkscrew twists, clashed against the fence, making the wires zing.

Becca's heart jolted and she winced, afraid that any minute they'd hear the sickening crack of a slender back leg.

The animal slumped again and Sully dropped his hand onto her shoulder. "Hold the light steady on its hind leg. Bit higher." His hand squeezed. "There."

The circle of light trembled over the kudu's rump and Becca steadied the torch's barrel with both hands.

Sully raised the rifle, shut one eye and aimed. There was a soft 'phut' and the neon pink dart reappeared bang in the centre of the torch light.

She tipped her head at him, impressed. "Dr Scott, the sniper. I'll have to include that in your bachelor bio tomorrow." She looked back at the kudu. "Now we wait," she said, remembering the caracal they'd rescued on her first morning.

He put the dart gun atop his holdall. "Now we wait," he agreed.

Like the men were doing outside the camp, standing around the bakkie, speaking quietly amongst themselves.

Becca hugged Sully's parka tight about her and jiggled her legs for extra warmth.

"You want to go back to the bakkie?" he said.

The concern in his voice made her shiver even more. "I'm fine. Until you've experienced a London winter, you don't know what cold is. Have you ever been?"

"To London?" He shook his head. "The closest I've been is what I see in the video calls I have with an old colleague who works at the Whipsnade Zoo in Bedfordshire. She's always trying to convince me to go out there and work with them in their African animal exhibit. It's never going to happen, but she tries her luck."

"You know Whipsnade is the biggest zoo in the UK? And that Gerald Durrell was a junior keeper there after the war?"

He smiled. "You know some weird trivia, princess."

"Mind like a sponge." An essential requirement for a concierge. She inhaled the cold, clean air and breathed a contented sigh. It was strange, but she wasn't missing The Rickford at all. "It's so quiet out here." Just the night insects singing and the wind sifting through the grass and a distant owl calling. "Not like London. I don't think there's a quiet square inch in that city."

"I'm not big on cities."

She wasn't either, to be honest. Her life in London was never dull, but the pace could get tiresome. She tipped her head back to gaze up into the inky black at stars so numerous they made the whole sky shimmer. "I'd forgotten how beautiful the sky is." She straightened her head and looked at him. "You're lucky to live out here."

"I am."

Something passed between them that made her breath catch and her fingers ball into nervous fists in his parka's pockets.

He broke eye contact first, grass crunching underfoot as he shifted. He blew on his hands and rubbed them briskly together. "That money Alek is giving us for the small predator housing?" He pointed into the darkness before resuming his hand rubbing. "It's the last portion we need to get started on building a whole habitat with a range where the small cats can hunt, extending all the way up into that foothill."

She followed the direction of his finger. "Small cats like the caracal?"

"Uh huh."

"Don't you release everything you rescue?"

"Not if their injuries make them too vulnerable to survive back in the wild." He put his hands into his jacket pockets. "If an animal can't survive on its own, I either have to euthenase it, or find it somewhere to live in captivity, and not all animals can cope with long-term caging. For those animals, euthenasia is the least cruel option. But once I get that range set up"—he looked away into the distance—"I'll have somewhere for the small predators."

She loved the way his voice sounded when it was brimming with enthusiasm. In the moonlight, his eyes seemed to shine, as if all the passion he felt for what he did was gleaming in them. She looked away sharply and began to jigger up and down, shifting her weight from one foot to the other, her stomach awash with a strange, zinging disquiet.

He reached behind her head then and pulled up the parka's hood.

Now she could smell him again. "Honestly, I'm fine." Her body chose that moment to tremor so violently her teeth clacked.

He stepped in front of her and drew the drawstrings to fit the hood snugly around her face. "That's better." He was avoiding meeting her gaze. "I don't want to have to treat you for hypothermia."

For the briefest moment as he adjusted the toggle, his fingers brushed the soft skin beneath her jaw and then he did look at her. She quivered with pleasure at his warm touch against her chilled skin and took a step back, unnerved. "We can't have that, no!" Her laugh was nervous. She fiddled with the hood, her fingers unsettled and shaky. "Imagine the headlines if the press found out you'd had to strip me naked and climb into a sleeping bag with me to warm me up?" She caught his eye as her brain finally took notice of what she'd blurted out, and she felt her cheeks grow hot.

His laugh broke the tension between them. "Imagine that," he drawled, channeling his Dr Sexy persona. "You and me, naked in a sleeping bag."

She whacked his arm through the thick padding of his jacket. "No, don't imagine that!" Laughter bubbled into her voice. "Put it right out of your head." An instruction she'd do well to follow herself.

Still smiling to himself, Sully glanced at the kudu, then at his watch. "Speaking of sleeping bags"—he motioned with his head—"let's go see if someone's finally asleep."

He waved to the men standing at the parked bakkies, then picked up the holdall and dart gun and set off ahead of her, keeping his strides shorter than usual as he crushed a path for her through the long grass.

She followed in his wake, looking over every now and then to the men filing in at the enclosure gate, carrying equipment and a tarpaulin and the kind of heavy-duty spotlight normally found mounted on the top of game-drive trucks.

A little way off from the kudu, Sully stopped and had Becca direct the torchlight over the animal's head. The light glinted off an open, fixed, unblinking eye. "Out for the count." He dumped his gear and signalled to the men.

The large spotlight, mounted now on a stand and connected to a car battery, flicked on. Someone ran up and pulled a patterned blindfold over the kudu's eyes, securing it behind large, shell-shaped ears.

Sully crossed to the trapped animal and removed the dart from its side. He paused and sniffed the air. "Blood." His eyes scanned the kudu, then he leaned against the fence and felt behind the animal. His hand came back covered in blood. "Shit. He's cut himself on something." He made a frustrated sound. "And we were going to release him tomorrow. Let's get him down."

All around the drugged kudu, men stepped into position. At Sully's call, they found a grip wherever they could and pulled, stopping to let Sully stretch up to work the wire over the kudu's splayed hooves. Minutes ticked by while the team tugged and stopped and untangled and pulled and grunted with effort. And then the kudu slipped free in a thud of limp limbs.

Becca threw up her hands, about to burst into applause, but stopped herself at the last second, afraid any loud noise might penetrate the kudu's drugged fog and cause a calamity. She settled instead for bouncing on the spot, her heart smacking hard against her ribs with a mixture of adrenalin and relief.

She looked up to find Sully watching her, a slight smile on his lips. Immediately she dropped her gaze, staring instead at the immobile animal. She'd never been this close to a kudu before. Was Sully still looking at her? She didn't dare look up to check.

Focus on the kudu. It was an impressive creature. Huge. With a white muzzle that made it look like it had been drinking from a saucer of thick cream. She risked a sideways glance and relaxed when she found Sully busy setting out the contents of his holdall on a tarp.

She moved to squat beside him. Like Sully had done with the caracal, someone had pulled the kudu's tongue out the side of its mouth and clipped a beeping monitor to it. "Anything broken?" she said.

Sully shook his head. "Luckily not. But that laceration's pretty deep."

A lurid red tear marred the kudu's rump, blood from a large torn flap staining its coat. Becca averted her gaze and took a slow breath. It was only blood. She exhaled with a determined huff and looked at Sully. "What can I do?"

Sully handed her a pair of surgical gloves. "You think you'll be okay to wash the grit out of the wound?"

Not instructing. Asking. A glow flared in her chest. "I think so," she said, tipping forward onto her knees and taking a large syringe and plastic bottle of liquid from him.

"Saline," he said. He showed her how to squirt away the dirt in the wound without spraying too hard and causing more damage.

"Like this?" Sand washed from the ugly gash.

His smile of approval made her handle wobble, but she kept rinsing.

"Perfect," he said. "Jonas, how's he holding up?" The man crouched at the kudu's muzzle gave him a thumbs-up. "Let's get to work then."

Sully's shoulder brushed hers as he leaned in next to her and her breath hitched softly. She glanced at him to check he hadn't heard, but he was in full vet mode. With her hands on her knees, she watched him work, clipping at coarse hair and tattered skin with sharp scissors. Then he began to stitch the wound. He had beautiful hands, even in surgical gloves. Strong, but gentle when they needed to be. Controlled. Skilled. They moved in a practised rhythm until the kudu's flank was once more intact.

Sully pushed back onto his haunches. "One kudu, fixed." He disposed of his gloves and surgical needle and stood. "Now we pack up and then I'll wake him."

Once the camp was clear of their equipment, Sully removed the kudu's blindfold and injected something into its back thigh. "Let's get out of here," he said, hurrying her ahead of him with a quick touch of his hand to her back.

Outside the closed gate, they stood side by side watching through the enclosure fence as the kudu scrambled to its feet on rickety legs and took a few hesitant steps, its head swaying as if it was trying to find where the upright position was.

"You were great in there," Sully said, keeping his eyes on his patient. "You're much tougher than you look."

"It was amazing," she replied. "Frightening and exhilarating all at the same time."

His answering smile warmed her, and then she felt the light touch of a finger against her hand. She stopped breathing. Another fingertip brushed her skin and a delicious sensation raced up her arm, right up into her nape. Her chest released and she exhaled softly through open lips. Sully's fingers laced through hers, and he enveloped her hand in his warm grip.

She looked up at him and he smiled at her, a smile that made her heart feel somehow too large for her chest. For a moment, she pretended there were no lies and deception between them. No ticking clock counting down the hours before she had to leave. No impossible distances separating their two worlds.

Just him and her. Uncomplicated. Safe.

The kudu had found its footing now. With a shake of its horned head, it slipped back into the cover of the dense bush at the back of its rehab enclosure.

Sully squeezed her hand. "I could do with something hot. You up for coffee?"

She wriggled her hand free of his and plunged it out of reach into her pocket. What was she thinking? There could be nothing hot between them. Not even coffee.

His expression turned puzzled, but before he could say anything, his cellphone rang. He glanced at the screen as he answered. "Hey, Jo."

In the quiet, Becca could hear Jo's raised voice through the speaker. "Where are you?"

Sully shoulders tensed, as if some trouble-detecting sixth sense had kicked in. "What's wrong?"

"Someone broke into the rehab centre."

Shock tensed his features. "What?"

"They took the pangolins."

Twitter

AnimalLuva
@mjs4eva

How dumb is this bitch? #GemStratton tipped off animal traffickers by posting a photo on Insta showing rescued pangolins at the Winterberg Wildlife Sanctuary. They raided the sanctuary last night and took the pangolins.

5:43 AM **2467** Retweets 670 Likes

Janet@janetvee 2h
Replying to @mjs4eva

How'd they know it was because of her Insta post?

AnimalLuva@mjs4eva 2h
Replying to @janetvee

The cops found a cellphone on one of the guys they arrested, with a screenshot on it of her Insta post. It'll be on News 24/7 soon.

VeggieBean@beascholtz 1h
Replying to @mjs4eva

Holy crap!! You'd think being a South African she'd know you never post location info about rhinos and endangered stuff. Dumb cow.

AnimalLuva@mjs4eva 1h
Replying to @beascholtz

I know, right! The sanctuary would be a lot safer if that stupid bitch just left!!

17

#FeelingLow

Becca huddled on a plastic chair in a corner of the rehab centre's reception, aimlessly running her eye over the posters and notices pinned to a board on one wall. An abandoned cat shelter wanted blankets. There was an upcoming benefit concert at the nearby Drakensberg Boys Choir School to raise funds for endangered vultures, sponsored by one of the brand's Gem endorsed. And a petition with horrifying photos advocated against fireworks.

Becca had been staring at them for so long, she knew them all by heart. Anything to avoid letting her gaze wander where it might inadvertently collide with someone else's.

"Shame, it must've been stuck in that drainpipe for ages," said a woman filling out a form at the counter. Becca peeped at the copy-paper box at the woman's feet. "Lucky my husband went to clear the gutters." Whatever was in the box scrabbled against the walls of its cardboard prison. "I won't have to pay for this, will I?"

"We treat all wild animals at no cost."

Becca lifted her gaze without thinking, catching the tail-end of the smile the receptionist directed at the walk-in, before being clapped full in the face by a disdainful glare. She looked back quickly at the notice board. It had been like this all morning, ever since she'd slunk into the rehab centre after a particularly uncomfortable breakfast in the volunteer dining hall where the whispers and hostile looks had ruined her appetite after just a few mouthfuls.

She'd dealt with plenty of irate guests in her time, who'd required the serious application of her concierge skills before they could be placated, but even her overdeveloped people-pleasing powers were of no use this morning. News of last night's break-in was on everyone's lips, and disgust at the person who'd caused it in every eye. No doubt Sully would look at her the same way once he got back from the pangolin rehabbers up north.

Head low, Becca hunched deeper in the chair. Guilt was a hot band around her chest. She wanted to tell everyone they had it all wrong, that it wasn't Gem who deserved their scorn, but that would prove even more disastrous for Gem's reputation. She'd never have imagined that one innocuous Instagram post could cause so much trouble, not only for the defenceless pangolins and the sanctuary, but for Gem.

Her pulse still hammered after Alek's call; UrbanROAD was threatening to cancel her twin's contract. The lifestyle brand had aspirations to up its planet-saving cred, and now the woman who got paid to endorse them had almost sent three pangolins to their doom with her geotagging prowess. She'd been so stupid.

The reception phone rang and the receptionist picked up the receiver. "Winterberg Wildlife Rescue and Sanctuary...You heard about it? I know, it was terrible. But they're safe now."

Becca sensed another toxic look burning into her from across the counter. *Terrible* wasn't a strong-enough word for what had happened last night. Seeing the wooden crates broken and discarded behind the rehab centre and knowing the little creatures they'd worked so hard to save were in danger again had made her want to throw up.

"Ayanda says she heard the shots from her house." The receptionist's voice thrummed with the excitement of re-telling the night's chaos. "The police stopped the traffickers at the freeway. They got away, but at least we recovered the pangolins. Mmmm, I know! Sully and Clare took them to..." The receptionist's voice dropped and intense whispering ensued.

Becca glanced up to see the receptionist angled away, her shoulder like a shield and one hand cupped around the receiver, imparting information that was most definitely not for the ears of the sanctuary's pariah. All Becca knew was that Sully and Clare had headed off well before dawn to a secure pangolin rehab centre some three-hundred kilometres north, near the border of the Kruger National Park. Sully hadn't wanted to wait until morning to transfer the recovered animals, not with armed traffickers on the loose. He wouldn't risk any of the sanctuary's staff getting hurt in another snatching attempt.

Gem's phone buzzed to life. Becca checked the display and answered. "Dad!"

"Bunny."

The familiar endearment made her throat clench painfully against a rush of tears. She could do with one of Dad's bear hugs right now. "Hey Dad. How're you feeling today? You managing without Mom?"

"Nothing a few painkillers can't fix."

Her heart squeezed at her father's dismissal of the chronic pain that had consumed him for months. "Soon, Dad. We'll have you back on your feet, I promise." Unless she'd completely blown things this time.

"You let me worry about myself. Right now it's you I'm worried about. I was listening to the radio and Gem's name came up on the news."

Becca's chin sank to her chest and she rasped into the phone. "How bad is it?"

"Not great. Some spokesperson from one or other animal group was saying the cops should charge you—her—with aiding and abetting animal traffickers."

Becca hugged her free arm around her middle and moaned into the phone.

"I know Mom issued me with strict instructions not to bother her and Gem, but I think they need to come back. This isn't fair on you."

She hung her head. "I'm letting you all down."

"No, my girlie, you're not. You're trying to pull off the impossible, in a world you have no experience in. I told your mother it wasn't fair to ask you to do this."

"Of course it is. I'm her sister. She needs me. And you need me too, Dad."

"I don't need you if it means you have to get hurt over it. You know we'll all still love you even if you call time and walk away from that sanctuary right now."

Dad's voice was soft and earnest, and it made her want to climb through the phone and into his arms. "I'm not going to quit, Dad." She could barely get the words out around the painful lump in her throat. "And don't bother Mom. You know you can rely on me."

"Everyone always relies on you, my bunny, but it's not right. This isn't your mess, after all. You're always the one leaping in to help, and I know you like to feel needed, but you shouldn't do it at your own expense. Come home and leave us to help Gem face the consequences. Or why don't I come stay in Winterberg for the week? Give you some moral support. I could even teach a few reporters a lesson."

She laughed through her tears. "Gosh, Dad, we can't have another Stratton making headlines." She wiped at her wet cheeks with the back of her hand and sucked down a steadying breath. "Don't worry. I've got this."

Her father made a resigned sound. "If you need me, all you have to do is pick up the phone and I'll be there."

She knew that. Dad had always been there for her. She twisted in her chair at the sound of the door pulling open behind. Clare. Looking less perky than usual, her ponytail at half-mast and her clothing crumpled.

Becca's heart clambered into her throat. "Dad, they're back. I need to go." She said goodbye, promising to call if things got too much for her. Even though they both knew she wouldn't.

She pushed up from the chair and checked over Clare's shoulder to see if Sully was bringing up the rear. But Clare was alone.

Clare's gaze raked over her, stopping at the safety shoes Sully had bought. She gave a wry laugh. "You can forget about doing community service today. Sully's gone home. We're exhausted."

"How are the pangolins?"

Clare's expression was acid. "They're fine, no thanks to you."

Becca's fingers scrunched the hem of her white T-shirt. "Is he still furious?"

Clare looked down her nose at Becca, her nostrils flaring. "What do you think?"

Becca exhaled a shaky breath. Sully had looked ready to tear the traffickers limb from limb last night if he'd come across them. Hiding out in her room seemed extremely appealing right now.

Clare thrust out her chin. "I heard him and Jo talking after we got back this morning. More like arguing really."

Becca's heart fell. "About me?"

Clare's expression hardened and her eyes took on the glint of polished knives, the kind serial killers liked to tote about in roll-up bags. "Who else? He wants you gone. Jo said she made a commitment to her brother, but Sully said he didn't care. He'll never risk this place, and if you mess up again, you could lose us our permits. The SPCA could charge us under the Animal Protection Act." Clare's cheeks were high with colour. "Sully said he'd rather sell his own body to raise the funds for the enclosures than have you here for one more second."

Becca's knees almost let out. This was even worse than she'd imagined.

Clare stepped in close to her and poked her hard in the chest. "Just go, Gem. You've out-stayed your welcome, so do us all a favour and fuck off."

Becca pressed her fingers to her aching breastbone as she watched Clare slam through the internal swinging doors into the back end of the clinic. Beneath her fingertips, her heart careened in a panic. It hurt to swallow, as if splinters of bone were lodged in her throat. This was the feeling she'd promised she'd never let herself feel again: the crushing shame of knowing she'd let someone down. That she was nothing but a disappointment. Unworthy. The way she'd felt that day in the back seat of Mom's car, driving home from the pageant that was to be her last.

She sank into a chair and propped her elbows on her knees, dropping her face into her hands. It would be so easy to pack up Gem's things and leave, but there was too much riding on this. She couldn't give up. Wouldn't.

She had to at least try and make things right with Sully, even if he refused to give her another chance and ended up throwing her out on her butt. She dealt with the impossible every day. Like that time she'd flown in a real Canadian Mountie on two days' notice for the birthday party of a sheik's son who was obsessed with them, running around the hotel in a tiny red jacket and wide-brimmed hat tormenting the housekeeping staff. Convincing Sully to change his mind might prove tougher than the negotiations required to secure an appearance of a member of the Royal Canadian Mounted Police, but she'd never been afraid of a challenge.

She would throw herself on Sully's mercy. Plead with him to let her stay, even if only for Dad's sake. A guy who'd quit his job and move to the other side of the country to help his mother through her grief wasn't someone who took family lightly.

She wiped her eyes on the sleeves of her T-shirt, glad she hadn't bothered with eye makeup this morning. With a loud sniff and her resolve set, she checked the time on Gem's phone. If she didn't go right now, she'd be MC-ing the auction in safety shoes and a messy pony. It was the last thing she felt like, laying on the charm at a church auction, but she wasn't about to disappoint one more person today, especially not when it was her fault that Mrs Abrams would now have one less bachelor turning up for her fundraiser.

In the parking lot thirty minutes later, primped and coiffed in trendy palazzo pants and an elegant cowl-neck top that kept her tattoo-free shoulder well covered, Becca beeped the remote on Gem's key ring. At a soft scuffling behind her, she turned to see Ella approaching in a slow amble, her tail swishing in an endless pendulum of good humour. Becca's heart gave a fearful blip and she did a quick sweep of the parking area, but the Labrador was alone.

Relieved, Becca bent to pat Ella on her silky head, her chocolate fur warm from the sun. "I'm sure your daddy doesn't like you to be wandering about on your own, girl."

The dog flopped her hindquarters into a slovenly sit beside the car, jaws working around her ever-present root vegetable, and stared up with expressive hazel eyes at Becca.

"I need your advice," Becca said, scratching behind Ella's floppy ears. "When you've done something naughty, like chew his shoes or pee on the rug, what's the best course of action to get him to forgive you?"

Ella cocked her eyebrows and panted happily, enjoying the ear rub.

"What do you do to get back into his good books?"

As if in answer, Ella's front paws slid forward in the dirt and she rolled onto her back, exposing her belly.

Becca smiled, the first moment of lightness she'd felt all day. "I would try that, but I'm not sure I could pull off playing cute as well as you do." She stooped to pat Ella's barrel chest and scrub her fingers over the Labbie's wide tummy, eliciting grunts of canine pleasure. "If it'll convince him to let me stay," she said in an undertone, "I might have to consider it."

"Are you trying to suck up to me by being nice to my dog, princess?"

Becca started and straightened. "Sully!" She scanned his face, looking for any sign that he was about to grab her by the scruff of her neck and toss her bodily from the sanctuary. But all she saw was fatigue. He looked drained, the dark shadows under his eyes in stark contrast to the pallor of his skin, as if he'd spent the night negotiating the release of hostages with bank robbers. "I thought you'd gone home to sleep."

Back on all fours, Ella trotted up to Sully and side-swiped him, rubbing her flank against his leg, her head bobbing as she rearranged her potato in her jaws. He stroked her head before he replied. "I went to shower and change."

Becca noticed his damp hair then. The indigo button-down shirt, sleeves rolled to his elbows. Dark, unfaded jeans hugging strong thighs. And his trademark scuffed work boots. She swallowed. If he'd been serious about selling himself to raise the funds he needed for the new habitat, he was going about it the right way. She returned her gaze swiftly to his face. "You're still coming to the auction?"

"I've had enough drama for one day. I hardly need to invite more by bailing on Edwina Abrams."

Shame heated Becca's neck and bile rose sharp into her throat. She averted her eyes, fixing her gaze instead on Ella, who was sniffing one of Sully's boots. She stepped back until her butt met the warm metal of Gem's car. Flattening her palms against the door, she gulped hard against the acid burn on her tongue. "I'm so sorry about the post on Instagram." She addressed Sully's chest. "It was stupid of me not to realise that animal traffickers might see it." She forced herself to lift her head and make eye contact. "And it was even stupider of me to leave the geotagging on, and mention the sanctuary by name."

Arms folded, Sully watched her with eyes that gave her no hint how he was taking her apology. She clamped her bottom lip between her teeth and gnawed for a second, not caring that she was probably smearing her teeth with plum lipstick. Unable to hold his dark gaze any longer, she returned her attention to his chest. "I wanted to do some good." Her voice was as small as her self-esteem right now. "I thought I could raise awareness about pangolins. Maybe inspire people to make a donation. Instead all I succeeded in doing was putting them and everyone here in danger." She leaned more heavily against Gem's car and lifted her eyes to his. "I understand completely that you want me to leave."

Her voice faltered. "I'd want me to leave too. But if there's anything I can do to make you reconsider..."

He unfolded his arms and shoved his hands into his jeans pockets. "I'll admit I was furious when we left the sanctuary this morning." He turned and rested his back against the car beside her. "But somewhere on the drive back, I'd calmed down enough to realise that you don't work with trafficked animals like we do. You weren't to know you were putting them at risk with that post. And you were only trying to help."

A spark of hope flickered in her, but she stamped it out. "It still doesn't excuse what I did."

He shifted and nudged her softly with the side of his arm. "There's a silver lining. The African Pangolin Work Group called me to say they've received almost a hundred grand in donations already."

She pushed off the car and turned to him. "No!"

"Yes. And I suspect Jo will find the sanctuary's bank account is looking healthier this morning too."

She looked at him, marvelling at the power her sister was able to exert through one post. "Does that mean you're not going to make me leave?"

"Leave?" Sully appeared not to know what she was talking about. "Why would I want you to leave?"

"I know about your argument with Jo."

"You do, do you? And what exactly were we supposedly arguing about?"

"Whether to honour Jo's commitment to Alek or send me packing."

He considered her words for a moment, his head nodding slightly. "You really do need to find a more reliable source, princess. Yes, we argued. But it was Jo who wanted you off the property."

Becca allowed herself to hope. "And you?"

"I want you to stay."

One day she'd learn not to trust a word that came out of Clare's mouth. Relief and something else softened her tense spine. Something that made her want to lean to the side until she could lay her head against his arm. Instead she stepped away from the car, putting distance between her and him. "Thank you, Sully." She risked a look at him. "I won't let you down again."

"You haven't let me down, princess."

The gentleness in his voice brought tears to her eyes and she pressed her lips together to keep them at bay.

Sully pushed off the car and patted his thigh for Ella. "We need to go. You have bachelors to persecute."

18

#It'sRainingMen

"What say we kick off the bidding for our next bachelor at five hundred rand?" The livestock auctioneer roped in by Mrs Abrams for the bachelor auction pointed his gavel at the crowd. There had to be a good two hundred women squeezed in around the tables in the church hall at St Matthew's, all knocking back tea and champagne and nibbling on baked goods.

An auction paddle shot up at the back and the auctioneer gave his lectern positioned on the stage a mighty rap. "Now do I hear one thousand? Imagine a morning of all-inclusive pampering at the luxurious Brookdale Health Hydro, followed by lunch with our muscled young rugby full-back here. I'm sure our gorgeous MC is itching to put in her own bid, aren't you, Gem? We all know you can't resist a rugby player." The auctioneer winked so hard at Becca it was a wonder his cheek didn't go into a spasm.

Becca lifted her microphone, with only the faintest tremor to give away how nervous she was. "You got me there, Jeff!" *Bit heavy on the enthusiastic game show host.* "I'm a sucker for a guy who knows how to handle his—" She snapped her mouth shut, before her babbling tongue could form the last word. *Balls? Really, Becca? At a church auction? Did you learn nothing?* She left her sentence unfinished and smiled inanely at the audience, attracting a bemused look from the auctioneer.

"Do I hear one thousand five hundred? Remember, we have to hit that target so the underprivileged kiddies get their amazing new playground equipment, so dig deep, ladies."

The audience was going to have to dig very deep indeed, now that two of the ten bachelors had rushed off to battle a veld fire. At such short notice, Mrs Abrams had insisted it was impossible to find replacements, a word that had rankled the concierge in Becca. But impossible or not, she was not going to get involved. No more well-meaning helping that ended up landing her in ever-deeper piles of crap.

She would just keep her head down and get through this auction. Do not engage concierge mode. After all, she didn't have any contacts here. Didn't know anyone. If this was London, she'd simply have consulted her long lists of contacts made over the years, called in some favours and *poof*, two more bachelors waiting in the wings. But this was not London.

Out in the middle of the stage, the rugby player had his white dress shirt off and was swinging it about by one sleeve over his head like it was a lasso.

"Yee haaaa," somebody called from the audience, promptly followed by a "Ride 'em, cowboy" that dissolved into giggles.

Cowboy.

Becca twitched as an idea sparked. That was it. The Dallas Cowboy. She *did* know where they could get a couple of stand-in bachelors after all. But she'd promised herself no more well-intentioned helping. Though what could a phone call hurt? She back-stepped into the wings, leaving the auctioneer to chase up the bids for the preening rugby jock.

She took out Gem's phone and dialed.

"Winterberg Wildlife Rescue and Sanctuary."

Becca wrinkled her nose in dismay. "Er, hi, Clare. It's Gem. Any chance I could speak to the receptionist please?"

"She's on lunch."

Perhaps she should call back later. No time. "I have a favour to ask. Not for me, for Sully's church," she added hastily. "Please could you ask a few of the male volunteers to pop round to St Matthew's? We're short of bachelors. There's that good-looking American, the one with the Dallas Cowboys shirt, and the tall German with the beard."

Silence greeted her request. It stretched out so long that Becca checked the screen. The call still ticked away the seconds. "Clare?"

"Did Sully approve this?"

Becca glanced across the stage to the other side where Sully and the remaining bachelors waited hidden in the wings. "I'm not with him right now, but I'm sure he'll be fine with it."

"After yesterday, you think you should be doing anything without his approval?"

Probably not. "It's for a good cause."

"You thought the same thing about your Instagram post."

"There are no endangered animals involved today, I promise." She smiled one of her reassuring concierge smiles, even though Clare couldn't see it.

"Cooper goes back to the States this weekend. And Hans is engaged. I can't see him agreeing to be auctioned off. I can ask Alan for you."

Becca screwed up one eye. Wasn't Alan the one who had the build of a scrawny fifteen-year-old? She'd prefer someone who looked like he was acquainted with the inside of a gym. Speaking of... "What about that friend of yours in your YouTubers forum? You said he had amazing abs. Is he single?"

"You want someone with abs?"

"Definitely." Clare's fitness jock friend would be perfect. "And if he'd be willing to go shirtless for a good cause, that would be even better. If the auction is going to hit target, we'll need a real show-stopper."

There was a long pause, and then, miraculously, instead of slamming down the reception phone, Clare said, "I'll see if he's keen."

"Great!" Becca hung up with the familiar feeling she got behind the concierge desk when she'd pleased the socks off a guest. And Mrs Abrams was going to be sockless soon. Cheering and clapping erupted from the hall then, and Becca peeped out of the wings to see the rugby player bachelor hop off the front of the stage and fold a beaming woman into a hug.

Becca clicked on her mic and stepped out on stage to see the victorious bidder squeeze a bicep on her brawny bachelor. "Now now, that sort of tackle is offsides until your date," Becca said, wagging a scolding finger in jest. Laughter bubbled through the audience. She pulled back her shoulders and straightened her spine...yep, Becca Stratton was back.

The next hour saw more bachelors fall under the hammer, but now, with only Sully left on the auction block, and Clare's gym bunny nowhere in sight, they were still several thousand rand off the auction target. Becca looked at the organiser's table, where Mrs Abrams was fretting over her clipboard.

Becca cast one more hopeful look at the hall doors, but there was no broad-shouldered, narrow-hipped gym jock in sight. All she could do now was turn up the heat and inspire the audience to throw huge wads of cash at Sully. Which shouldn't be that hard. She stepped to the edge of the stage and cocked a hip. "Hold onto your paddles, ladies"—*and your panties*—"because our final bachelor is a total catch." A murmur of anticipation rippled through the hall.

Becca lowered her voice to a sultry purr. "Does he love sunsets, Barry White ballads and long walks on the beach? Or is he into French noir films and tearing off into the mountains on his motorbike? The only way to find out is to get out that paddle and make him all yours." She aimed a smouldering look at the assembled women.

Some of the older women exchanged amused glances.

Becca cleared her throat and fiddled self-consciously with the scoop of her cowl-neck top, before continuing in her normal voice, "As seen in *The Sunday Star*"—Sully was going to kill her for that, but now was the time to pull out all the stops—"it's Bachelor Number Eight. Come on out, Dr Sullivan Scott!"

Eager shouts and jokey cat-calls erupted from the audience, and a group of women in their twenties cheered and clinked their wineglasses in the middle of their table. From the pole-mounted speakers came the rousing anthem of "It's Raining Men". A chorus of *hallelujahs* came from the wineglass-clinking table, before the women collapsed into fits of giggles.

On stage, there was a conspicuous lack of anything resembling a tall, built bachelor in an indigo shirt.

Becca tried again. "Come on out, Bachelor Number Eight!"

Nothing.

The twenty-somethings began to bang slowly on the table, their cake forks clanking on their side plates as they upped the tempo.

"It seems everyone's favourite wildlife vet may have gotten spooked," Becca said. "I'll go backstage and coax him out for you."

A shout of "Here, kitty, kitty!" rang out, followed by a tiger-like growl, and the hall dissolved into laughter.

If Sully had heard that, he was probably halfway to the Ranger by now. Becca flicked off her microphone and darted into the wings, ready to kick off her high heels and dash off in pursuit.

A stocky man in black trousers and a black mesh top stretched taut over bulging muscles blocked her path. "Gem!" Bleach-whitened teeth grinned Cheshire-cat-like at her. "I recognise you from TV." The man held a boom box that looked powerful enough to blast the clothing right off whoever was listening. She stared at him bewildered. "How did you—" She looked over her shoulder in the direction of the hall.

"I came in the stage door," the man said. "It's better for the surprise if they don't see me."

"Surprise?"

He held out a meaty hand. "Devon. Clare asked me to come. She said you wanted a show-stopper." He grinned and jiggled his pecs under the mesh shirt. "I am so your guy!"

Becca peeled her gaze from his flexing chest muscles for a surreptitious glance lower down. That was some set of abs too. She gave his hand a vigorous shake. "Thanks so much for coming. You're up next, right after this bachelor I need to track down."

He winked at her and struck a body-builder pose with one arm. "I'm gonna bring down the house."

"Can't wait!" She patted the bulging arm and scooted past him.

She found Sully deep in the wings near the backstage door, pacing like a wild cat. Ella lay to one side, her head following him in a slow panning arc.

Becca stepped into his path and brought him up short. "You're going to wear a track into the floor." She gestured with her head to the stage. "You're up."

"I heard." His breath came in short, anxious bursts, and there was a sheen of sweat on his forehead. "I can't go out there."

When he'd told her he wasn't good in front of crowds, she'd thought he might have been exaggerating a little, but the man was well and truly freaked out. She glanced at Ella, and the dog thumped her tail and tilted her head as if in helpless resignation.

She touched his arm. "Come on, it'll be fine. Just a few minutes and it'll all be over."

He shook his head violently. "I'll freeze if I go out there."

"And they'll still bid on you, trust me."

"That doesn't make me feel any better." His eyes were tortured, and he raked at the bracelets on his wrist. "How do you stand having people always looking at you?"

She had no idea how Gem coped with it. She'd never forget how it had felt as a kid when she'd been standing backstage like he was now, waiting for her name to be called, with butterflies that felt more like budgies smacking about in her stomach. *In the Tiny Miss division, it's contestant number twenty-two...Becca!* She knew all too well that urge to bolt.

She wanted to put her arms around him now and hug him until the pulse she could see racing in his neck slowed, but she settled for squeezing his arm. The material of his shirt was soft, the muscle beneath it warm and solid. "I know exactly how terrified you feel."

He looked down his nose at her. "Please. You do this for a living."

Once again she'd forgotten who she was meant to be. A little truth was needed now though. "I hated it as a kid. All those pageants I told you about? I was dying inside."

He looked at her as if he didn't believe a word she was saying.

"I'm serious. I dreaded going out on stage. I only did it because it made Mom so happy. But I was a nervous wreck every time. Once, when I was nine, I was posing at the end of the runway during the sportswear section, and my hands were so slick with nervous sweat that when I did this energetic backhand stroke, the racket flew out of my hand. It ploughed through all the trophies on the awards table in front of the judges and got stopped by a judge's head."

One corner of Sully's mouth lifted. "That probably scarred you for life."

More than he could know. That had been her last pageant. She hadn't placed that day. She'd never expected to, after her grand-slam fiasco. But neither had Gem, for the first time ever. Not even the Miss Personality consolation prize. In the car on the way home, Mom had told her she didn't need to be in any more pageants. That it was okay, that for the next show, Mom would just take Gem. Twenty years later and Becca could still recall the way Mom's gaze had caught hers in the rearview mirror only to slip quickly away, as if Mom couldn't bring herself to even look at her.

She shoved aside the memory and slapped on a glib smile. "I think it scarred the poor judge more. But look at me now. I'm out there on stage in front of everyone. You can do this." She gave his arm a little shake. "You rescue kudus from fences and make cross-country drives through the night to keep pangolins safe. You stare down frightening things every day, and this is no different, only now you're doing it to help children instead of animals." Outside in the hall, the noise was rising, and a gleeful chant of *Su-lly, Su-lly, Su-lly* was picking up in volume and momentum. She rubbed his arm in encouragement. "Come on, we'll do this together. Before they storm the stage."

He held her gaze for a long moment, then he expelled his breath in a rush. "Fine." He smoothed the front of his shirt. "Do I look okay?"

We'll be beating them off with a stick. She gave a non-committal shrug. "You'll do. Worth at least a few bucks."

"Cheek." He offered her his bent arm and she took it, enjoying the feel of his hair-roughened forearm beneath her fingers.

"Don't worry," she said, as she tucked her hand into the crook of his elbow. "If no one bids for you, I'm sure I have some loose change somewhere."

She was glad to see him smile.

The auctioneer's voice boomed over the speakers then. "Looks like I'll have to go back there with my cattle prod, ladies. What do you think?" The audience whooped.

"Chin up!" Becca said.

Sully squared his shoulders and they stepped out of the wings together, Ella's claws clicking behind them.

The crowd burst into applause, and the woman at the sound desk tapped at her laptop. A second later, Right Said Fred's "I'm Too Sexy" reverberated through the hall.

Sully's steps grew shorter and shorter, and Becca had to bear forward with all her weight against his arm until the sheer size of him dragged her to a stop before they could quite make centre stage. Over the speakers, Fred, or whoever it was who was singing, had got to the part about shaking his little tush. "Go on then," Becca said into her mic, and bumped Sully with her hip. "Give us a little shake." His glare was so fierce she couldn't help but laugh. *Keep it up, boy, because that glare is sexy as hell.* And sexy meant more bucks for the underprivileged children.

She motioned to the sound desk to drop the volume, then launched into her introduction. Keeping her arm hooked firmly through Sully's to discourage any thoughts of escape, she rattled off the few vital statistics she'd gleaned from him the day before. She earned a heart-melting 'aw' from the audience when she introduced Ella, who flopped at Sully's feet and rolled over, potato dropping from floppy jowls.

The auctioneer took over at her cue. "Let's get this bidding started, shall we? Now this date will include dinner for two at the romantic Rawdon's Hotel, with the reluctant—though rather famous, if the newspaper cutting stuck to my teenaged daughter's bedroom wall is anything to go by—Bachelor Number Eight."

Sully's arm tensed beneath Becca's fingers, and she gave him an encouraging squeeze and leaned into his side. He straightened his arm and tried to step away from her, but she clung on. He wasn't escaping on her watch.

"*Hot*," he said, his eyes fixed somewhere on the back of the hall.

Another common symptom of stage fright. "That's the nerves."

"No. There." Sully inclined his head towards the back of the hall.

And then Becca saw her, standing in the doorway with the photographer from Sunday. Cassie Govender from *Hot* magazine. Becca's gut clenched and she released her grip on Sully's arm and took a hasty step sideways.

The photographer lowered his camera.

Becca's stomach fell. More photos to contend with. Though Cassie's editor had better be happy with photos of 'Gem' standing beside a man who looked so terrified he might as well have had Pennywise the Clown on his arm, because that was all they were going to get out of her today. She threw a confident smile at the press contingent and sang into her mic, "Let the bidding war commence."

The auctioneer whacked his gavel. "Who'll start us off at a thousand bucks?"

Paddles rocketed into the air. Becca tossed out rallying cries to the bidders, but she kept her gaze firmly off the goods. There would be no photos claiming any stolen looks between her and Sully. After a heated round of bid and counter bid, the gavel fell and the auctioneer leaned into his microphone with a lusty "Solllllllld!".

Ella had to trot to keep up with Sully as he made a bee-line for the wings. Becca looked over at the doorway. Cassie was slouched against the doorjamb watching her and the photographer was fiddling on his phone, camera at last hanging neglected around his neck.

Becca smiled sweetly at the reporter. *You can push off now, Cassie. Show's over.*

"Well, folks, that's all we've got for you today, I'm afraid," said the auctioneer, and the audience moaned their disappointment.

Becca held up a hand. "Actually, I have a little surprise for you all. Someone I know is going to knock your socks off." She scanned the crowd and smiled reassuringly at a frowning Mrs Abrams who was looking in confusion from her clipboard to Becca. "You'll usually find our last bachelor in the gym, but I've coaxed him away from his weights today. He's into staying fit. He's, er..." She had no idea what Devon was into, but it wouldn't matter what he liked, not once the audience got a load of the muscles beneath that mesh shirt. "Please give a warm Winterberg welcome for Bachelor Number Nine...Devon!"

Before she could signal to the woman at the sound desk, music throbbed behind her. The tonsil-vibrating, pulsing beat of—

She froze.

That track was from *Magic Mike XXL.* Why was Clare's fitness nut with great abs doing his walk-on to Ginuwine's "Pony"?

A dreadful gnawing sensation clamped its teeth into her stomach, as if there were a small burrowing animal trying to claw its way out. She'd booked enough tickets to Dreamboys shows for guests wanting some girls-night-out fun not to know what men usually did on stage when that particular song came over the speakers.

And from the stunned expression on Mrs Abrams's face and Cassie Govender's ecstatic grin, Devon was doing precisely that.

Becca turned as if in a trance to see Bachelor Number Nine gyrating centre stage, hips jerking about as if he were keeping an invisible hula-hoop up, while he peeled the mesh vest from his chiselled chest.

But he was a fitness jock! He was meant to pump iron, not his hips. Clare's fitness nut with the great abs had officially gone nuts.

Oh God.

Clare'd mentioned a stripper too.

The small burrowing animal had made its way into Becca's chest, where it was making it particularly hard to breathe. She clutched the microphone so tight her fingers hurt. She'd asked Clare to send the guy with great abs, but wouldn't a stripper also, of necessity, have great abs?

She had to stop this, before it got way, way worse. She launched herself across the stage as the awful ripping sound of Velcro reached her ears. With an exuberant flick of his arms, Devon whipped his tearaway trousers from his thighs.

And the hall erupted.

In what felt like a slow-motion sequence, Becca took in the black vinyl pouch between Devon's thrusting legs, that was restraining something she could only hope was several pairs of chunky winter socks.

Hands settled on her shoulders then and Sully's voice spoke in her ear. "I don't know how you do it, princess, but it looks like it's time for us to flee the ball again."

19

#CrackedOpen

"You missed the turnoff." Becca swivelled in the passenger seat to look back through the bakkie's rear window at the sanctuary's signboard as it grew rapidly smaller.

"Nope," Sully said, without taking his eyes off the road.

From her post between the front seats, Ella gave Becca's tear-streaked cheek, now within easy reach, an opportunistic lick. Becca nudged away the dog's snout and turned back in her seat. "Please just take me back, Sully." She wiped at her wet eyes. "I need to phone Alek and—"

"You need to take a moment first before you have to deal with him," Sully said, without taking his eye from the road.

Without answering, Becca stared out her window. The natural grassland gave way after a few minutes to commercial pine forests, neat rows of towering pine trees stretching away on either side of the bakkie, their trunks stripped clean of the lower branches so they resembled Christmas trees atop telephone poles. As the bakkie flashed by, the uniformly spaced trunks seemed to flicker like moving barcodes. "If you're planning on taking me deep into a forest and abandoning me to the elements, then I'm all in." She leaned her head against the head rest and groaned. "God, that was a complete disaster."

Sully looked at her, his expression flickering between sympathy and amusement, a grin attempting to lift the corners of his mouth.

"On the bright side, it was the most exciting auction the church has ever had. People are going to be talking about it for years."

Becca groaned all the louder. "That's where you're wrong. They're going to be talking about it *forever*, because that's how long things last on the internet."

Sully's face sobered. "It wasn't that bad."

"You're right. It was horrifying."

He laughed and Ella shoved her muzzle into his neck, huffing as if to get in on the action. "That vinyl thong was horrifying, I'll give you that," he said, fending off his dog with a hand. "But it could've been worse."

"How?"

He fixed her with a somber expression. "Devon could've been wearing one of those novelty elephant thongs."

Laughter thick with tears earned Becca an eager nuzzle from Ella. "Oh God, don't even go there," she said, pushing Ella's wet nose away. "And stop trying to make me laugh. None of what just happened was even remotely funny."

"Not even a priest with tearaway pants on her head?" Sully chuckled.

"Especially not that." Becca covered her face with her hands and moaned. "Social media's going to break over this." She had no idea how she was going to fix things now for Gem.

The clicking of the indicator filled the cabin and the bakkie slowed. Becca lowered her hands to see that Sully had turned onto a dirt road that ran into one of the pine plantations. "I was joking about the forest," she said, her voice juddering as the bakkie jolted over the corrugated surface.

"You were?" Sully looked crestfallen.

Her smile felt like a wrung-out dish rag. "Where are we going?"

"You'll see."

They followed the forestry road in silence for a few kilometres. It grew steadily steeper as the plantation angled up into the foothills, until eventually both the rows of trees and the road came to an end and the plantation gave way to open grassland.

Sully parked the Ranger. "Come. I want to show you something." He opened his door and got out with Ella close on his heels.

Becca left Gem's stilettos on the floor and climbed out. She picked her way over dried pine needles and twigs to the front of the Ranger. "Wherever we're going had better be close, because I'm not dressed for hiking."

"Don't worry." He patted his shoulder. "I'll piggy-back you."

She searched his face, looking for signs that he was kidding, but he seemed in earnest. She frowned. "I can't get on your back."

"Why not?"

The eager leap of her stomach was why not. "I'm too heavy."

He snorted. "If I can carry a full-grown warthog in my arms, I'm pretty sure I won't even break a sweat carrying you." He went down into a crouch.

"Did you just compare me to a warthog?"

"Come on," he said, patting his shoulder. When she didn't move, he looked back at her, his eyebrows lifting. "Unless you'd rather I carry you warthog-style."

And be cosied up against his chest? Heaven forbid. She stepped up to him and placed her hands on his shoulders, trying not to notice how wide she had to span her fingers to cover his broad muscles. As she jumped, Sully caught her under her thighs and rose effortlessly from the ground, pulling her in tight against his back. A slip-slidey feeling like silk through fingers unspooled low in her belly.

Oh hell.

At his call, Ella emerged from the pine trees she'd been investigating and trotted into the open veld, as if she knew precisely where they were headed. Sully set off after the Labbie at a brisk walk, and Becca's arms looped instinctively around his neck and folded over his upper chest, bringing her flush with his back.

She tipped her head to the side so her cheek wouldn't brush against his dark hair, but that didn't stop the smell of him from reaching her, all freshly washed and citrusy and sun-warmed. "How far are we going?"

"A few minutes' walk."

Pity she wasn't a pearl diver, then she might have had a chance of holding her breath that long. It wasn't only his hair she could smell. She was acutely aware of the spice of his deodorant and the scent of his cotton shirt heated by his body, and it was doing alarming things to her. She turned her head away to inspect the scenery and keep his thick dark hair out of her field of vision. Tussocks of wild grass covered the ground, protea bushes held gnarled fire-blackened branches and silvery leaves against a blue sky, and wild veld plants showed off their delicate spring flowers from between stretches of rock exposed by time and weather. "It's beautiful out here."

"It's my favourite part of the world." Sully planted a boot on a cluster of rocks embedded in the path and powered up the sloping track, his shoulders flexing beneath her arms. "You haven't told me yet why you booked a stripper."

Becca heaved a sigh. "I was trying to get a replacement for the missing firefighters, so Mrs Abrams could reach her target."

He grunted as he hopped a rock in the track. "And you thought Strippers-R-Us would be a great place to find one?"

"No! I was expecting a sexy gym bunny. That's what we spoke about."

Ella had stopped ahead of them with her inquisitive snout buried in a clump of grass and her thick tail jutting out straight behind her. Sully stepped around Ella off the track and clenched one arm to keep Becca from slewing sideways. "Who's 'we'?"

"Me and Clare. The gym bunny's in her YouTube—"

"Clare?" Sully stopped abruptly, his hands tensing under her thighs, and twisted back his head so he could see her out the corner of one eye. "Clare sent a stripper to my church's charity auction?"

"It was probably a misunderstanding." Improbable, but possible. She hadn't been that specific about which of Clare's YouTube friends she'd wanted. "I said we needed a show-stopper who wouldn't mind showing off his abs. I meant the fitness jock, but she obviously thought I meant Devon." A show-stopper indeed.

Sully started walking again, but she could feel his anger in the hard line of his shoulders. "Unless Clare thought you were MC-ing a hen party, I fail to see how she could've thought you'd want a stripper at a church event."

Okay, so it had been deliberate. "It wouldn't have happened though if I'd focused on being MC instead of trying to help Mrs Abrams hit her target."

"Why do you care about pleasing Mrs Abrams? The only person you should be worried about is yourself. Finish your hours and forget about everyone else. Put your own needs first."

Not so easy to do, when she'd been putting other people's needs before her own for as long as she could remember. And what was wrong with that? She was good at helping people. She liked it. It was what people valued about her, that she was always there for them. That was why she'd gone into the hospitality industry in the first place. She shifted on his back. "Is it much further?"

"See those rocks?" He gestured with his head. "There."

Good...because she wanted off this horse. The feel of the muscles moving in his back and the flex of his shoulders and the jolt of his hips as his boots devoured the sandy track were getting too hard to ignore.

Ella spotted something ahead and darted off after it, disappearing between the rocks Sully was aiming for. Sully followed, making his way over the rocks until they flattened out into a wide outcrop from which the world seemed to fall away.

Becca inhaled a slow, appreciative breath. An uninterrupted vista of mountains stretched out on the horizon beyond the valley before them. Velveteen foothills lay like plush blankets in haphazard folds. A grey ribbon of road appeared around one of the ridges before disappearing into a dip. Water glinted mirror-bright where a narrow river carved its way along the valley floor. And above them, banks of white cloud trailed their fingers through a sky as blue as a summer hydrangea.

Becca relaxed against Sully's back, her cheek coming to rest against his thick warm hair. "It's breathtaking."

His hands beneath her legs tucked her in closer to him. "This is where I come when I need to unwind and get away from humans."

"That would be often then?"

"Since you came back to the sanctuary? At least once a day."

She smiled. "Touché, Dr Scott."

He chuckled and looked out over the landscape. "That's Cathkin Peak in front of us, with the flat top. And that"—he pivoted to the left and nodded his head at another stretch of mountaintop—"is Champagne Castle."

"You can put me down now."

He spent another moment taking in the view, then his hands slipped from her legs and he crouched until her feet touched the ground.

The rock was rough and warm beneath her bare feet, and she wrapped her arms around her body against the slight breeze that stirred the grass between the rocks. A flock of tiny birds flitted away in a whirr of beating wings from a protea bush that was growing in a gap between the rock.

Ella ambled over to them and deposited her potato on the toe of one of Sully's boots. It balanced there for a second before sliding off, leaving a trail of spit behind it.

Becca shook her head in amusement. "What is it with Ella and potatoes?"

Sully gave a good-natured shrug and nudged the Labbie with his shin. "It's a Labrador thing. They often carry things around. But as for why a potato, only she knows."

He dropped onto the lichen-dappled rock and extended one leg in front of him, bending the other and hooking his arm loosely about his knee. "She found one in my pantry when she was a puppy. It was so big I swear she almost dislocated her jaw fitting the whole thing in. When I took it away, she yapped at me until I returned it."

Ella pressed her head into his chest and he roughed her around with affectionate hands. "You've been carrying them with you ever since, haven't you?" He worked his fingers into the thick fur behind Ella's ears. "It used to drive Alisha nuts."

The fiancée who'd left him for the farmer? Becca folded herself onto the rock beside him, tucking her legs to one side. "Your ex-fiancée?"

Sully nodded, staring into his dog's eyes as she grunted her satisfaction at his attention. "Alisha used to throw out El's potatoes. I'd replace them. It was a good thing we never ended up together, or the cost of potatoes would've bankrupted me."

His voice was light, his tone joking, but Becca sensed that talking about it still got his hackles up. "It must have been devastating. And to leave you at the altar? That's cruel."

He made a dismissive sound deep in his throat. "Mrs Abrams was overstating things, as usual. It was actually five months before. We'd booked a venue, hired a photographer, that sort of thing, but we hadn't sent out the invitations yet."

As if that were any better. Anger for the way he'd been treated flared in her chest. "That doesn't let her off the hook. It must still have been a blow."

"It was. But with hindsight, I dodged a bullet." He settled back on his palms and looked out over the vista of mountains, the wind lifting the hair at his forehead. Ella collapsed along his outstretched leg and rested her muzzle on his thigh. "After my dad died, I had a hard time coming to terms with myself really. I have this protective side that I usually channel into the animals I work with. But when my dad died, I felt like I'd let my family down by not being able to protect him too. Which was totally irrational, I know, but I couldn't help it, especially seeing how his death affected my mom. When I moved here, I was still a mess. And then I met Alisha and her neediness fired up that protective part of me. Deep down I knew she was taking advantage of me, but taking care of her made me feel back in control of my world again."

Sully shifted his weight onto one arm so he could stroke Ella's head. "I could see later that we weren't right for each other, that I asked her to marry me for all the wrong reasons. To this day though, I've never worked out why she said yes, since she was already seeing him behind my back. A carrot farmer, of all things." He flapped one of Ella's ears with his fingers, looking into the dog's amber eyes. "That was the worst, finding out that she'd been lying to me for so long. And that she'd taken our relationship to the next level, knowing full well she was eventually going to end up tearing out my heart." His jaw tensed and he smoothed a hand over Ella's fur in a long slow stroke.

Becca shifted on the rock, tendrils of guilt snaking through her like venom spreading from a snake bite. Here she was lying to him, doing the same thing to him that Alisha had done, just without the cheating and the need to return an engagement ring. She drew her legs up in front of her and belted her arms around them. "I'm sorry." It was as much an apology as it was sympathy.

He shrugged. "Life lessons. I think that's why you and I got off to such a rough start last week. You reminded me of her. She put on this whole fragile, helpless act to get me to fall in line with whatever she wanted. And last week, that's how it felt, like you were trying to manipulate me so I'd take it easy on you. And I was damned if I was going to be manipulated like that again."

Becca dropped her chin into the dip between her knees. Her guilt was a palpable weight now, a thick, coagulated mass that squatted cold and heavy in her chest. She splayed her bare toes on the warm rock and turned her cheek against her knee to look at him. "I'm sorry again about that." *And for what I'm doing now.*

The smile was back in his eyes, which only added to her guilt. "Forget it. You've redeemed yourself." He patted Ella on her flank and she rolled onto her back with a happy grunt. "And I was an arsehole too. Animals do weird things when they're hurting, and I forgot that humans aren't much different."

Becca broke eye contact. If the guilt heaped on any thicker, she'd have to lie down under its crushing pressure. For a long moment, the only sound to break the silence between them was Ella's contented huffing.

"So what's your tale of woe, princess? I told you mine, now you tell me about Mandla."

Becca kept her expression neutral, despite the sinking feeling Sully's question had caused. It seemed overly cagey to say she didn't want to talk about it, after he'd been so open about his own past. But answering would mean more lies, even if she spun her answer in a way that would absolve her, technically, from lying.

"Hey, it's okay," Sully said. "You don't have to tell me. You probably both signed NDAs."

"Something like that." She hadn't meant to sound so relieved. He'd picked up on her reluctance, always so alert to what was going on beneath her facade. It made her feel warm in the deep centre of her chest. She crossed her legs and grinned at him. "Actually I was just thinking back through all my failed relationships to find one that could match your own sob story."

Sully laughed and settled back on his hands. "Go on then. Give it your best shot."

She couldn't believe she was about to launch into a story about Kevin the Bastard with a smile on her face. Something about Sully seemed to make everything feel better. "I met Kevin in a bar." A new place she'd been checking out to see if it was worth recommending to The Rickford's guests. "He'd just got laid off from a tech company and was sitting at the counter, staring into a beer. I guess his misery appealed to my naturally helpful nature." Sully snorted at that and she raised her brows at him. "Rude. Do you want to hear it or not?"

There was laughter in his eyes as he gestured for her to continue.

"We'd been seeing each other for a couple of weeks when he announced he couldn't afford his rent anymore, and I, being, as we've established, the naturally helpful type..."

Sully shook his head. "You let him move in with you."

Becca hunched her shoulders in a self-deprecating gesture. "Yep."

"And let me guess...he spent all his time lying about on your sofa watching Netflix while you went off to work in the coal mines."

She nodded and opened her palms in defeat. "What can I say? I'm a total sucker."

Sully gave a regretful sigh, like he had bad news to deliver. "I hate to tell you this, princess, but my story outdoes yours. I was definitely the bigger sucker."

"Just wait, Dr Impatience. I haven't got to the best part yet." She smiled as Sully held up his hands in surrender. "I meet a lot of people in my work, and one day, I got Kevin an interview with a woman who ran a blockchain startup, whatever that is. But like all the other interviews he'd been to, nothing came of it. And then I saw the same guest again a week later. I mentioned I was sorry things hadn't worked out with Kevin, and she looked surprised and said he'd never shown for the interview. And after a little detective work, I discovered that hadn't been the only interview he'd blown off or just plain made up. I was so angry, I went home at lunch to ball him out over it, and caught him having energetic sex with my neighbour on my kitchen counter."

Sully winced so hard that Ella pushed to her front paws and tried to lick his face. "Shit, I'm sorry," he said, deflecting the dog with his arm.

Becca inclined her head. "They didn't even have the courtesy to wash the dishes before they got down to it." She let her gaze drift to the lichen she was absentmindedly picking off the rock surface. "I shouldn't be surprised. Guys have only ever liked me for what I can do for them."

Sully patted the ground beside his leg and Ella flopped down obediently and draped her head over his thigh again. "Well, princess, I like you and you haven't done anything for me except force me to swim in an ice-cold dam, turn me into a national pin-up and send me off on a pre-dawn road trip."

Becca lifted her chin and eyed him as if he were being deliberately obtuse. "Have you forgotten I'm your cash cow? I'd say that's the very definition of quid pro quo."

"You can't count the money."

She snorted. "How do you figure that?"

He shifted Ella's head off his lap and folded his legs to the side so he was sitting facing Becca. "Nowhere in the terms and conditions of that bribe did it say I had to be the one to help you finish your hours. Clare was begging for me to assign you to her."

"So why didn't you?"

"We've already established I'm a sucker, in this case, for punishment."

"Nice."

He smiled. "I am, yes."

She propped a hand beside her and leaned a little as she scrutinised him, eyes narrowed. "You weren't very nice to me at the police station. Or after I valiantly rescued that Scottie."

"I was freezing my arse off and you were being so bloody stubborn." His smile faded as he considered her in contemplative silence for a beat. "I won't lie. You weren't my favourite person when you were first here. But that night at the station, it was like you were someone else."

A jolt of alarm fired through her, followed by a now-familiar guilt. "Prison will do that to a person." She leaned forward on her arm to peer at his watch. "It's getting late. We should probably head back."

"Such a little work horse. Who'd have thought it?" His smile deepened and warmth filled his eyes. "You surprised me that night. And you keep on surprising me. With your concern over the caracal. The way you mucked in to clean the monkeys and hurled yourself into a dam after a dog. Even today at the auction, MCing an event for people you didn't owe any allegiance to. You let me see the real you." He brushed a light touch across the hand she held braced against the rock. "And I happen to like the real you."

He has no idea. Becca shut her eyes so he couldn't see the corrosive guilt burning into her soul. If he ever found out about the real her, he'd think she was just another woman who'd manipulated him for her own ends and then betrayed him, and he would hate her for it.

"What's going on in that head of yours?"

You don't want to know. There were so many reasons why she should leap up and flee barefoot back to his bakkie, but his fingers had found the sensitive skin of her wrist and the light caress over her skin was making it hard to hold onto even one of them.

"I should add that I liked the way it felt when you kissed me after you crashed your car."

She opened her eyes with a surprised laugh. "Hardly a kiss." Laughter was good. Anything to dispel the charged tension in the air. She straightened and tucked her hands into her lap, out of his reach. The skin on her wrist still tingled. "Might I remind you that you were horrified? You looked like I'd slapped you across the mouth with a dead fish."

He laughed at that. "I'm not used to having gorgeous women flinging themselves at me."

Warmth settled low inside her at his compliment. "I wasn't flinging. I was tripping."

"Whatever it was, I was too taken aback to make the most of it."

His joking tone meant it took her a second to grasp the full meaning of his words. She looked into his eyes and saw a sudden intensity that made her bones feel rubbery. It wasn't right, though. She didn't deserve to have him look at her that way. "I'm only here until Friday."

"I know."

She wet her lips. "I'll be going back to my real life then. Thousands of kilometres from here."

"Joburg isn't actually thousands of kays away."

But London was. "You know what I mean." Her lips parted and she felt herself leaning in towards him, as if her libido-driven body were staging a coup d'état over her mind. She reeled herself back in and looked away from his hypnotic eyes. "We live in two different worlds."

"Princess?" The soft resonance of his voice made her breath catch. "Would you please stop tossing obstacles in my way and let me kiss you?"

A rush of goosebumps prickled up her thighs and her gaze found his. The steady hold of those dark eyes transfixed her. Sully paused, reading her face, and then he reached out to cup her chin with one hand, his fingers feathering beneath her jaw as he drew her so close she could smell the tang of his aftershave and taste his soft breath.

And then his mouth touched hers. Just the soft, warm press of his mouth at first, and then his lips parted on an inhale. Her eyes slipped shut and she opened her mouth to the slow hot slide of his tongue.

Without relinquishing his hold on her jaw, Sully slid his other hand up the back of her neck and into her hair. His fingers fanned out across her scalp and he angled her head and deepened the caress of his tongue, each stroke shooting an answering pulse between her thighs.

She caught his face in her hands as she kissed him back, the heat of his skin beneath her fingers and the roughness of new stubble stoking the sweet ache inside her. She wanted to sink into him. Wanted to feel his mouth on—

Sully recoiled with a sharp yelp and his hand yanked her hair as he withdrew it. "What the..." He felt his neck and looked in confusion at his wet palm.

Gleaming potato clamped between her front teeth, Ella smiled her wide, Labrador smile at him and shoved the slob-covered vegetable into his neck again. "El!" he protested, holding the big dog off with both hands.

Becca's laugh was breathless, her heart still clattering in her chest. She sat back to avoid Ella's thick whip of a tail. "It seems no female can resist the charms of Bachelor Number Eight today." Least of all her. But she had to. This was a colossal mistake and nothing good could come of indulging these feelings he fuelled in her.

Ella grunted with canine delight as Sully wrestled the potato from her jaw and flung it off into the long grass.

The big dog charged off in pursuit and Becca scrambled to her feet. "We should go. Community service awaits."

She felt his eyes on her for a beat before he pushed to his feet with an ill-concealed sigh. "Curse this new work ethic of yours, princess."

Ella galloped back over the rock, panting triumphantly, and disgorged the retrieved potato at Sully's feet. He levelled a playful scowl at the dog. "You're a useless wing man."

"She makes a pretty good chaperone though," Becca said, sending her silent thanks to the dog. That kiss would not have stopped where it had without divine—or in this case, canine—intervention.

Sully growled his disapproval. "In future, I'll leave her at home."

And then he caught her around the waist and pulled her flush with his body, lighting up every nerve ending all over again and making her forget why there could never be an *in future* for them.

Instagram

163,874 likes

hotmagazine_sa Causing a scandal again! Gem Stratton really knows how to get a rise out of an audience...literally! Everyone's favourite celeb-to-watch brought a bachelor auction for a church charity to a screaming halt, after Gem's surprise stripper took it all off in front of a packed church hall. Check out more hot pics and scandalous vids at hotmagazine.co.za or in the link in the bio.

#hotmagazine #gemstratton #southafricancelebs #fashion #celebnews #celebsbehavingbadly #bachelors

View all 3,246 comments

iamjason You have to watch the stripper video on Hot mag's site. Swear to jaysus this is the funniest video I've ever seen. I'm dead!

misstwinkle @iamjason i know, right? That stripper? Gem's eyes are like, OMG!!!!! lol That was some package in that thong!!!

jenalicious Is it just me or is Gem getting chunky? That's serious muffin top oozing out over those trousers of hers. Girl's letting herself go. Diet time, Gem!

Add a comment

20

#BringingDownTheHouse

Becca folded the last corner of toast into her mouth and chewed. It was like eating a bath loofah, and the peanut butter didn't help, sticking to the roof of her mouth like glue. She'd have preferred cereal, but what with all the snickers and whispers filling the sanctuary's volunteers dining hall, breakfast to go had seemed preferable. She pushed open the door to the rehab centre's reception, licking peanut butter off her fingers.

The receptionist was turned in her chair, phone wedged between jaw and shoulder as she dug through a drawer in a filing credenza. "My mom says it was chaos...I know! I would've peed myself laughing. She says Mrs Abrams split her trousers scrambling up the stage stairs to cover the stripper's junk!"

Becca cringed.

"I know! She's such a disaster."

Becca cleared her throat and the office chair swung round. She greeted the receptionist's scornful expression with a benign smile. "Is Sully in?"

"Second treatment room."

Head high, Becca crossed reception and was about to push through the internal swinging doors into the clinic when Clare barged through from the other side, her face tight and her eyes bright with moisture.

Clare stopped dead, her nostrils flaring. She took a lunging step forward and Becca flinched back. "Thanks a lot, Gem." Clare's eyes flashed, the anger in them hinting there'd been an implied *you bitch* at the end of that sentence.

"What did I do?"

"As if you don't know." A bead of spit flew from Clare's mouth. "Sully laid into me over Devon, when I was only trying to help you."

Becca stiffened and held her ground as Clare took another step into her personal space. Adrenalin spiked her pulse and twisted her stomach, but she put on the calm façade she always used when handling a confrontation across the concierge desk. "I can't say I blame him, Clare. You did ruin his church's auction."

"You asked for my friend with the abs."

"I asked for the fitness guy."

"Let me jog your memory." Clare brought her face in close, and Becca resisted the urge to back away. "You said you wanted someone with abs who wouldn't be afraid to show them off, someone who'd be a total show-stopper. Your. Words." Clare jabbed a finger into Becca's chest with each word. "And that description fits Devon."

Becca widened her stance and lifted her chin. "Oh come on, Clare. I don't buy that you thought I was asking you to send a stripper to a church auction. Not for one hot second."

Clare's only response was a growl. She bulldozed past Becca, smacking her shoulder hard against Becca's arm as she broke into a jog and hurried from the rehab centre.

Becca watched her go, her heart beating a painful rhythm in her chest. Then she leaned her shoulder on the swing door and went in search of Sully. She hadn't got far up the corridor when Gem's cellphone vibrated in her pocket. She groaned softly.

After Alek's understandable hand-wringing yesterday before he'd launched into crisis management mode, this was not a phone call she wanted to take. She pressed the call-answer icon. "Alek. Tell me you have good news."

"Nope." There was a tinge of mania in his voice. "You just lost Clearly Beautiful."

The floor fell away under Becca's feet and she clutched at the wall. "Oh God."

"They've decided the face of their brand shouldn't be constantly embroiled in scandal. And UrbanROAD is hanging by a thread. Explain to me, Gem, why the fuck you got involved in that fucking auction in the first place?"

Becca flinched, even though she'd been on the receiving end of worse yesterday afternoon when she'd phoned him to tell him what had happened. "I'm really sorry, Alek. I can't say that enough. But I just got dragged into it."

"And you couldn't say no?"

"Not without disappointing everyone."

"Why would you care about disappointing a bunch of people you didn't even know existed a week ago?" Alek gave a disgusted snort. "Here's a thought, Gem. Why don't you concentrate on not disappointing the brands you endorse?"

"You said I still have UrbanROAD?"

"Only thanks to some unashamed begging by me on your behalf. But one more strike, Gem, and they'll pull out too."

Becca leaned against the wall, her lungs snatching for air as she dug deep for strength she was no longer sure she possessed. "Don't worry, Alek, I'm not going to put another foot wrong. I promise I won't leave the sanctuary until my hours are done."

"That promise will be hard to keep. You remember those animal conservation benefit concerts they wanted to get involved with now they're launching their new sustainable clothing line?"

"Of course," she lied. Hadn't she'd seen their logo somewhere recently, and not just on Gem's clothing?

"There's one happening today," Alek said. "At the Drakensberg Boys Choir School."

That was it. The poster on the reception notice board. "The concert in aid of the Cape vulture."

"Some shit like that, ya," Alek said. "Now I know we agreed you wouldn't get involved in anything while you were doing your community service, but as a show of your continued commitment, I've convinced them to let you represent them there. Just to prove to them you're still the Gem Stratton they signed, and not this disaster-stricken mess they keep seeing in the media."

Wow. Harsh. "I'm sure I can sit through a concert without causing a scene," she said, managing somehow to keep any hint of sarcasm out of her voice.

Alek's response was a scoffing sound. "You're not going as a guest. *Carte Blanche* is covering the concert for World Vulture Awareness Day in September. Now that you're back on the scene, they're standing down their usual presenter to let you present the segment as UrbanROAD's ambassador."

It took a few seconds for Alek's words to sink in. She had to be Gem in full presenter mode in front of TV cameras? And for *Carte Blanche*, the current affairs show that exposed scammers, conmen and people who switched places with a famous sibling to deceive the public? Her knees concertina-ed and she sank down the wall onto the floor. "Holy shit," she whispered.

"I was expecting something along the lines of 'Thank you, Alek'. I've just saved you from losing another endorsement deal."

She ground the heel of her hand into her chest. This must be what a heart attack felt like. "No, of course, thank you, Alek. Only it's short notice, don't you think?"

"Not for a pro like you."

"But I've got to get changed and then there's travelling—"

"The clue's in the name, Gem. Drakensberg Boys is only fifteen minutes outside of town. The concert's at one, but they need you there earlier to walk through your positions with the producer and meet the bird. I assume you packed some UrbanROAD pieces in your luggage. And Sylvia's emailed the script."

Alek rattled off a litany of details, but Becca couldn't keep her mind on any of them. Her breath came quick and shallow, her thoughts skittering. She needed Gem. Gem would be able to talk her through this. But Gem wasn't here. She grimaced as panic filled her. This was it: the game was up. She was going to let down her family. Unless she could get out of it...

She could fall ill. Feign food poisoning from breakfast. Or take more of the pills in Gem's car. If she was half-comatose, they couldn't expect her to present the *Carte Blanche* insert. But then Gem would lose UrbanROAD for sure. Though that had to be better than giving away the whole switch.

"Hey."

She looked up with a start to see Sully standing over her. His face was shadowed with concern.

"Something wrong?" He dropped to his haunches before her.

She glanced at Gem's phone in her clawed hand. She checked the screen. Alek had hung up. She opened her mouth and her tongue came away from her palate with an audible snick. "I lost..." Her breathing was getting in the way, quick and harsh. "I lost..." There was so much air. So much. "And UrbanROAD." So much air and yet she felt like she was suffocating. "They want to..." Strange spots were forming at the edges of her vision.

Sully's concern morphed into something serious. Clinical. "Gem, stop. You're going to hyperventilate." He stood and pulled her like a rag doll into his arms. "Hold your breath. Hold it." His arms were an immovable band around her body as she did what he instructed, her heart pounding, her chest still heaving even though she held her mouth tight shut. "Just like that," he sang in an almost whisper. "A little longer. That's it. Just hold it. Good. Now let it out slowly."

Becca released the air from her lungs and sagged face-first, inch by deflating inch, against his chest, relying on his arms to keep her from falling, her own arms hanging like wet string at her sides.

"Now tell me what's happened."

"I lost the Clearly Beautiful endorsement," she whispered into his T-shirt. "And I'm about to lose UrbanROAD too. And now I have to present a segment at Drakensberg Boys. For a vulture benefit concert. A televised concert. Today." A sob tinged with fresh hysteria gargled up into her mouth. "With no warning." How the hell was she going to do that? There was no way! She had to tell Alek. Admit to this whole disastrous scheme. She snatched for air again.

"No, princess, slow down," he said, speaking against the top of her head in the quiet steady voice he used around frightened animals. "Just breathe. In." He paused. "And out. You're okay."

She noticed then how tight his arms were wrapped around her, the only thing keeping her from crumpling to the ground. How he was rocking slightly from side to side. She shut her eyes and forced herself to synch her breathing to his, exhaling when his chest rose, inhaling when it fell. In and out. Until the sounds of the world around her began to register again. The swing doors opening. Voices. Beeping monitors. Claws on a metal examining table.

"What's going on?" His breath was warm against her crown. "Why the panic?"

Her arms lifted and snaked around his waist like he were a lifebuoy in a violent sea. *Because I'm not Gem.* The words were right there, crowded together at the front of her mouth just waiting for one of them to have the courage to blurt itself out and then they'd all topple out in a rush. *I'm not Gem. I'm not Gem.* She forced back the truth and tipped her head up, her chin digging into his chest as she looked into eyes full of bewildered concern. "I don't have time for this." *Or the skill or the experience or—* She was choking again on tears and guilt. "I need to be here. I can't do this!"

He released one arm, still holding her close with the other, to wipe her hot wet face with his fingers. Then he cupped her chin and angled her gaze to meet his. "Don't say that. There's nothing you can't do. Haven't you proved that to yourself this week? You've done all sorts of things that I bet you never thought you'd ever be doing. So yes, you can do this, and you will. Get the presenting out of the way, and then we'll get back to working off your hours, even if we have to work nights."

She rolled her chin out of his grip and turned her face against his T-shirt. He had no idea. She drew in a shaky breath that was heavy with his scent...cotton and shaving cream and unwavering strength. No idea at all, and yet he was still right. She *had* done all sorts of weird and wonderful things since getting here, and she'd come out okay. Even the auction yesterday had been going perfectly until she'd inadvertently introduced the world's most inappropriate bachelor to grace a church auction stage. Maybe she could do this vulture benefit too. She'd seen Gem in action so many times, maybe she could wing it enough to just about pass muster. And there'd be no twerking bachelors involved this time.

She took another deep breath, pulling him deep into her lungs before looking back at him. "You're right." Her voice still wobbled. "I can do this."

"That's the spirit." He cupped her face in his hand. "You want me to come with you? There are likely to be vultures involved. Live ones."

Alek had said something about meeting a bird, and she could do with Sully's calm, quiet brand of moral support. She sniffed noisily and wiped her nose with the back of her fingers. She attempted a smile, and it must have worked because he smiled back at her. "I'd like that. Thank you."

He nodded and loosened his hold around her, letting her find her balance before moving back from her. "You want to put in a few hours now?"

"Sure." She felt like a wrung-out towel, but she wasn't going to give up just yet. "If you can help me hammer a script into my head while I work?"

By mid-morning though, her nerves had become so snarled that she'd broken a digital thermometer, knocked an open tin of formula meant for an orphaned banded mongoose pup's morning snack off the prep-room counter, and let a bat loose in the hospital ward, so she'd escaped to her room to begin the transformation from animal-rehabber Gem to TV-star Gem.

Now, thirty minutes before show-time, Becca touched up her lipstick in the illuminated mirror of one of the many dressing rooms at the back of the auditorium where the famous Drakensberg Boys Choir performed their regular concerts.

"If you put on any more of that stuff, your lips will be too heavy to form words." The picture of nonchalance, Sully sat behind her on a plastic chair with his legs sprawled out before him, arms folded lightly across his chest.

She caught his eye in the mirror. "TV lights are unforgiving. I have to look perfect."

"You do." He did a quick sweep of her body before returning to her face. "Now stop stressing. I thought you'd be loving this, being back in your element."

She looked away and fumbled the lipstick tube into Gem's makeup bag. "Even pros get nervous."

From dressing rooms along the corridor, the laughter and easy chatter of boys accustomed to appearing on stages around the world seemed to put the lie to her statement. She stared hard at her reflection. Everything was going to be fine. Thanks to all the time she'd spent on TV sets after school once Gem had got into commercials and kids TV, she hadn't come across as a rank amateur when she'd walked through the segment with the producer. And with Sully's help running her lines, she had the script nailed. She could do this.

A woman with a wireless headset looked in at the dressing room door. "Fifteen minutes, Gem. And your co-star's here."

Nerves exploded in her gut. In the mirror, she adjusted the collar of the green velvet UrbanROAD blazer she'd found amongst the clothes Mom had packed. "Electrocuted on power cables—" she mouthed. She looked at Sully's reflection in the mirror. "Is it power lines or power cables?"

"Lines," he said, without consulting the script he'd folded and stuck into his back pocket when they'd left the sanctuary together earlier. "Does it really matter?"

"It has to be perfect." Gem would've delivered no less. She turned to Sully. "You know the script better than me. Maybe you should go out there instead."

He laughed. "To stare transfixed at the camera?" The chair grated as he stood. He crossed to her and put his hands on her shoulders, holding her gaze in the mirror. "I know your confidence has been rattled lately, but you've got this."

She looked at herself, and for a split second, it was Gem's reflection in front of her. She caught his eye again, and he dipped his chin in a brief nod that said he had complete confidence in her. At least one of them did. But despite the clawing doubt, some of the tension left her body. With a bit of luck, she was going to pull this off.

A scritch-scratch sound drew her attention to the doorway. A vulture bigger than a turkey hopped into the room, its talons slipping and skidding on the smooth concrete screed. A woman in the khaki getup of a game ranger followed close behind the huge bird, lobbing what looked like small chunks of meat for it.

Sully beamed at the bird and let go of her shoulders, crossing the room to introduce himself to its handler.

"This is Bryan," the woman said, doling out more meat to the massive bird that bobbed from one taloned foot to the next like a sailor on a storm-tossed deck.

It scooped up the morsel off the ground with a lethal-looking hooked beak.

Becca reversed into the counter that ran beneath the mirrors. She hadn't expected the vulture to be quite so menacing, with its scowling amber eyes and bully-boy walk, its head slung low and swaying between hunched shoulders.

Sully though, was looking at the vulture as if it were a baby love bird he was itching to cuddle. He beckoned Becca closer with the fingers of one hand. "He won't hurt you."

Becca edged forward, keeping Sully between her and the vulture. She leaned to look at it around his comforting bulk. Its body was covered in soft cream feathers, and its long grey curved neck, rising from a feathered ruff, was bare save for a light covering of pale down. It was surprisingly beautiful. Regal. Haughty. Like a—

Becca made a startled squeak as the vulture flicked open vast grey wings big enough to cow an avenging angel and lunged for a piece of meat.

"Easy," Sully said, in his low animal-wrangling voice. "He's not going to hurt you."

Just in case, Becca stepped closer to the safety of Sully's back. "I never realised Cape vultures were so big." Even with his arms stretched wide, Sully wouldn't have been able to match the bird wing-tip to wing-tip. "What if it pecks me?" That beak looked like it could strip muscle off bone in seconds.

Sully drew her out from behind him. "He's not interested in you, princess. As a rule, Cape Griffons prefer their meat dead." He dropped an arm across her shoulders and hugged her to his side. "Just stay calm, don't make any startling moves, and you'll be fine."

Becca leaned into him and took a fortifying breath. She'd been around plenty of wild animals this week—admittedly all in cages or comas. Even with a huge carrion bird galumphing around at her feet, she *would* be fine. For Gem...for Dad...she was going to turn things around.

Outside in the corridor, the choir boys filed past, dressed in their distinctive powder-blue waistcoats with white ruffles at the throat, chatting and joking together as if they were off to the beach. A minute later, applause sounded from the end of the corridor and the headsetted woman stuck her head around the dressing room door. "Places."

Becca's stomach felt like a bucket of worms on a fishing expedition. This was it. Do or die.

The comforting weight of Sully's arm lifted from her shoulders, leaving her feeling strangely bereft. "I'll be in the auditorium," he said. He turned in the doorway and smiled. "Break a leg, princess."

If only.

The walk down the corridor to the closed auditorium door felt at once as slow as if she'd been running the London Marathon, and as quick as if she'd been whisked there on rollerskates. At the door, vulture snapping about behind her, she blew out a stream of air through pursed lips, grappling for control. She rolled her shoulders like a boxer about to enter the ring. *Talk to the camera. Smile. Chin up.* The litany of instructions she'd heard countless times when Gem had been on set jabbered in her head. *You've got this.* And for the moments when she didn't, 'Gem' would simply develop a sudden fear of vultures that would explain away any out-of-character, stilted behaviour.

The woman in the headset opened the door and peeked out into the auditorium. Through the narrow gap, Becca caught a glimpse of the auditorium. The long rows of choir boys ranged on tiered steps. The choir master conducting in front. The packed rows of seats. She gulped, which wasn't easy to do around a heart that was lodged somewhere near her voice box.

The boys, singing with the purity of Benedictine monks, sang the last line of their opening number and the woman at the door looked back over her shoulder, one hand pressing the headset into her ear over the applause.

Becca's heart felt like it had stalled. She was up.

Spotlights snapped on and the woman gestured with her hand—*go, go, go.* Becca took a deep but shaky breath, conjured up her most celebrity-worthy smile and stepped out from behind the choir like she'd rehearsed earlier.

Faces in the audience turned to her like sunflowers tracking the sun. So did the large glinting lenses of the *Carte Blanche* TV cameras. The segment producer signalled to her from the side of the auditorium.

"The Cape vulture." Her voice barked out as if she'd been punched in the stomach. The producer's face contorted in alarm.

A cube of meat sailed past Becca with the vulture in hot pursuit. It trundled out in front of the rows of choristers to a collective murmur from the crowd, buying Becca a moment to collect herself as cellphones lifted and flashes went off.

A door at the back of the auditorium opened and in the glare of light, she saw Sully slip in and move to stand in the shadows along the back wall. Her spirits lifted. Gem always said the trick to looking relaxed on camera was to imagine the camera was a single person, and talk to that one person. She would talk to Sully. She'd forget about the audience and the TV crew and tell Sully about the plight of the Cape vulture.

She cleared her throat. "*Gyps*"—she heard Sully's voice in her head, rolling the Latin words off his tongue when they'd rehearsed her script—"*coprotheres.*" His face was hidden in darkness, but Becca imagined his smile as she aced the scientific name. The thought fanned her courage.

At an impatient gesture from the producer to get on with it, she stepped closer to the vulture, looked into the camera and launched into her lines, imagining Sully mouthing them along with her from his vantage point at the back. "The Cape vulture. South Africa's only endemic vulture, yet sadly, this magnificent, hardworking bird is fighting for its very survival."

She ignored the cubes of meat raining around her, and the eager vulture bobbing and weaving like a cat after a bead of light, and focused instead on hitting the marks she'd been instructed on earlier and trotting out her lines with Gem-like flare. "Cape vulture populations have been in steady decline for decades."

The vulture reached the end of the row of choir boys and the handler wheeled it around with a deftly thrown bit of meat. The bird lumbered after the snack, giving its wings a little flap as it started the journey back towards Becca's side of the auditorium.

"Poisoned by poachers and farmers."

Hop.

"Electrocuted on power lines."

Flap, hop.

Becca stiffened. It had been less intimidating when it had been hopping away from her. "Drowned in reservoirs."

Hop-flap-hop. People in the audience were rising from their seats to snap photos.

"Today, there are fewer than five thousand breeding pairs left, making the Cape vulture critically in need of our help." This was going so well. A few more lines and she was in the clear. "That's why initiatives like the UrbanROAD Cape Vulture Preservation Fund—"

A piece of meat sailed through the air and landed with a wet slap at the toe of her high-heel.

The vulture opened its Grim-Reaper wings and scrambled in pursuit.

Becca took a hasty step backwards, her heart banging about like a pinball. Her stiletto glanced off something hard and her foot came down skew on the floor. She stumbled and caught a flailing hand on something cold and metal positioned behind her. A three-legged light stand.

A *tipping* three-legged light stand.

The heavy stage light clamped to the metal stand nose-dived towards the ground. A thunderous crash rolled through the auditorium as hot glass shattered over the polished floor.

The vulture drew back its curved neck in fright and a prehistoric shriek that sent Becca's teeth on edge erupted from its hooked beak. The handler made a swipe for the bird, but it threw open its immense wings and broke into a lumbering run, beating at the air as it clambered into flight.

In the chaotic seconds that followed, the only intelligible words, once the choir boys added screaming to their repertoire, were the producer's strangled cries of "Cut! Cut!"

21

#TakeTwo

Hiding out in her room, Becca tensed at the knock on her door. It was more a rapping of fingers than a determined application of knuckles, so hopefully whoever it was hadn't come to drag her off to a public execution party. "Hello?"

"It's me."

Sully.

Her pulse leaped even as relief settled through her. She looked at Gem's phone in her hand, at the social media feeds she'd been mindlessly scrolling through ever since they'd got back to the sanctuary and she'd barricaded herself in her room, too drained to even contemplate working off more hours.

The videos and photos posted online from the concert however, couldn't outdo her own vivid and mortifying flash-backs from the afternoon. The vulture thundering into the open grand piano, panicked talons plinking against the piano strings. UrbanROAD banners toppled by massive thrashing wings. Choir boys in tears. Parents in uproar. Sully and the incensed producer yelling into each other's faces. The choir master unleashing his inner diva.

Her stomach convulsed in anguish again and she pressed a fist into her solar plexus. "One second." She dumped the phone on the bedside table, threw back the covers and went to open the door.

Sully stood on the other side with a tray loaded with covered plates and cutlery and a thermos flask. “They told me you didn’t come for dinner.”

She looked at the tray and his thoughtfulness almost brought her to tears. The cold night air gusted in through the door and she pulled the long cardigan she wore over her pyjama top tighter around her body. “Thanks. Though I don’t think I can eat.” Her stomach had other ideas, reacting with a none-too-subtle rumble to the rich meaty smell of whatever was on that covered dinner plate.

Sully held out the tray. “Try. We’ll have to pull a long day tomorrow to catch up the hours you missed today. You’re going to need to keep your strength up.”

The man had unfathomable reserves of perseverance. “What’s the point? I haven’t got much of a career left to save.” It wasn’t like her to be defeatist, but then this week had little to do with being herself.

He shifted the tray onto one forearm. “Your dinner’s getting cold.” He looked past her into the room and raised his eyebrows in question.

She hesitated, hand on the door. She should take the tray and tell him she was tired. Close the door. Let him walk away, like he would most certainly do if he ever found out what she’d done. She left the door open and padded back to her bed.

The door clicked shut behind her and Sully deposited the tray on the bed. He retreated to the door and shoved his hands into the deep pockets of his navy fleece. “Eat something.” He directed a pointed look at the dinner tray. “Doctor’s orders.”

Becca uncovered the dinner plate. Beef stew with carrots and mashed potato. She picked up a fork. Her stomach growled as the thick gravy hit her tongue. She speared another piece of the tender meat and popped it in her mouth. Sully stood like a sentinel, watching her eat. "You're giving me indigestion." She nodded at the end of the bed. "Sit."

He crossed the tiny room. The mattress creaked as he sat, turning to lean against the wall, his legs stretched out across the bed's width.

The muscles in Becca's abdomen tightened. The room, already so small, contracted to the size of a closet, the space consumed by broad shoulders and dark hair and long, muscled legs. Sully on her bed... Probably not one of her better ideas. She stabbed at the stew.

"Jo tells me you've lost the UrbanROAD contract," he said.

She gave a tight nod, her mouth full. It had been inevitable. She swallowed, the food like a golf ball in her throat. "And I'll have to pay for the broken light, and those things cost a small fortune." Add it to her tab.

"You should've told me."

The concern in his eyes was precisely why she hadn't. Tears she'd been holding at bay all afternoon rose stinging into her nose. She sniffed them away. If she cried, Sully would comfort her, and if she ended up folded into his arms, she wouldn't want to leave on Friday. And she had to leave. For Gem.

Sully lowered his head for a second, and when he looked up, his gaze was weighed down with regret. "If I made things worse for you earlier, at the concert, with the producer, I'll go grovel to whoever you need me to apologise to."

She shook her head. "Trust me, I'd ruined everything all on my own before you told that producer to back off."

He didn't seem entirely convinced, his fingers opening and shutting against his jeaned thighs. "You still have *Luxe Life*?"

Becca picked at the stewed beef with her fork, rolling a cube through the gravy. "Only thanks to Alek talking the production company around. He's not the best entertainment agent in the country for nothing. If I finish the hours, *Luxe Life* will honour their promise to reinstate me."

"What do you mean 'if'? You're not thinking of bailing on me again, are you?"

The thought had crossed her mind. Just get in Gem's car and leave before she could engineer another catastrophe to ensure her sister's career was well and truly scuppered. She speared a bit of meat and put it in her mouth to avoid answering him.

He hummed knowingly. "Don't think I won't go after you this time, princess. I won't let you give up again. You're getting your job back, end of story."

The pressure that had been crushing her ribcage since the disastrous concert eased a little. How could she not keep going, in the face of such determination? While there was even still a scrap of Gem's career to be saved—and *Luxe Life* was no scrap—she would keep at it. She reached to touch his leg. "Thank you, Sully. Always saving my butt."

"It's a cute butt." His warm hand flattened hers against his thigh and he leaned in, his eyes locked on hers. A note of anticipation resonated through her, but he dropped his gaze and stole a piece of meat off her plate.

He returned to his position against the wall, chewing, his hand still covering hers. "You're not eating. Need me to feed you?"

Becca pulled her hand from under the warm weight of his and fumbled for her fork, managing only to knock it off the tray onto the ground. Dispensing with manners as he had done, she took a chunk of meat with her fingers and shoved it into her mouth, sucking her fingertips clean with a loud smack. She swallowed and looked at him. "Satisfied, Dr Scott?"

Sully's gaze was heavy as he looked from her mouth to her eyes. "Not even close." His low voice sent heat curling in her chest to pool in her belly. *This all ends on Friday.* She sat up straighter and reached for the thermos. Unscrewing the lid, she breathed in the steam of the hot tea. "I could get used to someone looking after me like this." She'd meant her words to be light-hearted banter but her observation only made her unspeakably sad. The one man she could never have. She capped the thermos and returned it to the tray. "Lucky I'm good at looking after myself."

His eyes grew apologetic again. "I didn't mean to go all alpha male on that producer. I just couldn't stand seeing them all laying into you like that."

"Everyone was a bit overwrought." She smiled wryly. "Even the vulture. Having to be extricated from a musical instrument would have that effect on a bird."

His lips twitched, but he didn't smile. "It's no excuse, but I feel..." His gaze roved over her face, seemingly unable to settle. "I feel protective over you, and, well..." At last his dark eyes found hers. "It's not like before. With Alisha, I mean. I know you can take care of yourself. Insist on it. Hell, you wouldn't even let me save you from imminent drowning. But you're special, princess, and I don't want anything or anyone to hurt you."

Her heart swelled and the strident voice in her head with all its excellent reasons why she had to keep this man at bay fell quiet. She lifted the tray and shoved it haphazardly onto the bedside table. Then she scrambled across the bed, took his shoulders in a fierce grip and kissed him.

He pulled her into his lap so she straddled him and kissed her back. His mouth was hard and demanding on hers until he broke away, breathing hard. "I've been wanting to do that all day."

The roughness of his voice made her blood sing with a delicious anticipation that simmered right down to her toes.

He cupped her butt and pulled her hard against him and she inhaled open mouthed, the ache of her nipples against the fabric of her pyjamas matching the heavy ache between her thighs where her pelvis met his.

Sully left one hand on her butt and twined the other into her hair, bringing her face to his. When he kissed her again, the hungry stroke of his tongue on hers making her squirm with the pleasure-pain of need, a desperation that was only fanned by the feel of his hard denim-restrained arousal against the flimsy material of her pyjama bottoms. She rocked her hips, digging her knees into the bed and rolling against him, groaning into his mouth.

His hand slid from her butt and under the back of her T-shirt. The touch of his palm on her skin was electric, the slide of strong fingers up her spine sending maddening tremors through her.

Her breasts ached for the same attention his fingers were showing her back. She arched against the support of his hands and he abandoned her mouth and kissed his way to the hollow at the base of her throat, the wet heat of his tongue and the scrape of his stubble on her skin sending jags of sensation shooting downwards.

She needed his mouth on her. Everywhere. She rocked into him again, gasping at the need that pulsed between her legs...there especially, she wanted him there. His tongue, his lips, his soft hair brushing her inner thighs. She moaned at the thought and curved back further against his hands.

He shifted her weight so he could bring a hand to her neck and skim his fingers down her throat. "I want you, princess." His dark gaze held hers, his pupils so dilated his eyes gleamed black.

She could only shiver in response.

Without breaking eye contact, Sully swept aside the edges of her cardigan and gathered the neckline of her pyjama top into a fist, as if he were planning to rip it off her. And with the power of that hand, she didn't doubt that he could if he chose to. "Do it," she whispered.

"Don't tempt me." His voice was gravel.

"I'm not attached to the bottoms either." It was time for new PJs anyway.

His growl made her nipples twinge so hard he might as well have had them between his teeth. Which was precisely where she wanted them.

She sighed his name and he released her top and flattened his hand, spanning his fingers wide as he drew his palm in an agonisingly sweet descent over her breast bone until the tips of his thumb and little finger grazed over her nipples through the fabric. Her hips bucked and he pulled her upright to devour her moan with his mouth.

The taste of him...she couldn't get enough. She wrapped her arms around his neck to bring herself as close to him as possible, her thighs squeezing into his waist.

He was vibrating.

Literally.

Against her inner thigh.

Vibrate.

Stop.

Vibrate.

She broke the kiss to pant out, "Your phone."

He groaned and tried to recapture her mouth. "Voicemail."

"It could be important."

"*This* is important." The vibrating ceased. "See? It stopped." He reached for her, and his pocket vibrated to life once more.

Becca raised her eyebrows. "See? Told you it was important."

He growled in frustration and lifted one hip beneath her to fish in his pocket. He removed his phone, checked the display and swiped. "What?"

She'd never heard him answer so brusquely.

He listened. "Where's Clare? Or Lerato?" At the muffled response, his chin dropped to his chest and he sighed. "I'll be there in five." He smacked his phone facedown on the duvet. "Sometimes I hate my job."

"Liar." Becca rolled off his legs and hopped off the bed. With shaking hands, she tucked her cardigan around her. "Thanks for bringing me dinner."

His smile was slow and sincere. "The pleasure was mine, princess." He rose from the bed and rearranged the front of his jeans with one hand. "And dessert was rather good too."

She laughed and pushed him towards the door. "Go. They need you."

The gust of night air through the open door was an icy caress on her heated skin. She filled her lungs with the cold, tamping down the fire he'd fanned in her. Tomorrow she had to do a better job of resisting him.

He stepped outside and zipped his fleece to his throat. Then he leaned in and planted a kiss on her forehead. "Next time, it's no dogs *and* no phones," he said, with his lips against her skin, "Third time lucky."

She shivered and wished she could blame it on the cold.

22

#Q&A

Thursday unfolded—mercifully—without drama. Just cleaning cages. Filling hungry mouths. Bandaging the walking, crawling, flapping wounded. Now, while Sully finished some long-neglected paperwork in his consult room, Becca busied herself with one extra job she'd managed to shoehorn into the day: bottle-washing in the clinic scullery. That made almost eleven more hours in the bag. Another eight tomorrow and she was good to go. *Had to go.* But she didn't want to think about that right now.

Two warm hands took her by the hips and Becca jumped and dropped the bottle brush into the soapy water in the sink.

"It's after six." Sully's affectionate voice so close to her ear lifted the hair at her nape. "Time to call it a day, princess."

"I'm almost done." A shiver travelled up her back as Sully spanned his hands wide and his fingers found the gaps between her jeans and the hem of her pistachio wrap top. For a second, she sank into the blissful sensation of skin on skin, but then the bang of a cage door somewhere reminded her that despite the hour, there were still people about. And she could not let this go anywhere, much as every fragment of her being might want it. She pushed at his hands with her wet palms. "Behave."

He tightened his grip on her hips and coaxed her back against him "Almost everyone's gone home already."

His mouth was against her neck. She squeezed shut her eyes and summoned her self-control. "Do you want to end up all over the internet again?" And become a laughing stock when 'Gem' left town and ghosted him publicly? She couldn't let that happen to him. He was a good, kind, sensitive man and it wasn't his fault he'd crossed paths with a deceiving liar like her.

He kissed her quickly beneath one ear and removed his hands. "Move over." He nudged her along the sink's edge with his hip and began emptying and stacking the clean bottles that were soaking in a solution of disinfectant in the adjacent sink.

Nerves still thrumming, Becca retrieved the bottle brush and whisked it about inside the last of the dirty feeding bottles. She popped the bottle into the disinfectant. "You'll be pleased to know that you only have to put up with me for eight more hours tomorrow."

"And why exactly would that make me pleased?"

The tenderness in his voice made her want to lean over and rest her head on his shoulder, but she resisted the urge to touch him, an urge she'd been resisting all day. She let out the dirty water and wiped her pruned hands on her jeans. "What time does dinner end in the dining hall?"

Sully placed the last clean bottle on the draining board and turned to her, resting one hip on the edge of the sink. "Have dinner with me tonight. My place. You can test out my skills in the kitchen."

And in other rooms, promised the caress of his eyes.

She found a cloth beside the sink and set about running it over the wet surfaces. "Thanks, but I don't much feel like fried egg for dinner."

He smiled a devilish smile. "I can do way more than fry an egg."

"Oh really?" She couldn't resist his grin and matched it with her own. "Such as?"

"Well, for starters…" He closed the small gap between them, hooked a finger through a loop of her jeans and kissed her.

A day's worth of concerted resistance fell away at the stroke of his tongue over her lower lip. Becca hummed with pleasure and parted her lips, breathing in the smell of his skin over the disinfectant that hung in the air. His mouth felt like heaven.

Quick footsteps in the corridor beyond the scullery made her stiffen.

"Sully?"

Becca whirled away from him as Clare appeared in the doorway.

Clare scanned the room with the thoroughness of a sniffer dog at the luggage conveyor assigned to a flight from Colombia. "What're you guys doing?"

Leaning now with his butt against the sink and his legs crossed casually at the ankles, Sully handed the wet bottle brush to Becca, his gaze catching hers and dropping quickly to her mouth before he looked at Clare. "The usual housekeeping. We're done though."

"Good. Because we should leave." The cheery skip in Clare's voice was at odds with the sharpness of her gaze. "My car or yours?"

Sully looked confused. "Where're we going?"

Clare's smile grew taut. "The Brewhouse? It's quiz night finals."

Sully's shoulders sagged. "That's tonight?" He pushed a hand through his hair. "It completely slipped my mind."

Clare's eyes sought Becca's, the blame in them explicit. She looked back at Sully. "We have to annihilate the Beer Boyz, or we'll never hear the end of their gloating."

"I'm not up to it tonight."

Clare pouted at him. "You can't ditch us. You're our only guy and you know they always have at least one rugby question. So your car or mine?"

He gave a deep sigh. "I'll meet you there. I need to go home first to feed my dogs."

Clare's ponytail licked around her jaw as she smiled, all teeth, and bounced on the balls of her feet. "Awesome." She patted the door jamb as she stepped into the corridor. "Night, Gem. See you tomorrow for your last day. Bet you're excited to be seeing the back of us."

Becca smiled and hung up the wet cloth over the sink's edge. She wiped her damp hands on her jeans. "I'll see you tomorrow then."

Clare's footsteps were still receding when Sully caught Becca by a belt loop again. "I seem to remember you know some weird trivia, princess. Mind like a sponge, you said."

Becca raised a cautioning finger and laughed. "Don't even go there." She attempted to back away from him but didn't get very far with his finger hooked tight to the loop. "I'm going to eat dinner and go to bed."

With a quick tug on the loop, he brought her shuffling back to him until her legs were flush against his. "You can still do both those things. Just with a short diversion in between."

Judging from the turnout, quiz night was a big deal in Winterberg. The Brewhouse was bursting at the seams, noisy with the chatter and clatter of people socialising and eating. Becca slipped into Sully's slipstream as he made his way past the cramped tables and crowded booths, passing a bar counter where bartenders pulled glasses of foam-topped beer from polished draught beer taps.

They stopped at a booth where Clare sat engrossed behind a menu. Clare looked up and directed a full-toothed smile at Sully, before her gaze shifted sideways and she spotted Becca.

Her smile extinguished. "Gem. You came too." Clare cracked out the teeth again, then directed her attention to Sully. She motioned to a glass and a bottle of beer on the table and patted the bench next to her. "I ordered you a beer already."

He shrugged out of his jacket and tossed it over the back of the bench. "Thanks." With a hand on the small of her back, he ushered Becca in at the bench opposite Clare and slid in after her, either ignoring or not noticing the way the skin around Clare's eyes crimped in veiled frustration. He reached across the table for the beer, passing on the glass.

A waitress appeared and they ordered more drinks and a pub basket of batter-dipped nibbly things for them to share.

"Sorry I'm late." A jovial voice cut through the din, and Becca looked to see a short woman in her early forties beside their booth. Dr Nomsa Gumede, the vet Becca had met at the town practice. "Had an emergency perforated gut."

Sully stood and hugged Nomsa. "We only just got here ourselves. I hear our Scottie patient is home."

"Hopefully he'll think twice about throwing himself into dams again." Nomsa looked over at Becca and smiled. "Nice to see you again, Gem. My wife'll be glad you're here. She's been saying all week she wanted to stop round at the sanctuary, but work's been crazy."

Another journalist?

Before Nomsa could explain further, two arms wrapped around her from behind.

"I hope you ordered me a glass of wine," said a woman's ebullient voice, "because I need one after the day I've had."

Nomsa looked back over her shoulder. "Guess who's in our quiz team tonight?"

A face framed by a halo of black curls popped around Nomsa's side and Becca's stomach nose-dived into her shoes. No more navy blue school tunic and blazer, and a tattoo of a koi fish on her wrist that would never have passed uniform inspection. But there was no question: that was definitely Livhu.

"Gemmie!" Livhu, dressed in the smart pants and branded jacket of someone in sales or customer service, threw her arms wide.

Mouth agape, Becca stared at the one person in town who knew enough about the Stratton sisters to bust them. The one friend from their high-school days who could always tell which Stratton twin was which.

Now would be a good time to develop a migraine and take an Uber back to the sanctuary. Flee to the loos and escape through a stall window like people were always doing in the movies. Instead she stood and waited while Sully left the bench, then she side-shuffled out and threw her arms around Gem's old friend like her sister would have. "Livhu! Long time!"

Livhu was bouncing up and down in the bear-hug like they were eighteen again. "God, it's been years!"

"Absolute eons!" Becca extricated herself and placed a steadying hand on the table. Was a decade long enough to dull Livhu's uncanny ability to tell one twin from the other? Becca's heart pounded and yet for all its efforts, it didn't seem to be pumping any blood around her body. Black spots were beginning to dance before her eyes. "I'm sure I've changed a ton since you last saw me."

A broad smile cleaved Livhu's face and she held Becca away from her by the shoulders and looked at her. "You're still as gorgeous as ever, Gemmie!"

Becca laughed with dizzy relief and flopped back onto the bench. Inspection passed. Now to make a convincing-enough show of being Gem for the rest of the evening.

She scooted over to make room for Sully, while Livhu dropped in across from them next to Clare with Nomsa beside her.

"How do you two know each other?" Sully asked, reclaiming his beer.

"We were friends at high school." Livhu held up two crossed fingers. "We were like this, weren't we, Gemmie?"

Becca's answering grin felt brittle. "Total BFFs."

Sully touched her leg. "You okay? You look pale."

"It's stuffy in here."

He handed her his beer. "Have some."

She took a long sip before returning the bottle to his hand, her fingers brushing his. The slightest touch could make her insides flip. She looked up in time to catch the expression that passed between Livhu and Clare: the lift of Livhu's eyebrows, and the flash of jealous irritation in Clare's eyes.

Becca shifted deeper into the booth, putting more space between her and Sully. She glanced around the pub to see if anyone else was watching them, phone raised for an opportunistic photo. Nothing. She widened the gap between them a little more, just in case.

"So tell me all your news." Livhu's eyes skipped to Sully, then back to Becca. "Have you and Mandla really ended it?"

The waitress appeared at the end of the table and offloaded their orders. Becca reached for her glass of white wine. "Forget my life. You can read about it online. What about you? What are you up to these days? Did you ever open up that boutique you were always talking about at school?" Becca slurped at her wineglass.

Nomsa nudged her partner and raised her brows. "A boutique?"

Livhu chuckled. "Teenage dreams. No, I'm a drug rep for an animal pharmaceutical company."

"Gosh. Quite the change." Becca took another gulp of wine. *Slow down.* She had to keep a clear head.

"Wouldn't you rather have tequila, Gemmie?" Clare asked, all innocence, mimicking Livhu's nickname for her sister.

Sully snagged a buffalo wing from the pub basket. "Play nice, Clare."

Clare reddened under his scrutiny.

Livhu nudged Clare with her shoulder. "You should've seen us at high school. The parties we used to have!"

Becca's hand tensed on the stem of her glass. "I'm sure no one wants to hear stories about us in high school, Livhu."

Clare's toothy smile matched the predatory glint in her eye. "I do."

Livhu put her elbows on the table and leaned in. "Gem used to play this drinking game with the guys that involved a bottle of tequila, a deck of cards..."

Becca folded a French fry into her mouth, then slipped a hand behind her neck to work the muscles.

"...and an Energizer battery."

Sully clunked his bottle on the table and Livhu stopped abruptly. "Did you ever manage to get me that out-of-stock midazolam?"

Livhu looked at him in confusion, as if she were mentally changing lanes. "That came in two weeks ago. I delivered it myself."

"Ah." Sully lifted his beer to his lips and took a contemplative sip. "Must have missed it in the drug cupboard. Nomsa, what happened with that horse you were treating at the De Langes' place?"

Becca dropped her hand below the table and squeezed Sully's thigh in thanks. He swung out his leg to touch hers and his lips ticked upwards around the mouth of his bottle as he took another sip of beer.

While Nomsa ran through the horse's treatment with Sully, Livhu took a French fry and looked at Becca with her nose wrinkled. "How are you surviving at the sanctuary? The stuff vets get up to can be super disgusting."

Becca shrugged and gave the sort of answer Gem would've given. "It's pretty gross."

Livhu shuddered theatrically. "I have no idea how you're coping, babes."

"Only barely, as it turns out."

"Bull." Sully had stopped talking to Nomsa and was listening to their conversation. "Of course she's coping. She's tough."

Becca smiled at his praise, but just so she didn't come across all GI-Jane-y, she flapped her chipped manicure before Livhu's face. "Pity my nail polish isn't as tough. And don't even look at my cuticles."

Sully turned slightly in his seat so he could see her better. "You shouldn't downplay what you've done. You've worked hard this week." He spoke to Livhu. "She even helped me stitch up a kudu."

Wineglass lifted to her lips, Livhu snorted explosively and pressed her fingers to her nose. "She did what?"

Oh. My. God.

Becca groaned inwardly and snatched blindly at the basket for a crumbed chicken strip. "It was a tiny flesh wound," she said to Livhu, motioning nonchalance with the chicken strip.

Sully scoffed. "Its flank was torn open on a fence. There was blood all over."

"So do you ever hear from the rest of the gang, Livs? Life's so hectic, I've been really bad with keeping in touch with everyone." Becca popped the chicken strip into her mouth.

Livhu was dabbing at her face with a paper serviette that Nomsa had handed her, her eyes watering from the alcohol she'd inhaled through her nasal passages. She looked at Becca, then turned her attention to Sully. "Are we talking about the same Gem Stratton? Because my Gem was seriously the most squeamish person you'd ever meet."

"God, I still am," Becca said, picking up another chicken strip and gesticulating with it. "I totally almost barfed."

"You did?" Sully said, confused. "But you seemed fine with it."

"With blood? Gem?" Livhu laughed. "You're lucky she didn't faint on you. Her boyfriend in Grade Eleven got his nose mashed in during a rugby match and the paramedics almost had to stretcher *her* off instead of him."

Shit! "I'm way less dramatic these days," she said, darting her eyes to Sully while fumbling in the basket for another piece of crumbed chicken.

Livhu sobered and took a sip of her wine. "I guess we all grow up eventually."

Becca nodded sagely and bit into the chicken piece.

"I mean, if this were ten years ago," Livhu continued, "no ways would you even be sitting here. You'd have switched with Becca for sure."

A morsel of chicken relocated itself with force into Becca's lungs. She coughed violently and pounded on her breastbone, her eyes watering. "We were such idiots back then," she spluttered, taking a gulp of beer from the bottle Sully held out to her. This conversation was heading south fast. She looked between Livhu and Nomsa. "So how did you two meet?"

"What's a switch?" Clare said.

Could we not, Clare? "Teenage silliness," Becca said. "Does anyone else want a chicken strip?" She held up the basket, but all eyes were now on Gem's loose-lipped friend.

Livhu chortled. "Gem and Becca would switch places with each other, usually whenever Gem wanted to get out of something."

Becca's blood roared through her veins and her head felt hot and giddy as if she might pass out. If it would shut Livhu up, bring it on.

"Who's Becca?" Clare said.

"Gem's identical twin sister."

"Hold on. You're an identical twin?" Clare looked at Becca with an expression that was part shock, part disgust, her top lip slightly curled as if to say she couldn't believe there were two of these bitches on the planet.

Livhu nodded. "Double trouble."

Sully was watching Becca intently, his body turned in to her, one elbow resting on the bench's backrest. "You told me you didn't switch places with your sister."

Livhu guffawed the big laugh that Becca remembered from their school days. "They did it all the time. It was hilarious!"

Becca feigned calm and rummaged about in the rapidly emptying basket of fried nibbles. "We did all sorts of stupid things at school." Onion ring. She waved it at the table. "It was a long time ago." She slotted the entire onion ring into her mouth to ward off further speech.

"Where is your sister now?" Clare said. "What does she do? I've never read about her online."

Mouth full, Becca mumbled about concierges in London until an amplified tap-tap-tap cut into the music that played over the Brewhouse speakers. Swallowing the onion ring in a painful gulp, Becca looked in the direction of the bar, where a short, balding man stood with a cordless microphone. "Looks like we're about to get started," she said, swivelling her body away from Clare to face the man.

"But—" said Clare.

"Welcome everyone!" The man's voice boomed over the speakers. "Are you ready for the finals of the Brewhouse Winter Series Quiz?"

A cheer went up, and Becca sent up a silent prayer of gratitude. For the second time that night, Sully asked her if she was okay. She smoothed her hands down her jeaned thighs and huffed a quick breath. "I'm just antsy. My present is full of enough newsworthy stories without adding my past to it."

Sully's hand found hers under the table. His fingers and palm were cold from the beer bottle, making her skin tingle. He gave her a reassuring squeeze and she returned the pressure.

"Want to get out of here?" he asked, close to her ear. "I'll say I'm too tired to stay, which wouldn't be a lie."

She shook her head. "That would really give them something to talk about."

He conceded the point with a tip of his head, then his hand abandoned hers and he sat back, hand once more on his beer.

"Okay, settle down all of you." The quizmaster consulted his phone. "First question. Who discovered penicillin?"

"Easy," Livhu and Clare chorused in whispered tones. "Alexander Fleming."

Clare wrote the answer on the quiz sheet they'd been handed earlier. "We can win this, guys. I know we can."

"So what's it like being famous, Gemmie?" Livhu put her elbows on the table and leaned in expectantly, chin propped on her fists. "I always said you'd be the one who'd crack it."

"Quiz now, interrogation later," Sully said. "We need to focus. This is the finals and we have a score to settle."

Clare beamed at him in surprise. "Finally someone who takes this as seriously as I do!"

Under the table, Becca nudged his foot in another show of silent thanks. He side-eyed her and returned the gesture.

For the next hour or so, the quizmaster's questions kept Livhu at bay. How long do elephants gestate? Who won the last FIFA World Cup? Which African state is the largest? Eventually, the quizmaster consulted his phone and bellowed, "And here's our final question, ladies and gents! What is the national animal of Scotland?"

Livhu sat back on the bench and motioned to her spouse. "Animal questions are yours, babe."

Nomsa shrugged. "How would I know? A haggis?"

Sully snickered. "Scottish terrier?"

"It's a unicorn."

The whole team snickered then.

"I'm not joking," Becca said. "Scotland's national animal is a unicorn."

Four sets of eyes stared at Becca.

Clare snorted. "You sure you don't mean the Loch Ness Monster, Gem?"

Becca lowered her chin and looked at Clare. "Trust me, it's a unicorn. I know because I once had to organise a cake shaped like a unicorn for a Saint Andrew's Day party. That's Scotland's national day."

Sully lifted his empty beer bottle in salute. "Told you that weird trivia of yours would come in handy, princess."

Clare scowled. "So now you're a party organiser too?"

Becca held her breath at the top of an inhale. She'd walked right into that one. "We were doing a Scottish-themed episode on *Luxe Life* and they asked me to sort out the cake."

"Write it down, Clare." Sully waved his hand at the answer sheet. "I'm tired. I want to go home."

The wait staff gathered up the question sheets and Becca excused herself to go to the loo. Now that quiz time was over, interrogation time might start again. When she finally returned to the booth, Clare was poring over the team's marked answer sheet.

"Seventeen out of twenty." She scowled at Becca. "You got the Westlife question wrong, Gem."

She'd been worried she might. Boy bands had been Gem's thing, not hers.

Livhu gave her a surprised look. "But you knew everything Westlife, Gemmie."

"Not tonight she didn't," Clare grumbled.

"I told you, high school was a long time ago," Becca said, raising her voice over the pub's din and the pounding of her heart. "And I did get the unicorn one right for you." She stabbed a finger at the sheet.

Sully tipped his head as he read the answer sheet upside down. "I also got one wrong. Algeria's the biggest country in Africa, not Sudan." Sully yawned expansively then and took out his wallet. He tossed a few bank notes on the table. "Guys, I'm beat." He picked up his jacket. "Thanks for a great evening, but I'm off."

The microphone tap-tapped again. "And now, with a score of seventeen out of twenty..."

Clare's eyes widened to saucers. "Oh my God, that's us. We did it! We won!" Her voice was a strangled squeak.

"We have a tie between the Beer Boyz and the Village Vets! Which means..."

The crowd whooped. "Tie break!"

Sully stood abruptly and Clare held up both hands like a traffic cop stepping from behind a bush at a road block. "You can't go now! It's the tie break."

"Which could go on for ages," he said. "Give you a lift, Gem?"

The look Clare shot Becca as she slid from the booth promised that if Clare had happened to have a unicorn horn on hand, she'd have liked to shove it somewhere particularly painful.

23

#TruthBeTold

The Ranger pulled into the sanctuary's visitor parking, the broad headlight beams washing over Gem's parked car. Becca unclipped her seat belt and had her hand on the door release before the bakkie drew to a full halt.

"I'm sorry to bail on you so early." Her eyes avoided Sully's. "Coffee would've been great, but..." The only coffee that would've passed their lips would've been tomorrow morning, standing in his kitchen, with guilt shredding her insides to ribbons. It was a mistake to even think about what could've been. They had no future. This would be a one-night stand, at best. Probably an insanely hot one-night stand, but that would only make it harder to say goodbye.

"You've had a busy day. I get it." Sully's easy smile said he had no hard feelings, but he shifted in his seat as if other parts of him weren't quite as relaxed about having the evening cut short. He engaged the handbrake and killed the engine. "Might as well check on things at the centre while I'm here."

Becca climbed from the bakkie and shut the passenger door. Sully was waiting for her and together they crossed the grass to where the path began. He slowed to let her step onto the concrete track ahead of him, and for the sweetest moment, his fingers found the small of her back through her jacket, sending shivers of anticipation through her. Then he fell in beside her on the path.

She hated that she noticed how he was shortening his stride to match hers. Worse, that it made her feel like she meant something to him. But the worst was that she loved that feeling. "You think we won the quiz?"

He shrugged and made a disinterested grunt.

"You're not even slightly curious to know whether you beat your archrivals?"

Sully's sideways glance gave her goosebumps. "Not even remotely."

Becca gulped. His hand was so close to hers, his arm swaying loosely at his side as they walked. If she extended her fingers a fraction— She angled away, hugging the outside of the path.

But he was still too close, and every cell in her body seemed acutely, almost painfully attuned to him. The tantalising hints of his aftershave. The slight swing of his shoulders. The way his heavy boots scuffed on the pathway. She fumbled for something to fill the electric silence between them. "Livhu and Nomsa seem like a nice couple."

"They are." Without breaking stride, he turned a questioning look on her. "Did you and your sister really switch places like she said?"

Up shot her heart rate. She evaded his gaze, taking an excessive interest in the dark garden beds beyond the pathway lights. "We did, but not as often as Livhu made out. It's really hard to keep a switch going without someone giving away the game. But it was a fun prank."

"Did you ever do it to your boyfriends?" His fingers played with the bracelets on his wrist.

She turned her head to him and stuck out her tongue in disgust. "I draw the line at kissing my sister's boyfriends."

"Good." A quick glance at her and then back to the path. "Because I don't like to share."

Every fibre in her drew tight. If she didn't make a break for her room now, she was going to grab him by the collar of his fleece and manhandle him into the nearest bush.

They'd reached the split in the path where it branched away from the rehab centre to the rest of the sanctuary's buildings. She clapped her hands. "Oh well. Busy day tomorrow." She yawned for emphasis. "I'd better get some sleep." *Alone.* There could be no repeat of what had happened in her room last night, no matter what the insistent throb between her legs said.

"I'll see you at seven then."

"Yep. Bright and early." Her tongue darted out to wet her bottom lip and his gaze followed the movement before he lifted his eyes to hers.

Something in her leaped at the wild, almost feral need she saw in that gaze. *Walk away.* She hadn't noticed him move closer, but the space between them had narrowed to where she could almost feel the heat coming off his body. "Sleep tight."

He swallowed so hard she could hear it over the soft buzz of crickets hidden in the dark vegetation. His hands were fists at his side, as if he were physically restraining himself from reaching for her. He stepped back onto the grass to let her pass. "Same." It was more a croak than a word.

"And thanks for the lift." *Could you draw it out any longer, woman?*

The low hoot of an owl floated through the night air, a soft questioning note followed by a second more haunting one. Becca paused and peered towards the sound.

"Spotted eagle owl," Sully said.

"You can tell from the call?"

"The double hoot, that's the male. He's calling for his mate." Sully's gaze felt like a physical touch before he turned and scanned the dark gardens. Another call came, lonely and plaintive. Sully looked back at her. "Have you seen a spotted eagle owl before?"

She shook her head and he gestured for her to follow him.

She hesitated.

He stopped after a few paces and turned back. "You okay?"

Every minute alone with him was another minute of willpower she had to dredge up from a rapidly diminishing pool of resolve. "I hope it's not as big as that vulture was."

He smiled. "Not quite. And I'll beat it off if it decides you look tasty."

There was an enigmatic look in his eye that she chose not to dissect. She followed him up the path towards the block that housed the volunteers.

The owl called again to his missing mate and Sully veered off the path onto the lawn. "There he is." Sully stopped and pointed directly up from Becca's room to the roof two storeys above. A large shape inspected them from the ridge, prominent ear tufts making the owl look like a feathered Batman against the night sky.

And then a call drifted from the trees near the building. A quick double hoot, sharper and more urgent than the male's, followed by a drawn-out third note. A shape sailed from the top branches and swept in complete silence over their heads to land on the roof's lower edge.

"And there she is." Sully's voice was soft, almost reverent. He tipped back his head, hands buried deep in his jacket pockets, and peered up at the owl where she sat bathed in the glow of the building's outside lights. "Hey, beautiful." The eagle owl's head swivelled and two wide golden discs around huge pupils looked down at him. "Are you keeping my rat population in check?"

The golden eyes stared, unblinking.

"Such a gorgeous girl."

Becca knew he was talking to the owl, but that didn't seem to make any difference to her body's reaction. The low resonance of his voice lit up every nerve-ending and stoked a deep swell of need in her. There was something about all that gentleness, wrapped up in such obvious, tethered strength that made her toes scrunch in her shoes. That made her yearn to fit herself against his chest and be enfolded in his strong arms.

She shoved trembling hands into the back pockets of her jeans. Her fingers closed on her room key. She pulled it out and jangled it. The owl's head jerked to follow the sound, and Sully looked around. "I'd better go," Becca said.

Sully took her hand, trapping the key between their palms. "Don't."

"I have to."

His eyes were as wide and focused as the owl's, as if he feared she'd dash off to her room if he dared to blink. "Do I get a good-night kiss?"

Her gaze flitted to his lips and back. "Sully, we shouldn't do this. We're setting ourselves up for hurt. This all ends tomorrow." A pain stabbed through her chest and she fixed her gaze on his hand, willing him to let her go.

"It doesn't have to."

She didn't bother replying. It did have to. Her lies had ensured that. "We have to be sensible, Sully."

"What if I don't want to be?"

"It's not a choice. It's inevitable. I leave tomorrow."

"We'll figure something out."

Her laugh was like glass cracking. "Why would you even want to?"

His brow furrowed. "Seriously?"

She avoided his gaze, looking instead at the eagle owl perched like a gargoyle above the downpipe. "I've caused so much hassle this week."

"And yet here I am, seconds away from pulling you into my arms and never letting you go."

She wanted that too, so much it hurt thinking about it. But imagining a future with him was an exercise in futility, not to mention self-torture. "You don't even know who I am."

"I know you really hate marmalade."

She choked on a snatch of laughter, her throat thickening with unwelcome tears. "Ah, well, that's me summed up in a nutshell." She spun away from him then, but his hold on her hand stopped her short, pulling her arm out straight behind her. She gave a half-hearted tug. "Let me go, Sully."

"I don't think I can, princess."

She heard his footfall in the grass at her back. His hand fell away from hers, and he slipped his arm lightly around her shoulders, his hold so loose and tentative she knew she had only to step forward and he would let her walk away. Out of his life forever, which was the only place she deserved to be.

Her feet hesitated. Her chin dipped until it touched his arm. A little more and she'd be able to press her lips to his skin. To stick out her tongue and taste him.

He eased her against his chest and she felt the rough slide of his stubbled cheek across her hair until he stopped with his mouth at her ear. "From the second you locked eyes with me through that cell door, princess, you've confounded me." His voice was soft and low with a dark sensual thrum to it that made Becca's thighs clench. "I've watched you all week, hopelessly out of your depth, falling on your arse more times than I can count, and you just get up and carry on. There I was all geared up to keep disliking you, only to find I'd completely misjudged you."

He turned his face into her neck and hugged her close, filling his lungs as he did. He cleared her hair with a scrape of his chin so he could kiss her bare neck, the feel of rough stubble on her skin making her eyes drift shut and a traitorous whimper escape her lips. "In case you haven't noticed, I like you, princess. You're strong and resourceful and sincere and genuine"—he kissed her behind her ear, sending sparks of anticipation over her skin—"and you feel so good in my arms."

His words twined around her heart and slipped in under the fortifications she'd been diligently manning all day. Instead of fixing things, all she'd done all week was mess up. And yet somehow—seemingly impossibly—he still liked her. Not for what she'd done for him, but for who she was. This man filled her soul right up to the brim. And in return she was lying to him.

She wasn't genuine at all. She was a liar. A fraud. Caustic guilt dug its claws into her and she stiffened, her back growing rigid, her shoulders setting like concrete. "It's getting late."

The circle of Sully's arms loosened, but he didn't immediately let her step away. Instead he slid his hands onto her upper arms and turned her to face him. "Tomorrow really doesn't have to mean goodbye, princess."

She looked up into eyes so warm with trust that her gut twisted. All she could do was shake her head, her throat thick with approaching tears.

Sully bent his knees until his eyes were level with hers. "I drove a six-hundred-kilometre round trip the other day, and that was for a bunch of pangolins. And I like you a whole lot more than those pangolins."

The stab of pain in the region of her chest made her hunch her shoulders. He was making this pure agony. "It's too difficult."

"Anything worth having is usually difficult to get."

Difficult, yes. But this was impossible. She pushed against his chest, a tangled panic of guilt holding her conscience in a stranglehold. "Let's just walk away from whatever this is." Her voice was a scratching rasp.

"Walking away isn't my strong suit," he said, tipping his head forward until it came to rest against hers. "But okay." He lifted his head and his hands fell away from her arms. "I won't push you into something you don't want."

Bereft. He looked— "I do want it," she said, one hand grabbing for him on its own volition. She snatched it back. *Just let him walk away!*

He shoved a hand up to fist in his hair. "Then I don't understand. Why won't you at least—"

"I'm not Gem!" Becca slapped both hands over her mouth, but it was too late. The words were out, and from the way Sully had stilled, they were careening about inside his brain punching holes in all the good feelings he'd just recently confessed about her.

"What do you mean you're not Gem?" His eyes narrowed in concentration, as if he were trying to formulate a sentence in a foreign language. And then his expression cleared. Hardened. "You...switched?"

For a fleeting moment, Becca rolled a lie about on her tongue. But she couldn't deceive him anymore. Wouldn't. She nodded.

"You're Becca."

Another nod. "I'm so sorry." She took a stuttering breath. "Nobody was meant to get hurt by this. I never for a minute expected"—she gestured at him with a wave of her hand—"you." She hitched a laugh, curling trembling fingers around her throat as she stifled the urge to reach for him. "A week ago you were the most impossibly annoying man I'd ever met, and now..." Her hand slipped from her throat as she crossed her arms around her chest, squeezing the soft flesh of her arms in a desperate attempt to keep hot tears from spilling over.

Sully looked as if she'd just slapped him. Hard. "You're Becca." He exhaled a *Fuck*, drawing the word out until his breath ran out.

When he didn't move for several seconds, she reached for him, but he threw up his hands as if to fend her off. "Just..."—he took a step back—"give me a moment to process this." One hand raked back through his hair. "You're the concierge. From London."

"Yes."

He scrubbed a big hand over his features. "And you've been lying to me all week."

Another *yes*, even softer than the first. She looked down at her feet, which were blurry through a sudden sheen of tears. "I'm so sorry, Sully. I never meant to deceive you. Well, I did, obviously. That was the plan. Though not you specifically. Everyone." She exhaled hard. "This is coming out all wrong. I just mean I expected to work the hours and leave, with no one any the wiser or worse off. Falling for you was never part of the plan."

Her breath caught and she glanced away. She hadn't meant to say that. Hadn't even realised how deep her feelings for him had become until now. She looked back to find him watching her, his expression unreadable. "I didn't want to lie, but my mom was so worried about Gem. All the hatred and trolling and death threats broke her, Sully. How could I not agree to help her? She's my sister. And it wasn't all lies." Her fingers dug harder into her arms. "For what it's worth, I hated lying to you. Although most of it wasn't lies. Not about the things that mattered, anyway. I've made such a tit of things precisely because every time I tried to be Gem, I just ended up being myself."

His eyes were hard. Unyielding.

Say something. Please.

The first tear streaked like fire down her cold cheek. A second was close behind. Then a third. She stepped backward. "I'll go and pack my things." She spun, nearly tripping over her feet, and broke into a jog across the lawn.

He didn't come after her, which both relieved and devastated her.

At her door, she stabbed the key blindly at the lock until at last it slid home and she fell into the room. She shut the door and leaned against it, her chest rising and falling in a panicked rhythm. What the hell had she done? She had one job this week and she'd blown it, and not even by accident. Wilfully. She'd just opened her big mouth and spewed out the entire sordid deception. And now she'd hurt her whole family. And what felt even worse right now, she'd hurt Sully.

She went down on the floor to pull out Gem's suitcase that was stowed under the bed. A short, curt knock at the door brought her bolting upright on her knees, her heart drumming madly in her chest.

She rose and crossed to the door, taking a deep breath before she opened it, though it did nothing to settle the churning riot inside her.

Sully stood outside, hands buried in his jacket pockets, shoulders hunched as if against the cold, but the hard set of his jaw told her what was really responsible for the rigid lines of his body.

His eyes locked on hers and she had to steel herself to not step backward into the room and bang the door shut, dragging the wardrobe across it to keep him out.

"Did I say I wanted you to leave?" he said.

She hugged herself to keep from splintering apart. "You didn't have to."

He broke eye contact, his gaze turning distracted as he looked away up the deserted corridor outside the rooms. His jaw worked as if he were testing out words before committing them to speech. When his eyes met hers again, they were hooded and troubled. "This whole week..." He shook his head as if he couldn't quite accept it.

She let her gaze drop to the floor between them, guilt and regret tipping her back to the edge of tears. "I'm so sorry. Honestly." Not that he'd ever believe that honesty was a quality she possessed.

"It explains a lot though," he said. "Why I could go from wanting to strangle Gem Stratton to wanting to kiss the hell out of her."

Her eyes met his and the unexpected heat in his gaze made her swallow hard. This is what she could have had if things had been different.

He considered her in silence for a moment. "Why did you tell me the truth? Why didn't you just keep up the ruse until tomorrow and walk away?"

She lifted one shoulder. "You opened your heart to me and in return, I pushed you away. And then it just came out."

He huffed, his breath white in the cold air, and he looked away, his brow furrowing as if he were wrangling with something. When he looked back at her, his gaze was like flint. "I don't like being lied to, princess. Considering my past, I think you can understand that."

Unable to hold his gaze any longer, she dropped her eyes to his chest. Rolling her bottom lip inwards, she bit down with her top teeth, focusing on the sharp pain in her lip rather than the pain that filled her heart.

“Look at me,” he said.

Reluctant, she obeyed, her lip still caught between her teeth.

Hands still buried in his pockets, he leaned almost imperceptibly towards her. “But while I hate being deceived, I would also do almost anything to protect the people I love.” His gaze was a physical force holding her in place. “Did you mean it when you said you were falling for me? Or was that one of the lies?”

How she wished it had been. Wished she’d never been drawn to this man who made her feel so alive. So wanted. She shook her head. “It wasn’t a lie,” she said, her voice a croak. “Though it’s unlikely you’ll trust anything I say now.”

“Perhaps this is a time when actions would speak louder than words,” he said, his voice a low rumble she could almost feel in her chest.

Her breath caught and a flash of need arced through her, hot and desperate. She licked her bottom lip. He wanted her to show him how she felt?

He straightened his arms, bracing his hands deeper into his pockets. His eyes, dark and magnetic, seemed to reel her in.

Becca hesitated on the threshold, then took a small step towards him. She swallowed hard and flattened her palms against her thighs to control the trembling in her hands.

Another step closer. She could feel the energy coiled in him, could almost sense the vibration in the air around him of leashed power.

She ran her tongue over her lips and he stiffened and breathed in slowly, the rising of his broad chest his only movement. She lifted her hands and dropped them carefully onto his shoulders, as if the slightest movement might break the spell and rouse him from his stillness. Her fingers closed over the broad muscle, and she felt his shoulders flex through his jacket. She went up on her toes, and her gaze dropped from his hypnotic eyes to his full mouth. Closing the space between them, she brushed her lips against his.

A tremor ran through him, but still, he didn't move. His arms stayed locked, his hands jammed into his pockets.

Holding herself mere millimetres from him, the warm heat of his breath played against her upper lip and his scent twined around her, making her stomach flip-flop. Her legs began to tremble, a shiver slipping deliciously up her spine as she stood, stretched up on her toes, breathing him in. For another second—two, three—she hovered there, so close to his mouth she could almost taste him, until she looked up and found him watching her with an intensity that made her rub her thighs together. *No more waiting.* Trembling on her toes, she ran her tongue along his bottom lip.

And he moved.

Hands flying from his pockets, he lifted her off her feet with one strong arm cinched around her waist, crushing her against him, hand sliding along her jaw and into her hair as he angled his mouth over hers in an open kiss that said his self-control had just hit empty on the tank.

Becca met his demanding tongue with hers and let the current pull her under.

24

#SexySleepover

The morning light through Becca's eyelids seemed determined to hook her up from the depths of slumber. She tried to roll away from it, but something warm and solid held her pinned to the bed. She lifted a languid hand to the weight draped over her chest. Her fingers touched warm skin roughened with hair, then slipped along the contours of resting muscle until she arrived at the hard jut of a wrist bone, the warm smoothness of copper and leather, and finally a sleep-limp hand.

Sully. Her smile was sleepy and sated. She pushed at his arm until it lifted and he rolled onto his side to let her snuggle in against the wall of his chest and tuck her head under his chin.

He murmured in contentment and closed his arm around her back, pulling her snug against him. His chest rose and fell in a deep sigh before his breathing settled back into the slow rhythm of sleep.

Becca relaxed into the warmth of his body, loving the weight of his arm holding her close and the feel of his warm, rough calf beneath the sensitive skin of her in-step. She inhaled the scent of his skin. He smelled so good, like sex and rumpled sheets and something uniquely him. She splayed sleepy fingers over the muscles that sculpted his chest. Turning her face to press her lips to his skin, her mind strayed back to last night.

To the way he'd kissed her in her doorway, so thoroughly and deeply that she'd been hot and wet before he'd even bundled her in at the door and banged it shut behind them. The way he'd dispensed with her jacket with one quick slide of his big hands over her shoulders. The way he'd slowed then to undo the ties on her wraparound shirt, his pupils dilating as he laid bare each new inch of her until his eyes had seemed almost black with desire.

You undo me, princess.

And then his fingertips had traced the edge of her lace bra, his mouth closing over one nipple and sucking it through the fabric before his fingers had hooked over the lacey edge and pulled it all the way down. The feel of his tongue and his hands on her skin had knocked the strength from her legs, which had been just perfect, since the only place she'd wanted to be right then was under him.

Now she wanted him again. And from the hardness digging into her stomach, he was rousing from sleep with similar thoughts. She nuzzled into his chest and tasted the salt of his skin with the tip of her tongue.

He hummed in satisfaction, rolled towards her and then winced, reaching for his shoulder. "This bed isn't big enough for a toddler." He hissed through his teeth as he worked the muscle. "I could have chosen a more comfortable location."

He could've spread her out on the floor for all she'd cared last night. She tingled at the memory and peeked up at him through her lashes.

His gaze swept her face. He nudged her onto her back and rose above her on an elbow. His morning stubble made him look dangerously sexy. "I haven't said good morning properly." Her stomach rolled over in delight as he lowered his face to hers.

The sweep of his tongue over hers sent shudders of pleasure through her. She could get used to being greeted like this each morning.

He rumbled his pleasure against her mouth and caressed his hand down the side of her body until his fingers curved over the swell of her hip. He relinquished her mouth enough to let him murmur against her lips. "Good morning"—another firm press of his mouth—"Becca."

Hearing her name in his deep, contented voice made her feel all light and trippy and glittery. So much better than having him braced over her and calling her *Gem*.

At the thought of her sister, Becca came instantly wide awake, her sleepy, sexy, melted-chocolate-y mood sent hurtling off a cliff by a swift kick of horror. The consequences of what she'd done crashed down around her. Last night, she'd let herself sink into the bliss of being with Sully, but now, there was no hiding. She'd exposed the switch. There would be no more hours now. No more job for Gem. No more hip replacement for Dad. She'd failed her family. She covered her face with both hands and groaned.

"What?" Sully said.

"I've ruined everything." Her remorse was a physical pain. "I've let them down."

"How? You've only got nine hours left. It'll be a long day, but nothing we can't handle."

Becca spread her fingers and looked at him through the gaps. "You want me to keep up the charade?"

"You've come this far, haven't you?"

She dropped her hands from her face and struggled up from under him onto her elbows. "I'd never ask you to sign off on our lie."

"I know you wouldn't. That's why I'm offering. But with one proviso. You can finish the community service today, so that Gem meets the deadline, but she'll have to come back and work it off herself. Step up like you have. Say she loved it so much, she's back for round two."

Becca threw her arms around his neck and pulled him down on top of her. "Thank you, Sully," she said into his neck.

"You're most welcome, Becca."

"I don't know how I'll ever thank you enough for this."

He chuckled and his eyebrows lifted. "Really? You have no ideas?" He worked one knee between her thighs and she laughed up at him. "Because I can think of a few."

There was a knock on the door.

They looked at each other for a beat before Becca lifted her head. "Hello?"

"Gem? Have you seen Sully? His phone's going straight to voice-mail." One of the vet techs. "There's an SPCA inspector at reception who's been waiting over half an hour already to see him."

The mattress juddered as Sully lunged for his wristwatch on the bedside table. His eyes widened and he turned the display to Becca.

After nine.

That had to be wrong. Becca craned an arm backwards to snag Gem's phone from the bedside table. The screen was blank, and pressing the power button did nothing. They exchanged a look. Charging their phones hadn't been high on their list of priorities last night.

"Gem?"

Becca set down the phone and called towards the door, "Uh, no, sorry. I have no idea where he is. I overslept, so he probably gave up on me and went out on a call by himself."

A muttered oath sounded through the door. "If you see him, will you tell him to come to reception? Urgently."

"Absolutely."

Footsteps angled away from the door, growing steadily fainter. Sully rolled off Becca and onto the floor. "My dogs are not going to be amused that I've left them locked inside until now. I shudder to think what they'll have shredded in revenge." He stepped into his boxers and reached for his jeans. "How the hell did we manage to sleep so late?"

Becca dragged the blanket off the bed as she stood and wrapped it around her body. "All that physical activity might have had something to do with it."

Sully's hands stilled on the buttons of his jeans for a moment as he caught her gaze. "That inspector better have brought me a ruddy unicorn, dragging me away from you like this."

Remembered conversations about the animal-welfare organisation and permits sent anxiety slip-sliding into Becca's gut. "What do you think the SPCA wants?"

Sully bent to retrieve his crumpled shirt off the floor. "Probably dropping off a wild animal they've confiscated. Couple of weeks ago they brought me an emaciated banded mongoose that someone had been keeping as a pet." He roughed his hair into shape with quick fingers. "I'd better ask Andile to go round to my house and sort out my dogs." A lunge for the bedside table and he pocketed his cellphone and car keys, before collecting his discarded jacket.

Becca unlocked the door and poked out her head to survey the corridor. "All clear."

Sully stepped through the door, then turned back to her. "I'll see you at the rehab centre." He planted a hard kiss on her mouth.

"And don't look so anxious. Nine hours. That's all you've got left. It's all plain sailing from here."

25

#SurpriseSurprise

Becca leaped in and out of the shower, threw on yesterday's jeans and the first top she could lay her hands on, and left for the rehab centre at a fast trot. As she drew nearer, she saw the SPCA's white van parked out front, with a large blue cross emblazoned on its bodywork. A wiry man in navy trousers and a white shirt stepped out from behind the van's open back door and banged it shut.

She noticed Sully then, standing near the back of the van. From his wide-legged stance and tight-crossed arms, he and the man weren't discussing the weather. As she stepped off the path, her footsteps crunched on the gravel and Sully looked up.

He lifted his chin in distracted acknowledgement before returning his attention to the inspector. "But our last inspection was perfect, Zweli."

The man fanned through a wedge of official-looking documents clamped onto his clipboard. He closed his hand on his belt buckle and stood a little taller. "It's out of my hands. The director says we must investigate."

"But investigate what?" Sully scrubbed a hand over his unshaven jaw. "You know the kind of place I run."

"That was before."

"Before what?"

The inspector pushed past Sully and headed to the rehab centre's doors, swinging his clipboard at his side.

Sully growled softly in his throat. He caught Becca's gaze and huffed out a breath heavy with exasperation. "I do not need this shit today."

Becca squeezed his arm before remembering they were standing right outside reception. She dropped her hand. "I take it he didn't bring you a unicorn?"

The lines on Sully's brow relaxed a little and he gave her a half smile. "More like a pissed-off zebra intent on kicking me in the nuts."

"Ouch."

"Figuratively." Sully gestured in the direction of the rehab centre and they set off across the parking lot. "Though an actual zebra would be better. I really don't have time for all the inevitable paperwork that comes with an impromptu inspection." He leaned his shoulder on the door to open it and flattened himself against the glass to let Becca through first.

The inspector stood at the counter, busily filling in the topmost form on his clipboard.

Sully yanked the door shut so the rushed hydraulic hinge hissed in protest. "I think I have a right to know why you're springing this inspection on us."

The inspector didn't respond, but kept writing. When his scribbling pen got to the end of the page, he finally looked up. Straight at Becca. "We got an anonymous email warning us about your celebrity volunteer."

This was about her? Becca frowned.

Sully stiffened, his expression growing even more thunderous. "Warning you about what?"

"That more animals would be in danger if Gem Stratton stayed on the property any longer. The person listed dogs being drowned and the endangerment of pangolins, amongst other incidents."

"The dog didn't drown!" Becca's protest brought all eyes in the room to her. "It only went under a few times before—" She broke off at Sully's brisk head shake. Becca pressed her lips together and retreated a step.

"The dog was an accident," Sully said, his tone measured. "It could have happened under anyone's watch. There was no malicious intent when it came to the pangolins. And what other incidents?"

The inspector lifted his chin. "I'm not at liberty to discuss all the matters in that email."

"You know this is all bull?" Sully said.

The inspector held out his hands, palms up, as if the whole matter was above his pay grade. "We can't have the public accusing us of not doing our jobs. Unless you've got something to hide that's got you being so uncooperative."

"You know I don't. And I'm not being uncooperative. Just does it have to be today?"

The inspector stared back at him in silence.

Sully ran a hand over his hair and sighed. "Come on then, let's get it over with." He turned to Becca. "Maybe you can find something to do in the scullery. Or help the Bat Squad." He squeezed her upper arm. "Even if we have to work until midnight, we'll finish your hours." He turned to the inspector and gestured with an outstretched hand to the internal swing doors. "After you."

The door swung shut behind the two men, and then almost immediately swung open to reveal Clare. The young vet waited for the doors to shut before she sauntered up to Becca. "In a bit of trouble, are we, Gem?"

Becca was in no mood. "Not today, Clare."

Clare's eyebrows lifted. "Tiring night? Enjoyed it so much, did you, that now you're trying to screw him again this morning?"

Becca tensed. "Excuse me?"

"I saw Sully's bakkie parked in the visitors parking when I got in, and the night staff say it was there all night." Clare smiled a smile that was sharp-edged in its feigned innocence.

The receptionist was watching their exchange with intense interest and Becca shifted to turn her back on the woman. "So? I'm sure it's not the first time he's worked late."

"Uh huh." Clare's eyes grew suddenly fierce. "Is your twin a man-eating slut like you? Does she also get off on stealing other women's men?"

Becca managed to keep her shock at Clare's venom from appearing on her face. "He isn't yours, Clare."

"He could've been if you hadn't come here and ruined everything. Couldn't be satisfied with one boyfriend, you had to find yourself a bit on the side."

"I don't have a boyfriend, Clare."

"Oh? That's not what Mandla Ndungane thinks." Clare touched a fingertip to her chin and narrowed her eyes in thought. "I'm pretty sure he called you his girlfriend on the phone this morning."

Becca's blood congealed. She took a step backwards. "You spoke to Mandla?"

Clare's smile was somehow lethal and gleeful all at once. "Yep, He tried to get you on your cell, but I guess you were otherwise engaged. So he phoned the sanctuary. I was first in, so I answered. Lucky me: two celebrity encounters in one week."

Foreboding slicked across Becca's skin, her hands turning clammy. "He called from Australia?"

Clare affected surprise. "You don't know? Mandla's here!"

Half expecting to see Mandla filling the front doorway of the rehab centre, Becca looked behind her so violently that she twanged a muscle in her neck.

Clare laughed. "Not here. Not yet anyway."

"What does that mean?"

"Some girlfriend you are. You didn't know he dislocated his shoulder in his last match? They flew him back home. He landed this morning. You can kiss it all better when he arrives, which I'm sure should be any minute now."

Becca's mouth dropped open. "He's coming to the sanctuary?"

"I assume so," Clare crooned, "since he asked me to drop him a GPS pin."

"What the hell did you tell him?"

Clare looked affronted. "Nothing. He wanted to speak to you, but I told him you hadn't come in yet, and that the last I'd seen you was before you and Sully went home together from the pub. He seemed rather upset by that, to be honest."

Becca's hands were clenched into fists at her sides. "Are you insane, Clare? You told a rugby player in peak physical condition—even with a shoulder injury—that Sully is sleeping with his girlfriend? Precisely how do you think that confrontation is going to go down?"

Clare's vengeful bravado cooled instantly, and doubt crept onto her face.

Becca nodded. "Didn't think of that, did you?"

Clare's mouth worked and the sugary nonchalance slipped away. "This is all your fault. I wish you'd go back to where you came from."

"I'm going to." Becca's voice was strained with anger. "This afternoon."

"Fucking finally." Tears glittered like glass fragments in Clare's eyes. "And I hope Sully gets tied up all day with Zweli so you never finish your hours and *Luxé Life* fires you. Then I won't have to see your shit-eating face on TV again." Clare spun on her heel like an indignant child and slammed both palms against the internal swing door, shoving through with such force that the door smacked against the corridor wall.

Becca stood in shocked silence. If someone had hit her on the back of the head with a garden spade, she couldn't have felt more stunned. Her mind grew oddly empty, and the world seemed to pause. She became aware of the steady *tick tick tick* of a wall clock. Muffled voices in the clinic. Faint beeps of an oxygen monitor. The creak of the receptionist shifting in her chair. Then the moment snapped, and Becca surged into motion. She had to get to her room. To Gem's phone. Because there was a remote chance that Clare was only yanking her chain.

She hit the glass door at a run, almost crashing into a vet tech who was coming the other way. She side-stepped and called out an apology over her shoulder.

"Gem! Wait," the tech called back. "Someone's here to see you."

Becca ground to a halt. *Mandla!* Her heart relocated to high in her throat and she spun around. "Who?"

"She wouldn't say."

Becca's knees weakened with relief at the tech's use of the female pronoun. *A reporter?* She looked about the parking lot. "Where's she?"

"Waiting in the gardens. You were inside with the inspector and she didn't want to interrupt."

A reporter who didn't want to interrupt. How noble. And unusual. She thanked the tech and hurried past the SPCA van, sending up a quick prayer that Sully would be able to defuse the nuclear countdown she'd activated at his sanctuary. Her mind was a cacophony, like a babble of news reporters trying to out-shout each other as they sought a comment. Would Mandla realise she wasn't Gem? Would he tell? And this mystery woman lying in wait...paparazzi? Reporter? Stalker fan? Animal-rights zealot? "Just please don't let it be Cassie Govender," she said out loud to the sky. *Anyone but Cassie. Please and thank you.*

The volunteers block loomed ahead of her. Becca quickened her step, then stopped short. Standing in the shadows near the building's staircase was a woman, skulking about like a sneaky-assed, celeb-spotting journo would. But even from behind, Becca could see it wasn't *Hot*'s resident celebrity hunter—the woman was too tall and had a pageboy bob of copper-red hair. Her prayers had been answered. Though *Hot* wasn't the only title that loved a little celeb scandal.

Becca cast a worried look at the outfit she'd carelessly tossed on. There was a grubby mark on one leg of her jeans that she hadn't even noticed in her haste this morning. And she didn't have a stitch of makeup on, not even mascara. It wasn't just *Hot* that would love a photo of Gem looking this disreputable.

If she could get into her room before the woman turned around and the long-lens camera came out...

Becca stepped off the path onto the grass to muffle her footfalls and set a trajectory as the crow flies to her room. She'd just got her key out at her door when a voice behind her spoke her name. And not the name they called her at the sanctuary.

Her real name.

Becca spun in the doorway, almost choking on her tongue, and wondered if it was too late to retract her earlier request for divine intervention, because she would take Cassie Govender over this any day.

26

#TimeTravel101

"What on earth are you doing here?" Becca's eyes were bugged so wide, one of her eyelids went into a spasm.

She held the offending eye shut with one hand and turned her back on her twin as she tried desperately to insert the door key into the lock. "Have you forgotten the most basic rule of switching?" she hissed over her shoulder. Two more fumbled tries and the key slipped into place. Becca threw open the door and bundled her sister into the room. She slammed the door behind her and leaned on it, breathing hard. "We can't be in the same space at the same time. It's like time travel."

"Relax." Gem smoothed a hand down the red page-boy wig that obscured her dark hair. "It's a solid disguise." She removed the enormous sunglasses that swallowed up much of her face and set them on the bedside table. "I wore it at the airport and not a single person looked twice at me. Usually I'd be inundated with requests for selfies. And the guy in the parking lot didn't recognise me at all, and he's presumably been working around you all week."

"But why are you here? It's the last day. Nine more hours and then we're home and dry."

"Isn't it obvious?" Gem pulled off the red wig and set it on Becca's unmade bed. "Because I'm not going to let you suffer for even one more minute." Practised fingers slid bobby pins from the edge of the wig cap. "Look how stressed out you are."

Becca forced herself to stop compulsively glancing back at the locked door as if a SWAT team was going to kick it in at any moment. "I'm not stressed out. Or I wasn't until you showed up!"

Gem dumped the cap and bobby pins on the rumpled bed sheet and set to work freeing her hair. "You haven't even made your bed, and you always make your bed. It's an efficient-concierge rule."

"We overslept."

Gem's fingers froze and an elated grin stretched her pink glossed lips. "We, hey?"

Becca groaned and snatched up the wig cap. "I don't know why you're taking this off. Put it on again, because you're leaving right now. How did you get here? Uber?"

"Rental." Gem tossed more bobby pins onto the bed and shook out her hair. "And don't change the subject. Who was he?" Gem shimmied her hips. "The hot German?"

Becca was vibrating with tension, her fingernails digging into her palms. "Gem, you can't be here. Why didn't you just stay in Thailand?"

Gem's expression sobered and she crossed to Becca and cupped her shoulders. "Because I finally came to my senses, Bex. I got my hands on a computer to check my social media and when I saw what you've been going through here, I told Mom we were taking the next flight home."

"Mom's here too?" Becca shot a frenzied look at the door, still mercifully free of a splintered crack from a SWAT officer's boot.

"No, sweetie." Gem gave Becca's arm a reassuring stroke. "I put her in an Uber at the airport and sent her home to Dad. Our flight landed at four thirty this morning. The last thing we need today is our sleep-deprived mother banging around." Gem squeezed shut one eye and examined Becca like a stock farmer sizing up a new stud bull. "Can you even imagine the grief she'd have given you for this outfit?" Gem smiled and pulled a horrified face, as if that might be able to lighten the mood.

Becca shook Gem's hold loose and began pacing. "Mom would be giving me grief for more than just this outfit." She stopped pacing and slumped onto the edge of the bed, making the mattress bob. "Oh God, Gem. I'm so sorry." A sob escaped on her next breath. "I've let you all down so badly."

"No, Bex." Gem dropped onto the bed and tucked a leg beneath her, turning to face Becca. "I'm the one who owes you an apology."

Becca stared at her twin as if she'd grown a second head. "You've seen the news, right? Seen the mess I've got you into?"

Gem snatched up Becca's hands in hers. "And how did you get into that mess in the first place? We manipulated you."

"You're my family."

"And yet we took advantage of you like everyone else invariably does."

"I signed up for this, remember?"

"Only after Mom gave you the old we're-all-counting-on-you-Becca speech. And after I'd bombarded you for days with my tearful video-call pity parties. What else were you going to do?" Gem used the sleeve of her blouse to dab at Becca's wet cheeks. "It was manipulative of us. Mom should never have suggested it, and I should never have gone along with it. When she told me you were game—which, frankly, wasn't a surprise—I should have put my foot down." Gem stopped dabbing and met Becca's gaze. "Instead I let you abandon your job while we buggered off to Thailand where you couldn't even get hold of us when things went pear-shaped."

"Of course you had to go, Gemmie. You could hardly put one foot in front of the other last week. You needed help."

"But not at your expense. I know you'd do anything for me, but you don't have to. I love you. And not just because you were prepared to rush over here to try and save my butt. I love you because you're my sister. There hasn't been even the briefest moment in my life when you haven't been a part of my reality. I love you because...because I just do, okay? Because of who you are and what you mean to me." Gem took Becca's face in her hands. "And it doesn't matter what you do or don't do, I'm always going to love you, you dummy."

The love Becca felt for her sister in that moment threatened to crack open her chest. She put her arms around Gem's neck and hugged her so hard one of Gem's vertebrae clicked.

"Thanks," Gem said into Becca's hair. "Had that crick in my neck ever since I got off the plane."

Becca's laugh was teary and wobbly, but for a long blissful moment, the switch and all its stress receded.

Gem straightened from the embrace. "Right, down to business." Gem clapped her hands and blew out a shaky breath. "I'm now going to do what I should have done from the beginning." She stood. "I'm going to fix my own mess. And you're going to put on the wig and sunglasses and go back to Joburg."

And like a skillfully thrown boomerang, Becca's anxiety careened back. Her shoulders caved. "I can't leave."

"No arguing." Gem picked up the wig and shoved it into Becca's hands. "You're going to spend some time with Mom and Dad, and I'll see you tomorrow when the deadline is over."

"He knows, Gem." Becca tossed the wig onto the bed and clutched distractedly at the neckline of her T. "About the switch."

Gem's eyes grew wide. "Who knows?"

Becca bunched her T-shirt in her hands, her fingers working the fabric. "Sully."

Gem let her head fall back and exhaled a swear word before looking back at Becca. "Sullivan Scott? He knows?"

Becca nodded.

"How? And when is he going to bust us?" Gem surged up from the bed. "He's totally going to, you know? He's a dick like that. God, he's probably rubbing his hands in glee, just waiting for the perfect opportunity to expose us. Bet he's busy setting up a press conference as we speak."

"He's not going to say anything." Absent-mindedly, Becca smoothed her hand over the sheet where his big body had slept mere hours ago.

Gem's eyes caught the movement and her brow twitched. "Oh my God." Her mouth fell open and she slapped a manicured hand over it and inhaled through her fingers. "It was him. In your room. But he's a dick, Bex."

Irritation prickled through Becca. "He's a really good man, Gem. He comes across as brusque and surly, but he's really impossibly kind and thoughtful and gentle and smart and caring and—"

Gem inhaled another horrified breath through the gaps between her tense fingers. "I thought the press was being sensational. I never thought there might be actual fire behind all that smoke. Please tell me you haven't fallen for him. Tell me it's just because he's hot in bed."

Becca hesitated as something light and warm expanded in a rush inside her. "He *is* hot in bed, but..."

Gem groaned and dropped to sit on the bed beside Becca. "What were you thinking, sis?"

"I wasn't thinking. He crept into my heart and by the time I realised it, it was too late. And last night, I just couldn't lie to him anymore. I just couldn't risk hurting him."

Gem swore under her breath. “And now? There’s not a chance he’s going to sign off on this week.”

“He will, so that you meet the deadline for the original fifty hours. But then you have to come back and work it off properly yourself. You could spin it that you wanted to make extra sure the public knew just how sorry you were.”

Gem’s sigh sounded like she’d dredged it up all the way from her toes. “Poetic justice, I guess. Seems he’s not such a dickhead after all. But what will you do now? You can’t give up your job and your dreams. And I really can’t see him ever leaving the sanctuary.”

A shard of pain splintered from Becca’s heart like a calving iceberg. “I don’t know. We haven’t figured that out yet.”

Gem’s eyes were soft with sympathy. “And how’s he going to take looking like the jilted rebound guy when Mandla and I get—”

“Mandla!” Becca shot up from the bed as if she’d been launched from a catapult. “Shit! I forgot all about him.” She dropped to her knees to fish out the charging cable from under the bed.

“What about Mandla?”

“He’s coming.”

“Coming where?”

It took a few tries to get the end of the charging cable into the phone, Becca’s hands were shaking so much. “Here! Now!”

It was Gem’s turn to launch herself off the bed. “Who told you that?”

“Clare. Did you know he injured himself on tour?” The phone was taking its sweet time to begin its start-up routine. She blurted out the details of the confrontation she’d just had with her unintentional nemesis, ending with Clare’s sending Mandla directions to the sanctuary.

“That bitch.” Gem’s face was the colour of chalk, despite the acid in her voice.

"There's a good chance she's lying just to freak me out." Becca entered Gem's security code and the phone blinked awake. "Fingers crossed." She slid down the notifications screen. "Shit." She shoved the phone into Gem's hands and flopped face down on the bed, groaning into the duvet.

"Tried to call you, baby," Gem read. "You're not answering." A pause. "You're sleeping with the vet?" Gem made an annoyed sound in her throat. Another pause. "Taking the off-ramp now. Shit, Bex, that one was sent fifteen minutes ago."

Becca bolted upright and Gem leaped off the bed and hurried to the door. She unlocked it, cracked it open just enough to look outside, then banged it shut and leaned against it, eyes wide with horror. "He's here!"

27

#GameOver

Becca scrambled off the bed and joined her sister at the door. An enormous bear of a man in a dark green tracksuit with the gold emblem of a leaping springbok on the jacket was coming up the path towards the volunteer block. One thick arm was strapped into a black sling that spanned a chest that appeared to be composed of bowling balls.

Holy crap, but he was huge in real life. Sully was a big man, but Mandla...he looked like an American football player about to run onto the field, except his bulk didn't come from any strap-on padding.

Every so often, Mandla would stop to let another excited sanctuary worker rush forward to take a selfie with their hero, his un-strapped arm draped across their shoulders, his mouth in a superstar-bright grin.

Becca closed the door and locked it. Her gaze met Gem's and they grabbed onto each other and bounced up and down mouthing *fuckfuckfuckfuckfuck*.

Several frantic f-bombs later, Gem stopped, gasping. "What are we going to do?"

Becca's clamouring mind felt about as useful in the thinking department as cream cheese. "Hide?"

"After driving all this way, he's not going to just go home."

Outside, some of the sanctuary workers were clapping and chanting "Mandla, Mandla, Mandla", coming steadily closer to the accommodation block.

Becca felt about in her head for the lever to engage concierge mode. She solved problems for a living and this was like any other problem. She took a deep breath and cast about the room, as if inspiration lay in the sex-tossed bed and old-fashioned wardrobe. Got it! Apparently that was precisely where inspiration did indeed reside. "Have you decided to forgive Mandla and take him back?"

Gem's expression softened and she looked wistfully at the locked room door. "All that stuff about absence making the heart fonder seems to be true."

"Okay. So we let Mandla in and tell him about the switch and then you sneak off with him when the coast is clear."

"No. He'll flip. The golden boy involved in a deception like this? Never going to happen."

"Even if it's to save your skin?"

"He won't risk it. Trust me. What if I go out and work this last day, like I planned? You said Sully won't say anything."

"But one wrong move and Clare will." Becca winced at the remembered conversation at the pub. "You won't believe who lives in Winterberg now. Livhu. And I spent last night on a team with her and Clare and Sully for the local pub quiz finals."

Gem made an annoyed sound. "Murphy's bloody Law. I suppose she isn't any less blabber-mouthed than she was at school."

"Her favourite story was how we used to switch places at school."

"Of course it was."

"So we can't risk it, not now that Clare knows it's a possibility."

"Hiding doesn't sound like such a bad idea then," Gem said.

The door vibrated as a heavy hand knocked against it. "Baby? You in there?" The deep rasp of a grizzly bear. "They told me in reception you were here."

So much for hiding.

"Um, babe?" Gem said, lifting her voice so it would travel through the door. "I'm just getting dressed."

"Please, Gem, I'm on my last legs." The door handle levered up and down. "I just got off a nineteen-hour flight from Perth and then climbed straight into a taxi to come find you."

"One minute, okay?"

There was a heavy bump on the door, as if Mandla had thudded his head against the wood. "Fine. Sixty seconds. One, Mississippi. Two, Mississippi. Three, Mississippi."

Gem turned back to Becca and spoke in a whisper. "Please tell me you've thought of something."

Becca needed more time. More minutes and seconds so she could think through all the possible solutions and consequences. She chewed her lip.

"Seventeen, Mississippi."

There was no time. Becca glanced from the door to her sister. "You need to not be here anymore. Leave me to finish your hours, and you disappear the same way you arrived"—she snatched up the wig and thrust it back into Gem's hands—"incognito. Let Mandla in and tell him you've finished the hours. That you can't wait to head back home with him. Say you're exhausted after this terrible week and you just want to slip away without any fanfare and put all this behind you."

Gem nodded like she was an undercover agent getting a new assignment. "Right. Let Mandla in. Wig on. Sunglasses on. Leave."

Good. This could work.

"Where are my car keys?" Gem said, looking around the room.

"You have to leave here in the rental."

"Oh right. Otherwise who's stealing Gem's car?"

"Precisely. And don't go with him to the parking area. The dirt road runs right behind this building, so give him the rental's keys and have him meet you on the road when he drives past."

"Check."

"Fifty-nine, Mississippi. Sixty, Mississippi." The door shuddered on its hinges from a knock that sounded as if it might split timber. "That's one minute, babe."

Becca opened the double-doored wardrobe that stood in the corner and climbed in, batting Gem's hanging clothes out the way. She looked up at her sister. "You got this?"

Gem replied with a tight nod and closed the cupboard door.

Sitting in her dark hiding place, Becca held her breath in a bid to slow her cantering heart. Her body had dumped so much adrenalin into her blood stream that her limbs were jittering. She pulled up her knees and wrapped her arms around them. The cupboard was small and cramped, and one of Gem's heels was poking her in the bum. She slid it quietly aside, and let her breath ease from her lips. This would work. It had to.

She heard Gem clear her throat, and a beat later, the room door clicked open.

"Finally," Mandla sighed. "A second more and I'd have had to start signing more autographs."

Heavy footsteps moved into the room and then the door closed.

Becca waited for the sound of the lock turning.

"So is it true?" Mandla said. "All that stuff in the news about you and that fucker?"

Her sister laughed. *Lock the door, Gem.*

Mandla was right outside the cupboard now and Becca held her breath.

"Of course it's not true. You know the press." Gem's voice.

"I do. But they wouldn't just make up something like that based on nothing."

"Trust me, Mandla. Nothing happened between me and Sullivan Scott."

A deep exhale filtered through the crack between the cupboard doors. "Jeez, you don't know how happy that makes me."

"Hold off on the happy dance for a minute, big guy. I haven't forgiven you yet."

An aggrieved noise. "What do I need forgiveness for?"

"You men!" Becca could imagine Gem spiking her hands onto her hips. "You've been a total dick about all this. You weren't supportive of me at all!"

Yep, her sister was definitely in the power pose right now.

"I was embarrassed, baby." There was a distinct wheedling tone in Mandla's voice. "All that negative publicity! You know I have a reputation to uphold. As the captain of the Springboks, I can't be involved in stuff like that."

"But you're meant to love me for better or for worse." Gem's voice had an indignant edge to it.

"We're not married, babe."

An incensed squeak from her sister threw Mandla into full grovelling mode. "But I do love you, gorgeous. How could I not love the most beautiful girl in the world? I'm sorry I didn't stand by you. I see now that I totally should have."

"I deserve better, Mandla." From the sound of her voice, Gem was in full pout mode.

"I know you do, and I'll do better next time. Not that there'll be a next time, will there?"

"I don't plan to do these things deliberately, Mandla." Irritation was a sharp bite in Gem's voice.

"No, for sure, I never said that. Look, let me show you just how sorry I am."

A big grunt was followed by a giggle, and then a soggy, sloppy sound like somebody slurping a peach filled the room. Becca sighed inwardly. *Keep it PG, sis!*

"Hold on," Mandla said. Peach consumption stopped abruptly. "The chick on the phone said you spent the night with that vet last night. You're not lying to me about him?"

"Does this feel like the kiss of a woman who slept with someone else last night?"

Mandla's laugh was like gravel in a blender. The noisy kissing resumed, and then the bed creaked as if its worn-out springs were in danger of snapping.

Becca leaned her head against the back of the cupboard and poked an index finger in each ear. The cupboard doors didn't quite meet in the middle, allowing for a slivered view of the room if she closed one eye. She closed both. She was as close to Gem as any sister could be, but watching Gem reconnect with her boyfriend wasn't the kind of closeness Becca needed.

As if Gem felt the same way, the tongue-smacking stopped and Gem said, "Let's get out of here. Right now!"

"What about your community service?"

"All done. But I'm exhausted. I just want to go home. As in right now!" Keys jangled. "Take the blue Renault in the parking lot. But don't tell anyone I'm leaving. I don't want any fanfare when I go."

Mandla was silent for a second. "But you're not packed, baby."

They hadn't thought of that. *Busk, Gem.*

"I never want to see these clothes again. They're all ruined by mud and shit. I deserve pretty new things after this ordeal."

"And where's you Audi? What's this Renault you're—"

"Anyone would think you don't want to take me back to Joburg and strip me naked so I can give you a proper welcome home, champ."

Good girl. And now they were kissing again. Becca tipped carefully onto her knees and brought her eye close to the crack of light. She could just make out the green of Mandla's tracksuited thigh atop the bed, and Gem's white jeans on top of that. Could they *please* get a move on?

There was a knock on the door and Becca started, bumping the wardrobe door with her forehead. She froze, staring at the gap that had widened to almost a centimetre.

The knock came again and then a handle cranked and the door creaked. "Princess?" Sully's voice. "The inspector wants to—" A beat of silence hung in the air like the fading, lingering note of a crystal bell. "Gem." His voice was flat. He knew. Of course he knew.

"Did he just call you 'princess'?" Mandla sounded incensed.

Becca winced silently and held her breath.

"Mandla, leave him. It's actually how he likes to insult me."

Not anymore.

The slice of Springbok green through the gap moved. The bed creaked and heavy feet hit the floor.

"Just leave it, okay?" Gem said. "I want to go. Now!"

If Becca didn't breathe soon, she was going to pass out. She tightened every muscle in her torso to control the slow release of the stale air trapped explosively in her lungs.

"Here you are!" A female voice sliced through the tension. "And how cosy! The whole love triangle together."

Kill me now. At the familiar voice, Becca clamped a hand to her mouth as the last few molecules of air gasped out of her lungs. Cassie freaking Govender. She shifted deeper into the corner of the wardrobe and rested her forehead on her drawn-up knees. *Damn damn damn.*

"What are you doing here, Cassie?" Sully asked.

"It's Gem's final day!" Cassie sounded undeterred by Sully's clipped tone. "I wanted to capture the last few hours of messy fun for our readers and subscribers. And look, it's just got messier!"

"You need to leave, Cassie." Sully's voice was edged with steel. "I don't want strangers tramping around here, frightening the animals."

"It's your sanctuary, Dr Scott. Before I go though, tell me how you feel about Gem and Mandla getting back together?" A sly quality had insinuated itself in Cassie's voice. "Especially after a source tells me that you and Gem got up close and personal last night."

Becca clenched her hands, fingernails biting into her palms. Someone had been busy on the phone. There was a special place in hell for people like Clare.

"I have no comment," Sully said, "except to tell you to get off my property. Now." There was quiet menace in his voice.

"And Mandla, any comment from you?" Cassie's voice sounded thoroughly un-menaced.

"Cas, darling." Gem's controlled, assured voice entered the confrontation. "You of all people should know: tacky source, tacky story. You should ask whoever told you that supposedly juicy, though entirely fabricated fake news, how long she's been trying to get her claws into Dr Scott. Jealousy can make people so nasty. Oh, hello, Clare."

Inside the wardrobe, Becca opened her mouth in a silent howl of protest to the universe. Did anyone else want to join this party?

"Do you need something, Clare?" Sully asked.

"The inspector. He wants to go up to the camps. And it's not fake news!" Clare's voice turned sharp with indignation. "Gem was all over Sully. But you mustn't blame Sully, Mandla." Sudden worry now. "Gem told him she'd broken up with you, and then she threw herself at him. It's all on her. She's a total slut!"

"Baby?" Hurt and accusation tainted Mandla's voice.

"Not only spreading fake news, but now you're slut-shaming," Gem said. "How progressive."

"Come, Clare!" Sully's voice had gone full authoritarian boss. "We have work. And Cassie, let me escort you to the parking lot." *Or frog-march you*, his tone implied.

If climbing out of the cupboard wouldn't have ruined everything, Becca would have leaped out and kissed him.

"No, hold on."

Now what, Mandla? Becca could have screamed in frustration.

"If it's not true, then you're slandering my girlfriend's name to the press, and that's not on," Mandla said.

Really? Mandla had to choose now to be the supportive boyfriend?

"It's not a lie." Clare wasn't going to let this go, boss or no boss trying to drag her away. "Sneaking around behind your back is exactly what I'd expect from someone like her. Has she told you about the times she used to sneak around, switching places with her twin sister?"

Becca plastered her hands over her eyes, as Cassie made a sound like she'd finally worked out how electricity worked. "Oh God, I forgot Gem has a twin sister!"

"Uh-huh. Identical," Clare said, triumphant. "So they used to switch. Deceiving their teachers. Probably cheating on tests and—"

Gem cut Clare off. "You're being rather dramatic, don't you think? *Deceiving* our teachers. And what we did as children doesn't have any relevance."

"What if they still do it?" Clare bulldozed on. "How do we know this is even the real Gem?"

Outside the wardrobe, Gem laughed, seemingly unrattled by this scene from a Hercule Poirot movie that was unfolding before her. "Oh God, that's hilarious. Becca and I used to do that in high school, but the last time I checked, I was twenty-nine, and my sister lived in London."

"They don't have planes in the UK?" Clare replied snidely.

"Enough," Sully barked. "This is crazy. Let's go. We have an inspection to get through."

"No, Sully, it's fine," Gem said. "I'd like to knock this little conspiracy theory on its head. Here. Look."

Becca whipped her hands from her eyes and peered through the crack between the wardrobe doors. Gem's hand was holding down the shoulder of her top to expose the flower wreath tattoo, stark black against her skin.

Cassie sighed her disappointment. "It would've made for a sensational story, Clare. But that is definitely Gem. She won *Hot*'s Top Tattoo on a Celeb last year for that tat."

"Could be a fake," Clare said.

"Could you not touch my girlfriend?" Mandla said.

"Clare! Now!" Sully's tone suggested he was about to pick her up and remove her from the room slung over his shoulder if he had to. "You too, Gem. Go find some work to do. And since there's no story here, Cassie, I'd appreciate it if you could leave my sanctuary."

"Oh, but there is a story," Cassie sang. "I'd love to hear more about these childhood switches, Gem. It would make such a fun, throw-back-to-the-past story."

"If you want the unvarnished truth, you should speak to her friend, Livhu. All sorts of things came out at the pub quiz."

"Quiz? How fun," Cassie said. "I bet you were great at that from your pageant days."

Clare made a scoffing sound. "About the only question she got right was the national animal of Scotland."

"Now, Clare." Sully's voice was a little removed, like he was talking from the corridor outside.

"Fine, I'm coming."

Becca bit back her relief as footsteps travelled across the carpet.

And then Mandla spoke. "What is the national animal of Scotland, babe?"

"The Scottish terrier," Gem said, all confident authority.

From outside the room, Clare shrieked in triumph.

Becca's head might have clunked against the back of the cupboard then. Or the loud bump that echoed through the room from the wardrobe could just have been her exhausted, shock-depleted heart tumbling from her chest like a boulder clattering down a mountainside.

In hindsight, trying to hide behind the skirt of a geometric-print sheath dress was never going to work, but when Clare almost wrenched the wardrobe door clean off its hinges, Becca tried it nonetheless.

28

#Goodbye

In the passenger seat of the rental, Gem roused herself enough to look out the window. "You sure this is where he said to meet you?"

"I'm sure." Becca pulled her attention back to the road, slowing as she searched for the turn Sully had taken that day into the pine plantation. When she spotted it, she put on the indicator and slowed.

Gem looked around her. "In a forest?"

"Uh huh. No one's going to take photos of us out here." The pine trees whipped past the rental's rattling windows, the illusory flickering of the symmetrical rows feeling somehow ominous this time, as if they were lifted straight from a Tim Burton movie.

Gem turned back in the seat and rested her listless head against the headrest.

Becca's own head was a maelstrom of noise and images, the bedlam that had erupted when Clare had flung open the wardrobe doors replaying on an endless, cacophonous loop. Mandla, looking like a fish hooked out of water, gaping and spluttering and flopping his way to the door and sweet escape. Clare, looking so pleased with herself she had seemingly eaten the proverbial cat after it had eaten the proverbial canary. Cassie, looking like her ship had come in, and not some paltry fishing trawler either, but the freaking Symphony of the Seas.

And Gem, opening her fist to reveal the keys to her rental car.

The doorway of the room had already been crammed with intrigued gawkers who'd materialised at the scent of blood, but they'd taken hands and shoved their way into the growing crowd. A hand had caught at her wrist and she'd tried to shake it off until she realised whose hand it was. Sully's. Telling her to wait for him at the mountaintop lookout, as he body-blocked a salivating Cassie.

And then they were through and running.

Wait for me.

But she couldn't bear the thought of a tearful farewell. It would be better to let him hate her for bailing on him. The quicker he put her out of his mind, the better. For them both.

And so they'd fled, the Renault spitting up dirt and gravel as Becca had roared away from the sanctuary like she was a stunt driver in *The Fast and the Furious*.

But somewhere on the freeway, several kilometres north of the Winterberg onramp, she'd pulled to a whiplashing stop on the hard shoulder, her heart clawing inside her chest like a wild animal trying to outrun a fire, fingers white on the steering wheel.

"Turn around," Gem had said.

She'd looked at Gem, like she didn't understand English.

"Go back and end it right, Bex."

"It'll hurt too much."

"It'll hurt more if you leave without saying goodbye."

She'd sat for a long while, the rental car getting buffeted by the wind of the huge trucks thundering by. Then she'd checked her mirrors and joined the northbound traffic again until she could cross over the freeway at the next exit.

Forty minutes later, here she was, negotiating the dirt road through the pine forest. Up ahead, she spotted the white Ranger parked beside the road. This morning, seeing his bakkie would've provoked a surge of spontaneous joy. Now all she felt was suffocating dread. She pulled in behind the bakkie and killed the engine. She forced her fingers, gripped tight around the steering wheel, to uncurl. She lowered her hands into her lap and dragged clammy palms along her thighs. "I don't want to do this."

"And yet you know you have to."

"But how am I going to say good-bye?" Her laugh was bitter. "I suppose I should have thought about that before I lost my heart. I've fucked everything up." She squeezed her eyes shut against tears that were already threatening. "And I only had one job. One!"

A hand on her thigh made her open her eyes. Gem was watching her, her head turned against the headrest. "You know I don't blame you for this?"

"You should."

"No. This was a cluster fuck waiting to happen. All the odds were stacked against you."

A sharp flare of guilt had Becca pushing aside her own desolation and scraping together the last of her optimism. "I'm sure we can fix this, sis. As soon as we get back to Joburg, we'll sit down with Alek and work something out."

Gem gave a hollow laugh. "Even if Alek doesn't fire me as a client, there's nothing to work out, Bex. It's all gone. The endorsements. *Luxe Life* for sure. And you can bet I won't be getting the *From Hell to Hotel* contract now." Gem turned her head and stared into the rows of trees outside the passenger window. "It's also safe to say that Mandla's publicist has probably already announced our break-up on social media. Damage control, before news of my treachery breaks the internet."

Her voice was small. Thin. Resigned. Anything would've been easier to bear than Gem's resignation. Anger. Accusation. Hysterical crying even. Becca closed her hand on her sister's leg. "I'll tell them it was all my idea. That you didn't even know about it. That I arranged it all with Mom."

"Becca. Stop." Gem's hand found Becca's face. "When did you start thinking that all the world's problems fell on your shoulders? Look after you for a change." Gem's hand fell away and she unclipped Becca's seat belt. "Now go and find him already."

A lone tear tracked down the cheek still warmed by her sister's palm. She wiped it away with a hurried swipe. "I love you, Gem."

"Would you go already?" Gem laughed and pointed an imperious finger at the pathway that opened from the grassland onto the road.

Becca took a haltering breath. She felt drained. Hollow. Her pulse so hard and quick she could feel the vibrations of it in her chest. She opened the car door and climbed out.

"And Bex?"

About to close the car door, she paused and ducked her head down to look at Gem.

"I love you. Forever and ever."

Becca couldn't reply, her throat suddenly too full of emotion and dammed tears, so she just smiled and closed the door.

She crossed the dirt road to the grassland that opened out behind the last row of pine trees, and found the footpath. It wasn't terribly steep—Sully had managed it effortlessly with her on his back—but her legs felt as if she'd come out of an all-day charity spinathon. The need to concentrate on drawing enough oxygen into her lungs took the edge off the accusatory voices in her head though, which was an unexpected blessing.

After some ten minutes of steady uphill trudging, she looked up to catch her breath and saw Sully, still a way ahead, standing on the flat rock he'd brought her to after the auction. His back was to her and he was gazing out over the mountains, legs braced so she could sense his tension even at a distance. A dark shape detached itself from his side and moved to the edge of the rock. Ella. The big dog barked, a joyous *You came!* that broke the silence, and Sully turned.

Ella scooped something off the ground—her potato no doubt—and leaped off the rock, heading down the slope at a gallop, her master not far behind her.

A deep, raw sadness split Becca's heart open like bruised plum. If things had been different, she'd have broken into a run herself and met Sully halfway, letting him catch her up in his arms. But this was the only reality she had, and it was a harsh, cruel, ill-timed one.

Ella waded through a grassy tussock and cavorted the last few metres down the sandy path, her tail a wagging declaration of happiness. Becca shut her eyes on a slow blink, marshalling her pain. "Hey you." A potato landed between her feet, and Becca went down on her haunches to rough the dog's chocolate-brown head in her hands so she would be otherwise occupied when those big boots came into view. With each approaching footfall, Becca's pulse grew more agitated. This was going to hurt so much.

"I thought you weren't coming, princess."

The word, a week ago said only with scorn, and now an endearment, made her gut twist with sorrow. She looked up into his beautiful face and her throat constricted around a knot of pain. "I wasn't sure I could bear saying goodbye." She cut her gaze back to Ella and redoubled her patting. "It's lovely to see *this* friendly face one more time though."

A soft smile lit Sully's eyes. "I went home earlier to get some paperwork the inspector wanted to see. Ella was sitting waiting at my bakkie when I came out of the house."

"She hadn't seen you all night. She missed you." *Like I'm going to.* "Has the inspector finished?"

"He's with Jo."

"You should be there too."

"It'll be fine. I run a tight ship."

She lifted her face. "And having the villainous Gem Stratton off the property can't hurt."

He smiled and held out his hand to pull her to her feet, but she turned her attention back to Ella, upgrading from simple head patting to ear massaging. "Thanks for trying to protect our secret back in the room."

He shrugged as if it were nothing. "I had no idea Clare felt that way about me."

"You're an easy man to fall for." *Fuck.* Saying things like that was not going to help. She pushed to her feet and set about brushing her hands vigorously on her jeans. "Gem's in the car. I don't want to keep her waiting too long; she's pretty fragile right now."

"And you? This can't be easy for you either."

"I'll survive. It's Gem I'm concerned about."

"Then it's a good thing you've got me to worry about you. Let me come with you back to Joburg."

"No, Sully. This weekend is going to be full-on crisis control. It's going to get brutal."

"All the more reason for me to be there."

She shook her head. "I won't have you dragged through all that. Getting you onto the front page of *The Sunday Star* was bad enough."

"I don't give a damn what they say about me."

"But you should. If the press sees you supporting me, they'll jump to the conclusion that you were in on the deception all along.

That could do huge damage to the sanctuary, if your funders think you're unethical."

"I'm prepared to risk it."

"For what reward? I fly back on Sunday night."

"Becca."

He reached for her, but she stepped back, hands raised to keep him at bay. A sadness so acute she had to hunch her shoulders against it swept through her. "Please, Sully," she said. "This is already so hard. I know you were all for having a long-distance relationship when that distance was only from here to Johannesburg. But this is to London. Even couples who've been married for decades wouldn't last over that sort of distance."

Ella sank with a grunt to her belly in the grass at Sully's feet and he looked down at her, silent for a long beat. When he looked up again, the earnestness in his eyes twisted the knife already plunged deep into Becca's heart. "I don't want to lose you, Becca. I know it's been a whirlwind this last week, but I really feel there could be something good between us. Something lasting. Something that we both need. And we can't just let that slip through our fingers."

"We're not letting anything slip. We're choosing. I have a great job at a top hotel, and I have my dream of becoming a member of the Golden Keys. And you have the sanctuary, and those animals need you as much as you need them. We can't just give all that up. You'll forget about me eventually."

"I won't."

"But you should. Like when you're on holiday and you meet people who feel like they're your long-lost best friends. And you exchange numbers because you are absolutely going to meet up the second you all get home. Yet when that first text comes through, the last thing you want to do is ever see them again. I bet that's what this week will feel like soon enough."

But she knew that of all the lies she'd been telling this week, that was the biggest one. That she could ever forget him.

His gaze hardened. "You think that's what's going on between us? That you were just some sort of holiday fling for me? Because need I remind you that this week was no holiday for me. And I don't do flings. If you think I'm that sort of man, then I'm insulted."

She'd lost control of this farewell. Like everything else this week. "I didn't mean it that way." She bit into her lip against mounting tears.

"So how did you mean it? And what is it you want me to do? Just say 'Cheers, princess, it's been great, have a nice life?' and wave? You want me to let you go like you mean nothing to me? Let you walk out of my life and go on as if you were never here?"

"I don't want any of that. But it's what has to happen. Please, Sully, don't make this harder than it already is. I can't stay. We both know that. And you can't go." She looked down at her feet, blurry and indistinct through a sheen of tears. "I shouldn't have let myself get carried away and fall for you. It was selfish and unfair and unforgivable, because I wasn't the only one at risk of getting hurt."

His hand closed on her shoulder and squeezed gently. "I didn't walk into this blindly, Becca. I knew how difficult pursuing this would be. If I wasn't prepared to risk things, to make sacrifices to have you, I could have walked away last night."

"I don't want you to make sacrifices for me."

"Isn't that my decision?"

She rolled her shoulder out from under his grip and stepped away. "I just want you to say goodbye."

His chest rose in a slow, fighting-for-control breath. "You're sure about that?"

She nodded, unable to speak around the pain in her throat.

His face took on the quality of granite, as if every muscle in it were clenched. "Goodbye then," he said, his voice as strained as his face.

She took a step back, then another. "I hope you'll eventually be able to put me and the last seven days behind you."

"If that's what you want, princess, then you're already forgotten."

It was precisely what she'd asked of him, to let her go back to her life and her dream, but his words still cut deep. Wiping savagely at tears she could no longer keep in check, she turned and stumbled over the uneven grass to the worn path that would take her back to the car and out of Winterberg, and Sully's life, forever.

YouTube

#CassieGovender #HotMagazine #SpillTheTea #GemStratton

Spilling the tea with Cassie: an exclusive tell-all with Gem Stratton

436,231 views • Aug 15

Hot magazine

359K subscribers

Hot celeb reporter Cassie Govender scoops an exclusive tell-all interview with TV celebrity, Gem Stratton, after the twin switch that rocked the nation! Gem and her identical (they really are!!) twin Becca Stratton, sit down with Cassie to 'fess up about switching places, and the online hate that caused Gem's near-breakdown and sparked the deception that's got everyone in South Africa talking!

Leave a comment and tell us if you think Gem deserves another chance. Do you want to see her back on *Luxe Life* or is it time to cancel this celeb?

2,568 Comments

Tay-tay_H

I'm shook. How could Gem's mother even suggest a crazy idea like that? And how could the sister go along with it?! Sure, Gem wasn't coping and was going to lose her job, but to even think that the sister could take over Gem's life like that and actually not totally mess it up! They must be delusional!

- 32 REPLIES

Ginger Snap
OMG, I am so so moved by this video. I so get Gem on the trauma of online haters...so relatable. I was bullied online when I was in high school and I still have scars. Gem, it was so brave of you to talk about this and what it has done to you and how it triggered your depression again. Sending you virtual hugs and so so much love.

- 17 REPLIES

Ashe
I was all for cancelling Gem after that leopard cub post, but now I've seen this, I can see she never meant it the way we all took it. I have so much sympathy for her now. She's been through hell and clearly just wants to put things right.

- 11 REPLIES

29

Earl's Court, London
Friday, 26 August

Becca re-read the email on her computer screen, inhaling slowly through her nose as her irritation levels rose. She'd been struggling all week to maintain her usual calm professional demeanour behind the concierge desk, and emails like this weren't helping.

What sort of a prat thought a bloody six-ton African elephant wandering down the aisle of a packed West End theatre was something Health and Safety would green-light? The same kind who thought that since she'd told him *The Lion King*'s stage version was just *like the movie, only in real life*, that she now owed him a refund of hundreds of pounds because his kids had been so looking forward to seeing the "lions and tigers". The idiot clearly had *The Lion King* and *Tiger King* confused.

She made a note on her Rickford-branded notepad, her pen strokes uncharacteristically savage. She'd organise him a few comps to the London Zoo. Or Whipsnade where he could pile his disappointed spawn into a safari bus and they could all pretend they were on safari. Though sadly, he wouldn't find the lions and tigers housed together. He'd just have to complain to management. Pity she couldn't send him off to the sanctuary and let Sully explain to him which continent tigers actually came from.

Her larynx worked painfully as she swallowed. Almost two weeks since leaving South Africa and Sully was still never far from her thoughts. So much for her holiday fling theory.

She put down the pen and reached for her mouse, piloting it with efficient strokes, though anyone looking over her shoulder would soon enough see she wasn't doing anything vaguely productive. She switched to the tab she'd had open on her browser ever since she'd returned to work last Monday and refreshed the page. Almost three hundred more likes since lunch.

Giving Cassie an exclusive had been a stroke of genius, proving that Alek was worth every percentage point of the commission Gem paid him. As the media frenzy had spiralled that Friday night after Cassie's breaking news tweets, Alek had gone into full-steam negotiation mode with *Hot*. By the time the first reporters had started phoning for comment, Alek had nailed down an exclusive, tell-all interview with *Hot* that not only meant he could better control the narrative, but Gem would even get paid for it.

And so, come Sunday, sitting in Gem's living room with Alek watching on, she and Gem and Mom had talked about everything. The online abuse. Sleeping tablets guzzled faster than sweets at a children's party. Anxiety attacks and long-overdue hip replacements and sisters who'd do anything to make things right.

The consequent media coverage had been scathing, as they'd expected. *Stratton Sisters' Scandalous Switch. Gem's twin deceives a nation. How celeb's twin conned us all. Becca: Pretty Little Liar.* News articles. Social media posts. The hashtag 'twinswitch' trending for days.

But slowly, as *Hot*'s exclusive did the rounds, things had started to change. Swept up in a growing wave of sympathy, public opinion—fickle beast that it was—had begun a steady about-face. And with the up-swell of support for Gem, *Luxe Life* could do little else but tear up the waiting severance letter.

Nothing about the switch had gone according to plan, and yet it had all worked out in the end. Gem had her job back and Dad would have his operation, sooner rather than later, thanks to the money from *Hot*. She and Sully hadn't been as lucky, but two out of three wasn't bad. She'd achieved what she'd set out to do, and finding love had never been one of those objectives. Not all love stories had a happy ending.

Her fingers itched to take out her phone and read Sully's final text to her, like she'd done so many times since touching down at Heathrow. She really should delete it so the temptation was no longer there, because reading his text over and over was only preventing the hole where her heart had once been from scarring over. Not that deleting Sully's text would help, because lengthy as it was, she had every word and punctuation mark memorised.

> *Becca, I'm sorry about how we left things between us. You're not forgotten and never will be. I wish you'd stay, but I know you have to go. You have a career and a dream and I won't be one of those people who expects you to put your own needs second...you've had enough of that in your life. But if you change your mind about what you want, and if what you want is us, then I promise you I'll move heaven and earth to find a way to make it work.*

Becca hunched her shoulders and let them fall on a deep sigh. Work. She needed to stop thinking about what couldn't be and do what she did best. She opened her email program and ran her eye down the subject lines of the never-ending influx of emails that dropped into the concierge inbox. *Needtickets for Les Misérables*. Let her guess...for tonight. Good luck with that. *Flowers for my wife.* Probably to ease his conscience after checking in with his mistress.

She wrinkled her nose at her uncharacteristic cynicism. It was time for this persistent ache in her chest to stop. When she did the next duty roster, she'd put herself down for all the weekend shifts too. Then she'd get back to normal.

30

Earl's Court, London
Monday, 12 September

It was a rare moment of peace, that brief hiatus that sometimes came after the rushed requests of the business guests and before the requests began flowing in from the slower-rising tourism guests. Becca stood beside a picture window in a corner of the lobby across from the concierge desk. Fingers wrapped around a branded Rickford mug, she sipped her steaming tea, watching the busy pedestrian traffic on the pavement outside and trying not to think of a certain someone.

She needed a distraction. Releasing her mug with one hand, she reached for her phone and called up Gem's number, then tapping the video-call icon.

Gem answered with a burst of sound that had Becca turning down her phone volume. "There goes our twin telepathy again! I was about to call you, Bex. I have the most fabulous news." From the jolting of the video, it appeared that Gem was bouncing on her toes. "Alek's managed to pull off a miracle with UrbanROAD. They're keeping me on as brand ambassador, and I'm going to present a livestream for them called *The UrbanROAD to Recovery*, all about wildlife rehabbing. We're shooting it at the sanctuary."

Becca ignored a twinge of irrational jealousy. "Sounds good."

"Good? It's totally awesome. Everyone wins! Your man's sanctuary gets publicity and in between streaming, I can put in the hours I still owe him. UrbanROAD's also sponsoring some or other housing project that Sully has for wild cats. Once it's built, there'll be a live webcam showing what the animals get up to."

"That really is great. I'm thrilled for you both," she said, and blanched. That had sounded like she was congratulating them on their engagement. Sully in a wedding tux... She gulped a sip of tea. Now that was an image she really hadn't needed her brain to serve up.

"Hey." Gem cocked her head. "What's up?"

"Just lonely. Missing you. Missing him." She took another sip, but now it hurt to swallow.

"Aw, sweetie," Gem said. "I'm sorry. If it helps, I'm going to be seeing him on Monday."

"Er, no, it doesn't help. It actually makes me jealous as fuck."

Gem laughed. "You know what we need? Another switch. I'll come and charm your guests, and you come here and climb a certain someone like a tree."

Becca's hand clamped down on her mug. "Mmmm. Tempting as that sounds, I think I'll pass." Her eye caught movement at the concierge desk and she looked over to see the Rickford's general manager speaking to one of the juniors, who nodded in Becca's direction. "Got to go, sis. Shahid's looking for me."

Becca stowed her phone in a pocket as Shahid drew up to her. He had an odd little smile on his lips, as if he'd chanced upon a stray turndown chocolate and had popped it surreptitiously into his mouth where it was melting at this very moment. The silver buttons on his double-breasted jacket winked in the downlights of the lobby.

Becca pressed the still-warm mug to her chest and smiled at him. “You need me?”

Shahid tapped the side of his nose and edged in close to her. “You didn’t hear this from me, but a source tells me that someone is about to get some very special keys.”

“Keys?” She tipped her head, a mystified smile beginning to creep onto her until—“You mean *the* keys?” She extended her thumb where it held her mug and crossed the index finger of her other hand over it, forming the X of the Society of the Golden Keys lapel pin.

Shahid patted his own lapel and winked. “You’ve been accepted.”

Accepted? She blinked at him. “You mean I’m in? I’m a Golden Keys concierge?” After the media coverage back in South Africa? The decision must have been made before the shit hit the fan, or otherwise the Society’s background checking department had been asleep on the job.

Shahid’s face shone with pride and he reached for her hand, forcing her to do a hasty swop of her mug, and began pumping it up and down like he was trying to lever it off her. “My little protégé. From housekeeping to the hallowed ranks of the most elite concierge organisation in the world. I’ll bet you’re ecstatic.”

“I...” She *was* ecstatic, wasn’t she? Elated? Jubilant? But where were the squadrons of bejewelled butterflies doing celebratory swoops inside her? Where was the urge to fist-pump the air while jumping up and down shrieking like a contestant on a home-makeover show as they took off their blindfold? It was as if someone had dialed down the intensity of her emotions.

She caught Shahid's hand with her other one to stop his enthusiastic congratulations before her shoulder required weeks of physiotherapy, slopping tea over the brim of the mug. "I am super excited!" she gushed. But the words didn't connect with anything inside her. Maybe it was simply because she'd imagined this moment so many times over the years, that the reality would naturally pale in comparison.

Shahid patted her firmly on her shoulder. "Good job, Becca. This is everything you ever wanted."

"Absolutely."

Then why did everything suddenly feel like nothing?

31

Earl's Court, London
Tuesday, 27 September

Becca's cellphone was propped against a potted succulent on the table in The Rickford's employee break room. It was way too early for a tea break, but she couldn't resist catching the last minutes of Gem's livestream.

It was becoming something of a guilty pleasure, sneaking off to the break room whenever one of Gem's livestreams was on, and it wasn't the animals or even her sister she was there for. It was the possibility of catching a glimpse of a certain vet that kept her sneaking onto YouTube instead of manning the desk. (And judging from the comments, she wasn't the only one who was "just here for the hot vet".)

Gem's face filled Becca's screen, her eyes bright, a rhinestone and gold flower clip over one ear holding back her hair. "It's a gorgeous spring day here at the Winterberg Wildlife Rescue and Sanctuary. If you're only joining us now on *The UrbanROAD to Recovery*, you're just in time to meet the most adorable spring baby ever." Gem stared into the camera and hugged herself with a theatrical shiver of excitement.

The camera cut to a wider angle and a woman in her mid-thirties, black hair in a neat ponytail, wearing a sanctuary tunic over jeans, came into shot. Verusha, the new vet who'd replaced Clare. Good riddance, though Gem hadn't been able to tell Becca why her nemesis had left.

The camera panned down. On the lawn at Gem's feet was a baby rhino. It stood just higher than Gem's knee, its three-toed feet splayed on the grass under the weight of its compact body. Heavy, blocky head down, black eyes blinking in curiosity, the calf investigated Gem's designer sneaker with a wide, square lip.

"Is that you with a baby hippo?"

Becca turned away from her phone to see one of the front desk clerks, empty coffee mug in hand, stopped behind her chair.

"That's my twin sister. And that's a rhino."

"You have a twin? How cool is that! But where's its horn?"

"Er, horn?" Becca glanced back at the screen, confused.

"On the baby rhino?"

Ah. "They're not born with horns. They grow later."

The clerk shook her head in wonder. "Too awesome. And how exciting that you have a twin! I bet you two got up to all sorts of pranks at school."

"You don't want to know," Becca said wryly.

The desk clerk patted her on the shoulder and made a maternal clucking sound at the screen, then headed for the coffee machine on the counter.

Becca returned her attention to her phone. Gem was squatting beside the baby rhino, waggling one of its Shrek-like ears. "Say hello to Vikela," Gem said. "He's an orphaned white rhino calf that's been getting back on his little feet for the last few weeks, under the eye of Dr Sully and his team."

It didn't matter how many times Gem mentioned Sully's name, Becca felt a little jolt of electricity every time. She propped her elbows on the table and angled in, her body wired with anticipation.

Gem addressed her unseen audience. "For security reasons, I haven't been able to mention Vikela before now. But he's off to his new home at a rhino orphanage today, so you finally get to meet him." The calf nuzzled Gem's leg with his boxy muzzle, and she bent to pat his sturdy back. "Before he gets on the road, we're going to give his little legs a stretch. If you've never seen a baby rhino running, you're going to want to stay with us. I'm talking cuteness overload!" Gem made an exuberant follow-me gesture to the camera. "And speaking of cute, here's Miss Ella."

If Ella was there... It felt as if her heart had just done an actual cartwheel.

Sully's chocolate Lab padded into view and promptly spat out her potato. Gem stepped back with a squeak. The rhino calf had no such aversions though. It scooped up Ella's cherished potato and crunched it with relish between its jaws.

Off camera, a deep male laugh turned Becca's insides to a treacle-y mush. She willed whoever was holding the camera to pan in Sully's direction, but apparently a rhino calf chomping on a root vegetable made for far more compelling viewing.

After what felt like eons of potato pulverising, the camera lifted from the rhino to Gem and she patted her thigh. "Let's move out, troops!"

Gem set off down a dirt road with a pint-sized rhino and a potato-less Labrador at her heels, effortlessly weaving facts about the rhino poaching crisis into her easy chatter.

Where is he? Becca peered into the back of the shot, leaning as if changing her angle might afford her a different view.

Around a curve in the road, the old manor house came into view in the background, and Becca gave up the hunt for Sully to focus on the rundown building. With a coat of white paint, that gabled front would be truly beautiful, set off by the towering oak tree to one side and the mountains beyond...

"Yay, he's doing it." Gem clapped her hands. "Galloping rhino!"

The manor house dropped out of the shot as the camera swung to follow the rhino calf as he bounced after Ella on toes that seemed to be fitted with springs. "Told you it was the cutest thing ever," Gem called, and the camera moved back to her.

And there he was. Sully. Bringing up the rear several paces behind. Becca's cartwheeling heart became a full Catherine wheel, shooting off sparks of light. She'd never known how sweet yet painful yearning could be.

Sully walked with unhurried steps, his work boots kicking up puffs of dust on the road, arms hanging relaxed at his side. He looked straight into the camera before he seemed to realise he was being filmed and dipped his head abruptly.

"Aw, come on, Dr Sully." Gem's voice was a teasing sing-song. "Say hi. You never know who might be watching."

Becca touched a fingertip to the screen and froze Sully's image. Longing crept along her nerves, tightening her stomach and putting a wistful hitch into her breath. She really should stop watching these livestreams.

32

Earl's Court, London
Thursday, 29 September

"What a wanker!" Becca's colleague scowled across the lobby at a retreating guest. "Like it was your fault he didn't set his wristwatch for local time and missed his airport shuttle. Who uses a watch anyway these days?"

Sully does. Becca swallowed a sigh. She appreciated her colleague's indignation on her behalf, but to be frank, she'd barely registered Room 127's temper tantrum. It had just blended into the general feeling of indifference that had settled over her life these days. Like this morning, when she'd managed to source an exact replica of one of Princess Kate's hats for the guest in Room 422 who wanted to wear it to a weekend wedding. It had earned her such effusive praise that she should be floating right now, but she'd just smiled and said she was only doing her job.

And that was the problem in a nutshell. Being behind the concierge desk had never felt like she was only doing a job. It has always felt so much more than that, like a calling. But now something had shifted, and she had a nagging fear that even once her uniform lapels were weighted down by her new Golden Keys pins, she might never get back to that place again.

Her phone vibrated on the counter, the video-call icon pulsing. She answered and Mom appeared on the screen.

"Sorry to bother you at work, love," Mom said without preamble, "but you don't by any chance have a phone number for a silversmith? Gem's broken that necklace with the moon pendant."

Silversmiths. In Johannesburg. Unreal. "Um, not offhand, no." Becca glanced over the counter to see the space in front of the concierge desk blissfully devoid of needy guests. "I'll find out for you. Give me a sec." She leaned her phone against her computer screen and opened her browser.

"Thank you," Mom sighed, as if a crisis had been narrowly averted. "Always such a lifesaver." Mom's head tipped and she studied the screen. "Are you alright? You're looking rather pasty."

Thanks. Becca curved her mouth enough to mimic a smile. "I'm fine," she said, her attention on the search results on her computer screen. "There's a manufacturing jeweller in Sandton."

"But you don't look fine. You look even paler than usual," Mom said, bringing her face closer to the screen for a closer inspection. "And those dark rings under your eyes... Have you been getting enough sleep?"

Becca released her mouse. "Avery?" She caught her colleague's eye. "Will you hold the fort please?" She scooped up her phone and headed to the luggage room at the other end of the concierge desk. "Mom, really, I'm okay," she said. "A few too many shifts, that's all." She stepped inside and pulled the door shut behind her.

"You might have picked up a bug. Have you seen a doctor?"

Becca balanced herself on top of an upright black clamshell suitcase parked at the back of the luggage room. Maybe Mom was right. A seasonal bug would explain the lethargic weight in her limbs. The difficulty getting out of bed each morning. The effort it took to keep a how-may-I-help-you smile nailed to her face all day. Who was she trying to kid? She squeezed her temples between her thumb and fingers before wiping her hand down her face and looking back at the screen. "I'm not sick, Mom," she said. And more's the pity, because the flu she could treat with a handful of pills and a few days of sick leave. "I just...I miss home." *I miss him.*

So much that even her teeth seemed to hurt. And it would appear that nothing—not time nor extra shifts—was making a blind bit of difference in getting over him.

"You could always come home, you know," Mom said. "I'm sure there are plenty of hotels here that would be thrilled to hire an internationally accredited concierge."

"I somehow doubt that, Mom. Even a set of Golden Keys lapel pins isn't going to make people forget that I'm the twin who deceived the whole country."

Mom flapped a dismissive hand at the screen. "It'll be old news soon enough."

"And I already have a great job here."

"I'm just saying," Mom said. "And it would be nice to have both our girls back home."

Becca's smile was wry. "Easier for me to get you any contact numbers you need."

Mom clucked her tongue. "You know that's not it."

Dad's face appeared over Mom's shoulder then. "Oh, hello, bunny," he said, looking into the screen. "I thought I heard your voice."

Dad's smile warmed Becca's heart like the sun coming out from behind a cloud. "Hey, Dad."

"You look a bit worn-out, my bunny." He shifted closer to Mom, an almost imperceptible wince crinkling the skin around his eyes as the movement hurt his hip. "Too much stress at that concierge desk?"

Soon she wouldn't have to see that pain on Dad's face, and that at the very least was worth a genuine smile. "It's all good, Dad," she said. "Don't worry about me. You know I love it." *Just not as much as before.*

Dad placed a hand on Mom's shoulder as he leaned in, bringing their faces together on the screen. "Why don't you go outside into that park on the other side of the road for your lunch break, instead of staying cooped up indoors?"

"I'm not actually on a break right now. I'm just getting a phone number for Mom."

Dad pulled back and angled a stern look at Mom. "This is what I mean.

"Oh Richard," Mom said, exasperated. "It's not some terrible imposition. She's just better on Google than I am."

"Anyone would think you were a tech-phobic Boomer."

Mom swatted at him. "Rude. I could absolutely look it up myself."

"Exactly what I'm saying. It's just easier to get Becca to do it." He wagged a finger at Mom. "We've spoken about this," he scolded, before he kissed her on the top of her head. "I need to get a move on. My appointment with the ortho's in an hour." He looked into the screen again. "Bye, bunny. Just tell Mom *no* next time."

"Bye, Dad." Becca waved at her departing father before giving her mother a look. "And that?"

Mom sent her gaze skywards. "Dad's been giving me grief ever since the whole Winterberg fiasco. He says it's all my fault." Mom pouted at the screen, showing exactly where Gem had picked up the habit of pouting whenever she wanted something.

And now, that pout said Mom wanted Becca to ease her conscience. To tell her that of course all the drama of that week and the chaos that had come afterwards hadn't been her fault. But today, Becca couldn't find the energy to make things all better for her mother. "It kind of is, Mom." *Kind of totally is.*

Mom tutted and her gaze swung away. "I just suggested it, and I had only the best of intentions. You two girls should have stopped me."

A sudden impatience pricked at Becca. "Look, Mom, I've got to get back to the desk." Inhaling quickly, she stood up from the suitcase and aimed a simulated smile at her phone. "I'll text you that number for the jeweller."

"Becca," Mom said. "I *am* sorry. You know that."

"I know, Mom." There'd been so many apologies in the weeks after their secret had been exposed, she couldn't stomach any more. "Don't worry about it. It's water under the bridge." She paused with her hand on the doorknob, waiting to end the call before going back to the desk. "You know I'm always there if you need me."

"I know. And we love you for it."

Becca's hand tightened reflexively on the knob. "Yep, that's me. Helpful Becca." *Carve it on my headstone.* "Bye, Mom."

"That's what I told Dad," Mom said. "It's who you are, so how can it be taking advantage? You're never happier than when you're stepping up and mucking in." Mom tittered. "Literally, as it turned out in Winterberg."

Becca hooked a finger under the knot of her pin-dotted scarf and pulled it away from her throat. "You're triggering my trauma,"

Becca said, with a stiff chuckle. She turned the polished brass doorknob and tugged open the door. "I have to go, Mom."

"Do you remember how you used to do Gem's homework at high school when her catalogue schedule got so busy?" Mom said, laughter in her voice as she took her trip down memory lane. "And how you'd make dinner when we were at late auditions. So much pasta! You were always such a helpful kid."

"Because that's all I had to offer." Becca froze, hand on the doorknob behind her, about to pull the door shut. Where had that come from?

"That's just silly," Mom said.

The tightness in Becca's throat was getting worse, as if something were crowding up from the inside, something that was desperate for air. She released the knob and reached instead for her scarf, shoving her fingers in behind the knot and tugging until she could yank it loose, pulling the ends out from inside her pressed shirt.

"Becca! What are you doing?" Mom said, her shrill tone causing Avery to turn and her gaze to zero in on Becca's dishevelled neckwear.

Becca stepped back into the luggage room and shut the door with a little too much force. Her skin felt too hot, like she'd opened an oven door and released a blast of hot, steamy air into her face. *That's all I had to offer.* She didn't really think that. Did she? She swallowed hard around a painful lump in her throat, gulping futilely against a swell of hurt clawing up from her chest. What was happening? She fanned her face and fumbled the black clamshell closer, dropping onto it off shaking legs.

"Becca, you're frightening me," Mom said, from somewhere down the side of the clamshell where Becca's hand hung, the phone caught in numb fingers.

She was frightening herself. There was a pressure building inside her, as if a roiling geyser of super-heated steam was beginning to escape around the edges of a chunk of concrete that was blocking the vent. Becca lifted the phone so she could look at her mother.

"What's going on?" Mom said, her voice and eyes showing the concern that her Botoxed forehead couldn't.

An excellent question. "Do you remember the last pageant I was in?"

"Your last..." Mom laughed. "With the tennis racket? Who could forget that?"

Hard to forget a moment where your daughter had so shamed you. Becca didn't want to go there though. She squeezed her eyes shut and bit down against the pain spreading through her chest as she tried to shove the memory back into its box. Why had she even brought it up?

"What about it, love?"

Leave it. Forget I said— "I felt like the world's biggest failure that day. I remember looking at Gem and feeling like a defective copy. Redundant." The words tumbled from her mouth, exploding up from the shallow grave they'd been buried in all these years. "And I've spent my whole life trying to feel otherwise. Trying to feel needed. All I ever wanted was for you to see me. My whole life I've been trying to get your attention. Trying to be enough for you and for everyone else."

Becca's face felt hot and cold at the same time, chilled in the cool air of the luggage room. She lifted a hand to her cheek to find it wet with tears. Was this why? Why she put together itineraries for guests over her weekends instead of chilling? Why she would always stand in for a colleague or be the one to take on an extra shift? Why she hadn't even thought twice about the possible repercussions for her own life of switching with Gem? She'd always been proud of how nothing was too big of an ask, how nothing was too hard, how nothing could prevent her from putting a smile on someone else's face.

Her people-pleasing superpower. It wasn't a power at all, was it? It was a symptom of her own need. She'd even chosen a career where she could indulge that need, bending over backwards for anyone and everyone so that even complete strangers wouldn't be disappointed in her. For the rest of her team, guest satisfaction might be a job, but for her, it was validation. *Like me! Need me!* Because only when people did, did she feel worthy of love.

Mom was saying something, but it took Becca a few seconds to tune in to it. "How can you even say that, Becca?" Mom said. "That you aren't enough. Of course you are. And you always have been."

Right. "So you weren't ashamed of me that day?" Becca said, the first notes of anger stabbing into her voice. "You're telling me you didn't look at me and see only a disappointment?"

"Absolutely not!"

"You've forgotten then how in the car going home, you couldn't even bear to look me in the eyes?" Becca said. "How you kept catching my gaze in the rearview mirror and then looking away?"

"No!" Mom looked pained. "You were a child, Becca. Children see the world in strange ways." One hand fluttered at the base of Mom's neck and her gaze skittered away for a moment. "Okay, so I was a little ashamed," she said, her eyes returning to the screen, "but in my defence, you *had* just given a pageant judge a concussion."

"It was an accident!"

"I know." Mom took a deep breath as if she was steeling herself, the fluttering hand now gripping her throat. "And if you really must know, I was actually more ashamed of myself than of you."

Wait, what?

"I've never forgotten your sad little face that day." Mom looked away, and when she looked back, her eyes were bright with moisture. "And I was ashamed that it was me who'd put you in a situation like that. I'd turned a blind eye to how much you hated being out there with Gem. I'd been so caught up in being the mom of the most gorgeous twins in the country that I'd lost sight of one of them." Mom's hand kneaded at the column of her throat. "I've done that a lot, haven't I?" And Mom began to cry.

There were no more words left in Becca. Just tears, the strange feeling of disorientation that came from seeing her life from a different perspective, and rather more snot than should ever be allowed to come anywhere near a concierge uniform. Becca wiped her eyes with the back of her hand, attempting to stem the tide. "No, Mom, you haven't." She was doing it again. Making things right for everyone else. "Okay, yes, you have done that a lot."

"Oh God," Mom wailed, "I'm the world's worst mother."

"And yet I still love you." Becca hiccupped teary laughter. "Warts and all."

"I hope not," Mom said. "The warts part, I mean." Her smile was shaky and she blotted at her eyes with a tissue. "I love you, Becca. So much. I'm sorry I ever let you doubt that."

As Mom's words sank into her heart, Becca lowered her chin to her chest and let the tears flow.

When Becca finally ended the call and emerged from the luggage room, her scarf retied after she'd used it to pat her face dry, she felt like she'd just binge-watched a Nicholas Sparks movie marathon. Wrung out. Hollow. Raw. As if the skin she'd been living in for most of her life—this false impression she'd laboured under that had seen her spending so much of her time and effort trying to prove her worth, even to strangers—had been scoured off. It was an alien concept, that perhaps the people who truly mattered did already know her worth, even if she couldn't quite see it herself yet. That it might be okay to put herself first, to do something for herself, without losing the love of the people who mattered to her.

Two men stood waiting for assistance behind a guest who was consulting a brochure with Avery. Becca checked her scarf was properly tucked in before she hurried back to her workstation. She motioned to the men to step forward. "Sorry to keep you waiting, sirs," she said. "How may I help?"

"What time do they change the guard at Buckingham Palace?" said the one in a navy coat.

"The New Guard leaves Hyde Park Barracks at half ten, sir, and arrives at Horse Guards Parade at eleven."

The man turned to his companion. "If we leave now, we'll make it."

"Oh, it's not on today, sir," Becca said. "From August to May, the parades aren't daily. You can catch it tomorrow though."

Navy Coat scowled. "But that's ridiculous! We're not here tomorrow."

Experience kept Becca from reacting with anything more than a sympathetic smile. "How unfortunate, sir."

"But that was one of the things we specifically wanted to see." He clamped a hand on the edge of the marble counter. "Does England want tourist revenue or not?"

"I'm sure it does, sir," Becca said, her voice a soothing hum. "Unfortunately, we're moving out of peak season now and—"

"When was the last parade?"

"Yesterday, sir. Every Monday, Wednesday—"

"So if you'd told us this yesterday, we could have gone then."

Becca stared at him in silence as she squashed her rising anger into a tight dense ball and swallowed it down. "Indeed, sir. Had you but asked."

The man shook his head. "Unbelievable. It seems everyone's right about England's crap customer service." He crowded up to the counter and eyeballed her. "You can sort this out. I know you can. For what we're paying per night for our suite, it's the least you could do."

"I don't think I'll be able to help in this case, sir."

"Why not?" he barked. "You people are supposed to have contacts. Unless you're also second-rate like everything else in this place."

The self-control that had been keeping Becca's smile attached to her face snapped. "I suppose I could phone the Palace and ask to have it moved up for you, sir. I'm sure they wouldn't mind completely altering their schedule for you."

The man's mouth fell open. "Excuse me? Are you allowed to talk to guests like that?"

"Oh, you thought that was sarcasm, sir? No, no, no. Like you say"—she tapped the side of her nose—"we people have contacts. One moment." She picked up her mobile and swiped it awake, ignoring the frantic drumming of her heart as it realised she'd just veered dangerously off her usual script. "Let me see. Charles." Swipe. "Charles." Swipe. "Charles. Nope. Oh, hold on. Silly me." She looked up and did an exasperated eye-roll. "I saved him under King, not Charles." She tapped at nothing on the screen and lifted her phone to her ear. "Hello? Your Majesty? It's Becca here from—" She clucked her tongue and waggled her phone at the men. "Voicemail," she chuckled. "Gets me every time."

Both men gaped at her.

"Avery?" Becca slid her mobile into her pocket. "I'll be taking my tea break outside. And I might not be back exactly on the hour."

"Take your time," Avery said, clapping her hands silently beneath the cover of the counter, and whispering *bravo* as Becca passed.

"Gentlemen," Becca said, sailing past the two scandalised guests and heading off across the lobby. As Becca reached the Rickford's double front doors, she smiled. She did love being a concierge. Loved thinking on her feet and pulling off miracles and wowing people with the impossible made possible. But it demanded a lot, and not just of her time, but of her heart and soul too. She was all give, give, give, fulfilling what everyone else wanted, never expecting anything in return, not even a thank-you. But she deserved more than that. After living her life for other people, perhaps it was time to finally figure out what *she* wanted.

33

Winterberg, South Africa
Friday, 28 October

The sun was warm on Becca's face as she followed the dirt road that led to the sanctuary's stables, passing in and out of the soft shade cast by the overarching trees in their fresh spring foliage. It was a bit of a walk from the rehab centre, and she could've driven, but she'd left Dad's car where she'd parked Gem's that first night—without mowing down the fence this time—and had set off on foot, enjoying the warmth of summer after the winter bite of London. As she walked, a breeze heated by a morning of lazing about on sun-drenched roads wrapped up her jean-clad legs and played with the untucked hem of her soft floral-print blouse.

She'd spent yesterday at her parents', wanting to wish Dad well before his operation in the coming week. She'd have loved to give in to Mom's cajoling requests for her to stay the whole weekend so they could spend time together, this time without the stress of a baying pack of reporters at the door. But there was only one place Becca wanted to be right now, and these past few weeks, she'd been trying something new: saying 'yes' to herself.

As she passed the line of cages where the recuperating monkeys were housed, a volunteer with a shovel over one shoulder called out Gem's name and raised his hand in greeting. It had been like that with everyone she'd crossed paths with since she'd arrived. She was Gem again.

A month ago, she'd felt a little like her sister. Spontaneous. Leaping without first looking. Every responsible, dutiful fibre in her had shrunk back in horror at her impulsive decision, and she'd come close to retreating into her comfort zone of people-pleasing obligation when Shahid's face had crumpled in disappointment at her unexpected resignation. Finding an impeccable replacement for the concierge desk had helped placate her mentor, and by the time she'd finally headed to the airport, it had been with his promise to be there for her when she needed him. And with the ambitious project that—hopefully, if she did her proposal correctly—lay ahead of her, she most certainly would.

Two vehicles were parked in front of the barn-like stables, one of them Sully's Ranger. Excitement tinged with trepidation quickened Becca's pulse. She paused in the big doorway that opened onto the stable to breathe cool straw-scented air into her jittery body. Her hand was clenched tight on the strap of the leather messenger bag over her shoulder, and she consciously released her grip as she let her gaze rove over the barn's interior. Four open-air stalls with sliding wooden gates set into a chest-high wall looked out onto a wide concreted corridor. Light spilled in from strip windows set just beneath a low ceiling that lent a close, protective feel to the space.

A woman stood with her arms folded on top of the wooden gate of the furthermost stall. She had on one of the sanctuary's veterinary tunics, her black hair tied in a plait that hung down her back to her bum. Becca recognised her from Gem's livestreams.

Verusha, was it? Yes, she was pretty sure that was the new vet's name. So engrossed in whatever was going on inside the stall, Verusha hadn't yet noticed Becca.

Someone else had though. At a heavy thumping just inside the doorway, Becca looked down to see Ella, stretched out on the concrete floor, front paws bracketing her potato. She opened her arms to the big dog, and Ella scrambled to her feet, whipping up her potato on the way, only to dump it in enthusiastic welcome on Becca's right foot.

"Ew," Becca mouthed, and tipped the spud off her shoe, toeing it back to the delighted Labbie. She caught Ella's heavy head in her hands and rubbed the dog's ears while she searched the barn for Sully.

"He's much perkier this afternoon," Verusha said, to someone out of sight inside the stall.

Becca's pulse skipped. Equal parts anticipation and nervousness turned her insides into a churning barrel of eels. "Is that where Daddy is?" she murmured to Ella.

As if her words had conjured him up, Sully appeared, his head and shoulders rising into view over the chest-high stall wall. Becca's stomach somersaulted and her hand slowed to a halt on Ella's plush head. He was faced away from her, his dark, somewhat scruffy hair brushing the neck of a faded black tee. He stretched to hang a drip bag from a hook set in a beam that ran above the stalls, the muscles in his back and forearm flexing.

Sully squeezed the drip bag. "Monique's going to watch him today, and Gunther will take over tonight."

Goosebumps tracked across Becca's skin. She'd heard that deep voice every night in her dreams, but it was so much better in real life. She blew out a soft breath and looked down into Ella's upturned hazel eyes. She smiled and gave an exaggerated shiver.

In response, Ella jammed her vegetable-filled muzzle against her leg, and Becca chuckled.

"Gem?"

Becca glanced back at the stall to find Verusha looking in her direction. "Busted," she whispered. She lifted a hand to wave, before giving Ella's head a last pat and setting off towards the stall, the soft chuffing of an ambling Labrador falling into step behind her.

Unlike his new employee, Sully didn't turn to look at Becca. Instead, he kept his attention trained on something at his feet. "Come on then," he said. He bent and there was the soft thump-thumping of a hand patting an animal's side. "Up you get."

There was a loud rustling of straw and then the patchwork head of a baby giraffe rose into view, borne aloft on a graceful neck. One ear hung down under the weight of a bandage that kept the drip in place. Half a foot taller than Sully, the calf angled its head, blinking at him with enormous, liquid eyes protected by the sort of thick, ebony lashes Gem would've killed for.

"Gosh, that's even cuter than you, El, which is saying something," Becca said, looking back at the dog as she walked. She moved in beside Verusha and settled her arms on top of the gate. "Hi," she said.

Sully turned his head enough to see her out the corner of his eye, before the baby giraffe pulled his attention back.

"I thought you were only back on Monday." Verusha said.

Shooting commitments for *Luxe Life* had taken Gem away from the sanctuary for the last month, but she was back next week to pick up with the UrbanROAD livestreams again. "I decided I might as well get a head start on prepping for the next episode."

"Missed us that much, did you, Stratton?" Sully said, head down as he fiddled with the bandage wrapped above the calf's knee.

Becca smiled. He'd called her sister *My Little Pony* when she'd first returned to the sanctuary to re-do her service hours, just to get a rise out her, Gem had said. He'd eventually switched it up to a brusque *Stratton* for the livestreams, as his relationship with Gem had mellowed. "I missed being a thorn in your side, Dr Scott," Becca said, teasing him like she'd heard Gem do on the livestreams and eliciting a chuckle from Verusha.

"Giant pain in my arse, that one," he muttered into the giraffe's neck.

"But what an arse it is." In those worn blue jeans... "Have you read some of the comments for the last livestream?" Grinning at Verusha, Becca fanned herself, adjusting her stance against the stall gate as heat unspooled low in her belly and slip-slid down to between her thighs. "People are fangirling over you, Dr Scott." And she was the head of the fan club. After so many weeks of not seeing him, it was a wonder his clothes weren't beginning to smoke from the friction of her gaze.

Ella sat down heavily at Becca's feet, her rump rattling the stall gate.

Verusha jerked her chin at the baby giraffe. "Isn't he the most gorgeous creature?"

The calf nuzzled Sully's neck with its velvety sock-puppet mouth and he laughed and fended it off with gentle but firm hands. Becca sighed, the kind of sigh Gem made when she saw a to-die-for pair of shoes in a shop window. "So gorgeous." And the baby giraffe was cute too.

"Let's do the next episode on him."

"Sounds like a plan," Becca said, her chin propped in her hand and her gaze fixed on Sully. If he felt her unblinking stare on him, he made no sign of it, still not giving her more than that first cursory glance.

He checked his watch. "He's due for a feed in the next hour." He checked the drip again, his metal bracelets shifting against each other on his wrist as he twisted the bag. "Looks like I'm done then." He patted the calf's rump, making its muscles ripple beneath its patchwork coat. "I'm going to head off." Sully brushed off his hands on his jeans and turned to Verusha. "Thanks again for volunteering to look after my dogs."

Becca's shoulders lifted as she stiffened to attention. He was going somewhere? Probably off to deliver an animal to another sanctuary. She relaxed against the gate again.

Verusha released the latch on the gate and slid it open for him as he crossed the stall. "You know I love your dogs. Especially Ella."

At the mention of her name, Ella's tail thumped hard against one of Becca's feet.

Stepping out of the stall, Sully shut the gate behind him and dropped onto his haunches, opening his arms to Ella like Becca had done. Ella swayed into his embrace, her tail a slow-turning propellor of joy. "You be good, okay?" Sully said, and Ella jammed her spit-covered potato into his neck. He flinched back laughing and threw an arm around the thick brown neck, making Ella huff with delight and nuzzle him under his chin. "I'm going to miss you."

Becca eyed him with unease. Exactly how long was this trip he was going on?

He roughed Ella's ears and pushed up with a hand from the floor, his gaze rising up Becca's body until he reached her face. He halted, not quite at his full height yet, and stared at her, his gaze moving over her features. And then his eyes widened and he felt behind him for the top post of the gate, gripping onto it when he found it as if the ground were shaking beneath him.

"You okay?" Verusha said, concern in her voice.

He grunted and nodded, his eyes never leaving Becca's. "Stood up too fast." He released his hold on the gate.

"Well, let me get back to the centre." Verusha turned to Becca. "You want a ride back?"

"I'll walk, thanks," Becca said, tipping her head in Verusha's direction without taking her eyes from Sully's.

"Suit yourself." Verusha patted Ella's head and nudged the big dog with her leg. "You're coming with me, Miss. We don't want any tearful goodbyes when your dad leaves."

Tearful goodbyes? Becca eyed Sully with growing alarm. This was starting to sound like more than a there-and-back trip to relocate a rescued animal.

He broke eye contact then and watched as Verusha headed off across the barn, Ella at her side. Once they disappeared through the wide door, he turned his full attention back to Becca and his chest expanded on a measured inhale. "Princess," he said in a low whisper that lifted the hair on her nape and made her breath catch.

"Dr Scott." Her voice wobbled and she cleared her throat. "Sir."

Sully's mouth tipped up and Becca's blood became warm syrup. One short step forward and she could be in his arms. "I've come at a bad time, by the sounds of it."

"I have some travel plans, but I don't have to leave just yet."

"Dropping off a rescue at another sanctuary?" *Please, please, please!*

"Job interview."

Oh? Oh! One hand lifted to fist above her sternum. She had not expected that. "You're...leaving the sanctuary?"

"If I like them and they like me."

Her heart toppled from her ribcage and floundered about in her gut. He was really leaving? But she'd just got here. And she had plans. "Somewhere local?"

"Overseas."

Oh God. That would teach her for wanting to do this in person and not calling him first. For just assuming he'd be waiting here when she was finally ready to move forward. "Well, that's...um...great for you." Her voice sounded like she'd swallowed a hair ball. She fixed her eyes on the baby giraffe's head that was swaying gently over Sully's shoulder. "I... Wow." She coughed to clear her throat. "I never thought you'd leave the sanctuary."

"I would never have thought it either. But I found, after all the shit that went down, that something was..." He lifted one shoulder and let it drop. "Missing."

"Mmmmm. I found the same thing. It got really hard to keep delivering service with a smile." Outside a bakkie roared to life and she looked away at the stable door. "Verusha seems nice."

He nodded. "And talented. She fits in well here. And there's the added bonus that she doesn't have a stalker-level crush on me."

Something to talk about other than his impending departure. "Gem told me that Clare was no longer around."

"Ya. Some stuff came out after you left that made it impossible for me to keep her on."

"Stuff?"

"Like how the pangolin story got into the press."

"That was Clare?"

He nodded. "In the early hours after the raid, someone was gabbing about it on Twitter from an account that had only just been set up. Naming and shaming you." Sully leaned his back against the stall wall and crossed his arms, one hand gripping his biceps. "But Jo and I had no idea who it could be. Only the cops and a handful of sanctuary staff knew that it was your Instagram post that had brought the traffickers here. That there was a screenshot of your post on one of their phones. But at the time, I had no idea about her hostility towards you, so I didn't suspect anything. After everything blew up with you and Gem, I confronted her about it."

Talk about hell having no fury. "I feel bad that she got fired because of me."

"She got fired because she put animals and staff members in danger," he said. "But I doubt you came here to talk about Clare."

"No. I didn't." Just because he was leaving, didn't mean her new dream should get derailed. This was something she wanted. But she also wanted him. Maybe this new job he was interviewing for was only for a short time. They could try the long-distance thing. Not that that ever worked. Why did he have to be leaving! She had a desperate urge to excuse herself and dash outside for a quick cry.

Sully propped a booted foot against the rough plaster of the wall. "Speak, princess."

Deep breath and focus on one thing at a time. Becca swung the messenger bag around until it hung at her stomach. Opening the flap, she reached in for one of the file binders she'd prepared before leaving England. "I have a business proposal for you and Jo." She clasped the binder against her chest, surprised to find she was nervous. "The last few months were really difficult. I felt terrible about what happened here, and then even when everything started to click into place and come right for Gem and my dad, I didn't feel any better. It took a while, but finally I realised something. That for as long as I could remember, I'd spent so much of my time and energy trying to make other people happy, that I'd stopped trying to make myself truly happy."

The baby giraffe looked over the wall and Sully reached up an arm to stroke its flexible neck. "And what would make you happy?"

She opened her mouth, one word—*You*—on her tongue. A tiny head shake dislodged the pronoun and she took a steadying breath before answering him. "I always wanted to run a hotel."

"I remember," he said. "Before you got caught up behind the concierge desk."

He'd remembered their conversation from all those weeks ago. Really paying attention. And now she was going to have to say goodbye. For the second time. The dull ache in her chest intensified. But she'd come here for a reason, and she owed it to herself to follow through.

She thrust out the binder and he took it from her, holding it unopened, waiting for her to continue. She slipped her messenger bag off her shoulder and placed it on the floor at her feet. "Sully," she began. Nervousness had made her mouth dry, and she wet her lips. "This is a beautiful property you and Jo have here, and I think you could make it work harder." The focused way he was watching her, like every word she said was important, was making it hard to remember the opening lines of her pitch. "I want to restore the original farmhouse to its former grandeur and turn it into a boutique hotel."

His eyebrows lifted, but he didn't interrupt her.

"It's a truly beautiful piece of Cape Dutch Revival architecture that deserves to be saved. And it's not an impossible job. I watched the livestream Gem and Verusha did about the bats in the chimney, and while they were in there, they wandered all over the house and really, it's not a lost cause at all. Plus it's on a stunning part of the property. That view out over the mountains?" Becca put her fingertips to her lips and kissed them. "Chef's kiss, honestly. And with the river behind it? We'll put a deck out the back going down to the water. Just think of the weddings we could host there. It would be stunning. All it needs is love and vision."

As she spoke, the corners of his mouth had been curving slowly upward until he was looking at her in unreserved amusement. "Which I assume you have plenty of."

She gestured for him to open the binder. "Look. Everything's in there."

Without breaking eye contact, Sully settled back against the wall and flipped open the cover. Then he dropped his head and began to read.

Becca hugged her arms around herself and gnawed on her bottom lip as she watched him read, mentally running through the sentences she knew almost by heart.

He turned the first page and her nerves bubbled over. She spun away, unable to stand there watching him for a second longer. She walked to the barn door, where she did an about-turn and walked back. He had his head angled to the side now, looking at some of the rough drawings she'd made after watching and rewatching that livestream.

God, this was nerve-wracking!

He turned the page.

The giraffe calf sidled up behind him and leaned its head down to mouth at the back of Sully's T-shirt. Deep in concentration, Sully held up a hand to ward off the calf, which stuck out a surprisingly long, surprisingly black tongue to wrap around his fingers. "Hey," Sully said softly, craning his head back to look at the calf. "You're being a bloody menace. Go and eat some leaves." The giraffe just nibbled on Sully's hair with its prehensile lips. Sully chuckled and dropped onto his haunches out of reach of the towering baby. Settling his back against the wall and the binder across his thighs, he returned his attention to her proposal.

Becca did an about-face worthy of the King's Guard and headed off towards the barn door again.

"You're going to wear a track into my floor, princess," he said on her return journey, without looking up from his reading.

There was an empty wheelbarrow and a metal bucket beneath a rack of manure forks and spades hanging on the wall opposite the stalls. Becca turned the bucket over and sat on it. Her knees poked up and she hooked her elbows around them.

He turned a page. "And now you're jiggling your leg."

She hadn't even noticed her one leg hammering up and down like a sewing machine needle. "Sorry," she said, and pressed her heels into the ground. She should have emailed the damn thing. Why wasn't he saying anything? Did he hate it? She worried the inside of her lip. What page was he on? She drew herself up straight on the bucket and peered across the walkway at his lap, but his hand was blocking her view. She leaned over, trying to see around his hand and almost fell off the bucket.

"Princess, would you calm down and let me finish. I'm almost"—he checked the reverse of a page, then turned back—"done." He shut the binder and lifted his head at last.

Becca exhaled loudly and stood up from the bucket. "Well?" She could barely contain herself.

He drummed the fingers of one hand lightly on the back of the closed binder. "Well indeed."

Oh God, he hated it. "Before you say anything, I know it's an ambitious project, and it's not like I'm some big hotel developer." *Way to go, Becca! Just highlight your own inexperience.* "But I'm absolutely up for the challenge. Between my degree and my experience working with banqueting managers and front desk managers and housekeeping staff, organising all sorts of things for guests, I can do this. Plus, I have contacts you wouldn't believe."

"I wouldn't doubt it," he said. He bent an arm back to set the binder on top of the stall wall, then he rested his back against it and regarded her with a serious expression. "This new reality TV show Gem's going to present next year."

From Hell to Hotel, where teams of renovators and interior designers competed to transform a disused building into a functioning hotel, room by room. "The show that will make this whole dream possible," Becca said.

"Do you really think they'd be interested in using the manor house as the location?"

"They're more than interested," she said. "They were meant to start shooting early next year, but their original location fell through a few weeks ago, and they still haven't found a replacement. Gem's already mentioned the manor house to them and showed them photos, and she says they're desperate to come and see it, especially since the show would then be a project for a good cause."

"Sounds promising then." Sully tilted his head and pinned her with an assessing eye. "But tell me, princess. I need to be one hundred percent clear on one thing. You've resigned from your job in London?"

"Anything will be better than the current bat guano floors." Sully tilted his head and pinned her with an assessing eye. "But tell me, princess. I need to be one hundred percent clear on one thing. You've resigned from your job in London?"

Becca nodded.

"Even though you'd just been accepted into the ranks of the Golden Keys? Your dream. The one thing you wanted to achieve before you turned thirty."

He sounded as sceptical as Shahid had been when she'd told him her plans. "I decided it was time for a new dream. One where I could use my skills to fulfil my own needs, not just everyone else's."

A smile tugged at Sully's mouth. "Well then, I don't have any more questions. I think your new dream is impressive, Becca.

And once you're done, it's going to be an incredible asset for the sanctuary."

"So it's a *yes* from you?" she asked, channelling an *X Factor* judge.

He chuckled. "It's very much a *yes* from me."

A burst of relief and pride and excitement made her feel light right through to her bones. Impulsively, she closed the space between them, covered his cheeks with her hands and kissed him square on his mouth. "Thank you," she breathed against his smiling lips.

His hands found her hips and he drew her in. "You have yourself to thank, not me. This is all down to your own hard work and inspiration."

This man... Still holding him pinned between her palms, she kissed him again, and he answered her with a kiss so full of tenderness that goosebumps danced across her skin. How had she ever thought in those first weeks apart that she'd be able to get over him and move on?

But he's leaving.

Becca broke the kiss on an inhale as she remembered the one major flaw in her happily-ever-after plan. Her hands fell from Sully's face and she took a sharp step back, only to be stopped abruptly by his hold on her hips. She tugged against his hands and he released her, his eyes confused as he let her open up the space between them.

She bent to scoop up her messenger bag, her movements made jerky by the renewed stab of pain to her heart. "You'll have to come and visit us from wherever your new job is taking you. To see how it looks when it's all done." She threw the strap over her shoulder but kept the bag against her body, as if it could somehow shield her from the pain of this second, inevitable parting.

Understanding passed over his face. "Ah. That," he said solemnly. "Could I ask you a favour before you hang up your concierge hat?"

The baby giraffe was snooping on them from on high. "Sure," Becca said, aiming her answer at the calf because if she looked at Sully right now, she was going to tear up and that wasn't fair. If he wanted to follow his heart to a new job, after he'd just given her the green light to do the same, then she couldn't in all good conscience stop him.

"Here," he said.

Reluctant, she looked to see him holding out his phone to her. "Would you cancel this plane ticket for me please?"

She took the phone, one arm still pressing her messenger bag to her chest, and scanned the e-ticket on the screen. "London?" *But I've just come from there!*

"Outside Dunstable in Bedfordshire to be more precise," he said. "Overseeing the African animal exhibits at the Whipsnade Zoo."

Was he being serious? The job his former colleague was always trying to convince him to take? The job he'd told her he would never even consider? But then people could change. She had, after all. "Sounds exciting." For anyone but Sully, maybe. "It's actually not far from where I stayed."

"I know. Your sister is a wealth of information." He was grinning now. "That's why I agreed to finally go through and meet them."

Joy tinged with disbelief unfurled inside her. "You were going to leave the sanctuary for me?"

"So vain, princess!" he laughed and hooked his index finger into a belt loop on her jeans, pulling her towards him. "How do you know it wasn't because I've always wanted to work in a zoo with captive animals?"

She grinned back at him and swatted at his chest over the messenger bag that was now crushed between them. "I can't believe you were going to do that for me. That you'd even consider it, when your whole heart is here at the sanctuary."

Sully brushed the strap of her bag off her shoulder and dropped it without ceremony on the floor. "It used to be. Before it found a new home." Finger still hooked in her belt loop, he ran his other hand along her hip to the small of her back, sliding it under her thin summer blouse, his palm branding her with heat. "In that text I sent you, I said you needed to figure out for yourself what you wanted. But I knew exactly what I wanted. And I told you I'd move heaven and earth to make it happen."

He leaned towards her, but she held him off with a palm to his chest. "One second, Dr Surly. I need to be one hundred percent clear on something," she said, repeating his words from earlier. "You're not going to leave the sanctuary. You're staying right here. With me."

Sully peeled her hand off his chest and brought her palm to his lips, sending heat spiking into her belly. "That would be another *yes* from me, to all three of your questions. Now would you please shut up and just kiss me?" And before she could reply, he lifted her onto tiptoe and claimed her mouth in a rush of heat and want that told her precisely how long all those weeks had felt to him.

She twined her arms around his neck and wove her fingers into his thick hair, the deep stroke of his tongue on hers sending waves of pleasure down to her toes.

He moaned into her mouth and—

Crash!

Becca jumped in Sully's arms and they jerked apart.

The giraffe inspected them over the wall. On the ground lay the binder, knocked off the wall by the curious baby.

Sully dropped his head back and laughed like an indulgent parent, making the calf sashay back from the wall, a wary eye fixed on them both. When Sully lifted his head again, his face was wreathed in exasperated mirth. "What is it with us and animals, princess?"

"Hey, it has nothing to do with me, Dr Doolittle," Becca said, poking him in the shoulder.

He drew his shoulder back and pretended to flinch, before catching her jaw in one hand and kissing her hard and fast on her mouth. "Now I have a proposal for you."

Becca cocked her head. "Is it as brilliant as mine was?"

"Mmmm," he said, the low rumble sending an involuntary shiver tracking up her spine. "I think it might give it a run for its money."

"Already off to a good start," Becca said.

Sully smiled and stroked his thumb in a featherlight touch over her cheek. "What do you say we get out of here and get started on turning those seven days we had together into a lifetime?"

Instagram

Winterberg
Liked by **rohan.scott** and **57,678 others**

gem_stratton You guys know I don't often post pics of my family, but I couldn't resist. Three years ago, my gorgeous accomplished sister @beccastratton met her true love. Today, here she is, walking down the aisle to marry him, in the most romantic spring wedding ever. Totes looking fabulous, Bex, and to my new brother-in-law, @sullivanscott, mwah. I love you both to the moon and back. So blessed to have shared this happily-ever-after with you.

Off to the reception next @TheManorHouse boutique hotel...yes, as seen on DStv's @FromHellToHotel, presented by yours truly and overseen by sister dearest. And now here we are, in this jewel tucked away in the shelter of the Drakensberg Mountains. Stunning views, to-die-for decor, a wooden deck overlooking the river...it's swoonworthy! (And it all supports the amazing work done by @WinterbergWildlifeRescue.) The perfect setting for the perfect wedding for the perfect couple!

#gemstratton #couplegoals #wedding #bride #mysister #sisterlove #weddinginspiration #weddingvenues #HEA #countryretreats #fromhelltohotel

View All 2,746 Comments

weddingjunkie OMG so beautiful! I remember how good it looked on the final episode, but it looks even better now! Must, must feature this place in our next issue! I'll DM you for your sister's deets.

trishiero YAAAASSSSSSS!

patty.fitness Awwww no, another gorgeous man off the market :(

lauren_Y @patty.fitness Did you see the photo Gem posted with all the groomsmen? The groom's brother Rohan doesn't have a ring on his finger and he is S.M.O.K.I.N.G!

friedalovesbikes @lauren_Y u know he races motorbikes? In the MotoGP championship overseas. So hot!!!

swankygabs Stunning couple!! And you're looking fabulous as always. Luv you Gem.

naledi_k They look so in love. Congratulations to your sister and her new husband.

megan_jayne When's it your turn, Gem?

Acknowledgments

I used to think writing a book was a solitary endeavour. Then I started writing books.

Yes, there's a lot of sitting at a keyboard all alone, hammering out words (and then deleting them, muttering about your own inadequacies). But it's hard to create a book baby and send it out into the world without the talents, skills, inspiration and guidance of others. Without people who I could bounce ideas off. People who helped change the direction of the story for the better. People who found errors and helped to polish the writing. And probably most importantly, people who helped me stay the course when I felt like Frodo, crawling on all fours across the plains of Mordor.

First, to the people closest to my heart...

To Theo, my husband and my best friend, who has been in my corner from the beginning. Thank you for your endless encouragement and your belief in me, even when I didn't believe in myself. For telling me to follow my dreams and then giving me the space and the resources to do that. And for demonstrating to me every day what true, boundless love and kindness looks like.

To my mom, Chanel Brinkworth, for being the greatest cheerleader, support and companion any daughter could wish for.

You've been there through it all, unceasingly cheering me on and offering me a shoulder to cry on. Though if anyone was crying, it should have been you, after I asked you to read over the book for what must have felt like the millionth time! Thanks for always being there for me (and for never once sighing out loud when I said, "Mom, can you read this please?").

To my daughters, Ashley and Joanna, for helping me untangle plot snarls, showing me how to use TikTok, and generally putting up with having a romance author for a mother, even when I was making you both cringe!

And then to the talented authors, editors and designers who helped me take this novel from initial concept to published book.

To Suzanne Jefferies, my incredibly skilled ROSA Strelitzia Award mentor, who helped me navigate the wastelands of my first drafts, stopping this book from becoming a rehashed James Herriot novel and lifting it to the point where we could take home the award for best unpublished author.

Sophia Karlson, who's been by my side on this journey since that first 4 a.m. call from Canada to ask me how the final draft was coming along. I don't think you were quite prepared for the emotional rollercoaster that would ensue, but your advice, plot brainstorming sessions, and most of all, your friendship, mean the world to me.

To my editor, Whitney Ross, who helped me hone not only this story, but also my writing craft. Thank you for making suggestion after suggestion until the book was where it is today.

To my beta readers Sophia Karlson, Leigh McPhail, Nicolle Allison, Joanna Chronis, Tracy Tuck, and Frieda Levycky, for your sharp eyes, honest feedback when something sucked, and glowing praise when something made you laugh and kept you reading way past your bedtime.

To the romance authors of ROSA, the Romance writers Of South Africa. Without you awesome authors, I know I would not have a published book in my hands right now. I can't begin to quantify just how important these authors have been on my journey, the knowledge and experience they have shared with me, and the friendship and encouragement they've shown me along the way. A special shoutout to Sophia Karlson, Amanda Holly, Ashleigh Giannoccaro, Tamsyn Bester, Sian B. Claven, Toni Cox, Mik Hunter, Romy Sommer, Alissa Baxter and Sharonlee Holder for being my author tribe. And to Dr Marianne Lomberg, romance author and veterinarian...my apologies in advance for any dodgy veterinary procedure which might have slipped through, despite your input.

To my cover designer, Tallulah Lucy, who perfectly translated my vision into a cover that I'm proud to put out there for the world to see. And to illustrators Nada Qamber and Gregg Davies for bringing to life the characters that have lived in my head all these years.

Lastly, it's been such a long journey that I have doubtless failed to mention everyone who deserves to see their name here, so to anyone else who helped me reach my destination, my grateful thanks.

Animals in the book

While you're still here, I wanted to give the pangolins in *The Seven Day Switch* an extra mention.

Living in South Africa, rhino poaching is a frequent and horrific topic. But there's a smaller, less publicly visible animal that is suffering the same fate as the rhinos, and for the same senseless reason: as a scientifically unproven traditional medicine.

Pangolins or scaly anteaters are timid solitary creatures that trundle through the African bush seeking out ants and termites to hoover up with their long gummy tongues. And because their scales and bones are believed, like rhino horn, to have miraculous healing powers, they're being trafficked and killed to the edge of extinction.

As Sully tells Becca in the book, pangolins are the most trafficked mammal in the world. For a species that has lived in Africa for over forty million years, to now be facing extinction is a travesty.

If you feel inspired to learn more about these embattled creatures and perhaps even donate to help save them, you can visit these pangolin conservation groups:

Pangolin Africa, at www.pangolin.africa

Pangolin Africa has a beautiful HD documentary called "Eye of the Pangolin: The Search for an Animal on the Edge" on their YouTube channel; well worth a watch.

Connect with Pangolin Africa on Instagram at @pangolinafrica.

African Pangolin Working Group, at www.africanpangolin.org, or find them on Instagram at @africanpangolinconservation

As for the rest of the furry and feathered cast...

As a South African, wildlife is part of the fabric of my life, and I've loved getting to share some of our wild creatures with you in this book.

If you'd like to know a little more about some of the other African animals mentioned in *The Seven Day Switch*, I made a YouTube playlist containing some of the videos I found during my research. You'll find it on YouTube using this shortened link: http://bit.ly/3zUMuFv

What's in the playlist?

- Pangolins, including the documentary I mentioned earlier.
- Vervet monkeys at CROW, a wildlife sanctuary in KwaZulu-Natal that inspired Sully's sanctuary.

- Stunning GoPro footage of Cape Griffon vultures in flight, as well as a Cape Griffon vulture in a studio setting with talk-show host Conan. (Watch from 2:10 to see what Becca would have experienced.)
- Spotted eagle owls, a rescued giraffe calf (cuteness overload off the charts), caracals and kudus.
- Rescued baby rhinos (when they gallop along, they really are as cute as Gem says they are!)
- And last but not least, the bat scene in the book was inspired by animal rehabbers ReWild. They're on Facebook at @ReWildNPC...check out the posts about the "sky puppies" they rescue.

About the author

Meg lives in Johannesburg, South Africa, with her two teenage daughters and her engineering husband, who is a steadfast supporter of her dreams, brings tea without being asked, and never objects to finding another rom-com cued for viewing on Netflix.

She writes feel-good rom-coms full of charm, hijinks, and heartwarming happily-ever-afters.

Meg is an amateur violinist and a huge fan of MotoGP motorcycle racing.

- Visit Meg online at www.megchronis.com
- Follow Meg Chronis on Instagram and Facebook under the name @megchronisauthor
- Subscribe to Meg's newsletter and get her novella, *Second Fiddle*, as a welcome gift. Visit www.subscribepage.com/megsnewsletter

Also by Meg

Second Fiddle

"Exactly how grateful would you be if I took care of your baboon problem?"

Intern Sophie James is one weekend and one glamorous African safari wedding away from becoming a permanent member of the Star Weddings team. All she needs to do is not mess up.

But booking a wedding string quartet that turns up minus a first violinist would definitely count as messing up. She could fill in herself; after all, she knows her way around a violin. Except a dream-destroying mistake a long time ago saw her pack away her instrument forever, and the thought of playing again is almost as harrowing as the thought of slinking back to her parents' house after yet another career sunk in a sea of failure.

It's a good thing then that Sophie finds herself in the right place at the right time to rescue the delectable—and heaven-sent—violinist Nate Holt from a baboon that's holding him captive in his game lodge shower. Now she has all the leverage she needs to convince him to fill in at the wedding in the bush.

Which is problem solved. Or so Sophie thinks. Because it turns out that problems, like baboons, are seldom solitary. As Sophie rushes to put out one career-ending fire after another, there's another fire sparking into life between her and Nate. But there's something Nate isn't telling her. Something Sophie really should have noticed, if she hadn't been so wrapped up in her own insecurities.

Once she finds out the truth about him, will she turn and run, letting her painful past continue to dictate her life? Or will she take Nate's hand and confront what happened all those years ago, so she can finally grab hold of a future she didn't even know she wanted?

***Second Fiddle* is available free as a welcome gift when you subscribe to Meg's newsletter. Sign up on her website—www.megchronis.com—or visit www.subscribepage.com/megsnewsletter**

Printed in Great Britain
by Amazon

21377150R00212